ALL FRACKED UP......
A HORROR STORY

PART 1

Early October 2016

The Nightmare Begins

Chad Whitescarver loved hiking the Sauratown Mountains, an isolated Prehistoric Mountain range that is home to bald eagles, falcons, ravens, and vultures. In the fall, these huge birds loved to ride the wind currents. Chad was envious of their freedom and the ability of these creatures to defy the laws of aerodynamics and gravity. It was early October, and the canopies of colors in the North Carolina Mountains were almost overloading his brain's capacity to comprehend the brilliance of the leaves. The Oak tree that he was perched behind partially hid him, as he watched the happy couples ascend the mountain hand in hand, "yes, fall is definitively mating time for animals and humans alike" He thought. These thoughts intensified his feeling of longing for his wife Lynn, who had perished two months prior in a horrible car accident. Chad was standing on Hanging Rock; this peak existed only because of the erosion- resistant quartzite that lay beneath his hiking boots. Chad thought to himself, "What uncontrolled beauty!" as he stood on the pinnacle of the mountain.

He thoroughly enjoyed the serenity and tranquility of God's gift to humanity, but it was a moment of mixed emotions from conflicting values. Part of Chad's psyche was conscious of the environmental impact that hydraulic fracturing might have on an area that resounds with the creators' voice. Unfortunately, the majority of Chad's psyche was controlled by money, greed, and power.   As Chad made his climb up Wolf's rock, the hairs on the back of his neck stood up, his heart began to flutter and his breathing deepens. This was alarming to Chad because these physiological changes were not occurring because of fatigue, but by a deep fear that he was being stalked like a wounded animal by a lethal predator.

It moved with the grace and quickness of a wild deer, but it was a meat eater, not a vegetarian like that timid creature. It was a descendant of an ancient tribe that inhabited these mountains thousands of years ago. This was its home, the sacred land of its ancestors. It ran with the rage that comes from knowing that this sacred land was being raped by the white demons that plagued its dreams. These demons now wanted to bring forth the fire monster from the center of the earth. His fire would power automobiles, light their homes, and line their pockets with money. This final insult would destroy the one thing, its people cherished the most; fresh, clear water. The Great Spirit in the sky had bequeathed that gift to its people. Hi'cictawi'a would protect this gift with its life, if necessary. It had tracked this white man with ease, and Hi'cictawi'a would make this pale face pay the ultimate price for his obedience to the fire monster. It would not consume the man like a tasty morsel but would make an example out of him. The grotesque way in which he would die will strike fear in the hearts of those that wished to rape its ancestors' land.

Chad Whitescarver was Danbury's mayor, and he was enjoying his rare day off. He was the third generation of a very politically powerful family that controlled the small town of Danbury with bribes, threats, and police force if need be. The geologist who worked for Abbot Gas had informed the company of the large natural gas deposits that lie in the shale in the northeastern portion of Stokes County, which is in the Piedmont region of North Carolina. This deposit of natural gas could be larger than the Barnabas shale in Pennsylvania and the Harnett Shale in Texas put together. Chad could not resist the feeling of euphoric joy that spread to every cell in his body as he thought of the vast sea of natural gas that lay beneath his hiking boots. He and his family would stop at nothing to cultivate the riches and power that this precious resource would provide for his chosen family. Chad believed that his town and family had gained God's favor through their Christian living. No one was going to get in their way of retrieving God's gift to them, even if they had to kill a few environmental terrorists to get their precious reward!

Chad decided to walk to Wolf Rock. The bright fall day had energized him, and the light crisp northern breeze propelled him down the ridgeline from Hanging Rock to Wolf Rock, a mammoth cropping of granite that thrust out for a panoramic view of farmland two thousand feet below. At this majestic point, he could view his kingdom. Chad Whitescarver was a big man; he played offensive tackle on his high school football team. His girth made it difficult for hikers going in the opposite direction to pass on the trail, which is why, when a hiker nudged him with his elbow as he and his friends passed. Chad thought that the nudge was unintentional, but when the offender turned and shouted, "Hey fat boy, get out of the way!" Chad knew that he had been recognized. He wanted to keep walking and ignore the insult, but his rather large ego would not let the insult go. As he turned his massive frame to address the brazen insult, he noticed the Sierra Club patch on one pack back and a Green Peace on another, and it dawned on him that he was dealing with an environmental terrorist (probably funded by the KGB or some other Russian intelligence branch). Chad bellowed in his deep bass voice that petrified the city council members,

"What did you say, nature boy?" half expecting the young man to back off now that he had been challenged by an older, bigger, aggressive man.

"I said get your fat, pro fracking ass off our trail! he continued, you and your cronies are going to turn this beautiful land of ours into a waste land full of carcinogenic chemicals that are going to kill wildlife and pollute our aquifers and wells, you greedy fat dumb ass!"

Chads face turned a violent shade of purple. He started running at the group with a speed that surprised the young men, but they held their ground. When Chad got within five feet of the group, the biggest man produced a Smith and Wesson 45 caliber handgun and pointed it right at Chad's forehead.

"Always come prepared," the young gun wielding environmental thug said, grinning at Chad like some comedian delivering a well-rehearsed punch line.

Chad stopped so suddenly that the group started to laugh at him, which humiliated him further. "Do you have any idea who you are pointing that gun at boy? I will have you locked up so damn fast it will make your head spin. I own this damn town," Chad thundered in his deep bass voice.

The young man did not flinch as he replied rather calmly, "Dead men don't tell tales." These last words stopped Chad's rebuttal cold, as he suddenly realized that he was outnumbered four to one, and one of the four was holding a very large pistol. He also realized that it was late in the afternoon and they were at a remote place on the trail, mid- way between Hanging Rock and Wolf Rock.

"You're going to shut up. Part of me wants me to put a bullet in your forehead and save this beautiful place from assholes like you, but I'm going to let Karma and the laws of the universe deal with you," the young man calmly stated as if he was solving a complex math problem. Chad relaxed a little; as he realized that maybe, he would not be meeting the grim reaper this day.

"Listen we are going to leave and pretend this ugly event never occurred, but I am going to leave a lookout behind. In addition, if you come off this mountain in less than an hour, I am going to find you in this park and put a bullet in your brain. Do you Understand Mayor?"

The young man asked, as if he were speaking to a first grader. Chad slowly nodded his head, and with that affirmation, the ruthless environmental trash was gone, leaving Chad shaking with rage.

His first impulse was to rush down the brush in a head long reckless run, breaking through the underbrush with his wild off trail romp, but then he chilled and realized that would be suicide. He had never seen those young men before, and he knew that they were not local. He also read people very well and knew that the young heathen was dead serious about his threat. With that thought screaming through his subconscious, he suddenly felt eyes watching his every move. Even if he caught them and something violent happen, it would be their word against his. Although He was the mayor, there was a certain segment of Danbury's prominent society that did not care for him or his family, including the only judge in town.

Chad was still shaking with rage when he reached Wolf Rock, but the stunning view of his kingdom, combined with the crisp air and bright autumnal sun, calmed him. As the rage began to leave him, he noticed a young woman standing on the edge of the rock, lost in meditative trance. Her back was facing him, and she had her young son of two or three year's old sitting in a child-carrying backpack. The child smiled at Chad and tried to wave but was stopped by the strap holding him secure.

For one horrifying moment, Chad thought the woman was going to jump. He started to rush toward the women to save her, and He dreamed of the good press that he was going to receive for his heroic action. He was so focused on saving the women, he did not feel at first the uncommonly strong arms wrap around his torso, He fought his attacker, but the strength of the beast was superhuman. As his consciousness was fading, he felt the cool rush of the wind on his face as if He was skydiving. Chad knew instinctively that He and his abductor were locked into a free fall off a 1,000-foot cliff. Young Timmy Long screamed at the top of his lungs! His mother wheeled to face the terror that had ruined her meditation. She was ready to battle whatever had terrified her precious boy. Nevertheless, to her surprise, nothing was there except the lonely peaks of the ancient mountain. She un-strapped her boy and was shocked by what she saw: her sweet, good son was silent but his faced was distorted into a mask of revulsion. She cleaned his face with a Kleenex, and the slobber and snot consumed the tissue, instantaneously. After he had calmed down, she asked him what he had seen and in a small child's vocabulary, he kept repeating the word "monster". His mother had no way of knowing that the vision of this monster had been so entrenched in his young brain that the image of what young Tommy saw would haunt his dreams until adult-hood.

CHAPTER 2 CHAPTER 2/ OCTOBER 7

Chad was having a vivid nightmare. In his dream he was being carried by something not quite human, but not quite animal. It had superhuman strength and ran with the speed and grace of an Olympic track star. It was covered with hair, like an ape that he had seen in a National Geographic magazine. It appeared to be the famous missing link, the famed mystical beast that bridged the gap between lower primates and humans. The thing turned its head 360 degrees like Linda Blair in "The Exorcist", and Chad began to scream because the beast had the face of his newly deceased wife Lynn.

Chad had opened his eyes to utter darkness; the blackness was like the night sky over a desolate forest in a remote corner of the world. He could see nothing, but he heard the steady flow of water. He knew indistinctly that he was near the Mayo or Dan River, maybe in an abandoned textile mill. These mills had used the rivers as a transportation method to get their goods to urban markets. These mills, now long abandoned since the influx of cheaper imports from China or India, reminded one of a more prosperous time in North Carolina history. Chad laughed to himself and thought about what Tom Hanks said in his favorite movie Forrest Gump. "Life is truly like a box of chocolates, you never know what you're going to get". One minute he had been standing at the top of Wolf Rock and now he was in some abandoned mill listening to the eternal sound of an ancient river.

Chad heard the steps approaching before he saw the lantern moving his way. He half expected the hairy Bigfoot creature from his dreams, but it was a meager looking man in a white lab coat. The nerd had on bifocals that could start a fire, if the meek little weasel of a man stared at something too long. Chad began to laugh at the specter in front of him. The little man stopped about five feet in front of Chad and studied him with great intensity as if he was looking at a new life form. The focus of the man was so intense that Chad wondered if he himself had gone through some type metamorphosis and now resembled some alien life form.

"What you are staring at, you four eyed freak!" Chad screamed at the man, obviously unhinged by the little man's stare. The man was not fazed by Chad's emotional outburst and continued to stare at Chad, as if a one-celled organism under a microscope.

Finally, the little man spoke "How are we going to do it?"

"Do what you little freak?" Chad asked

"Well, Chad, since the human body is composed of eighty percent water, how are we going to drain it all from you?" the small man asked as if he was speaking to a cornered lab rat. Chad's eyes widened with terror, and he suddenly understood what his mother had told him many times that some questions are better not asked.

CHAPTER 3

William O'Toole as his name implied was a proud Irishman, and his physical appearance echoed his proud Irish lineage. William, or Bill, as his mates called him, was short but powerfully built, with bone crushing titan hands and bright red hair, which he kept in a burly ponytail. He had a properly trimmed mustache and beard but kept the rest of his face shaved. He looked like a Celtic king or god with his piercing blue eyes, which terrified anyone who brought forth his wrath. Bill O'Toole was a fourth-generation farmer and rancher, and he owned several hundred acres in Walnut Cove, that he, his wife, and five children lived on.

Bill did not believe in birth control. Besides, having a large family (especially boys) were a great source of free labor. Bill's wife Beth also believed in large families but for different reasons; she hoped that she and Bill's pure Irish stock could improve the genetic makeup of these ignorant hillbillies around them. She would never voice these sentiments, but all who knew her could sense her arrogance. Beth was taller than Bill by about two inches, which irked Bill all the way down his 5'8" frame. Beth was nice endowed with huge breast and had an hourglass figure, which did not help Bill's insanely jealous streak.

He had once beaten up a man who he thought was sleeping with his wife, but his lawyers had paid the man off with a substantial bribe. The gentleman, who was a member of the only Catholic Church in Walnut Cove, had been innocent of any adulterous affair. Bill, after calming down, had apologized profusely, and confessed his sins to his priest. The priest, speaking on behalf of God forgave him of his sins. Bill O'Toole was the salt-of-the-earth kind of man who would indeed give anyone the shirt off his muscular back. Bill O'Toole had a big heart and gave without pretense. However, Bill like most people with a huge heart, lived life with a high degree of passion, and that passion, if not checked, could turn into unmitigated rage. It had managed to get Bill into some serious quagmires in his life.

The O'Toole family estate, nestled up against the Saratown Mountains, was considered by many in the area to be prime real estate. Abbot Gas wanted just a fraction of the land for fracking development, since the three-year moratorium the community had voted on back in 2013 would expire October 15, 2016, Bill knew that it was just a matter of time before a representative of Abbott gas was knocking on his door.

Bill had been raised on this land and had fished both the Mayo and Dan River. He and his friend Johnny Bates hunted for deer, rabbits, squirrels, and sometimes bear that meandered through the mountains and along the riverbank of the crystal-clear water. This land was sacred to Bill, and he would protect it from hydraulic fracturing and horizontal drilling. He would preserve with his heart and soul the purity of this 300-acre tract of land. He would defend his childhood home for his grandchildren with violence, so be it. Bill prayed every night for peace, but he knew in his heart that these powerful gas companies would pit neighbor against neighbor in a propaganda war that would trick the citizens of Walnut Cove as if the serpent tricked Eve in the book of Genesis.

"Ah Dad, quite being such an old school alarmist, always viewing progress as an evil!" the author of these words was Bill Jr, now a young buck of twenty-one. Bill Jr was seeking his MBA in Business and Finance at Wake Forrest University in Winston Salem, NC.

"Junior, watch your tongue, boy! I will not tolerate your

insubordination since I am the one paying for that highfalutin education you're getting," Bill said, raising his voice a decibel. Bill was very proud of his son for being a prodigy and for his brilliance, but sometimes he did not appreciate the arrogance that came from the boy's intelligence. Bill knew that a brilliant mind combined with youthful impulsiveness could be a dangerous thing.

"Dad's right, Billy Boy, those damn gas companies have made Texas, Oklahoma, and Nebraska into carcinogenic waste lands. The flow back water has sent Benzene and Methane has not only poisoned the water and aquifers but the air, too." Junior's younger brother Shaun said, shifting his eyes defiantly at his older brother.

The men were sitting at a beautiful mahogany desk in Bill's study (the man cave or war room as Beth jokingly referred to it). Father and sons were discussing the attempted visit from the landsman representing Abbot Gas, but the visit had been quickly aborted in the driveway after the man saw the "order for cancellation" that was endorsed by Bill's sawed-off 12-gauged shotgun. Shaun's resemblance to his father was uncanny: The same piercing blue eyes and bright red hair, but unlike his father's it was wild and unruly-looking and gave the young man the appearance of an Irish Republican Army Terrorist.

Bill Jr., however, looked as if he might have been adopted; he had Brown skin and dark eyes and hair. Bill assumed that he resembled Beth's rumored Native American heritage. Bill would never mention to his wife that he suspected she was not to be pure Irish, for she would have flown into a rage. He would always agree with her that Junior took after the dark Irish clan from the Northern Belfast region. Bill had heard of the dark olive colored Swede, but never an Irish man, and sometimes he wondered if Beth were hiding some awful lustful secret. Junior sensed his father's rejection. Bill felt that Junior was his wife's bastard son conceived by sperm not of his loins.

"Come on, Dad, we have enough natural gas locked in the shale under this farm to make our family mega wealthy for generations, and besides you're always screaming how this country's dependence on foreign oil has driven up the cost of farming to a point that you can barely make a living," Junior stated profoundly. Junior had no way of knowing that his father's definition of, "barely making a living" was netting about 200,000 grand a year.

Bill Sr. was getting ready to reply to his know it all son, when the phone rang. Bill grabbed the home phone off the wall in one savage pull, and answered "hello" in a ruff, booming voice. The sons watched their father's reaction to the caller, his frown deepen, and his eyes blazed as he asked, "When did this happen?" and when the hapless caller response was not to Bill's satisfaction, he slammed the phone down. The boys had seen their father's reaction, and knew it was best to keep their mouths shut until he spoke.

"Seems as if our good Mayor Chad Whitescarver has disappeared while hiking near Hanging Rock," he said in an uncharacteristically quiet tone. Both sons wondered why the disappearance of a man their father obviously loathed would have such an impact on their stoic father. Bill sat transfixed by the news, as an ancient premonition of fear invaded his soul. He feared for his sons and his family because he sensed the firestorm of violence that this disappearance would bring to his front door.

CHAPTER 4

Black Bart Whitescarver, quite possibly the meanest son of a bitch in all of Stokes County, sat on the back porch of his monstrous mansion. Black Bart was a dark-skinned man with piercing coal black eyes that were shaped like the many lizards that scurried all over the primitive, isolated mountains that surrounded his plantation. Bart Whitescarver had a black beard, which meandered, down to his massive chest, and after a hearty meal, it would contain morsels of food, which Bart would consume as a midnight snack, much to the horror of his wife. She, however, took pride in knowing that he enjoyed her cooking even after several hours of "storage". Many of the town folk questioned his heritage or wondered if he could be the by-product of some union between Bart's mother and one of her many field hands. Many believed that Connie Whitescarver had a ravenous case of jungle fever. The cowardly conspirators would always gossip in hushed tones behind Black Bart's back, petrified of the short powerful, man with gigantic arms and equally massive hands. Bart Whitescarver owned the town of Danbury's soul, and his Mexican henchman enforced this wicked country king's decrees with violent intensity.

The twenty-room mansion, which rivaled the Biltmore House in Asheville, North Carolina, was built with old money, more specifically tobacco money. Bart's grandfather had owned two hundred acres of prime tobacco land. The big tobacco producers like Phillip Morris and R J Reynolds had paid top dollar for the fine one sucker and burley tobacco that grew at the intersection of Delta Church Road and Shepard

Mill Road, just north of the banks of the Dan River. Bartholo-
mew Whitescarver III hated his god given name, and nobody
but his nagging, conniving wife called him that, but even she
didn't call him that when he was in a bad frame of mind or
after a hard night of knocking back some moonshine with
his cronies, fellow rednecks, or country home boys. Gloria
Whitescarver knew that her loving husband of thirty years
would have her floating belly up in the Dan River, if she ever
forgot her place!

Gloria set the peach flavored iced tea in front of Black
Bart and calmly asked, "Any news on Chad yet honey?"

"What do I look like woman?" "CNN damn news! You stupid ass," a snarling Black Bart said answering his own question.

Gloria was on the verge of cleverly retorting something
about people answering their own question, when she saw the
extremely murderous look in her husband's slanted reptilian
eyes.

As he sat rocking on the wide cedar deck that circled
the massive home like a belt on a heavily obese man, he
thought about escape from this hellish purgatory, how the
winds of change were coming, and that he could hopefully
deposit his massive frame on some beach in Cancun, Mexico
or on the French Rivera. Bart Whites carver had an uncanny
ability to project into the future, and since the huge coal ash
spill on the Dan River a couple of years ago, he had started
to plan his great escape, like Steve McQueen did in that 60's
movie "The Great Escape." Bart knew that a perfect storm
was brewing, and that the combination of coal ash leakage
and hydraulic fracking would soon turn this fertile farmland
into a cancer ridden wasteland like Chernobyl in the Soviet
Union. It was clear that the current state government did not
give a damn about the environment and was stripping away
environmental protections faster than the pole dancer had removed her top at that exotic bar he and his cronies had visited

last night in Winston Salem.

He planned to be far away in some tropical paradise when that hexavalent chromium started turning all the fine town folk of Danbury into flesh eating zombies, like all the damn horror movies had been predicting for eons. Bart knew the hydraulic fracturing was his means to financial freedom, and his son Chad was going to make it all happen. Chad was his marionette, and Bart was going to control him like an evil puppet master. He rocked with a quickened intensity and peered into the pitch-black night and listened to the pulsating current of the Dan River hundreds of feet below him, and wondered if his demons were finally coming home to roost.

CHAPTER 5/
OCTOBER 8

The Dan River, named after a Saura Indian chief Dan-pa-pa, flows for about 214 miles from its point of origin, Kerr Lake in Patrick County and boomerangs backs into the Kerr Reservoir on the Roanoke River after passing into North Carolina's Rockingham and Surry counties. It is a river that technically travels nowhere, but it was vitally important for two reasons. First, it is a source of water and recreation for two large northern counties in North Carolina, but more importantly, it was ground zero in a battle between corporate greed and environmental preservation. Queen Power had located many of its coal ash retention ponds along the Dan River and in 2014 a pipe had ruptured, dumping chromium, arsenic and lead into the drinking water of the good folks of Virginia and North Carolina. The pristine Dan River now was an innocent collaborator of an environmental disaster.

The rivers toxic reputation did not matter to Hector Rodriquez, as he shouted with uncontrolled excitement as he cleared the last minor rapid on the shallow Dan River near Riverside Park. Many of his friends were cursing as their buttocks were slammed against the huge rocks that lined the bottom of the river. Hector was able to glide over the rocks because he was lighter than his older brothers. He was ecstatic! He had finally beaten his two older brothers in a two-hour race down the river, and he shouted excitedly, "Who's the King of the river?"

Either his brother ignored his question or they were too far away to hear. After all Hector, masterful tubing expertise had allowed him to beat them like an Olympic champion in some redneck summer games. Hector was about to get out and walk his tube up the great hill when he spotted a wooden canoe lodged against a tree on the opposite bank about 100 yards away. Hector was an average swimmer and knew better than to swim against the moderate current, which had been strengthened by a recent flash flood, but curiosity got the best of him, so he set off to claim his prize. He swam hard but soon was caught up in a surprising undertow. Hector could feel his body being tossed around like a towel in a washing machine, He panicked and began to thrash the water with a violent intensity, and he began to hyperventilate. He was sure that death was lurking for him right around the next turn in the river. As the sinister river pushed Hector toward his death, a spirit of a long dead Saura Indian chief possessed his heart and calmed him. He managed to grab a hold of the canoe or log that had initiated this brush with death. He began to pull himself up onto the log that had saved his life and was going to rest until help could arrive. As he began to squirm up into the center portion of this floating natural life preserver, he stared into two glossy lifeless eyes that resembled the eyes of Zombies, which he had seen in the movie "The Dawn of the Dead." Hector began to scream with a maniac intensity that would continue until the emergency crew from Danbury plucked him from this river of death.

Black Bart initially thought the high-pitched scream was a siren on a police car rapidly approaching to apprehend, and incarcerate some hapless tuber caught drinking alcohol on the river. This was a major offense punishable by a night in the pokie, because many folks along the river had complained about beer cans accumulating on their property. Bart thought it to be highly ironic that these same folks did not give a damn about the highly toxic coal ash byproducts tarnishing their water supply.

Bart stood overlooking the Dan River, and peered down into the darkness and listen to the Ancient River, as it seemed to whisper, "Your son Chad is gone forever, and you killed him with your greed." He suddenly heard the sirens as they pierced the darkness. A horrible premonition penetrated his awareness and he trembled with rage and yelled to his hapless wife Gloria, "I believe your baby boy Chad has just been found!" Bart instinctively knew that he was now going to play a more active role in unleashing the curse of fracking upon the innocent communities of Walnut Cove and Danbury, so he picked up his cellphone and called his enforcers.

"Hey Pedro, round up the boys and meet me down at Riverside Park in twenty minutes," he snarled.

"Boss, the men are mighty tired. We topped about four acres of tobacco today" Pedro sheepishly replied.

"Pedro. If you don't get that lazy group of parasites down to the park in twenty minutes, I will revoke your work visa and you will be back in Mexico before you can utter the words Santa Anna!" Pedro hated Black Bart with a molten passion, but he uttered the words. "Yes Sir" so fast he felt the bile build in his throat.

"Bet your ass, yes sir! " Black Bart bellowed as he hung up the phone. Black Bart relished the feeling of unbridled power that came from controlling a race of people with no advantage legally and no constitutional rights protecting them. These men were his slaves, his possessions, and like pawns on a chessboard, he would move them to achieve his diabolical plan. He then would offer them up as scapegoats to be punished for the lethal violence that he would soon release. Bart wanted vengeance for his son premature death, but more importantly, he was enraged by the vermin that delayed his escape plan.

CHAPTER 6

Ralph Barton was washing fire truck Number 21, when the call came in about a potential drowning victim on the Dan River near Riverside Park. He was the lead paramedic at Fire Station number 5, which was located on curvy Highway 8 about 10 miles from the site of the drowning call. He angrily threw the shami-cloth down and hurried to his ambulance. He was surprised to see that his partner Rod Lewis was already in the navigator seat eager to serve his community.

"Here it is mid-October, and folks are still tubing down the Dan," Ralph said in a high-pitched voice.

Rod Lewis, his partner for about five years, noticed that Ralph appeared to be agitated by having his chores interrupted, so he could not resist irritating his partner just a tad more.

"It's all because of global warming, October has become the new September!"

"Oh, Lord here you go with that global warming crap!" Ralph shouted back over the whine of the load ambulance siren as it sped down highway eight. Rod smiled to himself. The fish had taken the bait; now he was going set the hook.

"Yes, I have done massive research on this global warming and the number one culprit is methane gas, specifically the methane gas that is released into the ozone layer by hydraulic fracturing." Rod said with scholarly expertise.

Ralph Barton was a tall man, and the long arm that was not controlling the steering wheel waved in the air dramatically while he made his obvious point.

"What are you now a climatologist? Besides, methane gas occurs naturally and has been blamed for many coal mine explosions, particularly in West Virginia and Kentucky," he exclaimed triumphantly.

"I have studied methane gas levels in the earth's atmosphere and there was a tremendous spike in their levels in the late 1990's and early 2000," and with added dramatic flair, Rod concluded, which coincides with the legalization of hydraulic fracturing in the Midwest and Texas."

"Ah bullshit," an obviously flustered Ralph exclaimed, but before Rod could respond the ambulance arrived at the park and was greeted by a blinding array of colors emitted by Sheriff Paul Brown's squad car! Ralph tried to shout, "What the Hell?" because Sheriff Brown's car was blocking the route to the assumed drowning victim. But the words died in his throat as he caught a glimpse of Black Bart Whitescarver tearing Sheriff Brown a new ass.

CHAPTER 7

About the same time that Chad Whitescarver's severely dehydrated body was being fished out of the Dan River, David Barret was preparing his last report to Baker Gas, a large oil-refining outfit out of Jenkins, Pennsylvania. The company was currently using hydraulic fracturing techniques around the town of Jenkins, Pennsylvania that was right smack dab in the middle of the Barnabas shale. The Barnabas shale was about 104,000 square miles in area, and was contain in four primary states: New York, Pennsylvania, West Virginia and Ohio. It was the largest source of natural gas in the United States, and Baker Gas had legally fracking there since 2008. The fine townsfolk were forced to give up their land through forced pooling or by a lame excuse of eminent domain, thus causing great court battles over property rights. The townsfolk also were worried about health concerns because of the cocktail of fracking chemicals, many of them being carcinogens, that bubbled into wells and aquifers during back flow leakage around concrete containment areas.

The leaders of the small town had successfully silenced the protesters with more cash flow funded by Baker Gas, but when the citizens began to be able to light their water on fire the shit hit the fan. Baker Gas bought 2,000-gallon tanks, called Water Buffalo's, to appease the citizens of Jenkins, but many folks had had enough and smelled blood in the air as EPA agents were called in to investigate. Baker Gas was in a panic mode, and that is when they called the master manipulator David Barret, the miracle worker.

David Barret was working late in his office, which

was in downtown Denver, Colorado. He looked more like a rancher from the high plains of El Dorado than a man who possessed a Doctorate Degree in Psychology from Vanderbilt University in Tennessee. He had a large cranium with a protruding forehead, which he had explained to his wife contained a brain that was so highly evolved in divergent thinking skills, that he sometimes was accused of having extra sensory perception ability, or ESP. David Barret was a non-conformist and was now sporting a Mohawk haircut and a Fo Manchu mustache, which was quite hilarious looking until one looked into his deep penetrating stare and realized that he was gifted with an intelligence that is exceedingly rare in the human species. David had on a flannel shirt that concealed his washboard abs and wide muscular chest and arms. David had brown skin curiosity of his Mexican mother, which meshed with his light Brown eyes. His eyes were his most valuable weapon, emitting either an explosive passion or a hypnotic stare that would cause a stranger to do his bidding.

.   He had "Carp deim" tattooed on his left bicep, which in Latin means, "Seize the day." He had gotten the tattoo during his days in the Army, when he was attached to the US Army's second Battalion/7th Cavalry, during the second assault on Fallujah. Bush II had invaded Iraq in revenge for 9-11. David had been a captain attached to a squad of Special Forces soldiers, and he often felt like a kid brother tagging along with older, more dangerous brothers.

David was a unique animal. This special gift was influencing or convincing Iraq civilians to do his bidding through psychological subliminal suggestions. Through flawless Kurdish and Arabic, he could get civilians to give up vital information about the Al-Qaida insurgents in the area. David had been attached to Army's PYOPS division and he was the very best the Army had in psychological warfare. In fact, many referred to him as the" Mind Magician." He had used the information given to him by civilians to clear improvised explosive devices from the highways, or to send drones sent from thousands of miles away down the throats of many insurgents hiding in caves around the city. He had saved countless lives of both civilians and soldiers, but he had not gotten damn movie made about him. David loved glory, and he knew he had saved more lives than that Hollywood glorified sniper. These thoughts were parading through his mind when his cell phone chirped its secret ring tone "Money-Money Money" by the O'Jays. He answered, "Speak" with his strong bass voice. The voice on the other end explained that his services would be in Stokes County, North Carolina, and that he needed to get his ass there ASAP, and then the line went dead. He hated the arrogant bastards that ordered him around like a piece of mindless meat, but he would retire at forty with several billion dollars in numerous offshore accounts that were untraceable by the Internal Revenue Service. David would finish this last job in some God forsaken place in North Carolina, and then he would store the information on a 128 GB flash drive for Blackmailing and intimidation.

CHAPTER 8

"Now calm down. Bart" Sheriff Brown said in vain. "We are loading up Chad's body in this ambulance and taking it to Greensboro for an autopsy."

"The hell you are, Bob! I want to see my boy." Black Bart yelled at the top of his lungs. Alarming Pedro so badly, that he started to reconsider asking the boss for a small raise for himself and his gang. Ralph Barton pulled the ambulance around the confrontation and headed toward the nearest bank of the Dan River. He jumped out of the ambulance so quickly that Rod was winded by the time he reached the bank. Ralph was already administering first aid to the young Hispanic youth, who was obviously hyperventilating because of hysteria. Rod noticed the boy's cold, pale skin and began to check for other signs of hypothermia. As Ralph reached down to grab a blanket for the boy. He glanced at the newly deceased mayors' body. In the twenty years of being a paramedic, he had never seen a more hideous sight. Chad's skin was wrinkled like a mummy in a tomb found in the ancient Pyramids of Giza in Northern Egypt; his upper torso looked like that a man of 200 years old. Ralph would later learn that every cell found in Chad's vital organs, bones, muscles and tissues were completely void of water.

When Black Bart finally arrived at the scene, he fought past Ralph and Rod and sank to his knees, cradling the malformed body of his son. He rocked back and forth, cursed, and then started to laugh insidiously, for he knew that vengeance, for this murder would not be from God but from his own bloody hands. Ralph and Rod finally separated Black Bart from his dead son, but while doing so Ralph looked into the eyes of a man obsessed with revenge. For the first time in his life, he not only feared for his life but for the safety of his town.

CHAPTER 9\OCTOBER 15

The funeral for Chad Whitescarver was held one week later, after the autopsy confirmed what many of the townsfolk already knew; Chad Whitescarver had indeed been murdered. Doctor Brian Gilbert an expert in forensic pathology in Greensboro, describe the autopsy as the most bizarre he had performed in the last 20 years. All the body's fluids had been totally absent in the cadaver upon arrival at morgue. The typical adult male adult body is composed of around sixty percent water, and both inter-cellular and extra cellular fluids were completely gone. Doctor Gilbert had seen the fluid outside of cells absent in autopsies due to traumatic injury, but never the absence of inter-cellular fluid. Inter-cellular fluid makes up about two thirds of the fluid that is contained in the human body. The cells had cremated or shrunk to a point of almost disappearing totally; the only way he could see them by turning up the magnification on his powerful electron microscope.

"I bet he was abducted by aliens!" Harry Jenkins whispered to his fellow city council member Tammy White during the visitation night at Wake's Funeral Home, which was right in the heart of downtown Danbury.

"Naw Tammy replied. Damn environmentalist thugs got him. They've backed by ISIS, Taliban, or Al-Qaeda!" Tammy whispered in a slightly elevated tone, causing Bert Whitescarver to turn his reptilian stare toward them. Both Tammy and

Harry noticed the icy stare and shuffled out of the inner sanctum of the funeral home to continue their conspiracy theory ideas.

"Now why in the hell would terrorist organizations care about a back-woods mayor of a one-horse town?" Harry asked, almost shocked by Tammy's stupid uninformed remark.

"Because Chad was a big proponent of hydraulic fracturing, and as if speaking to a slow child she continued. If our vast amount of shale gas in the area were refined and cultivated, then the United States would not have to depend on oil from countries supporting global terrorism Tammy summarized like a member of the Senate Energy Committee. The money spigot would be turned off, no more using this country's addiction to fund the raghead terrorist camps in Afghanistan or Pakistan and all the other 'stans' in the damn Middle East."

"Damn Ragheads" Harry Jenkins echoed the approval of his friend's theory.

As they turned to go back into the viewing room, they noticed a man walking briskly into the funeral home. He was wide shouldered with an athletic build, and he walked with a confident strut. The men stared at his Mohawk and Fo Manchu mustache but kept silent because the man exuded a professional personification that demanded respect. The man wore a Rocco-Watt Ombre jacquard wool silk suit, and had golden cuff links blazed with the initials D.B. All heads turned to view this man who appeared to come out of nowhere like a sudden summer thunderstorm, and the rumors started circulating that he was a Philadelphia lawyer, or a hit man hired by Bart Whitescarver to seek revenge upon Chad's killer. David just kept walking, totally oblivious by their stares because to him they were invisible. He would recognize their presence, but the timing was not right.

David had needed to do a scouting mission, and this was the main reason for his appearance. He wanted to meet with

Bart Whitescarver in person during a high-profile time, and a funeral did certainly qualify as one. He had picked this time so the rumors would start;

"Who was this man?" He needed to lay his business model, and the unknown was the great breeding ground for the control that he needed... He walked right pass the judges, lawyers, politicians, and many gas company executives that had gathered to pay their respects to the dead mayor of a small rural city in near Hanging Rock He walked up to a grieving Bart Whitescarver, looked him square in the eye and calmly said,

"I'm sorry for the loss of your son, but we have some serious business to discuss" and with that he handed Black Bart Whitescarver his business card.

All eyes were on Black Bart, and some began to wager that the stranger would not make it alive out of the funeral home. Black Bart's face turned a crimson red, and his big hands began to ball into a fist... until he read the card. Unbelievably, Bart's face began to relax as he slipped the card into his suit pocket, as he did, the stranger turned and abruptly walked toward the door. Gloria Whitescarver's eyes never left the man as he strode out of the room, and she thought, the audacity of that rude bastard! She was engulfed with rage, but she could not deny that the strange, beautiful man had ignited her unsatisfied sexual desire.

The eulogy for Chad was given by the only pastor with a Doctorate in Divinity within a hundred miles' radius. Ben Jackson was an eloquent speaker who mixed several Bible verses from Matthew in the New Testament to exemplify what a Godly man Chad was. Harry Jenkins began to wonder if he was at the right funeral, because the saintly description of the man lying in the coffin did not remotely match Chad's vicious aggressive and personality. He looked over just in time to see his friend Tammy roll her eyes in disbelief, wondering how a man of the cloth could be guilty of such fabrication.

"Chad was a friend of the environment, but at the same time recognized God's great plan to cultivate the town's natural resources to advance his kingdom," Ben Jackson spouted with great conviction. The many gas executives in the audience collected responded by shouting "Amen," and Harry Jenkins had to excuse himself from the sermon because he could hardly resist the urge to shout "Bullshit" at the top of his lungs. At the conclusion of the eulogy, Gloria Whitescarver began to sob uncontrollably, finally realizing that her Chaddie was gone. Black Bart just stared ahead with dead eyes void of anything that resembled a soul.

On the ride home, Bart's young son Fred asked his Dad who the mysterious stranger was. His dad simply whispered, "That's my passport out of this hell hole, son." Being a young boy of ten, Fred didn't know what a passport was, but he didn't appreciate his Dad referring to his beautiful hometown as a hellhole.

CHAPTER 10

The town of Danbury was built along Highway 8 as it meandered toward the wind-swept cliffs of the ancient mountain, so the shadow of those prehistoric mountain peaks seems to engulf the town like a fat man eating a cheeseburger. The ancient mountain was like an omnipresent God staring down at the good people of Danbury as they went about their meager daily tasks. As David Barret crossed the street and walked toward the Shape Shiftier Cafe, he couldn't help but to think about his last trip to Naples, Italy to meet with some Italian officials that were in need of his special powers. He and his beautiful wife Eternity mixed business with pleasure, and visited the Ancient City of Pompeii, which had been engulfed, by lava and volcanic ash from a Mount Vesuvius eruption in 79 AD. As he peered up at the prehistoric Stone Mountain, he was almost knocked unconscious by the vision of a great man-made firestorm that was going to inflict this small quaint town with many casualties. When he entered the small cafe, the owner, Sam Blackfoot, met him at the front door, and offered a back-woods greeting of

"Howdy, welcome to our humble town," as he stuck out his big ole paw for David to shake. But David just stared at the Man's hand, and asked, "You're a Sara Indian correct?"

"Why yes I am, descended from the original peoples of this great land," Sam answered, still shocked by David's response to his friendly gesture.

"Where is Bart Whitescarver?" David asked not even acknowledging the big Indian's reply.

"He is waiting for you in the back room," Sam said, trying to subdue his feeling of great dislike for this arrogant pale-face.

David proceeded to the back room and knocked on the door. Black Bart opened the door and stared at David with a penetrating stare, which irked David to the core, because he, the "Mind Magician," was the only one allowed such a malevolent stare! No formalities of handshaking or goodwill were shown because that would have been a waste of time; this was not a social occasion.

"So you're the famous Mind Magician, huh"? A scowling Black Bart asked.

"Some call me that, and you're the man who wants to escape this town forever?"

"Damn, how did he know that?" Black Bart wondered, as if his last thoughts had been read.

"Don't worry your motivation for leaving this one-horse town is safe with me!" David Barrett said, then winked at Black Bart and grinned at him. The mind magician was enjoying playing with Bart's limited mental resources.

Black Bart was impressed and instinctively knew that their relationship would be crucial to executing his plan of disappearing like a white rabbit in a magician show.

"Let's get down to business," shall we?" David asked, eager to gather the facts necessary to laying the groundwork for a massive plan of mental propaganda and manipulation.

Black Bart stared at David with an intense gaze, and then asked him,

" Why all the cloak and dagger positioning?"

"You are my contact person, my point man, replied David, and then he added, you have lived here all your life, and your intimate knowledge of their meager existence will benefit the implementation of my plan."

David explained the Pennsylvania Supreme Court had ruled in favor of the environmentalists and forbade eminent domain (or taking of private land for public enhancement like highways or hospitals), so with the forced pooling option off the table many gas companies in that area must now convince owners to freely give up their land for fracking.

"So, you're concerned that my unworldly, unsophisticated neighbors now understand that big bad oil companies can't force folks off their lands? Black Bart smiled wickedly when he added excuses like forced pooling and eminent domain will no longer work on these ignorant back-woods hillbillies."

"You are one hundred percent correct," David drawled sensing that Black Bart was a flaming narcissistic personality that always had to be right about everything.

"I need to know their objections to selling their land to the oil companies, and Abbott Gas mentioned that you were the biggest supporter of hydraulic fracturing in the region."

David pushed his chair back and then calmly said

"List the top reasons for resistance in the area?"

"Well, let me give the three main reasons: health concerns, water concerns, and property concerns. And underlining those concerns is that the folks here have a complete and utter mistrust of big corporations and their total disregard of the environment!" Black Bart said as he spit some Redman chewing tobacco into a spittoon.

"Most of these concerns are stirred up by two rogue anti-fracking voices in the area: Paul Williams, who owns about 1,000 acres which he has set up as a damn nature preserve that protects damn mollusks for God's sake! Black Bart's voice raised a few decibels. His anger deepened the crease in his ample forehead. As he mentioned the name of his nemesis, dripping saliva cascaded out of his mouth like poisonous venom. Bill O'Toole is a large rancher up near Walnut Cove and has a lot of influence over the heathen in Walnut Cove. They revere him as some kind of God there, that old bastard!" Black Bart almost shouted with rage.

David witnessed a compete shift in Black Bart's personality and knew that the man seated opposite him was not only a raging narcissist but also had psychopathic tendencies. His professional training kicked in as he realized that Black Bart was obsessed with Bill O'Toole, because he suspected that Bill O'Toole had murdered his son. David knew that only a psychopath could generate that much rage, so he had to defuse Bart's anger immediately.

"Listen, I want you to stay away from Bill O'Toole. Your intense hatred of this man could derail any hopes you have of leaving this hellhole. He added, leave him to me." David spoke with such quiet force that it almost sounded like a command.

"THE HELL I WILL" but Bart's defiance died in his throat as David calmed his disobedience with a strange hypnotic stare. As Black Bart sank into a stupor of calmness, his mind became aware of two things. David Barret was controlling his mind without his permission, and the waitress that was serving them, was staring at him with an intense hatred. Black Bart should have recognized the unholy stare because it came from someone who shared his DNA.

"So, when are the city commissioners voting on repealing the moratorium on fracking in Danbury?" David Barret asked calmly. The question seemed to awaken Black Bart from the hypnotic trance that he was under. He answered, "October 15," in a sleepy voice.

"I would not worry about the outcome of that vote. My boy Chaddie has all those dumb asses in his back pocket." His voice trailed off as he realized his son was no longer among the living.

David Barret knew that Black Bart was still dealing with the trauma of losing his son, so he gently ordered Black Bart to get him a list of the commissioners who might vote against rescinding the moratorium, and a list of the five biggest families in Stokes County that owned land. Black Bart was not used to being ordered around, so he asked in a loud booming voice,

"Why in the hell do you need that information? Thought I told you everything is taken care of!" David could forgive Bart for his insolence given that he was in distress and anguish from losing his son, so he calmly said, "A human should not question the reasoning of a superior being." Black Bart shook his head and in puzzlement wondered what was going on, but he followed the orders perfectly like the mindless sheep David Barret knew him to be.

CHAPTER 11

Hanging Rock State Park had many hiking trails meandering through the oak and hickory forest; several led to beautiful waterfalls or cascades. The abundant limestone that underlines the soil cause great erosion forming several caves in the area. The limestone and iron ore lead to the development of mining companies that melted the ore by using giant forges or furnaces. The Moratuck Mining Company had supplied the Confederacy with tons of iron, until the mine was captured and closed by General Stoneman of the Union Army in 1865. As a testament to its great service to the Confederacy, the Moratuck Furnace was the centerpiece of Riverside Park. The colossal granite furnace had stood like a silent sentry guarding the park for eons. It was on eternal guard duty watching out for vandals or those up to no good, and its large semicircular arch at the base seemed to form a wicked smile that served to warn those with evil deeds on their minds.

A.J. Black stood at the base of the furnace, frantically searching the large open space at its base. "Damn it, I left my shit right here!" His mouth twisted up into a snarl. His "shit" was some of the finest homegrown weed in all of Stokes County; at least, that was what he told all his customers. Just as he was going to quit and hunt down the culprit who had the stones to steal from him, his fingers grasped onto a string and he pulled it hard. The "string" turned out to be bright red hair belonging to a decapitated head, its carotid arteries dangling down like hellish dreadlocks of some Jamaican rock star. The burnished stare of the eyes frightened A.J. so much that he heaved the head into the woods directly behind the furnace. He turned to his potential customer, Artie Branch, and bellowed, "Let's get the hell out of here!" Artie Branch, being a big fan of the hit shows "Criminal Minds" and "C.S.I." stood his ground.

"You can high tail it like the coward you are, but I'm calling the sheriff!" Artie bravely exclaimed.

A.J. Black couldn't believe his ears. "I am going to whup your ass!" He yelled as he started to run toward Artie with a murderous gleam in his eyes.

"Guess I will claim all the reward money for myself," then Artie managed to get out before the irate A.J. could carry out his mission of destruction of Artie's face. Now, A.J. was known for his love of money and his mommy always believed he would someday be a millionaire, but A.J being a high school dropout rather put a damper on his mother plans for him. Therefore, when Artie mentioned reward money, A.J. stopped in his tracks.

"What the hell are you talking about Artie?" he whispered, not wanting anyone in hearing range to learn of his new scheme to become wealthy.

"That head belonged to Shaun O'Toole, and I bet that his daddy will offer a vast reward for information leading to the arrest of the murderous bastards that killed his boy," Artie stated defiantly.

."How do you know that Shaun O'Toole's helmet?" A.J. asked interjecting his own vivid descriptive terminology.

"I went to school with him over at Walnut Cove High and could recognize that patch of crimson red hair anywhere," Artie said in a confident, cool manner.

"Okay I will go along with your plan, but we found the head in the woods, and if you double cross me Artie, Shaun O'Toole won't be the only headless redneck around here," A.J.

warned.

. Artie dialed 9 1 1 on his Generation 5 smart phone that he had just gotten for his birthday, and as one of Sheriff Brown's deputies answered the phone, Artie glanced at the imposing figure of A.J., who towered over him by three feet, and wondered if the cell phone would be the last birthday present, he would ever receive.

CHAPTER 12

Rhonda Hardy could not believe the beautiful early October day. The warm mid fall rays felt delicious as they massaged her delicate ivory skin. The late summer sun caressed her flesh like a gentle lover, while the harsh sun of the July and August had abused her like her daddy did many, many years ago. These thought were randomly penetrating her consciousness, when her youngest son squealed with delight as the cold waters from the lower cascades rheumatically flowed down his face. She and her two sons had braved the hiking trail, which started at the parking lot and slowly wove downward toward the waiting shallow pool surrounding the stunning waterfalls. The cascades themselves tumbled down a ragged cliff, but through eons of pounding the rocks near the base of the pool were smooth. The two boys of eight and ten years old were taking turns sliding down the rocks and squealed with pleasure as they entered the chilly waters of the natural kiddie pool. "The perfect baby sitter," Rhonda thought as she rubbed the sunscreen into her skin. But then her youngest son's howl of delight turned into a shriek of horror! Rhonda, being a natural protector, waded quickly across the shallow pool and put her arm around her trembling son as he pointed to something high above them dangling in the cascades. The blood of the torso was intermingling with the water. Rhonda, being a farmer's daughter remembered the many "hog killings" that she had witnessed as a young child. The violence and the blood had been terrifying to her. She always wondered if making her witness the hog killings was a method of convincing her to keep her mouth shut about her daddy's incestuous ways.

At first, she thought maybe this was Daddy's ghost playing some sick trick, tying a rope to a hog torso and lowering it down into the falls, but then her mind seemed to shake off its childish delusion and recognize that the torso was human and that she and her children were in grave danger.

Rhonda stayed calm, but she knew that her cell phone would not get reception in their current location. Therefore, she gently gathered her sons from the pool, and hiked to the parking lot in a rapid but relaxed pace. After about a quarter of a mile hike, they reached the parking lot. The parking lot was vacant, and this added to Rhonda's anxiety, but she quickly dialed Sheriff Brown's number with her trembling hands.

The CSI specialist handed Sheriff Brown a paper that had been recovered from the oral cavity of the decapitated head, the procedure had been accomplished by specially designed tweezers mostly used in autopsies. Sheriff Brown looked down at the neatly folded paper still with the teeth impressions made by the lock of the jaws when death sealed them like a vice. As he opened the note, he recognized a sequence of coordinates listed in longitude and latitude, which are used to pinpoint a location on the earth's surface. Through many years of police work, he knew distinctly that these coordinates were ghoulish clues to the location of various other body parts.

"Get this down to the crime lab in Greensboro, and check for latent fingerprints," he said solemnly. He was about to question his old friend A.J. when his cell phone began to vibrate Rhonda Hardy was describing her gruesome find at the lower cascades.

"Calm down, Rhonda, I'll have a patrol car out to you in five minutes," he vociferated into the phone.

He then downloaded the first coordinates of the note found in the mouth of the decapitated head onto the app on his cell phone, which was used to triangulate coordinates to a specific location in the county. Within a Nano second, the lower cascades of Hanging Rock State Park flashed onto the screen. Sheriff Brown's face transformed into a strained scowl as he realized that a macabre scavenger hunt had begun. He also knew if the chief medical examiner in Raleigh identified the head as belonging to Shaun O'Toole, hell was coming to this neck of his woods.

Sheriff Brown also knew that William O'Toole upon hearing about the grisly murder of his son would fly into an uncontrollable rage! After a twenty-year career of law enforcement, he knew that intense anger was the first symptom of grief. The feud between the O'Toole family and the Whitescarver family would intensify and he would have a remake of the Hatfield's and the McCoy s, except because of the current division in the county over frocking, this feud would into a bloody miniature civil war. He had to buy some time to find the rest of Shaun's body, and since no missing person's report was filed, he wondered if for some reason Shaun had an excused absence from the controlling arm of his father. Maybe he was on a camping trip or fishing trip, and was not expected home for a while! He had to find out why a missing person's report had not been filed.

CHAPTER 13

Sheriff Brown hated social media: Facebook, Twitter, and Instagram, but he had used information found on these sites to help solve crimes ranging from armed robbery to assault. He was amazed by the downright ignorance of some folk as they bragged about their crimes on Facebook or twitter. Just last week, some kids had videoed their beating of a handicapped white kid and put it on Facebook! He could not explain why people would incriminate themselves in such a way, but maybe it was because of the extreme narcissism that overruled these folk's natural desire for self-preservation. Ah well, that is a job for the shrinks. All he knew is that it made his job a helluva lot easier. Sheriff Brown had a great relationship with all the teenagers in the county, because he treated the youth as equals. He never chastised them or was critical or cynical about their teenage ways, so it was not uncommon for him to have many young people as friends on Facebook. He suspected the kids thought that he would give them a break if he caught them smoking weed or parking on someone's land. Now, all his townsfolk thought that his Facebook relationship with kids was unprofessional, but he rationalized that if a Facebook presence helped him to solve crimes in area, then to hell with what the sheep thought!

He opened his Facebook page and searched for Shaun O'Toole's page, and got the information he was looking for, Shaun was on a kayaking trip on the Mayo River with his best friend, Rusty Foster. He was not expected to be home until tomorrow night, so that would give Sheriff Brown about 24 hours to find the rest of Shaun's body; that was the least he could do for a man that he liked and respected. Sheriff Brown turned to his deputy sheriff Donny Miller and barked a couple of orders.

"Have the men assembly at my office in 20 minutes for a brief-in, and arrest A.J. and his buddy!"

"On what charge, Boss?" the confused Donny Miller inquired.

"Damn Donny use your imagination! I don't care, maybe on just being plain ugly," Sheriff Brown said jokingly. The sheriff knew that A.J. and his buddy wouldn't be able to keep their mouths shut about their discovery, so the best place for them was in the jail cell for the next twenty-four hours. The men then could be monitored, to prevent any leakages of their hideous find.

Just as Sheriff Brown got to his cruiser, he could hear A.J. rather boisterous appeals. "That's what I hate about cops, always wanting to lock me up for some bullshit reason!"

He was very amused by Donny Miller's reply " Oh hell, A.J., we have your old room reserved for ya, even have a chocolate on the pillow and a little towel doggie made up and put in the middle of your rack, that way you can pretend you're on a Cruise ship" chuckled Miller.

"Why don't you cruise on this?" A.J. shouted pulling on his little member.

Sheriff Brown smiled to himself, and thought, some things never change. He then remembered the definition of insanity: doing the same thing over and over again expecting different results. Suddenly he thought about retiring and getting off this crazy train.

PART 2

Rise of the Hi'aiatawi'a / October 2016

CHAPTER 1

Twenty minutes later, Sheriff Brown was at the sheriff office outlining the mission to recover Shaun O'Toole's missing body parts. It was 5:00 pm on October 10, 2016. The day's light was beginning to fade, and Sheriff Brown knew that the macabre scavenger hunt was going to happen in the nocturnal hours. He preferred to search by the light of the early day, but he knew time was of the essence. Leaks of crimes are more prevalent in small towns, and he could not risk the firestorm of Bill O'Toole's wrath. Assembled in front of him were Deputy Sheriff Miller, Deputy Mack Peters, and Deputy Rodney Gibson.

"OK, men, I have pinpointed the longitude and latitude coordinates that were left in the mouth of the victim," Sheriff Brown announced, careful not to tip the identity of the deceased. These locations correspond with some of the most hiked points in Hanging Rock State Park, so it's safe to assume this crime is very fresh." Sheriff Brown stated in confident tone.

"Why is that?" Deputy Gibson asked, again confirming that he was the slowest in the group. While the other deputies began to snicker, Sheriff Brown, being a very patient man answered Deputy Gibson's question professionally.

"Well, Deputy Gibson, because of the popularity of these hiking trails, if the body parts had been there longer than a day someone would have already found them."

"OH," was the intellectual response from Deputy Gibson. Sheriff Brown then explained to his men that the team of four would be divided in half. He and Deputy Gibson would search Hanging Rock and Wolf Rock, while Deputy Peters and Deputy Sheriff Miller would search Cook's Wall and Moore's Knob. A CSI specialist would accompany each team from the State Bureau of Investigation in Raleigh, North Carolina.

"The SBI boys are on route as I speak. We will reconvene here at 1900 hours," Sheriff Brown ordered.

He knew two hours was plenty of time enough to eat supper and pack their gear. As each man shuffled out the door, he seemed to sense a strange mixture of fear and excitement from each one, and He wondered if he should recruit more men. Brown then reasoned that they were on a covert operational status, like a Navy Seal or Ranger team; this was a mission of stealth and finesse. If Sheriff Brown had known what was waiting for him and his teams in those deep dark woods that night, he would have requested help from the National Guard.

CHAPTER 2

She was very restless, kicking off the sheets of her king-sized cedar bed. Her Brown, beautiful skin was glistening with sweat, her jet-black hair tied in a ponytail. She had a sweet angelic face, chiseled with high cheekbones, hinting to her Native American heritage. The full moon's light flooded into her room and cast its rays on her slender athletic frame, awaking the prehistoric spirit deep within her. She felt the quickening of the beast and knew that it would soon emerge from her like a butterfly from a cocoon. It resided in the temple of her body, like a visiting family member that would not leave. It had witnessed the massacre at Wounded Knee in 1890, when US Cavalry had killed 150 Sioux on a reservation in South Dakota. The great chief Sitting Bull had been murdered, and many women and children had been killed. Its anger was building to a boiling point, like a pot of water simmering on a stove.

It had been there when 5,000 of its people perished on the Trail of Tears in 1830, when the palefaces tricked its proud brothers and sisters once again. Chiefs of the Seminole, Chickasaw, and Choctaw Nations had been lied to, and had peacefully surrendered their land east of the Mississippi. Hi'cictawi'a cried as it remembered the 5,000 that had expired from hunger, disease, and exposure as they marched thousands of miles to the reservations in the West. Accalia's face began to transform into something not quite human, her body growing to mammoth proportions, fingernails lengthening into claws, teeth transmuted into sharp fangs. The rage erupted like a dormant volcano; it was hungry. It would consume the bodies of the pale face interlopers and send their souls to the Underworld! It awoke seething with anger, howling like the wind in a fierce storm. It opened the balcony doors that lead to the second-floor patio and leaped out into the pitch-black night. It would find the descendants of these hideous crimes against its people and do a ghost dance on their bloodstained bones.

CHAPTER 3

Brian Cox goggled Hanging Rock State Park as he and his Partner, Lisa Cohen, traversed the 120 miles from Raleigh to Danbury, and was surprised to learn that Hanging Rock State Park encompassed some of the unique geological formations in the Southeastern United States. The pictures of its white quartzite cliffs that surrounded and protected a diminutive lake amazed him. He browsed the hiking map and learned that many of the park's waterfalls, cascades, and caves could be viewed from the twenty miles of hiking trails throughout the 7,000-acre park.

He laughed as the tree hugger who had written the column spoke in awe of the whispering pines that are perched on these barren cliffs, and that only an individual gifted in advanced biology could appreciate the mixing of the Carolina and Canadian hemlock in the park. He learned that Stone Dam, placed on a tributary of the Dan River, was built back in the 1930's as part of Roosevelt's Civilian Conservation Corps. The dam created a small lake that lies beneath the cliffs of Hanging Rock state park. Cox threw his head back and laughed hysterically at the writer's claim that this Garden of Eden could cure the modern world's ills by providing an escape from the high-tech world of computers and the omnipresent cellphone.

Entire families enjoyed fishing canoeing, and swimming; even tech-crazed teenagers did not care about tweeting, texting, or face booking once they were in the park. Human beings connecting to each other and nature are the legacy that men working to feed their families passed down to future generations. The idealist writer had concluded his masterpiece by writing about two antique structures. Two trails that climbed nearly half a mile and terminated at Wolf Rock and the trail to Moore's Knob started behind the bathhouse on the lake and the amphitheater near the campground. These two antique buildings were like gateways to the past, a simpler, gentler time in which the quality of a job well done was more important than making large sums of money by meeting deadlines.

The fact that these buildings were still standing was a testimony, a shrine to the idea that quality is more important than quantity.

"Never heard so much bullshit in my life," Cox chuckled as he exited the website.

"Why do you think the bureau chief wanted us to investigate murders in such an isolated, back-woods town?" Lisa inquired, barely hiding her deep respect and slight attraction to the seasoned veteran agent.

"Well, my dear, this back-woods town is laying smack dab in the middle of a large shale area containing several million cubic feet of natural gas just waiting to be cultivated by colossal oil and gas corporations." Cox replied

"Oh, you mean by destroying the environment by hydraulic fracturing," Lisa stated with a smirk on her face.

"The State smells large revenues, and with the current administration abolishing many environmental protections, the goal of astronomical drilling is obtainable," Cox explained with a shrug of his massive shoulders.

Cox studied the map of the trails leading to the areas that Sheriff Brown had indicated as possible recovery sites for body parts. He read that many experienced hikers had twisted their ankles on the steep, rocky terrain in the broad daylight. This crazy back-woods sheriff wanted them to climb these trails in middle of the night! The thought sent a cold chill down the length of his spine as if he had had a premonition of the future, and that this would be his hike into eternity.

CHAPTER 4

Special Agents Cox and arrived at the Sheriff's Office at exactly at 7:00 pm and, as with most small Southern towns, the Sheriff's Office, jail, and court house were located right in the middle of the town square. Cox was amused that Sheriff Brown had gathered a massive group of four men to search 7,000 acres of land in the middle of the night, and upon walking into the meeting room, he immediately voiced his concern.

Cox loudly exclaimed, "Just how in the hell are we going to search 7,000 acres in the middle of the night with just six men?" He glanced quickly over at Agent Lisa Coltraine for any signs of a reaction to his referring to her as a man.

Sheriff Brown, shocked by the lack of protocol and the abrupt manner in which Cox had barged into the room, calmly replied, "Agent Cox, I presume?" holding out his monolithic hand.

Cox suddenly realizing that his entrance bordered on extreme rudeness and eagerly shook Sheriff Brown's hand with an equally big paw. "Sorry, I am Agent Cox and this Agent Lisa Coltraine". We are just concerned about the limited manpower that is assembled, given the large task of searching such an immense area for human remains," He concluded with the frown lines deepening on his massive brow.

"Well, I can understand your concern, but if you read my synopsis of the mission, you should have read that the killer or killers left exact longitude and latitude coordinates in the oral cavity of the victim's decapitated head." Sheriff Brown lingered on the last part of his answer for dramatic effects.

He was very encouraged to see no visible reaction to the gory details on either agent's face, because he needed nerves of steel and solid resolve on this mission to perdition.

"In light of all the public's perceived notions of police brutality, how do you know that the killer or killers are not just setting up an ambush?" Agent asked.

"A very valid point, and to be perfectly honest, I don't." The sheriff then explained that there had been two mysterious murders of sons of extremely prominent families in the area, compounding the fact that the families involved represented polar opposites on the pending hydraulic fracturing moratorium vote.

He added, "The whole town would erupt into a powder keg of violence, and I just want to the keep the lid on this as long as possible."

He concluded by telling both agents that they were free to leave if, they wanted to, and that there would be no animosity toward them if they chose to do so.

"Just hold on, Sheriff! The bureau is very interested in keeping these murders on a low profile given the gas reserves in the area, besides the bad publicity of two high profile murders might scare away large gas companies interested in cultivating this area," Brian Cox said, thinking that a gas company reversal might negatively influence his retirement.

"Well, I will take that as your commitment to this mission, so take a seat. I was going into my briefing of the mission when I was so rudely interrupted," Sheriff Brown stated sarcastically. Agent Cox and Agent Coltraine sensed the-agitation in the sheriff's voice and quietly assumed their seats in the back of the room. As the Agent sat down, she wondered if her outspoken, veteran partner has just sealed both their death certificates.

CHAPTER 5

Sheriff Brown started the meeting by introducing Agents Cox and to the deputies in the room, adding that all these men knew the area like the back of their hands. The men nodded at the state officials with a mixture of small town warm and curiosity. Sheriff Brown divided the room into two fire teams: Brian Cox, Deputy Miller and Deputy Mack Peters would be Team A, and that team would search Cook's Wall and Moore's Knob. Fire Team B would be Sheriff Brown, Deputy Rodney Gibson, and Agent Lisa Coltraine would search Hanging Rock and Wolf Rock.

He had drawn a crude map on the board of the area, with matching altitudes, longitudes, and latitudes. Cox noticed that the elevation ranged from 1,240 feet at Cook's Wall to 2,570 feet at Knob. Pointing to Hanging Rock with a ruler Sheriff Brown said,

"As you will notice, Hanging Rock is the furthest point east, and Cook's Wall is the western barrier." He continued laying out the plan with military precision. Fire Team A will reach Hanging Rock at 8:30 after a three-mile hike from the visitor center and will then proceed west toward Wolf Rock. Fire Team B will reach Cook's Wall at 8:30 after a three-mile hike from the lake and will proceed east to Moore's Knob."

Cox could ascertain that both teams would be directly across from each other at the end of the mission, separated by a mere two miles, but the distance was complicated by rugged downhill slopes and a small lake. The sheriff then turned and uncovered the items that were laid on the large table in the front of the room. Cox initially had thought they all were going to bond by consuming the Lord's Supper, but he let out a low whistle when he saw the vast military hardware on the table.

"I have taken the liberty of borrowing the following items from the local National Guard Armory," Brown said with a slight smirk of confidence on his face.

The eyes in the room lit up as Sheriff Brown described the arsenal would will be at the disposal of each fire team.

"Each team will have one MP/5 sub-machine gun, and a Remington 870 12 gauge shotgun, and each fire team member will have M4 carbine and a 40 S&W 10mm pistol," Sheriff Brown stated with a rogue gleam in his eyes. Both teams will be equipped with tactical body armor and the latest in night vision goggles," Brown continued, his voice elevated like a football coach firing up his team at halftime.

The room was deathly quiet, too shocked to make a sound, but a small female hand shot up in the back of the room. A very concerned Lisa Coltraine asked "Why all the fire-power? Are you anticipating an encounter with Bigfoot?"

Rodney Gibson muted his laughter, careful not to piss off his hero, Sheriff Brown. Sheriff Brown hesitated only for a second before he answered.

"If those freaks that killed my best friend's son are in those woods, they are in for a very rude awakening."

Cox, sitting in the back of the room, thought that Sheriff Brown might be a cheeseburger short of a happy meal. Brown also explained that in the body cameras worn by each member would have a microphone and a GPS tracking device, and finally that each team would have a flare gun, which was to be used only in an extreme emergency.

"Are there any questions?" Sheriff Brown asked, half expecting none because of his attention to detail.

Deputy Gibson raised his hand, and when Sheriff Brown acknowledged him he asked, what the others thought was a goofy question

"What happens if we encounter any Boy Scouts doing night hikes?"

Deputy Mack Powers quipped, "Unless they're giving merit badges for skipping school these days, most young folks should be in the rack, being it's a week night."

Sheriff Brown gave Powers a look that would strike fear in the heart of a wild beast, and then responded to Deputy Gibson's questions with patience and kindness.

"Good question Deputy Gibson, I have spoken to the park rangers and instructed them to prohibit any hiking in the park after 7:00 pm, and actually have had them place a curfew in the campground at 8:00 pm."

Agent Cox thought what great luck for those hapless campers, expecting the great freedom of the outdoors and being quarantined to the confines of the campground. He raised his hand and asked the question that was on everyone's mind.

"I am sure that the elephant in the room is why a nocturnal mission instead of waiting until morning?" The heads of all the other five-law officers nodded in agreement.

"Great question, Agent Cox. Let me give you the top two reasons. First, if the folks around here found out about the grisly details of this repulsive murder, there would be panic of epic proportions; folks would be terrified! Sheriff Brown said, his voice raising a decimeter. Second, this victim may be related to a family that is a strong pro-environmental family in Walnut Cove, and I don't want any damn conspiracy theories circulating prematurely until we know more about what the hell is going on!" Sheriff Brown said in an agitated voice.

"Well, the proverbial cat will be out the bag soon!" Deputy Powers voiced in a defiant tone.

"Of course it will, but I assure you the violent storm the media and Bill O'Toole will bring down on this community will demand all the facts, Sheriff Brown countered. He continued by saying, I'm sure if your loved one was lying up in these hills, you would want them brought home in one piece."

The entire room nodded in agreement. "Besides, by tomorrow, Bill O'Toole will be coming to my office looking for answers, and I know that hell will be coming with him." Sheriff Brown said with a twinge of apprehension in his voice.

The sheriff then glanced at the clock and announced that the briefing was over and that if anyone had any further questions, to get with their leader. He concluded by announcing that fire teams had approximately one hour to suit up and meet at the rally points which were pinpointed on their team leader's map.

CHAPTER 6

The moon was full shining down on, illuminating its path as it ran up the mountain toward Moore's Knob. Its mind was crawling with hatred for the white man. Its people accepted Mother Earth's gift of clear, beautiful land and abundant precious water, but the White Demon polluted the waterways, raped the land, and enslaved its people. Its people were the indigenous people of America, the Native Americans who were the protector of Mother Earth. Now the White Demons were building a large serpent to carry the evil liquid under vast rivers and sacred burial grounds in South Dakota, causing great dis-equilibrium and sickness in Mother Earth's womb. Its revenge upon the greed of the white man would be swift and without mercy, and the palefaces' interpretation of its action tonight would be vile and full of wrathful revenge.

It would be hunted, but the blood of the white man would be spilled and flows like the rivers that they polluted with their unbridled greed. The anger and rage quickened its pace as it reached the observation tower that sat on the 2,579 feet pinnacle of Moore's Knob. The building of the rage was too much to contain, so it howled and the gods of the wind carried its echoes down the mountain toward those who would soon feel its fury.

CHAPTER 7

Brian Cox stood on the banks of the small lake, watching the moonlight sparkle on the water. As he listened to the wind as it blew through the Canadian pines, a blood-curling howl echoed down the mountain ended his brief encounter with the rawness of nature.

"Ah don't worry about that, just some Coyote baying at the full Moon," laughed his team leader Sheriff Deputy Donny Miller. He quickly described the ascent up to Cook's Wall as a mile straight up, the path will be laden with rocks, bushes, and falling leaves. Donny Miller then ordered them to put on the night vision goggles, and suddenly Cox world was embellished with an eerie green light. Donny explained that these top-notch goggles had a range of 100 yards; He added the length of a football field in case anyone was measurement challenged.

"Okay guys since it's a full moon we shouldn't have to turn on our head lamps, I don't want to give away our position". Miller also explained the order in which they would proceed.

"Mack you get up front with your trusty shotgun, and I will bring up the rear with that nasty Machine gun, Oh agent Cox you can hang out in the middle."

Miller added, as if Cox didn't have the ability to figure out the obvious. Cox resented the insult to his intelligence, but he kept his mouth shut since his survival might depend on the navigational skills of this Neanderthal. The men started up the trail mostly in silence, each concentrating on his foot placement and thinking about the gruesome task of collecting a body part on top of a 930-foot headland.

"Too bad you're not climbing this in daylight, Agent Cox. You would be rewarded with an excellent view of the Blue Ridge Mountains in the distance." Deputy Peters said, trying to make conversation with the stern, serious agent. Cox was walking about 10 meters behind Peters and just grunted his reply, because he was out of shape and silently gasping for oxygen. Just when Cox thought his life might end from suffocation, Deputy Donny Miller stopped suddenly causing a chain reaction that made Cox almost bumped into portly Deputy Peters that could have knocked him off the precipice into a 930-foot free fall.

Agent Cox surveyed his surroundings, and the only emotion he could sense was a feeling of deep spiritual awe transmitting to every cell of his old body. The stars were emitting a phantasmagorical display of light, which bathed the tobacco below in a luminous glow. The intermittent light of the houses mixed with the darkness of the night gave Cox insight into what the angels must see when they peer down from heaven.

"Agent Cox, if you're done with your star gazing, could we get on with the task at hand?" asked an agitated Donnie Miller.

Cox regained his composure, turned up the magnification on his goggles, and searched the rim. The men searched every inch of the bluff with no luck, and Deputy Miller was about to throw in the towel when he suddenly remembered a crevice called the Devil's Chimney, which was directly below them. "This chute is a favorite of rock climbers, but it has been shut down for the past few years because of fatalities that have occurred here," Miller informed sounding like a seasoned tour guide.

He positioned his goggles down the massive chute and saw nothing, but then he turned on his head beam. He gasped

and let out an excited yell, because 20 feet below him, laying in the colorful wildflowers and pink lady slippers, was a
severed arm. He got to his feet and searched his backpack for
the climbing rope that he had brought for such an occasion.
He quickly tied the rope to the locking carabineer and inserted the steel anchor that attached to the face of the cliff. He
then disappeared over the cliff and repelled down the crevice
toward the arm. Cox was amazed by the mountaineering skill
of the young deputy.

Deputy Miller finally reached the bottom of the chute,
walked over, picked up the arm, and placed it into a partial
body bag. As the young deputy was placing the arm into the
bag, Cox could see that the middle finger on the twisted discolored hand was extended.

"Well, at least we're dealing with a killer that has a sense
of humor," Mack Peters muttered.

"Yeah, a sick sense of humor," Agent Cox said in queasy
disgust.

"Well, you all going to stand there all day or get me the
hell out of here?" yelled an angry Miller from deep in the crevice. Both men grasped the rope and started pulling the 140-
pound deputy up the steep cliff. Cox thought it was the tough-
est physical challenge of his life. He then looked over at the
portly deputy Mack Peters sweating profusely and thought it
could it have been worse!

After Deputy Miller had cleared the chute, he transmitted
the information via radio to Sheriff Brown, telling him that
they had secured a detached left arm. He also mentioned that
the brachial artery wrapped around the arm like a sleeve,
however he did not mention the eternal salute of defiance.
Sheriff Brown told the team to proceed to Moore's Knob approximately two miles away. Before he signed off, the sheriff mentioned his team's success on Hanging Rock. They had
found a severed leg, complete with the femoral artery hanging

out like a dirty sock on a boot, hidden among the shrubs and laurel.

CHAPTER 8

Brian Cox adjusted his night goggles and fell behind Deputy Sheriff Miller, who now took the lead. He followed with a new respect for the lawman after the demonstration of above-average mountaineering skills.

"Hey, Officer Miller, how did you learn to climb like that?" Cox asked in an almost reverend manner.

"I was raised in this area. My father instructed me in the fine art of climbing. We were going to climb Mountain McKinley together before the cancer got him." He added the last bit of information with a slight shrug of his shoulders. Deputy Sheriff Miller was a small man, but Cox guessed that he had extraordinary strength and athletic agility, which might be helpful in running down the occasional purse-snatcher in the small hamlet of Danbury. He had a darkened skin tone and aphotic hair and cartilaginous eyes, which hinted of a Native American heritage.

The most distinctive feature that one would remember after meeting Deputy Sheriff Miller was his eyes, not for color or shape but for the intense glow, they emitted. Miller turned and described in detail the short hike along the ridgeline to Moore's Knob.

"We will be walking along a ridge line which offers a panoramic, sweeping views of both sides of the Sauratown Mountains, best hiking trail in the park! Look to your left... great view of the distant Blue Ridge Mountains. Turn to the right and get a postcard view of the lake, beach, and bathhouse," added a suddenly euphoric Deputy Miller. Cox could sense a deep bonding between these two men and these remote mountains that seemed to magically appear, completely separated from the more popular distant Blue Ridge Mountains.

"A lot of folks believe the Sauratown Mountains are in fact ancient volcanoes, and that's how they have withstood eons of erosion by the wind and precipitation," Deputy Miller said to no one in particular. Cox was about to dispute the deputy's claim when he suddenly turned his head to the left, and half way between his location and the Blue Ridge Mountains stood Powder Mountain. Bathed in the moonlight, Cox could make out that the mountain was indeed cone shaped and that it did resemble a prehistoric, dormant volcano. Brian Cox made a mental note to bring his girlfriend to this place of geologic wonder, and proposed marriage; surely, she would not say "NO" surrounded by such beauty.

CHAPTER 9

The men silently but swiftly made the gradual climb to Moore's Knob; at 2,579 feet, it was the highest point in the Sauratown Mountains. They walked with a quiet intensity committed to the goal of bringing Shaun O'Toole body home. Even though the result would be grotesque, at least the dismembered limbs would not wind up as buzzard or falcon food. As they neared the next recovery point revealed by the note left in Shaun's cranium, a loud screech pierced the silence. Agent Cox involuntarily jumped back, and both deputies laughed in unison.

"Hey, State Bureau Investigator man, that was just a screech owl!" Deputy Sheriff Donny Miller said, laughing.

"They are quite numerous in this area," Mack Peters added. Cox did not have time to be embarrassed, because the beast descended upon them with unnatural swiftness. Mack Peter's head was quickly detached from his spine before he could bring his shotgun up to meet his attacker. Blood spurted from the carotid artery like a water sprinkler working overtime in late August. Cox and Miller were drenched in Peters' blood and resembled two bloodthirsty vampires in a low budget horror movie.

The men countered with a sub-machine gun blast and 9-millimeter fire, but the beast had disappeared into the night.

"Did you see it?" Miller asked, obviously still in shock, using it as a pronoun to describe the attacker or attackers.

"Naw! Damn thing came out of nowhere and was gone like a spring storm!" Cox echoed the use of an inhuman pronoun.

Both men instinctively knew that they were dealing with something instead of someone.

"Quick! Let us make a run for the observation tower, Miller yelled, heading for the 40-foot tall old fire tower. It will provide a good area to lay down suppressible fire!"

Cox started running for the tower, an old stone structure constructed during the 1930's. He ran toward the tower blindly firing his 9-mm into the blackness, because in his haste, he had forgotten to adjust his night vision goggles. As Miller ascended the double staircase, he noticed the severed leg lying in a large hole in the wall of the tower. The hole was a natural opening that was created by the many years of rain and wind pelting the tower during storms. Being the true professional that he was, he stopped to pry the leg out of the hole despite tremendous danger to himself and Cox.

"Forget that damn thing!" Cox shouted at the top of his lungs. Miller's final tug dislodged the leg and almost caused him to lose his balance, but Cox was only inches behind the deputy grabbed his arm, possibly saving the deputy's life for approximately the next twenty minutes.

Deputy Miller reached the platform first and set his machine gun up to fire on a down-slope trajectory, and then he reached into the backpack and grabbed the flare gun. He assumed the situation they were in qualified as a definite emergency, so he pointed the gun into the night sky and pulled the trigger. Deputy Sheriff Miller then turned his attention to the ground 40 feet below. He removed the safety on the machine gun and placed his finger on the trigger, eagerly waiting to avenge Mack Peter's gruesome death. Just as Cox reached the platform, he witnessed the most incredulous spectacle! This giant Tasmania Devil thing had leaped the 40-feet from the ground, and now stood between him and Deputy Miller. It was enormous, standing almost nine feet tall, covered with coarse hair from head to toe. Cox thought the creature seemed to be a cross between Bigfoot and a Werewolf. Its fangs protruded out at an obscene angle, and its claws, still matted with dried blood, looked like butcher knives protruding from its hands.

The beast stood between Agent Cox and Deputy Miller, so neither man could fire off a round in fear of striking the other; both men realized that they would have to engage the beast in hand to claw combat. The creature negated any reprisal because with its blinding speed. It took one-step forward and took a mighty swing at the midsection of Miller's body. The advanced woven fibers of Miller's soft body armor were no match for the lethal swipe, and the contents of Miller's thoracic cavity tumbled out onto the observation deck. The last thought that passed through Miller's dying mind was that the thing that killed him looked like an Ogre from one of Aesop's fables that he had read to his daughter the night before. Cox was horrified when the brute stooped down and picked up Deputy Miller's still beating heart and began to consume it. Cox was frozen with fear. He attempted a feeble roundhouse kick that struck the creature in the hindquarters, but the kick just enraged it. It picked him up, and Cox began to scream and kick with all his might. The kicks and punches had no effect on the monster; it was as if Cox was an insect buzzing around a lethal predator.

The eyes of the creature penetrated Cox's soul and, unbelievably, Agent Cox began to calm. Cox was suddenly aware that his thought process had been altered, and his thoughts took on a dark, ominous quality. The bloody images of Native American Indian women and children being slaughtered by white cavalrymen flashed across his mind like a movie playing in a theater. Cox began to tremble with deep sorrow and shame. Hi'cictawi'a then dropped Cox onto the deck. Brian Cox filled with shame and regret, walked quietly to the side of the platform close to the 2,570-foot drop-off, climbed the rail and jumped into the deep, dark abyss.

CHAPTER 10

Sheriff Brown's team had just recovered the last item of their macabre scavenger hunt; the arm had been stuck on a dwarfed Canadian Pine. These stunted trees somehow managed to grow in the harshest environments, as the little tree's presence on the 2200-foot cliff exemplified. The severed arm had been positioned in a precarious place directly over the edge, waving in the wind as if in salutation or goodbye, depending on which direction it was observed from. Being the slightest, Special Agent Coltraine shimmed out and retrieved it in spite of great peril to herself. Sheriff Brown's respect for the female agent grew staggeringly, as he assisted her off the tree. The flare lit up the sky like a Roman candle. In fact, Deputy Gibson thought it was someone shooting off illegal fireworks.

"Hey, Sheriff, I just saw someone discharge some illegal fireworks. Should we go arrest them?" he childishly asked.

"Naw, Rodney, that's a flare from over at Moore's Knob, but thanks for spotting it for me!" Brown replied, always trying to find a way to praise the slightly dim-witted Gibson.

Sheriff Brown tried to get Miller on the radio but was rewarded with only static for his efforts. He immediately knew something was wrong. Deputy Sheriff Miller was not prone to crying wolf. He would have not fired the flare unless under extreme duress. Brown considered calling the state police or park rangers, but then he considered that the covert operation had been his decision. He knew the consequences of failure on a mission so covert and knew he would kiss his pension and retirement goodbye.

"Deputy Gibson and Agent Coltraine, pack up the gear! We have to haul ass over to Moore's Knob!" he yelled as he started on the trail down to the lake.

The trail was twisting and steep, so all three turned their headlamps on so the high beams illuminated the rocky surface. They covered the downhill portion in twenty minutes. Instead of walking around the lake, which would have consumed more time, Brown ordered them into the canoes that were usually reserved for daytime trips. Sheriff Brown gave paddles to his team and commanded them to envision themselves as members of the Harvard rowing club and to paddle like hell! The paddling was difficult because of the lightweight body armor, but Agent Coltraine, who was built like an Olympian swimmer, used her massive shoulders to propel the canoe swiftly across the lake. Deputy Gilbert must have been impressed because he blurted out,

"Darn good fishing here 'cuz the rangers stock the lake in the spring with bream, shell crackers, and bass."

Sheriff Brown thought that this tidbit about a good fishing hole was the slow-witted man's attempt to flirt with female SBI agent. The attempted flirt went wide right as Agent Coltraine ignored him as she continued paddling, demonstrating her bulging forearms and pectorals. Although Agent Coltraine had brilliant blue eyes, she had several masculine features that at present were focused on their speedy trek across the small lake. They reached the other side of the small lake in ten minutes, and the team exited the boat quickly, causing Deputy Gibson to lose his footing and fall clumsily into the lake. Sheriff Brown had already starting the climb up to Moore's Knob, but turned and yelled unsympathetically,

"Let's go, Gibson! You can dry off running up to Moore's Knob!" Sheriff Brown checked his watch; 30 minutes had elapsed since the distress flare. This is taking too much damn time he thought to himself.

The trail up to Moore's Knob was steep and had several large cut stones that resembled a primitive staircase leading up the mountain.

"We're skirting the campground along the western boundary, so don't get alarmed if you spot a couple of camp-fires," Sheriff Brown explained.

"Yeah, got a real nice campground here while you're fish-ing," Deputy Gibson said, confirming his attraction to the tough looking female agent They would cross a small creek, then they would commence a steep climb from 1,500 feet to the 2,579-foot crest of the mountain.

"Turn your halogen lights on high beam; don't want ei-ther of you trekking off the side of the mountain," Sheriff Brown ordered as they neared the pinnacle of the Knob. They approached the area with extreme caution, straining to hear noises in the wind. The clouds were racing across the sky driven by the hands of the Gods, occasionally hiding the full moon. Agent Coltraine almost blew away a barred owl that had the audacity to hoot at them. As she leveled her 9-milli-meter clock at the feathered beast, Deputy Gilbert grabbed her arm and admonished her for being so jumpy, thus elim-inating any chances of a storybook romance. Sheriff Brown led the team armed with the MP/5 sub-machine gun. He si-lently walked to the fire tower, sweeping the area from right to left with his weapon. Agent Coltraine carried the 12 Gauge shotgun and was approximately 10 meters behind Brown, and Deputy Gibson brought up the rear armed with the M4 car-bine.

The tension was thick as they slowly proceeded toward the fire tower. The eerie silence is broken by a loud crash in the brush! A violent barrage of bullets was then targeted upon the beast that had the brashness to interrupt their intense fear. The assault lasted for almost two minutes, until Sheriff Brown came to his senses and ordered a cease-fire. He then ordered his deputy to check the area that had just received enough firepower to qualify for government disaster assistance. Deputy Gibson started to protest but didn't want to appear weak or scared in front of his new love interest. He slowly traversed over to the overgrown brush and carefully entered it. He was immersed in the brush for what seemed like an eternity, and then slowly emerged, pulling the bullet-ridden carcass of a 12-point white tailed buck! He had a look of total dejection and sadness, but still wanted to take the antlers to mount above his fireplace.

"Oh, damn, Rodney, we're not on a hunting expedition!" wailed Sheriff Brown.

Just as he began to admonish his dim-witted deputy, he saw some movement out of the corner of his eye. He slowly turned to his team and told them to cover him as he proceeded up the stairs to the observation deck. As Sheriff Brown cleared the last step, he sharply inhaled as his mind tried to grasp the repugnance of the scene. Two cone shaped pile of bones resembling Indian wigwams were resting on the observation deck. The bones were matted with dried blood, but the thing that horrified him the most was the two skulls placed directly on top of the bones. The skulls seemed to peer at him with deep cynical resignation as if blaming him for their deaths. Sheriff Brown noticed that cartridge, tendons, and tissue were still attached to the bones. As he looked closer, he noticed fang indentations on the bones.

A primal scream bubbled up from his soul, and as it resounded down the mountain Hi'cictawi'a began to howl in unison. Unnerved by the howling, Agent Coltraine and Deputy Gibson quickly ran to Sheriff Brown's location. When they arrived, Sheriff Brown had regained his composure and was radioing the park rangers, and the state police! Deputy Gilbert and Agent Coltraine were in complete shock and mortified by the spectacle that assaulted their senses. Deputy Gilbert overheard Sheriff Brown demanded the Park be evacuated and closed down. Sheriff Brown then requested an Evidence Response Team from the Federal Bureau of Investigation converge on the area before daylight. Finally, he ordered paramedics and emergency responders to their location.

He noticed a partial body bag blowing in the wind, which explained the movement he had seen from the ground. He peered into the bag and took a quick mental inventory: one severed arm and a leg. At least the team had completed their grisly mission. Simple-minded Rodney Gibson pondered three thoughts upon hearing the sheriff's orders. Why weren't there three piles of bones? How were the ambulances or bone wagons going to climb the mountain? Finally, to coin a commercial from the eighties, "Where's the beef?"

Several hours after the killings, Accalia stirred in her bed. A strong earthen scent assaulted her nose, and she felt a muscle twitch and something moved on her left leg. She pulled at the covers to try to stay warm, but the blankets made a crackling noise, and then dissolved in her hands like magic. She opened her eyes, and to her horror, she realized that she was totally naked, caked with mud and blood! She then realized that she was outside covered with oak and sugar maple leaves, and what she had thought was a muscle twitch was a large earth worm crawling up her thigh.

Accalia struggled to her feet and tried to get orientated her surroundings. As her eyes became focused, she realized that she had been sleeping in a shallow, muddy creek bed. The impression that her body had made on the soft ground was massive, much longer and wider then her small petite frame, as if something of massive size had been sleeping along beside her. Judging by the position of the full moon above her, Accalia thought that it was about 4:00 am, which meant she had been in the woods for approximately six hours. Had she really been wandering the woods for six hours? As a terrible fear invaded the middle of her soul, a large beetle crawled out of her long thick hair and traveled down the side of her face. Accalia aggressively swatted at the pest, and with the help of the lunar glow of the full moon noticed a crimson stain on her hands. She smelled her hands and they indeed had the coppery smell of blood. Accalia knew that her sickness had resurfaced, that the beast had committed another act of debauchery!

Accalia knew she had to escape from these woods, but she had no idea where she was and did not want to risk walking around in circles. As she began to panic, the whispering began inside her skull as if some ancient soul was trying to communicate with her. Was this some type of schizophrenic mumbo jumbo? Or maybe she had disassociate identity disorder like her mother. She had listened to the voices before, and they had led her to safety. This message was delivered in a chanting format and kept telling her that she was near the old three story abandoned hotel near Vade Mecum Springs!

Accalia knew these woods well and came to realize that the muddy creek bed that she was lying in was two miles west of Highway 8, the main highway leading into Danbury. She would hike to the road and hopefully a Good Samaritan would pick her up! She looked down at the huge oak tree and noticed the clump of moss growing on one side of the massive trunk. Accalia knew that moss only grew on the north side of trees, so she used that knowledge to hike in a westerly direction. As Accalia took each step toward safety and freedom, she realized that she was assisting a ruthless, vicious creature to evade capture once again, and she began to weep mournfully.

CHAPTER 11

She was caught in the same nightmare, which had plagued her dreams for about eight years now. The same giant hands engulfed her tender, vulnerable neck, cutting off the air circulating down her trachea. The sheet enshrined her body like a shroud as she struggled to get the air into her lungs, but the oxygen deprivation seemed to cause her to slip into an unconscious state. Her rational mind knew that it was the same recurring nightmare, but that knowledge did not nullify the terror that was pulling her toward the darkness! At the very moment she thought her heart was going to stop, she felt the strong arms of her husband wrap around her.

She then forced the air back into her lungs and screamed loudly enough to wake the dead, or at least to get the next-door neighbor's dog to howl in unison. Kelli Ryan became aware of Jake's firm embrace and his soft whispering in her ear. "It's going to be alright, baby, I have you!" She stared up sheepishly at her soul mate, protector, and muttered,

"Jake, you need to replace me with a sane wife."

Jake quietly replied, "Nonsense! Then I wouldn't have an excuse to give to Dr. Jennings when I nod off in front of my last period American History class."

"Oh, I'm just surprised it's you nodding off instead of the other way around!" Kelli laughed, knowing that Jake was one of the best natural teachers that Pinewood High had ever had. In fact, Jake had been named "Teacher of the Year" three times in the past ten years. As a testimony to his brilliance, Jake had been invited to work with the Governor's Scholars Program three years in a row. He was so proud to be able to work with the best and brightest students in the Virginia school system.

Kelli had suffered from nightmares and flashbacks since she and Jake had almost lost their lives on Portsmouth Island, North Carolina. The psychopathic killer Timothy O'Conner had almost ended her career at the bureau. She was terrified of the darkness in the shadows, and if anyone made a sudden move, her reaction was quick and aggressive. In fact, Jake had to warn many friends of her inner demons. She was suffering from Post-Traumatic Stress Syndrome, and her career with the FBI had gone in a different direction. The bureau recognized her intelligence, bravery, and skill, and rewarded her with a desk job; her official title was Administrative Officer.

Through her quiet persistence and dedication for obtaining her Doctorate in Criminal Justice, Kelli was now the top Administrative Officer at the Behavioral Science Academy located in Quantico, Virginia. Although Kelli was respected among peers as brilliant, she felt like her soul was dying a slow death. She controlled every facet of the operation of the school from appointing instructors to management of curriculum for an increasing complex global FBI presence, but in her soul and heart, she longed to be in the field tracking terrorists and apprehending the FBI's most wanted serial killers or rapists.

Dr. Sloan, the department's shrink, had been treating her for PTSD for the last eight years. He had been using "hypnotic subliminal suggestion" to replace the triggers and thoughts that caused her night sweats and flashbacks. He had also used breakthrough technology in virtual reality to help Kelli to re-enter the traumatic events of her kidnapping and deal with her terror from a "safe place". Through cognitive and exposure therapy Kelli began to stop using any anti-depressants, which she had relied heavily on in the initial stages of her recovery.

As she peered into her husband's deep blue eyes, her confession came bubbling out her soul.

"Jake, Doctor Sloan is going to recommend my return to field operations. I am going to be a field agent again, baby," she said uneasily.

There was a long silence as Jake took a deep breath, which turned into a sigh. "Kelli, you don't have to prove anything. You almost died on your last case," he replied.

"Jake, I am not going to let some freak show like Tim O'Conner, alias Hercules, stop me from doing what I was born to do." She continued, "Even though I have this awesome position and I am compensated at a high pay grade, my soul is empty," she said in an anguished, hushed whisper.

Jake stared at his beautiful wife for a long time, recognizing a kindred spirit, a warrior, that needed the stimulus of the chase and capture. He sensed that her warrior spirit, inherited from her Special Forces father, was slowly wilting away like a precious flower in an arid climate. He wanted her to reclaim her heart, so he calmly gave her his affirmation.

"You forgot to mention your strong, loving husband in your list of current positive material possessions in your life," and then he laughed and gave her his permission to follow her heart.

"Get out there, baby, and make our world safer for the sheep out there," he whispered in her perfectly shaped ear lobe.

"Oh, Jake, I love you so much!" and she hugged him so tightly that the air was forced out of his lungs. That one act caused him to flashback to the horror they had both faced on Portsmouth Island eight years before.

CHAPTER 12

Paul Jacobs called her into his spacious office around 9:00 am the next morning, many pictures of his long tenure with the FBI aligned the wall. He was a lanky man with a nose that was pointed and resembled the beak of a hawk. He seemed to have a perpetual scowl on his face but looks can be deceiving. Paul Jacobs actually cared a great deal about all 300 staff and 100 part time employees who magically turned average citizens into the finest criminal pro-filers in the world. He was going over a spreadsheet that outlined the financial cost of running such a sophisticated operation and comparing it to the funds that Congress had allocated to the school in the next year's fiscal budget. He scratched his head and was about to call his CFO into the office, when his secretary calmly announced over the intercom that Kelli Ryan was there to see him.

As Kelli walked into his office, Jacobs could not help but think such a tough, courageous, strong woman wrapped in stunningly beautiful package. He was well aware of her PTSD, but she had always performed brilliantly on any task he had assigned to her.

"Agent Ryan, I was expecting you. Have a seat," he said with a hushed professional tone.

Kelli was admiring the beautiful cedar desk, with the large, perfectly cut piece of marble that lay in the center. No matter how many times she had been in his office, the desk always caught her attention.

"I'm going over our budget for next year; looks like 2017

is going be a year of cutbacks for us." He tried to avoid the issue of Kelli's request for transfer to field grade grunt.

Kelli Ryan, always the professional, took the reports and calmly stated, "I will go over this budget and recommend cuts in our operational costs."

"You always taking the bull by the horns, Kelli. You are invaluable to me," Jacobs replied with a serious demeanor.

Like a dam breaking, Kelli had to bring the real issue of her visit to the table

. "Have you gone over Dr. Sloan's report?" she bravely asked. After a brief hesitation, Jacobs replied, "Yes, but I have not made the decision yet. I wanted to ask you some questions about your motivation for sacrificing all you have worked so hard for to go back into the lion's den."

"My first field case was a disaster! Without the interjection of Senior Agent Miller, I would have failed," Kelli defiantly stated, with a rogue look of intensity in her eyes.

"I have researched your file, and you barely escaped with your life. You required extensive dental surgery to replace the teeth that monster stole from you. Why put yourself in that kind of danger again?" Jacob inquired with intensity.

"Sir, with all due respect, I am running on empty here. I am void of any passion. I was born to be in the field!" Kelli pleaded.

"Nonsense! With your instincts, your knowledge of counter intelligence and victimology have led to the apprehension of several known FBI most wanted serial killers, terrorists, and scumbags around the world," he replied with strong conviction.

Kelli stared at Jacobs for a brief moment before she replied. She was beginning to sense that her request was going to be denied.

"Sir, that was all behind the scenes. I have the blood of a Special Forces soldier running through my veins, and it beckons me to be a warrior!" Kelli said with a volcanic intensity.

"Kelli, don't you think that away from therapeutic intervention your condition may worsen, causing you to have flashbacks?" He countered her passion with a strong dose of rationality.

"I can handle it! Doctor Sloan has provided me with several desensitization techniques," Kelli countered.

Jacobs, sensing that he was not getting anywhere with his brilliant but stubborn subordinate, calmly said,

"Be in my office tomorrow morning at nine, and I will give you my decision. And please get started on those cutbacks to the budget." he said sternly.

On cue, Kelli interpreted those orders as her dismissal. As she turned and made her way to the door, she wondered if she had just pushed Jacobs too far. Her brain told her that her request would be denied, so she went to the ladies' room to get her emotions in check because she knew that the bureau doesn't approve of whiners.

CHAPTER 13

On the Morning of October 11, Kelli woke up early with an urge to run, so she put on her Nike jogging attire complete with her Nike running shoes. Jake always commented that she looked so fine in her navy blue pullover shirt, that fat guys would run a four-minute mile to catch her!

Kelli and Jake lived in Manassas, Virginia, about 25 miles from her work in Quantico. Jake's commute to the high school was only five minutes from their spacious but modest home on Lancaster Avenue. Kelli opened the front door of the 6,000 square foot Colonial split-level home, and after properly stretching, began jogging swiftly pass the neatly manicured lawns and tastefully trimmed hedges. They lived in a subdivision that was controlled by an overly aggressive HOA, which sometimes seemed like a dominant big brother. The one good thing about the paranoid HOA was that security and surveillance cameras were ubiquitous.

Kelli was a big fan of modern technology that allowed witnesses, human or electronic, to capture the vile actions of demons cloaked in human camouflage. Her mind regressed to Portsmouth Island, and she began to run with a deeper intensity, her thoughts becoming fragmented. She knew she was on the verge of spinning out of control and began to implement the semi-hypnotic methods that Doctor Sloan had instructed her to use during such an episode. Kelli's breathing slowed as she envisioned herself defeating the monster Hercules with extreme prejudice. Kelli then turned her thoughts to the meeting with Director Jacobs later in the morning, and she felt a renewed strength in her conviction that she could indeed keep her private monster in its mental cage.

Jake was waiting for her with a towel and a cup of coffee in his large masculine hands. "Hey, baby, you should be on the cover of Sports Illustrated!" He smiled and handed her the towel

Kelli suddenly felt a twinge of guilt as she looked into the clear blue eyes of the only man that she would ever need. Kelli knew her desire to reenter the field increased Jake's stress level. Although he had fully recovered from his heart attack on Portsmouth Island, she didn't want to create any pressure on that vital organ.

"Jake, you're my private knight in shining armor, and I will be yours for eternity," she whispered in his ear.

"Ah, Kelli, you sound so needy and possessive. Let's just get through this life first!" He grinned that golden smile and playfully smacked her on her well-shaped buttocks.

He then gave her a deep sensual kiss, and in spite a burning desire to make love in the doorway in front of the bothersome probing cameras, she breathlessly whispered in his ear,

"I have an important meeting with Jacobs this morning, so unfortunately this copulation event will have to wait till tonight!"

Jake's eyes never left hers as he told her that he loved her deeply, and that he would be waiting behind the door ready to pounce on her with her favorite bottle of Chardonnay. Kelli would never forget the look of hurt and fear that emitted from those crystal blue eyes and wondered why she was being so self-centered. She briefly thought about reconsidering her request before the spirit of her recently departed warrior father engulfed her soul urging her to follow the passions of her life.

CHAPTER 14

Kelli was fifteen minutes early for her appointment with Jacobs. As she sat in the foyer, the muffled sound of an intense conversation drifted from underneath the door. Kelli looked inquisitively at Barbara Cates, Jacobs' executive secretary, who mouthed the words, "Doctor Sloan," and Kelli nodded her head, thanking her longtime friend for the helpful tidbit of information. Kelli knew instinctively that Dr. Sloan was on her side and was defending her with bellicose fervor. The door suddenly opened and Dr. Sloan himself ushered Kelli in. She glanced at Director Jacobs; he appeared to be in a state of upheaval, his eyes were red and were glazed over, and his usually neatly combed hair was ruffled. Kelli also was aware of another man whom she had never met, who was staring at her with an intensity that made her feel uncomfortable. He was a small man, maybe 5'6" tall, dark hair, and ruddy looking skin. Because he was so impeccably dressed, Kelli assumed it was his way of compensating for his small stature.

"Kelli, this is Jordan King, director of the State Bureau of Investigation in North Carolina," Jacobs informed Kelli. Kelli had an immediate flashback as she wondered if the soulless monster Hercules had resurfaced somewhere and was killing with impunity.

Mr. King quickly made it across the room and shook Kelli's hand with vigor.

"Damn glad to finally meet you!" Brian Cox talks glowingly about your intelligence and skill!"

"Oh, thank you! How is Brian?" Kelli asked, amazed by the

strong grip produced by the small man.

There was an awkward silence as Director King informs Kelli that Senior Agent Brian Cox was missing and presumed dead in the mountains of North Carolina. Kelli was stunned by the news and a wave of grief spilled down into her soul. Brian Cox was a dear friend and was the only reason Jake and she were still alive.

"When did this happen?" Kelli asked in bewilderment, because She and Jake had just invited Brian and his new love interest to their home the next weekend for a steak cookout.

"Last night, at Hanging Rock State Park near Danbury, North Carolina." "Brian Cox disappeared and the two sheriff's deputies who were with him were slaughtered," Director King said in a hushed tone.

Kelli shook her head back and forth, trying to negate the horrifying reality of Director King's words, and simply asked, "How?"

"That's what we're hoping you will find out for us, Kelli," Paul Jacobs surprisingly stated from behind his desk. Kelli suddenly realized that her dream was coming true. She would return to the field, but it was a bittersweet moment because her close friend was lost in the mountains of North Carolina and presumed dead.

"Kelli, last night I had decided to deny your request for reentry into the field because you're just too valuable a resource to this operation. But I was ambushed by these two gentlemen this morning." Paul Jacobs seemed to almost smile as he glanced at Sloan and King. He explained to Kelli that Doctor Sloan had almost convinced him to change his mind, and then Deputy King had flown in this morning to request her assistance.

"It seems that karma and the laws of the universe are conspiring on your behalf, but this video that we downloaded from one of the deceased sheriff's deputies' body cameras may convince you to reconsider," Paul Jacobs said with a sincere look of horror on his face.

After the file was uploaded on his powerful Hewitt Packard computer, Kelli watched in complete awe and disgust as a hybrid, wolf-like creature that takes a vicious swipe at the midsection of the hapless victim. The lycan moved so swiftly that its image appeared to be a blur, and Kelli wondered if the creature was an optical illusion. The lighting and camera angle may have conspired to create an apparition. After witnessing such a killing machine in action, Kelli almost reconsidered, but then she thought of Brian Cox. She simply said,

"What time do you want me to leave?" Both Jacobs and Jordan King were caught by surprise at the brave woman's quick response, but Paul Jacobs had anticipated Kelli's reaction and simply said,

"I have taken the liberty to book a flight for you on American Airlines, leaving at 5:00 am tomorrow from Ronald Reagan International Airport. Director King will accompany you. While you are in transit to Stokes County, he will brief you on what the state's evidence team has dug up in the last 24 hours. The rest of your team will meet you at Piedmont International Airport in Greensboro." Jacobs almost whispered the instructions like a man struggling to maintain his composure. Jacobs also informed her that her team would assume the lead in the investigation, and that all state law enforcement agencies would be at her disposal.

Kelli's mind was racing with complex issues such as procedures and compliance to FBI regulations for field agents, since she had been out of the game for eight years. She then realized that her main concern was Jake's reaction to her madness. As Kelli turned to leave her the office, her confidence is shaken by the look on Paul Jacob's face. The look resembled the expression on a judge's face when he sentenced a hapless soul to be executed.

PART THREE

Murder, Massacres, and Moratoriums

CHAPTER 1

Jake Ryan was a man gifted with a sixth sense; so during his sixth period American History class, he sensed that something was wrong. He had a sudden flash in the left temporal side of his brain, and then a vision of his dear friend Brian Cox lying in a casket. He quickly told his class to read the pages concerning the Tet Offensive during the Vietnam War and that there would be a short ten-minute pop quiz at the end of class. The short reprieve would allow him to regain his composure.

The group of seniors began moaning their displeasure but suddenly became deathly quiet when Jake turned and gave them a stare of such intensity that it would have intimidated Beelzebub himself. He then turned on his cell phone, and read a text send moments before from his queen. It read BRIAN COX IS MISSING IN THE MOUNTAINS OF NORTH CAROLINA AND PRESUMED DEAD. Jake sharply inhaled; this news had the same effect as having been kicked in the stomach by a dwarfish mule!

He suddenly felt the need to go to the men's room, so he instructed the brown-nosing Rachel Smith to watch the class. Rachel was one of the chief ass kissers in the class, and he knew that he could count on her to snitch on any violators of his class rules. He went to the nearest bathroom where he promptly and violently heaved up the last remnants of the lasagna that he had had for lunch. He had a planning period coming up, so he decided to go home early, and since it was only Tuesday, his assistant coaches could manage one day of football practice without him. He went back to the classroom, gave the short pop quiz to the grumbling students, dismissed the class, and grabbed his coat, hurrying to the principal's office to inform them of his decision. Along the way, he thought of his friend Brian Cox, and an icy chill went down his spine. Jake felt much grief for his friend, but the main reason for the cold chill was knowing that his beautiful wife, his reason for living, would cross the third dimension of hell to avenge their friend's death.

CHAPTER 2

Kelli noticed Jake's car parked in their driveway when she arrived home. She dreaded the confrontation that would ensue upon her announcement that she would be leaving for North Carolina in the morning. Kelli pushed the gadget above the driver's sun visor and the garage door opened like magic. She quickly parked her Monte Carlo in the spot reserved for her "baby". Kelli started heading for the side door leading into her home, when she noticed movement in Jake's man cave, an area reserved for his many woodworking projects. Jake was operating the lathe with expert precision, and she knew better than to disturb him. Kelli quickly disappeared into their home, knowing that Jake was using the woodworking as a distraction from the day's horrible events. Kelli knew that somehow her clairvoyant husband knew that she would disappear in the morning on another morbid adventure.

Jake worked in his man cave until 7:00 pm, when Kelli called him to dinner. He could hear Marvin Gaye's hit, "Ain't No Mountain High Enough" permeating the room. The mahogany table was like something out of Better Homes and Gardens, with the fine china reserved for only special occasions shining with a dazzling brightness. The centerpiece featured two candles burning brightly, and the scent of Jasmine filled the room. The atmosphere of the room was as if a telegraph sent to the cerebellum of Jake's brain: his wife, his anchor of stability and love, was going to be gone in the morning.

She came in the room with a radiant flush to her cheeks and a sparkle in her beautiful almond shaped green eyes as she set before him his favorite dish of filet mignon and lobster with garlic butter. He grabbed her, the intensity in his light blue eyes burning with a soul piercing stare, and calmly stated,

"You are leaving in morning, aren't you?" Kelli looked into the windows of Jake's soul. His eyes were emitting an image of complete and utter sadness, and Kelli tried to reply but promptly started sobbing on his shoulder. Between pitiful, gut wrenching sobs, she asked for his forgiveness for being so selfish.

The two lovers held their embrace for several minutes. Jake looked at her with tears in his eyes, and even through his heart was breaking, he whispered in her ear,

"It's okay, baby, I made a promise on our wedding day for better or worse, and that also includes for sane or insane." He broke off with that big-hearted "Jake's Laugh" of his that she knew and loved. Kelli held him with a rib spitting intensity and began to laugh, and when Marvin starting singing something about sexual healing, they both decided to take the conversation to the bedroom.

Their lovemaking was intense, like two souls reunited after eons of separation. Their eyes meet on several occasions while both were climaxing simultaneously, deepening their bond for eternity. As they held each other for several minutes, Kelli was the first to utter the most soothing words Jake had ever heard.

"Jacobs has agreed to allow you to assist in the investigation as a consulting expert," Kelli said with an upbeat tone.

Jacobs had read about Jake's strong contributions to Kelli's last case eight years before and was impressed with Jake's dogged persistence that had helped solve the case and eventually saved Kelli's life.

"So, you stoically insisting that I be part of the investigation had nothing to do with Jacob's decision? "Jake asked, trying to hide his amusement.

Kelli looked at him with shock and replied, "Maybe just a tad", again surprised by his sharp deductive reasoning.

"Well, maybe ten years with the Manteo, North Carolina Police Department and five years of being a private detective did assisted you a little bit in convincing Jacobs, my dear." Jake added.

Even though it was football season, he could fly to North Carolina on the weekends and give her some consulting and support. He never asked her to reconsider her decision because as a true soul mate, he wanted not to control her but to liberate her. He slowly caressed her face and massaged the small of her back with his other hand, and gently told her that he was behind her decision one hundred percent, and wickedly winked at her as "little Jake" announced its desire to start a consulting session immediately.

CHAPTER 3

The next morning, Jake was awakened to a very early breakfast in bed and began smiling to himself and silently congratulating himself on a fine performance the previous night. Kelli came back into the room, and as he was munching on his crispy bacon, she ruined his delusions of grandeur. His wife deflated his ego by asking, "How about a ride to the airport, lover-man?" Her green eyes exuded the residual passion from last night.

"Ah, this is all about bribery," he thought, but he could not deny his beautiful wife's request. Besides, the hour's drive would give him many opportunities to ask some deep, probing questions about the case.

"Sure, just let me call the school and tell them of my twenty-four-hour stomach virus," Jake said, smiling to his grinning wife.

As he opened the car door for his lady a short time later, Jake noticed that the morning was overcast, with low stratus clouds that hovered over the ground like a gray shroud. The clouds seemed to be laden with rain, as if at any moment, the floodgate would open, and to Jake the weather was perfect for a funeral setting on a movie set. The weather only added to Jake's gloom, but he stayed positive and upbeat for Kelli's sake.

During the hour's trip to Ronald Reagan Airport, Jake clasped her hand tightly with his non-driving hand, as if subconsciously he was expressing his desire never to let her go. Jake was in rare form, explaining to Kelli that he feared for her safety, and threatened to punch Director Jacobs in the nose for allowing her to pursue this madness. Kelli, knowing that Jake was just letting off steam, patted his hand in a gentle loving manner.

"Jake, it will be okay, because you, my great protector, will be there every weekend, helping to solve this case with your creative out-of-the-box thinking," Kelli said in her best calming voice.

"It's just that back to back strange murders of sons of prominent families in less than a week, combined with the passion ignited by the fracking moratorium vote, makes this place a powder keg ready to explode," Jake stated with great conjecture.

Kelli wondered about Jake's reaction. If he were to see the video of Deputy Miller's violent death, she knew that Jake would have barricaded her in the bedroom and forbidden her to go!

"I know part of the reason you're going is to avenge Brian's disappearance, but you have to promise me that you will come home if your PTSD rears its ugly head," Jake pleaded.

"I promise you Jake," Kelli whispered, secretly crossing the fingers on her free hand behind her back.

As they approached the American Airlines departure area, Jake pulled the car over and hugged his wife with a fierce passion, almost forcing the air out of her lungs.

"I will call you when I land in Greensboro," she said, fighting to hold back tears. I love you, Jake, and I hope that I will see you this weekend," Kelli said as she retrieved her luggage from the trunk.

Jake just nodded and blew her a kiss, not trusting himself to speak. He then watched as his soul mate disappeared into the massive crowd of travelers.

A loud honk from the Lyft driver dropping his clients off

behind him brought Jake out of his trance. Jake contemplated getting out of his car and giving that Lyft driver a lift with his left hook but knew that Pinewood High School would not appreciate the negative publicity. Jake pulled off in a slow manner to further infuriate the very fortunate but clueless driver-for-hire.

After showing her credentials to the TSA agents at the security check-in, Kelli was given VIP treatment and was processed rapidly through security, much to the displeasure of the masses who stood in line like obedient cattle. She scurried down Terminal B, and even though she was tempted by the robust aroma of coffee brewing at the Dunkin' Donuts café midway down the terminal, Kelli proceeded to her gate. Ronald Reagan was a very user-friendly airport that even had a rail service that deposited passengers directly to the airport from downtown Washington, DC. The only problem with the airport's infrastructure was that passengers had to take a bus or shuttle between terminals. Luckily, the American Airlines terminal was just past the security check-in. When Kelli reached her gate, Director King was waiting for her. She almost walked right past him because the lounge chair that he was ensconced in engulfed his small frame. The absurd subconscious desire to ask him if he needed a booster chair quickly passed, and Kelli began to wonder what random hemisphere of her brain had formulated such an insane urge to ask such a rude question.

"Director King, thanks for emailing the details of the investigation thus far. It appears that the state's response team did an excellent job processing the crime scene in the dead of night," Kelli said, as she strode up to shake his hand. Jordan King was surprised the strength of Kelli grip, but calmly told her that she could use his first name when addressing him.

"Likewise, Jordan," Kelli said, smiling broadly and thinking that it would be a pleasure working with someone who was not anal about professional protocol. The moment of bonding was interrupted by the spattering of raindrops against the terminal's windows, and just as Kelli was inquiring about the forensic and DNA evidence found at Moore's Knob, the announcement that Flight 8201 bound for Piedmont International Airport was now boarding.

Kelli and Jordan were seated in the comfortable first-class section, which boasted of excellent service from the flight attendants and better privacy for discussion of the case. As soon as they were seated, Kelli wasted no time asking Jordan about the unique or strangest qualities of the massacre at Moore's Knob. Jordan King was very impressed by Kelli's ability to bypass all the material in the report and get to the evidence that would help her to visualize the crime area in her mind.

Brian Cox had been on point about her immense skill to process a crime area from both an empirical and a psychic perspective.

"To me, the most bizarre thing is that the bones were placed on the observational tower deck in an anatomically correct position," King said in a hushed tone, conscious of prying ears around them.

"What do you mean 'anatomically correct' position?" Kelli asked wanting clarification.

"Not to quote an old song, but the clavicle bone is connected to the scapula bone..." Jordan King then added that the bones had a systematic placement all the way down from the shoulder to the metatarsus. Kelli realized that the unsub (or unknown suspect) must have some medical training, thus this tidbit of information helped her to formulate the profile that she would use to catch the mass murderer.

Jordan also stated that several campers had heard an inhuman howl around the time that coroners had established as the time of death of the men. Finally, he explained that the initial reports from the forensic lab indicated that the impressions left on the bones of the deceased appeared to have been made by animal fangs. As the big 757 taxied out to the runway, Kelli was lost in thought, thinking that the supernatural world was stalking her again.

Jordan King was the first to speak after the plane had slipped the bonds of gravity.

"This case has some unearthly overtones. I think that we have either a Bigfoot or some type of werewolf roaming the mountains of North Carolina. "King's quiet tone indicated that someone would think him mad for making such a ludicrous statement. Kelli looked at him with sudden mental clarity and asked, "So is that why you asked for me?"

"Exactly, you solved a case involving a 6'8" inch 360-pound psychopath, who was described as an inhuman monster," King replied with a look of solid admiration for his travel partner. Kelli reminded King that she had had assistance from several brave agents who lost their lives during the apprehension of the killers.

Kelli suddenly felt ill, excused herself, and hurried to the first-class lavatory. Unfortunately, the bold red letters on the door read, "Occupied." Kelli opened the curtains separating first-class from coach and proceeded down the aisle toward the restroom in the economy section. She was shocked to see Brian Cox sitting in the row nearest to the ladies' room. He smiled at her, and where there should have been teeth, blood-drenched fangs protruded out of his mouth. By some kind of mental telepathic communication, his whispers resounded through her brain.

"Kelli, you are going to dieeeee, and Hi'cictawi'a will munch on your bones!" and then Brian Cox stood up and disappeared through the aft side of the aircraft. Kelli immediately started going through Doctor Sloan's entire checklist of methods for fighting off this latest onset of her PTSD, and finally was able to calm herself enough to reach the bathroom. She breathed in a silent sigh of relief as she opened the door to her private sanctuary.

After several minutes of deep meditation, Kelli had calmed herself enough to return to her seat. When she reached her seat, she noticed the grave look on Jordan King's face.

"Jordan, what's wrong?" Kelli inquired.

"Brian Cox's body has just been recovered at the base of Moore's Knob. It appears obvious that he was killed by massive head trauma." King relayed the information stoically. He turned to look at the ashen, pale face of Kelli and said, "Looks like you have just seen a ghost." Kelli recoiled at the remark as she made the connection between her seeing the ghost of Brian Cox at the same time his body was discovered. The chill had not yet exited her spine when Jordan King said,

"Based on the positioning of Agent Cox's body, it appears that he may have jumped."

"Brian Cox would never have committed suicide!" Kelli said with conviction. Right before they landed, Kelli had a vision that what was awaiting her in those beautiful mountains was so terrifying that it had driven Brian Cox into madness. Had Kelli's had a flashback brought on by her condition, or had Brian Cox warned her from beyond the grave?

CHAPTER 4

About the same time Kelli was receiving her supernatural warning, David Barret was intensely studying the thick report on Tammy White, one of the city commissioners that Bart Whitescarver had identified as threatening to vote to continue the moratorium on hydraulic fracturing in Stokes County. He was reviewing the dossier which was sent to him by one of the many private investigators on his payroll. David was going to make an unannounced visit to Tammy's home, for like the Japanese at Pearl Harbor, he felt that a surprise attack was the best method to strike fear in the heart of one's enemy.

He was staying at River's Bend Bed and Breakfast, located at bottom of a sloping hill near the banks of the Dan River. According to the dossier, Tammy White was a big advocate of green technology including solar and wind power. David knew that solar technology utilizes solar panels to capture and magnify the ultraviolet rays of the sun, and that it was the champion of the grass roots environmental movement. Upgrades in the technology had improved the output of energy even in cloudy and stormy weather. David had even read of new solar equipment that would fold up during inclement weather and encase itself in the ground until a storm passed. As he was concentrating on his report, he heard the other guests chatting while eating breakfast served by owner-operated Pam Howard. David strained to hear the conversation.

He heard a booming voice bellow out, "Official notification from the park rangers were that toxic gases from a manufacturing plant over in Mayodan." David guessed that the author of the statement was the pot-bellied man that he had seen while checking in yesterday.

"Ah, that's BS, Marshall! Ain't no power fumes gonna travel that damn far, besides my brother Jed who lives at the entrance of Hanging Rock Park says he saw an ambulance with siren wailing speeding through the gates at the main entrance," another male voice boomed up the staircase.

David Barret just laid back on his comfortable mahogany bed and smiled, as he could sense the fear in the voices drifting up the stairs. What perfect timing he thought. Fear was best way to control folks. Just ask the Federal Government, which used the media to perpetuate myths about global warming, terrorism, and strange viruses in order gain control over the masses. Back in his undergraduate years, David had read that the Red Scare orchestrated by Senator Joseph McCarthy had led to so much panic and paranoid behavior from the general US population that the Cold War had intensified. Fear drove folks to build fallout shelters in order to survive nuclear war that the monsters from the Soviet countries were sure to initiate. David assumed that the Russian people were fed propaganda about the bloodthirsty Americans coming to rape their women and children. David knew that the fear tactic was an excellent way to build solidarity and that Adolf Hitler had used fear masterfully to build the blond, blue-eyed master race in Germany.

David's stomach growled for he had not eaten supper the day before, so he removed the jump drive from his computer and locked it away in the small cedar desk provided by the proprietors of the only B & B in town. He slipped on a bright red flannel shirt and some worn jeans, giving the appearance of some wayward hiker that had stumbled down from the Appalachian Trail. The River's Bend Bed and Breakfast was just a mile from the trail and treated many an exhausted through hiker to a nice comfortable bed and a delicious home cooked meal.

David used his stealth-like quickness to move down the staircase to the open foyer leading to the dining room and entered with the suddenness of a spring storm, causing the old pot-bellied Marshall to choke on his nice fluffy homemade biscuit.

"Well, hello, Mr. Barret, you almost missed this fine country breakfast!" Ms. Howard bellowed in a hearty voice. She was a perfect grandmotherly stereotype, with a heavy bosom and wide ample hips. David could sense that she had a heart of gold and knew that her maternal instinct was something he could exploit when the time came.

"Well, you shouldn't made the beds so dang comfor'ble!" David replied with a sudden good-ole-boy accent. He needed to fit in to extract as much information as possible from the two country bumpkins presently munching on their crispy bacon.

The two men laughed heartily at his witty remark. Pot-bellied Marshall pulled out a solid oak chair from the table as a gesture of welcome to the good-natured hiker.

As David had hoped, the two men let their guards down, chatting nonstop, as David remained quiet while wolfing down scrambled eggs, biscuits and homemade gravy like a starving hiker would. He listened as the men spoke of a massacre at Hanging Rock and the rumored firing of the local sheriff.

"I believe we have a Bigfoot roaming our hills," Pam Howard chimed in from somewhere back in the kitchen. The two men laughed for a few minutes, then chastised her for being such a busybody.

David Barret tired of listening to the two simpletons at the table and had already diagnosed them as having the mental condition of being idiots. He rose from the table and shook their hands, and they asked him if he was leaving to get back up on the trail.

"Naw, going be hanging around a while. Besides I'm kinda scared now with all that talk about a killer Bigfoot in the area," David replied in his best good ole boy accent. Both men thought that was hilarious and laughed like a couple of demented hyenas.

David mocked their laughter as he went up the stairs, using the comedy as a great exit strategy. He was in such a hurry to leave that he forgot to thank Ms.Pam for the fine home cooked breakfast. He would have to make amends for that slip in protocol by complimenting her vociferously at dinner, because all this psychic ability was screaming at him that she was going to be a vital ally in the very near future.

As he entered his room, he wished that he could take a hot shower to wash their stupidity off his body. He only hoped that some microscopic unit of stupidity wasn't wiggling its way through the epidermis layer of his skin. He had wasted too much time listening to the ramblings of two homosapiens from a diluted gene pool; that his appointment with Tammy White was less than an hour away.

He quickly changed into a 1,000-dollar suit, and the transformation from a hapless hiker to the Mind Magician was complete. One bit of gossip, which he learned from his housemates, had peaked his interest. The fact that the local sheriff had been fired for conducting a completely rogue and unsanctioned operation involving two agents from the State Bureau of Investigation. David guessed that Sheriff Brown was a sacrificial lamb in a vast cover-up. He believed that those at the top level of the SBI had approved the mission, and now that the mission had gone south, all those responsible had a bad case of CYA, or in layman's terms, COVER YOUR ASS! As he slipped a sealed envelope into his suit pocket, David smiled to himself, knowing that the breakdown of local law

enforcement would greatly enhance the chances of a successful mission because he local citizens of this small backward
area would never trust outside intervention by state or federal agents. The mouths of the God-fearing citizens of Walnut
Cove and Danbury would shut tighter than a clam in sub-zero
temperatures.

David unlocked the back door of the two-story colonial
style home and scurried down the back-porch stairs, careful
to avoid any contact with any other houseguest. As he approached the powerful black Ford Mustang GT that he had
rented at the airport, Ms. Pam yelled after him, admonishing him for not locking the back door, But David was already gunning the V8 engine, anxious to release he 550 horses
that hid under the hood. He pretended not to hear her as he
roared down the driveway because he was preoccupied with
the thought that his poster child for insanity, Black Bart, was
somehow responsible for the massacre at Hanging Rock State
Park. Ms. Pam hurried out into the yard and watched the
speeding car disappear over the hill, and suddenly she came to
the realization that a very dangerous man was sleeping under
her roof.

CHAPTER 5

David Barret was driving toward the entrance of Hanging Rock State Park like the proverbial moth to the flame. He had only fifteen minutes before his meeting with city commissioner Tammy White. Black Bart had set up the meeting between the two and had informed David that White had only agreed to the meeting out of kindness. Although White was not very fond of Chad Whitescarver, she did realize that to get on the wrong side of Black Bart was political suicide. David rounded the turn; he was meeting with a barrage of lights flashing from local, state, and federal vehicles. Several black SUVs blocked the entrance to the park, and various lawmen and park rangers stood in front with very menacing-looking automatic weapons. As he sped by, he did catch a glimpse of a stocky man with bright red hair tied in a ponytail. As David looked at the man, David was overwhelmed with the sensation of unbearable grief. Suddenly David had a premonition that this redheaded, powerfully built man was going to be a major roadblock in completing his mission.

As he turned his attention to the road winding up the mountain, he noticed an FBI drone hovering in the sky above Moore's Knob. David knew that the FBI was using its thermal scanners and biometric software to process a crime scene that stretched for several square miles. David also knew that many drones have facial recognition technology, so he gunned the powerful V8 engines and prayed the drone was blind to his presence.

As David drove, his eyes scanned the horizon for any more invasive drone technology that threatened his personal freedom. David was a true patriot who cherished his free-dom above all else. He reflected on his military days in Fallu-jah when large predator drones used to blaze hell fire missiles down on the army of the Mujahedeen and Al-Qaeda. While drone technology defended his freedom, David though that this technology in the hands of a narcissist dictator could bring forth a world envisioned by George Orwell's 1984, in which Big Brother watched your every move. He had read that Nano Hummingbird drones, which are only 6.5 inches long, were almost impossible to see with the naked eye. These thoughts concerned him, and because He has vast knowledge or psychological disorders, he wondered if he had begun to diagnose himself with paranoid delusions. He was so very glad this would be his last mission.

It was October 14, 2016. The sun was shining, brightly bathing the landscape in a blanket of clarity that was typical of a mid-fall day. David rolled down the window and breathed in the cool, crisp air. He dreamed of the day when he and his beautiful wife would go off the grid and disappear into the vastness of New Zealand. Suddenly his daydream was gone, when he realized that the vote on the moratorium that could end his mission prematurely was less than a week away. He mentally cursed those like Tammy White who always swam against the current like the capacious salmon that he caught in the dazzling, beautiful rivers in the frozen outback of Al-aska.

As he approached a rather sharp curve, his GPS device that was integrated into the muscle car began to squawk that he had reached his destination. David thought that the satel-lite controlling his GPS was a tad bit deranged, because there was nothing there but an old dirt road leading up into the desolate hills. David turned down the dirt road as ordered by the annoying voice, and admired the towering spruce pines that lined the private road on each side, beckoning him on-ward. After he had traveled about five miles into this remote area, he decided to end the seeming wild goose chase. As he was looking for a wide spot in the road to turn around, he noticed smoke billowing over the trees about a half mile ahead. He decided to drive a little bit further and was rewarded with an attractively built modern log cabin nestled up against some of the most exquisite landscape that he had ever seen.

Tammy was standing on the front porch waiting for him, wearing an expression of utter contempt on her round chubby face. The woman's plain dull facial features, gray dull eyes, took David aback and ashen complexion, which made her, look more dead than alive. He thought that he might have a wrong turn and had accidentally stumbled upon some type of back woods funeral home and was being greeted by a recently embalmed corpse. The corpse lady spoke.

"You have about ten minutes to explain what the hell you want! then about five more to get off my land!" Tammy said in a loud, aggressive manner.

David smiled because he could see into her soul, and he knew she was petrified of him.

"Now, Ms. Tammy, is that any way to greet a guest, especially when Bart Whitescarver told me what a friendly welcome that I would receive from you?" David cleverly retorted, reinforcing the fear by mentioning the menacing Black Bart.

He was now right in front of the manly, aggressive woman, using his mere presence as a weapon to subliminally disarm her.

"Listen, mister!" "You have wasted your time driving out here. I am voting to continue the moratorium on hydraulic fracturing in Stokes County!" Tammy stated triumphantly.

David fought back the urge to grasp her by her portly neck and snuff the life out of her. He was alarmed by that primal urge, but very calmly asked what her reasoning was in denying her neighbors the opportunity to become filthy rich?

Tammy looked David squarely in the eyes and replied,

"Well, Mr. Barret, when three million gallons of water are contaminated by benzene and radium and flows back into the Dan River, I don't want to explain to some poor mother why her baby boy or girl died of cancer at the tender age of three."

David recoiled as if bitten by a snake. He had just learned from that comment that Tammy White had either had a miscarriage or someone very close to her had lost a young child. He calmly filed that information into the deep recesses of his mind.

David could see that the fat woman's mind was made up, and that no amount of discussion about the limitations of solar and wind power would change her mind. He fantasized about entering her mind, making her go into the kitchen and slash her wrist with the largest butcher knife that she could find. He had the power to do that, but such an action would be impulsive and premature, thus destroying the systematic plan that he had devised.

"Listen, Mr. Barret. I believe that green technologies of solar and wind power are best for Stokes County now and in the near future. They are clean and natural technologies that are gentle on the environment." Tammy stated this with strong conviction. David stared at her, knowing he could control her thought process for that important moratorium vote, but he had to be within ten feet of her. He knew that when she was casting her vote at city hall in Danbury, that he would not be allowed into the assembly room.

"There are many limitations to solar power, the major one being that it cannot not keep up with the high demand of a technology-addicted society, including the rural counties of North Carolina," David said, trying to reason with this strong-willed vixen.

"Well, that may be true, Mr. Barret, but with the development of improved solar panels, the yield of kilowatts per hour can be increased. At least we don't have to worry about massive earthquakes and radioactive waste water getting into our wells and aquifers!" Tammy said with her voice rising, clearly becoming agitated by David's presence.

David, sensing that he was wearing out his welcome, decided to fire one last shot, "Certainly the cost of solar panels will make your brother a very rich man indeed. I heard through the grapevine that he is buying the old Walton building over in Walnut Cove and plans on being the sole distributor of solar panels to home builders in the area," David said, studying his nemesis for a reaction.

He had indeed struck a nerve; it was as if he was playing chess and had just declared 'Check Mate'. "Listen, I know that Abbot Oil sent you here to change my mind, but you have failed miserably, so I suggest you get the hell off my porch!" Tammy screamed, her face glowing like molten hot lava!

David was very entertained by her response and relished her rage, but it was time to play his trump card.

"Okay, I get the message, but before I leave can I use your bathroom?" "It's a long drive back into town," David said, faking the urgency with his body posturing.

Tammy considered his proposal for one brief moment and jumped at the chance to rid herself of this proxy for big oil. "Be my guest. The bathroom is down the hall and to the left. Just don't make me come in there and get you!" she said with a loud snorting noise.

David thought she sounded like a hog in heat, and he certainly intended not to be cornered in the house like Kathy Bates trapped James Caan in the movie Misery.

He silently walked down the hall, admiring the rustic allure of the stone fireplace that had produced the smoke signal that helped him find Tammy's home. He noticed the mounted

12-point buck on the wall glaring at him as he walked on the bearskin rug that lay on the cedar wood floor, like some monolithic dust mop. He stopped at the solid oak table, which was the centerpiece of the large dining room, placed his hand in his suit jacket, and laid a brown envelope on the table. He then hurried down the hall, having visions of Tammy White entering the cabin, foaming at the mouth with handcuffs in tow. He shuddered because of the repulsiveness of the thought. When he reached the bathroom, he quickly flushed the toilet and headed toward the front door like a saint heading for the Pearly Gates.

He opened the front door and hurried past this hog woman, offering no goodbye salutations. He had mentally dismissed her from his mind; she no longer existed on the same earthly plane. She was like an insect under his foot. Tammy White was not bothered by David's rude departure and felt a surge of pride in her soul because she had stood firmly against the uncontrollable greed that was slowly destroying the earth. Tammy didn't notice the envelope until she was setting the table for dinner. Her husband Jed always demanded his dinner at five thirty sharp, and Tammy paid a heavy price when she disappointed him. She picked up the brown envelope, opened it, and her face turned an even paler color as her eyes widened in fear. Inside was a glossy picture of her doing nasty, ungodly things with her preacher, Clive Ramsey. Her heart began to beat faster as she thought of Jed's enraged reaction if he should ever find out about her transgressions. Tammy shivered knowing that Jed would indeed set up a meeting between her and her Creator, if her secret was ever discovered. She suddenly knew that she would indeed vote to rescind the moratorium banning fracking in Stokes County. Tammy began to shake with unbridled fear as she realized that she had seemingly had an encounter with the devil himself.

David Barret was in a euphoric mood as he sped down Hwy 8 toward Danbury. He had just sent a message to all those who opposed him and his mission. He noticed the rolling hills bathed in their bright fall colors and his heart soared as he thought of his greatness and his intellectual prowess. These simpletons were no match for his intellect! He would always be one-step ahead of these country bumpkins. He rolled down the window and let the October breeze invigorate him, laughing out loud when he wondered if it would be sacrilegious to thank God for horny preachers.

CHAPTER 6

American Flight 8201 landed on time, and the giant 757 aircraft lumbered to its designated gate. Kelli, not one to be patient, started retrieving her luggage from the overhead bin. Director King glanced at her with concern, because he had witnessed a transformation in the young agent's demeanor. Director King, who prided himself in his observational abilities, was very concerned about Kelli's appearance after she returned from the lavatory in the back of the plane. He had been a lawman for thirty years, and he could recognize a look of sheer horror when he saw it. He considered calling Paul Jacobs and telling him that they had made a terrible error in judgment. He then glanced up at Kelli, and was shocked to see her staring at him with a look of total calmness and defiance as if she had read his thoughts.

"Director King, you need me on this case, not only because of this supernatural element, but because I loved Brian Cox and that gives me the most powerful motivation in the world!" Kelli said with strong conviction.

"Okay, Kelli, but promise me that if you can't contain your demons. And it interferes with your judgment, let me know immediately." King countered, knowing it would be his ass if anything went wrong.

Kelli looked King in the eye and calmly said, "Director King, I appreciate this opportunity and your trust in me, and I will not let you down." The intensity of her conviction eased Director King's mind, and he chastised himself for having doubted her.

Kelli was tense and agitated as she exited the plane and walked down the umbilical cord connecting the terminal to the aircraft. Kelli always thought that emerging from the vacuum like tunnel into the vastness of the terminal was like being reborn. As she exited into the waiting room, her fears subsided, because waiting there like a saint welcoming her home was the lanky, broad shouldered Sam Jenkins!

Sam walked up to Kelli and gave her a big bear hug.

"Kelli, you're a sight for sore and ancient eyes!" Sam Jenkins bellowed, waking up all those at the gate who had been hoping for a little shuteye before their next flight. Director King snarled up his nose. He was surprised by the breach of protocol from a man dressed more like a lumberjack than a federal agent. Sam Jenkins stood 6'2" tall in his casual attire of flannel shirt and blue jeans. Bulky hiking boots covering his size twelve feet accented Sam's big country appearance. After the air finally returned to Kelli's lungs, she managed to ask in a strained voice, "Sam, what are earth are you doing here? I thought you retired last year?"

"Well, you know news travels fast in the Bureau, and when I learned of your reemergence into the field and Brian Cox's disappearance, I knew that I couldn't let you have all the fun!" Sam replied with passion and enthusiasm resounding in his deep bass voice. Kelli's face drew up in a frown, and Sam wondered if he had said something wrong.

"I regret to inform you Sam, but Special Agent Brian Cox's broken body was found at the base of Moore's Knob by federal and state agents processing the crime scene this morning," Kelli's voice trembled slightly.

Sam Jenkins reacted to the news as if a hornet had stung him because he both liked and respected Brian Cox. Jenkins had learned several techniques on controlling his emotions during his long career with the bureau, so he reacted with a stoic face, but inside he was bursting with rage. Suddenly this case had become deeply personnel, and he would commit all his skills to finding Agent Cox's killer!

"Director King, I would like to introduce you to Sam Jenkins." Kelli continued, "Sam is the genius that theorized that we had been dealing with two psychopathic killers on the Outer Banks," Kelli said proudly.

Kelli almost laughed out loud as the diminutive Director King extended his pint-sized hand, which was rapidly consumed by the Brobdingnagian paw of Agent Jenkins. As King shook Jenkins' hand, he proudly announced that he was at the top of the food chain in the State Bureau of Investigation of North Carolina. Sam Jenkins, sensing that Director King was suffering from a bad case of Napoleon complex, eagerly shook King's hand and told him what an honor it was to meet him.

Kelli was anxious to get to the crime scene about forty miles due west of the airport, so after all the formalities and greeting she hurried off to baggage claim, with Director King and Agent Jenkins tailing her as if she were an international drug smuggler. As Kelli and Director King were retrieving their luggage, a muscular man, appearing to be of Native American decent, strolled up to them with his cuff-linked hand extended to offer a greeting. Sam Jenkins reached for his 9-millimeter Glock, fearing that some disgruntled Indian from Standing Rock was making an assassination attempt on a federal agent.

Suddenly Kelli turned abruptly, ingrained with a sixth sense that alerted her to any encroachment of her personal space, and smilingly extended her hand to quietly welcome Special Agent John Running Deer. She quickly introduced him to the team. Special Agent Running Deer was a large man, dressed impeccably in an Armani suit to which had he added his own personnel flare with a ten-gallon cowboy hat and worn leather boots. Agent Jenkins silently re-holstered his weapon, relieved not to have shot a federal agent, especially one with a cool name like that!

The odd squad made their way to the front of the terminal and clamored into the black SUV with official government tags that was waiting for them, making all the mere mortals who were waiting for taxi's and goobers from Uber very jealous. It was a bright fall morning with clear blue translucent skies, that allow one to see forever. As the driver pulled out onto Highway 65 heading due west, Director King pointed out the ancient primitive Sauratown Mountains, incredibly visible from 45 miles away! Director King spoke like a tour guide as he explained that the ancient Sauratown Mountains lie cut off from the distant Blue Ridge Mountains near the Tennessee line.

CHAPTER 7

Bill O'Toole was in his man cave, reviewing the information that the newly unemployed Sheriff Brown had left on his front porch late last night. The late-night covert delivery was an attempt to eliminate any electronic fingerprints left by emails. Computer forensic specialists from SBI or the FBI could now take computers, even those that were inoperable, and recover data from digital storage devices. Although he appreciated his friend for wanting to recover Shaun's dismembered body, he was seething with anger because he had not been alerted to the covert operation to recover his precious son's remains. Bill was alone. His broken-hearted, grieving wife Amy was resting upstairs after having mercifully been sedated by Doc Ray, the family physician. Bill Jr. was away at school, preparing for fall mid-term exams, and his twin daughters Amelia and Ann were with their older sister Cora at Bill's brother's home. Bill studied the document with disbelief, trying to find a connection between Black Bart and the gruesome murder of Bill's youngest and favorite son. If there were a link, he would find it! Bill knew that his resistance to hydraulic fracturing was somehow connected to Shaun's death, and he would move heaven and earth to prove that Black Bart was the mastermind behind it.

The chime on the old oak grandfather clock directly over Bill's head rudely announced that it was the top of the witching hour: Bill slammed his fist down on the desk in such a violent fury that it cracked the densely solid mahogany wood. Bill O'Toole then unleashed a wail so mournful that it would have chilled the blood of all the banshees in Ireland. His eyes overflowed with tears as the memories of his son flooded his brain... his boy, the young man with an uncanny resemblance to his father, was now gone, and discarded like trash on the peaks of the mountains that protected his home like silent stone soldiers. He would mourn his son, as age-old traditions from Ireland commanded he do, and then he would seek unholy vengeance against the vile demons that had murdered his son. No force from heaven or hell would stop him from avenging his son's death; he would seek out man, monster or demon and use lawful or unlawful means to vanquish them and sent their souls straight to perdition.

CHAPTER 8

While Bill O'Toole was grieving the loss of his youngest son, Kelli was traveling through the foothills of the Appalachian Mountains. The rolling tobacco, corn, and soybean fields lay barren after the fall harvest, but the explosion of colors from oak and sugar maple trees mixed with the brilliant blue sky uplifted her soul into a state of euphoric joy. Kelli knew that the joy in her heart would be short lived, because they were heading to the morgue in a small regional hospital directly across from the entrance to Hanging Rock State Park to meet with Dr. Drake, chief pathologist for Stokes County.

Sam Jenkins broke her deep thought process by comically retorting, "We're in the back country now, folks! I am half expecting some good ole boy to come out of the woods dressed in bib overalls with a nice string of catfish or crappie telling me that I got a prutty mouth!"

"Naw, just because they're country doesn't mean they're blind," Agent Running Deer cleverly retorted.

Director King was alarmed by the highly unprofessional banter between highly trained federal agents, but Kelli knew that comic relief was how males bonded. The phrase "Boys will be boys!" is apropos no matter the age or maturity level of the man.

Highway 8 whined through the town of Danbury. They passed the small southern town, dressed in its fall colors and looking like a Norman Rockwell painting with an old monstrous brick courthouse and a beautiful white Baptist church lining the highway. The architectural design of both buildings easily dated back to the 1800 has; law offices, a small cafe, and a funeral home added to the quaintness and charm of this small Carolina town. This quiet southern town had been jolted into the national spotlight after the brutal slaying of two of its civil servants, and an SBI agent. Crowds were milling the streets sharing gossip and intermingling with the media. Kelli counted at least five vans from regional and national television stations along the way to the hospital!

As they reached the northern edge of the village, blue lights from a State Police cruiser stopped them and the tall, lanky officer told them to turn around, that the road was closed to unauthorized personnel. Kelli and her team displayed their badges and were then nonchalantly waved through. Kelli had expected the trooper to stop the government SUV for a search of greater intensity, and she made a mental note to address his superior.

As they pulled into the hospital parking lot, an armed security guard told them to pull around back, and that he would then escort them to the basement morgue and Dr. Drake. As the group descended the steps, Kelli's heart began to speed up, and she began to sweat even though it was relatively cool in the subterranean chambers. As they reached the bottom of the stairs, a slightly built man with huge bifocals and features like a mouse greeted them with a timid handshake.

"Special Agent Kelli Ryan, I presume?" Dr. Drake inquired as he shook Kelli's still clammy hand. Kelli silently prayed that Dr. Drake would not reveal her nervousness to the others, as Director King would contribute her condition to her Post Traumatic Stress Disorder and replace her post haste.

Kelli was relieved when Dr. Drake announced that he had finished the post mortem examination on the two bodies from the tower, Brian Cox's cadaver, and the dissected body of Shaun O'Toole. He quickly handed each member of Kelli's team diagrams of each autopsy with a synopsis of his findings at the bottom of each page.

He silently moved into a large examination room and motioned them to follow him. Three large medical gurneys with sheets pulled over them were the only objects in the room. Kelli's feet tried to step into the room, but to her horror, she could not move! Fear had petrified her into absolute immobility. She was trying desperately to move forward when suddenly she saw Brian Cox's body twitch, then move. The corpse then sat up on the gurney. When it did the bed sheet slipped of the cadaver. Brian Cox's head swiveled 360 degrees like that of Linda Blair in the movie The Exorcist; the cracking of the vertebrae in the corpse's neck was deafening!

"Do you have any questions, Agent Ryan?" Dr. Drake asked Kelli for the second time. Kelli came out of her trance, and to her astonishment, she was standing in front of the remains of Shaun O'Toole. Her vision of Brian Cox had been a hallucination! Director King was staring at her with a very intense gaze, trying to discern any signs of in Kelli's demeanor.

"As I was saying, Shaun O'Toole was already dead when he was dissected with what appears to have been a chain saw." Dr. Drake's voice echoed off the walls of the sterilized autopsy room. As if to validate his findings, he pointed to the severed head and neck and pointed out the ligature marks and bruising around the neck.

"The subject's windpipe was crushed causing asphyxia, so whoever strangled him was quite powerful," Dr. Drake concluded excitedly before he moved to the next set of remains. Agent Jenkins wondered how anyone could get excited over a corpse, wondering if the chief forensic pathologist could be suffering from the pathological disorder of necrophilia.

Kelli then asked the question that had been invading her consciousness since she entered the subterranean house of horrors.

"How many days after Chad Whitescarver's body were found was Shaun O'Toole killed, Doctor?" Kelli asked, trying to set a timetable for the ghastly murders.

"Well, I don't have a crystal ball, but based on the color of the dermis and epidermis layers of the skin on the severed limbs, I would estimate death occurred about three days after Chad Whitescarver was found on October 8th." Kelli quickly typed the information into her generation Seven cell phone. The time of Shaun O'Toole death made the case for a revenge killing even stronger.

Dr. Drake promptly walked over to the skeletal remains of Deputy Sheriff, Donny Miller and Deputy Mack Peters, and in a voice filled with controlled emotion; he stated that both men had been killed by a sharp instrument. Mack Peters had been decapitated around the fifth vertebrae, and Donny Miller had his thoracic cavity sliced open, literally severing the heart from the body. Dr. Drake held up what was left of Donny Miller's heart in his gloved hand and grimly stated that both men had been consumed post postmortem by the most severe case of cannibalism that he had ever seen. Agent Jenkins wondered to himself how many cases the good doctor had seen, thinking maybe that being eaten by a cannibal was a common way to die in the back woods of Stokes County.

The coroner dramatically uncovered the remains beneath the sheet, and the group of seasoned agents let out a collective gasp; before them were bones that were completely void of any connective tissue, ligaments, cartilage, and blood.

"There was a fang embedded in the tibia and femur bones of Mack Peters, as if the killer or killers were eating a chicken leg at a restaurant," Drake said with a hint of a smile, trying to be mildly humorous.

"Where is all my DNA evidence, both trace and touch, from both the skeletal remains and the fang?" Kelli demanded, not amused by Drake's smile. Before Dr. Drake could respond, Director King injected, "Since the SBI was first to process the crime scene, all biological evidence has been sent to our crime lab in Raleigh. Agent Briggs will debrief you on that at about ten hundred hours." Kelli bit her lips trying to suppress her anger at not having the samples on site.

The final gurney was the stop that Kelli dreaded the most on this grotesque tour of the dead that was being led by the weirdest ghoul that she ever had the displeasure to meet. Jake's best friend's corpse lay beneath the final curtain, and in her mind, she could hear Bob Barker of the television show The Price is Right, exclaim "What do we have for Kelli behind curtain Number Three?" As if on cue, Dr. Drake pulled back the sheet revealing the repulsive face of the man who had saved her life eight years before! His swollen face had a purplish tint around the eyes and mouth.

"The abdominal cavity contains a ruptured spleen, lacerated liver, and punctured kidneys thus the heavy swelling and discoloration," droned on a now seemingly bored Dr. Drake.

Kelli was concentrating so intently on suppressing an urge to run out of the room crying uncontrollably, that she didn't see Brian Cox's left eye open as if to say,

"What the hell are you all gawking at?" Agents Running Deer and Jenkins jumped back instinctively and both men had a look of unbridled fear carved on their faces. Dr. Drake responded as if the peek-a-boo game the dead Brian Cox was playing was completed normal.

"Damn ocular muscle is always scaring the crap out of rookies," he said as he grabbed a piece of tape to secure the wondering eye. Sam Jenkins was scared but for some asinine reason was thinking about the good book's New Testament verse that said, "If the left eye offends you, pluck it out," and oh yes, he definitely wanted in the worse way to pluck out Brian Cox's wayward eye!

Dr. Drake's monotone voice calmly droned on, somewhat acting as a tranquilizer for the petrified group.

"The bones of the lower extremity starting at the hip are completely shattered, compound fractures of the femur, tibia, fibula, in addition to all the bones of the foot including the metatarsus are shattered, and in fact the only thing attaching the victim's legs to his upper torso is his skin. The victim landed on his feet after hitting a ledge just 40 feet down from Moore's Knob, and for that reason I'm ruling this death a suicide," Dr. Drake said with conviction in his eyes, daring anyone in the room to contradict him.

Kelli knew that Brian must have fallen while trying to escape from the maniacal killer. She quickly strode up to the mild-mannered mortician, looked him in the eye with an enraged stare that made the meek man tremble, and exclaimed in a voice, which seethed with anger,

"Brian Cox would NEVER commit suicide, and I will prove it before this case is over, and then I will make sure that you will be so discredited that you will be forced into an early retirement!" Everyone stood in shocked silence, and at this very moment, Director King terminated the meeting with the chief coroner; no one was more relieved than Dr. Drake was.

The team left the morgue and literally walked the street to the entrance of Hanging Rock State Park in silence, each one deeply pondering what they had just seen. Thus began an investigation that would take one of their lives and completely end the career of another.

It was October 15, at 0900 hours, when Kelli and her team arrived at the crime scene approximately 29 hours after the slaughter of the two Stokes County deputies. They were greeted by local, state, and federal agencies working diligently to process a mammoth outdoor crime scene. Kelli knew that valuable time had elapsed, but since the murders had occurred at night, the processing of the crime scene had to be completed, at the first light of morning or risk further contamination of the evidence.

Kelli took command immediately upon arriving, thanking and then relieving local law enforcement agencies. She was not trying to anger or alienate the local law agencies, but she was aware that too many investigators equaled too many feet trampling her crime scene. Many alpha males, which seemed to comprise the majority of law enforcement, don't take to kindly to a woman sitting in the catbird seat, but when Kelli showed them her FBI credentials, and then Director King asked, "Is there a problem, gentlemen?" The defiant stares and gestures of he-men quickly abated. Kelli walked toward the park ranger's cabin, followed by her team and several SBI agents. She would issue her first briefing from the confines of a building constructed from the very Canadian pine forest that at this very moment might be concealing a ruthless, violent predator.

Kelli stood in front of the rustic stone fireplace in the main meeting room, which served as a conference room for the several park rangers that served the three North Carolina state parks within the radius of 50 miles. A makeshift podium had been set in front of the room facing 15 metal chairs, part of which were occupied by Director King and a couple of state forensic pathologists, along with personnel from the Federal Evidence Response Team, that had recovered Agent Coxes body at the bottom of Moore's Knob. Kelli scanned the room and spotted Sam Jenkins and John Running Deer having a low conversation with photographers from the state crime lab in Raleigh.

High-ranking North Carolina state troopers rounded off the group and several local park rangers engaged in a heated debate in the back of the room. When Kelli made a slight clearing of the throat sound, the men instantaneously terminated their passionate discussions.

"Good morning, gentleman, I am Special Agent Kelli Ryan of the Federal Bureau of Investigation, and with the consent of Director King, my team and I will be taking over the processing of this crime scene. I have assembled this group to outline the procedural steps that will be necessary to investigate this slaughter and limit any further loss of life."

Kelli scanned the now silent room for any non- verbal body posturing that would indicate how these alpha males were reacting to a strong female personality taking over the investigation. She noticed that many in the room had their arms folded and displayed blank stares of mental noncompliance. Kelli ignored their efforts to distract her and asked Sam Jenkins to dim the lights in the room. After he complied, she downloaded the video from Deputy Donny Miller's body camera and played it on the large screen in front of the room. The transformation was instantaneous. Many of the blank stares were replaced with looks of horror and disbelief at the visceral dissection of Deputy Miller's chest cavity. The quality of the video was blurry and very grainy, but there was no mistaking the blinding speed of this creature. Kelly even froze the video in critical places, so these veteran lawmen could comprehend the viciousness of the attack. So in the future, they would never underestimate this dangerous genetic abomination when trying to apprehend it.

"Gentleman, what you have just seen are the last few seconds of Deputy Powers' life, and this video is to remain top secret. None---NONE---of what you just viewed this morning is to be disclosed to the press, peers, wives or girlfriends under any conditions!" Kelli spoke solemnly and forcefully, and no one in the room doubted her conviction.

Kelli then placed a large map of Hanging Rock State Park and surrounding area on the large screen and drew a large red circle around the 7,000-acre park from Vade Mecum Springs in the west to Piedmont Springs in the east. Kelli turned and announced that she was placing this entire area in lock down, quarantine, and if necessary, martial law until this genetic freak was apprehended! The silence that preceded that announcement was a product of shock and bewilderment. Trooper John Caper, senior in command of the Western North Carolina Division, was the first to speak.

"How are we going to literally shut down a very popular state park? I mean this is not Roswell, New Mexico. The federal government will not be able to keep this massacre a secret!" His booming bass voice echoed off the cabin walls. Johnson concluded by saying that the manpower required to shut down such a massive area would cost the hard-working tax payers thousands of dollars.

Kelli had anticipated this objection and coolly replied, "I wouldn't put such a massive undertaking squarely on the shoulders of the state police. That's why we have to convince the Governor to release the services of the National Guard." Kelli's announcement shocked everyone in the room including her team, because she had kept this information secret even from Director King, opting to unleash it at the perfect time.

Kelli explained that the security of this mission relied on the cooperation of the National Guard, state police and the park rangers assembled at this meeting.

"The two local newspapers in the area will print articles that a massive manhunt for the killers of two Stokes County Sheriff's deputies is underway, and that Hanging Rock Park and the surrounding vicinity will be closed for the safety of the general public. There will be security points manned by National Guard personnel and law enforcement around the perimeter of the park, and any violators or trespassers will be prosecuted to the fullest extent of the law," Kelli summarized.

"So, no specific details of this hideous slaughter will be released to the media," Director King added.

"We will never be able to stop all the curious hikers from entering the park. Your method of check points is just too porous; what we need is a frigging wall!" Chief Park Ranger Brent Jones complained with great passion.

"Good point, Ranger Jones, and that's why the state police and your staff will be patrolling this area on all-terrain vehicles to firm up this porous border that you're so worried about." Kelli replied.

Agent Running Deer smiled to himself as Ranger Jones' face turned bright red in an attempt to suppress his rage toward this slight, aggressive, female pawn of an overreaching federal bureaucracy.

Kelli walked to the large screen, and pointed to the beast dissecting Deputy Miller's midsection and stated the obvious.

"Bottom line, Gentleman, this beast must be contained! Imagine the consequences if we fail!" Kelli said her face flush with excitement. All the personnel in the room nodded their heads in agreement, suddenly envisioning one of their loved ones crossing the path of this hellish creature on a moonless night.

CHAPTER 9

SBI Senior Agent Joel Briggs walked into the small room adjacent to the main conference area, and Kelli could see by his ramrod posture and his purposeful, disciplined strut that the agent had spent many years in the armed services, most likely the Marines or Army. Briggs conducted the initial processing of the very complex, large outdoor crime scene, and had been tapped by Director King to bring Kelli up to speed on every facet of the operation thus far.

Kelli and her team were seated in the front of the room, with several of the crime scene techs seated behind them. Agent Briggs stood like a robotic statue, his serious, steely gaze pierced the collective consciousness of the room. He had a wide face, with deep-set brown eyes that emitted a burning intensity that could only have only been forged on the field of battle.

"On October 13, at 0300 hours, my team arrived at the crime scene on Moore's Knob. We immediately cordoned off the observation tower and did a grid search 100 yards around the tower," he said, as he circulated around the room photos and diagrams of the carnage.

In the photographs taken by the tech, Kelli noticed that Deputy Donny Miller's and Mack Peters' bones were in cone-shaped piles sitting in the middle of the observation deck. To Sam Jenkins, the two piles of bones were shaped like miniature tee-pees that he had seen on an Apache reservation a couple of years before.

"Those bones were placed in exact anatomical order,

from the cranium all the down to the metatarsus," Agent Briggs said in a hushed tone. Techs from our crime lab in Raleigh gathered trace and touch evidence, such as blood, hair, and a fang that was embedded in the femur of Deputy Mack Peters. DNA samples have been fast-tracked in our crime lab and are being analyzed as we speak."

Briggs hesitated only a minute before Kelli interjected, "I want those fang DNA samples run through a sophisticated test called Bio-geographical Ancestry Analysis, which will determine the ethnicity of the killer."

Agent Briggs stood at the podium with his hands locked behind his back as if at parade rest, and calmly asked, "Why do you feel that expensive test is necessary?"

His intense eyes emitted arrows of extreme annoyance at the slight FBI agent.

"After viewing the photos of these piles of bones of the two officers, I think we are dealing with an example of tribalism, possibly Native American Indian," Kelli replied, totally oblivious to Brigg's stare. Agent Briggs was on the verge of responding aggressively and with a degree of condescension when King interjected.

"The state does not have the resources to do a BGA, but I have instructed our lab personnel to expedite the fang DNA to Quantico post haste," Director King said with a stern glance at Briggs, daring him to object.

"Why didn't you expand your grid search further than 100 yards?" Agent John Running Deer inquired, locking eyes with the agitated Briggs. Agent Briggs was not used to having his judgment questioned and instantly responded.

"After viewing the crime scene, I feared a greater loss of life if my men tried to track that creature into the dead of night." Both Kelli and Director King thought that Briggs had exhibited excellent judgment in an emotional, crucial moment!

Pausing briefly for dramatic effect, Agent Briggs proudly announced as he was unfolding topographical maps, that he had indeed tracked the killer using modern drone technology, thus minimizing the loss of human life. He went on the explain that special drones that can detect body heat were being used to track and find endangered species of animals in the wild all over the world.

"These drones are equipped with infra-red cameras and are being used to track Koala bears in Australia, so we used a drone that was launched within 30 minutes after we were notified of the slaughter to track our suspect." He then downloaded the contents the HD cameras onto the computer hard drive and displayed the route taken by the beast onto the topographical map of Moore's Knob.

"We picked up the suspect traveling west down the ridge line toward Vade Mecum Springs, but unfortunately the trail stops cold at the abandoned three-story hotel." Agent Briggs continued his briefing. "Because of heavy fall foliage and the darkness, we were not able to get a clear picture of the Humanoid creature." Briggs concluded his briefing by shuffling his papers like some big shot prosecuting attorney.

Kelli knew that Vade Mecum Springs had hosted many tourists back in the 1800s, as the hot mineral water was of great therapeutic relief to those suffering from everything from arthritis to muscle deterioration brought on by neurological disorders. She wondered why the creature would make a beeline to the springs. Was it trying to cleanse itself from the blood and gore of the slaughter?

After a moment of silence, Agent John Running Deer asked,

"Agent Briggs, why do you refer to the killer as a 'Humanoid creature'?" As Agent Running Deer asked the question, his faced tensed up as if he knew and feared the answer that was coming.

"When daylight broke, two other agents and I followed the escape route that the drone had produced, and unfortunately no animal or human tracks were visible until we reached Drake's Creek. The muddy banks of the creek allowed us to see large prints, like a large coyote or wolf had recently made a visit to drink from the creek, but on the other side as the creek those large paw prints transformed into a human footprint!"

The volume of Briggs's voice peaked at the word footprint for great dramatic effect. The room was silent as each agent digested the weirdness of Briggs's tale, all except John Running Deer, who involuntarily let out a low Cherokee war chant. John Running Deer at that very moment knew the complete and utter horror that they all would face, and he knew that several of his peers would likely be sent to the afterlife before this case was over. Kelli glanced over at John Running Deer as he let out the low guttural sound; his almost black eyes were blank and focused on an object in the room that was invisible to the pale faces present.

Kelli knew that Running Deer would be an integral part of the investigation because he was a full-blooded Cherokee Indian and had been using his abilities tracking Mexican aliens entering the country illegally via the Rio Grande for the last ten years. The US border patrol had borrowed his services frequently from the bureau, when either a capital crime like murder or human trafficking was involved. The CBP used modern technology like drones and surveillance cameras to catch aliens and smugglers alike, but a full-bloodied Cherokee had tracking abilities that were almost supernatural. John Running Deer was no exception to that rule. Kelli would question why he reacted so strangely to Brigg's report while hiking up to the crime scene.

CHAPTER 10

Ranger Brent Jones drove like a maniac up the road, which led to the trailhead leading to Moore's Knob. Kelli guessed that the hairy big-armed man who resembled a large ravenous grizzly bear was still agitated by Kelli's proposal that his staff patrol the perimeter of the crime scene on all-terrain vehicles.

"This being an outdoor crime scene will be difficult to process any further because of the length of time that has passed," Agent Briggs complained in a loud, authoritative voice.

"Agent Briggs, if you are alluding to the fact that my team is a day and half late to the scene, I agree. That's why I hope that your initial grid search and processing lives up to Director King's expectations." Kelli countered and was rewarded by a suddenly stoic and silent Agent Briggs. Before the conversation peak in entertainment value for Sam Jenkins, who was sitting right next to Agent Briggs, the big ole grizzly man stopped the jeep very abruptly, almost throwing John Running Deer out onto the secluded road.

Kelli guessed that maneuver was another payback from the Neanderthal who was clutching the steering wheel with a death grip.

"Moore's Knob is about 2,500 feet straight up, so please watch your step," the park ranger big-dumb-ass Neanderthal said as he chuckled copiously. Kelli was first out of the jeep, followed by Jenkins, Running Deer, and Agent Briggs, who got out last at an extremely leisurely pace, perhaps not wanting to part company with his new manly friend! Kelli smiled at the random thought as it came screeching out of her subconscious.

"Don't smile too much, buttercup," the brazen ranger exclaimed, staring at Kelli and wishing for a sharp rebuttal. Kelli just grinned even wider as her athletic frame gracefully jumped over a huge boulder that was blocking the trail after a sudden fall storm had brought it crashing down the mountain. As Agent Jenkins cleared the boulder, he wondered if the Gods knew of the carnage on the peak of this lonely mountain and wanted to protect hikers from the visual that was waiting for them. Agent Briggs stepped over the huge rock with a quick pace to overcome Kelli and demonstrate that he was the alpha male who would lead this group of novice hikers. Just as he was overtaking Kelli, he noticed John Running Deer leaving the trail behind as he started to bushwhack through the heavy fall foliage created by large sugar maples and other deciduous trees. Agent Briggs, frustrated and alarmed at Running Deer's complete disregard and noncompliance to his leadership, yelled,

"You will never make it to Moore's Knob, and then we will have to allocate precious time trying to find you!" Agent Briggs's anger intensified as he heard Running Deer's faint echo of laughter already far above them. Kelli was exhausted by the time the trail peaked at the summit of Moore's Knob, because Agent Briggs had set a fast pace, hoping to make Kelli beg for a break. Kelli's father was an Army Special Forces officer and had instilled in his only daughter the heart of a warrior that would rather have death than dishonor. Her father Jim had taken her on many long-distance hikes, including one at the tender age of 13 in the French Alps with a forty-pound rucksack on her back, and she always out hiked her older brothers.

Agent Briggs secretly admired the strength and stamina Kelli demonstrated on the uphill hike, but his positive demeanor shifted when he saw a fully rested John Running Deer standing on the observation deck.

"Hey! Was going to send a search party after you, but I then heard you all moving up the trail about thirty minutes ago," bellowed the proud and cocky Cherokee Indian.

Agent Briggs was amazed by the climbing skills of this muscular, broad shouldered man, then he thought about the auditory abilities that allowed Running Deer to hear them coming from about a half mile away, and his amazement turned to hero worship. Sam Jenkins was about 100 meters behind Kelli and was huffing and puffing, obviously out of shape but refusing to quit. The Federal Evidence Recovery Team had set up a defensive perimeter about 100 yards around Moore's Knob, insuring no wanderlust hiker would stumble upon an active crime scene. Kelli and Sam Jenkins had been stopped at one of the checkpoints. The brief rest had allowed both agents to catch their breaths before proceeding to the observation deck.

Kelli was awestruck by the kaleidoscope of fall colors as she peered down the steep cliff to the shimmering lake bathed in the clarity of a resplendent blue sky. A complete calmness engulfed her soul, and the quiet solitude sharpened her empirical senses as she scanned the area for clues. Kelli had decided while on her morbid tour with Dr. Ghoul, that the modus operandi differed in the murder of Shaun O'Toole and the massacre at Moore's Knob, and that they were looking for two separate killers! Kelli and Sam hurried to the tower and climbed the thirty stairs to the observation deck and the grisly scene of butchery.

As Kelli reached the summit of Moore's Knob, she felt as if she just climbed the stairway to heaven because before her was 360 degrees of unparalleled majestic beauty. Her trance was rudely interrupted by Agent Brigg's rude inquiry

"He rudely asked, "Earth to Agent Kelli Ryan, anyone

there, anyone at all?"

Agent Running Deer glared at Agent Briggs as if he wanted to hurl a tomahawk at him! Kelli was quickly brought back to reality as she peered at the darkened stain that saturated the cedar wood below Brigg's feet, and she realized that Agent Briggs was standing on the spot where the human tee pees had been constructed!

"Get the hell off my evidence! You're contaminating the crime scene!" Kelli at Briggs with a look of sheer horror

. "As I already informed you, we have already gathered touch DNA and all trace evidence from this crime scene. It has been swept clean, and frankly, you are just wasting your time here, Agent Ryan. I went over this area meticulously." Briggs concluded his tirade with a smirk Kelli had an 'ah-ha' moment...Briggs was intimidated by her and was afraid she would find some additional evidence, thereby making him appear to be incompetent in Director King's eyes. Kelli also knew that from this point forward, Agent Briggs would try his best to impede and obstruct her investigation, so she calmed down and said firmly,

"Agent Briggs, this is now a federal investigation." "You are dismissed; I will use you in a consultant capacity only." The look of deep resentment and hatred spread over Brigg's face like a grim mask. The veins were alive in his neck, pulsating with barely restrained rage.

"I will go over your head to the Director King. He was the one responsible for getting your incompetent, overbearing ass here anyway!" As he shouted, he inched closer to Kelli.

John Running Deer quickly stepped in between the battling agents.

"I think you heard the lady, Agent Briggs!" Running Deer said in a calm tone void of any hostility.

"This is none of your business, Chief'!" yelled Briggs. "Get the hell outta my way, or I will…" but Agent Brigg's words trailed off as he peered into darkest, most vicious eyes that he had ever seen. He then thought of the almost supernatural way that Running Deer had climbed to the peak of Moore's Knob, and he decided that he would indeed obey Kelli's orders. As he stomped down the stairs, he shouted, "This isn't over, Agent Ryan, not by a long shot!" they watched Agent Briggs angrily retreat down the mountain. As Briggs disappeared from view, Sam Jenkins quipped,

"Ah, Kelli, that's what I like about you. Always trying to win friends and influence people!" Kelli had indeed read that bestselling book, but was not entertained by Jenkins' reference. She had a faint smile on her face, but also had a nagging notion that she had just pissed off the wrong man.

Kelli walked over to the side of the platform that offered a commanding view of the backside of the mountain. She peered over the guardrail, which was about two feet from a sharp vertical drop off to the final resting place of Brian Cox. His broken corpse had been found at the base of Moore's Knob, his face turned up, eyes open as if peering toward the gates of Heaven.

Kelli turned around and made eye contact with her team, and then she voiced what her training as an FBI profiler was telling her.

"Gentlemen, we are dealing with two crime scenes blended together, and I think that both scenes represent some type of hideous example of what can happen if you cross the killers."

"So, the murders were a warning?" Sam Jenkins asked the obvious question.

"Yes! Kelli answered However, for two different reasons. I believe the killings of Shaun O'Toole and Chad Whitescarver were related to the hydraulic fracking issue, since the town is passionately divided over it." Kelli's voice was filled with a deep, dark, foreboding tone.

Running Deer then picked up the chain of thought. "Since Shaun's family represents one extreme side, which is pro-environmental, he may have been murdered and dismembered by the pro-gas cronies to demonstrate what happens to you if you're passionate about your tree hugging tendencies."

John Running Deer's description of a staunch environmentalist amused Sam Jenkins, especially since the Native American culture views the land, sky and water in a sacred manner.

"Exactly, John," Kelli said, looking at Running Deer like a teacher looks at her favorite students.

"Chad Whitescarver may have been murdered by the opposite side. The massacre, however, represents a deep pathological hatred toward authority or a group, which, in the killer's opinion, represents too much power and control. I would not be surprised if the second killer belongs to a minority or a group of people that has been suppressed for a long period of time."

Sam Jenkins looked at his boss as if she had lost her mind.

"Kelli, you saw the pictures of this thing and what it is capable of. I mean, the Wolverine on The X-Men could not have sliced and consumed these deputies as this thing did! Yet you refer to this creature as human?" Jenkins' tone expressed his disbelief.

"I know, Sam, but the killing procedure was so vicious, yet the bones were not scattered along the observation deck like an animal would leave the remains. They were systematically arranged in correct anatomical order, which demonstrates some kind of logical and rational thought process." Kelli summarize, with her voice taking on a cryptic, eerie tone.

She stood in silence, thinking about the disappearance of Chad Whitescarver and the murder of Shaun O'Toole almost the hapless tuber had found a week after Chad's shriveled up body. Could Shaun's have been a revenge killing?

As Kelli stood at the edge of the abyss looking down at the final resting place of Brian Cox, a mental image formed in her brain of a man consumed with so much hatred for the O'Toole family who, in his mind, had murdered his beloved son, but also for opposing the plan that would indeed make him filthy rich! Kelli turned back to her team, her green eyes ablaze with passion and her cheeks reddened by the sun or by the boiling desire to apprehend Brian Cox's killer and voiced her plan of action.

"Gentlemen, while we wait for the DNA, trace, and touch evidence to be processed in Raleigh, we will do more investigating. Sam, you and I will go question Bart Whitescarver at his home overlooking the Dan River while John retraces the path taken by the killer down to Vade Mecum Springs. John, you will be escorted by three National Guardsmen."

Kelli was already moving down the steps toward the stony face of Moore's Knob when she experienced a mental jump in intuition and turned to ask Running Deer about his reaction earlier.

"Why the guttural war chant upon viewing the photographs of the bones that were placed to look like human tee pees? You know what we are dealing with here, don't you, Agent Running Deer?"

Running Deer hesitated for only a few seconds, but it seemed like an eternity for Kelli and Sam.

"Yes, he replied. Its name is Hi'cictawi'a and it's the most terrifying skin-walker of all, because it uses witchcraft to hypnotize and control the minds of its victims."

Kelli looked at the dark skinned Indian in disbelief and then she thought about Brian Cox's death leap off the observation deck at Moore's Knob. Suddenly her flesh crawled as if someone had taken a hypodermic needle and inserted worms under her skin.

CHAPTER 11

David Barret was euphoric when he returned to Ms. Pam's bed and breakfast, because he had eliminated Tammy White's threat to his divine plan in the most devious way possible! Broad-hipped Pam Howard met him at the door, and at first, David thought that he was going to be admonished for the brazen way that he had squealed out of her gravel driveway. Her face was flushed with a feverish excitement as she exclaimed,

"There has been some kind of mass murder on top of Moore's Knob! We have been listening to the police scanner all morning. Ambulances and police vehicles with their lights blazing have been whizzing by the house all day!"

As his host spoke these words, his memories regressed in time, and he thought of the spectacle he had seen in front of the entrance to Hanging Rock Park as he had sped down the highway toward his successful meeting with the preacher-humping Tammy White.

"I even heard that it was some kind of werewolf that killed those deputies!" Pam said in a loud and excited voice.

David was lost in thought as he remembered the stocky powerfully built man obviously in a state of emotional upheaval standing at the entrance of Hanging Rock state park, his powerful intuition KNOWING that this man that resembles a Celtic God would be his chief nemesis.

"No news reports have surfaced about these killing, not a peep Pam, how do you know it's a mass murder scene involving Sheriff Deputies and werewolves?" David asked locking his hypnotic eyes into Pam's baby blues.

"Well these hills have eyes, and besides a lot of supernatural stuff happens in these backwoods" Pam then proceeded with some tall tale about an apparition that would appear assisting her Grandmother with household chores. The specter would always appear after a sharp rapping on the walls of the outhouse in the backyard, as if it did not to alarm or frighten her grandmother as it floated through the back door.

"Sounds like your grandmother was just having delusions of owning an automatic dishwasher" David joked dismissively,

Pam apparently did not hear or chose to ignore David's rude remark, she continue to speak of her heroic mother, a devout Christian and rebuked the ghost by quoting scripture when she heard the rapping noise outside. David really had to get upstairs to his room and escaped this outbalanced women, but his curiosity got the best of him, so he reluctantly asked, "What scripture did she quote?"

Pam stared at him like he was an unschooled heathen, "Why she said, get behind me Satan" and poof the rapping spirit parted and never appeared again Pam concluded rather dramatically. David was frozen for a moment pondering the physiological disorder of the women, who just might murder him as he slept.

"Well that is a very entertaining tale Ms. Pam, but it's been a long day and I really must get some rest, David said smiling as he turned to go, and Ms. Pam stop spreading gossip about what happen on Moore's knob yesterday."

"OK Good night Mr. Barret" Ms. Pam called after David as he climbed the stairs to his room, thinking that he was the strangest man she had ever met.

"Good Night Ms. Pam, always a pleasure chatting with you" David replied so relieved to shut his bedroom door to complete and utter silence. As he shut the door behind him,

David wondered If Ms. Pam would have been alarmed to know that he probed her brain with his powerful extra sensory perception ability and discovered that she knew nothing of the slaying on Moore's knob, in fact her Brain was void of almost any kind of intelligence at all.

The vote on banning the moratorium on hydraulic Fracking was less than three days away, and David still had to persuade Bob Miller, the lone vote of opposition allowing hydraulic fracturing in Stokes County, to change his mind. David's cell phone began to ring, and before He even picked up the Phone David knew it was Black Bart.

"How did your meeting with Council women Tammy White Go?" Black Bart asked already knowing the answer because Tammy White had already called him and explained that she had a change in heart and would definitely be voting to allow fracking in Danbury and the surrounding vicinity. Black Bart knew that David the mind Magician had worked his legerdemain, and this frighten women phone call was like holding a white flag, the universal sign of surrender!

"Oh I have a feeling, you already know that Ms. White will not be a problem," David said confidently into the phone. David wanted Black Bart to know that he would always be one-step ahead of him, and that he would be the puppet master controlling Black Bart like a meaningless tool. Black Bart hated the arrogance in David's voice, and calmly said,

"Bob Miller will not be such an easy target of conversion to the dark side," Black Bart said laughing insanely into the phone.

"Why is that"? David asked humoring this evil, controlling psychopath. Black Bart delayed his response for a brief moment, imagining David mind squirming like an insect

"Well, He is Bill O'Toole's neighbor, and Bill, the biggest

environmental nut in the County. He has been filling Bob's head with the evils of fracking for the past two months" Black Bart exclaimed with a triumphant tone.

David already knew of Bob Miller's property, line ran adjacent to O'Toole's land, and that convincing Bob Miller to reconsider is stance on fracking would indeed be more demanding than with the adulterer Tammy White. David knew that he could always count on good old fashion greed as a prime motivator in changing minds. Bribes have always been very useful in human History, and the folks in this back wooded, isolated town were just as money hungry as a New York stock Broker.

"Ah Blackie, I wouldn't lose any sleep worrying about Bob Miller"

David said as he pulled up Miller's trucking company balance sheet and income statement that he had downloaded on his Mac Lab top, which showed a company that was about to file a chapter 13. David also noticed that the Bob Miller had put a second mortgage on his home, and foreclosure was intimate. Black Bart was shocked no one had ever dared to call him Blackie, and he was sure that David Barret had found out about his Mother's infidelity. He could barely suppress his rage, when He growled into the phone

"What makes you so damn cock sure about everything?"

David was silent for just a brief moment, then calmly replied

" Listen Blackie, you are like some insect on my shoe, I am far more advanced in intellect than anyone that you have ever met in your meager existence, So when you question me, it's like a retarded person having a conversation with a Rhodes Scholar."

Black Bart face began to transform into a hideous mask of molten rage, he screamed atrocious threats into the phone, and when he finished his rage even intensified because he realized that he had been yelling at a dial tone for the last three minutes. Black Bart knocked the lamp off his desk with one violent swipe of his hand, and swore to his recently departed son Chad that David Barret was a dead man. He then calmed down enough to realize that David Barret was his ticket out of this hellhole, and then after further reflection Black Bart was just grateful that David Barrett, the mind magician was on his side. Black Bart was still angry, so as he climbed the stairs, his rage building with each step, and he began to wonder if, his unsuspecting wife had any idea of the wrath that was speeding toward her like a runaway train.

David wicked smile twisted his face into something other than human, and his eyes glowed with an evil intensity as he envisioned Black Bart's mental meltdown. Just as he was contemplating calling Bart again, his cellphone vibrated his theme song for" For the Love of Money by the O jays," the eighties song summarized the reason for David's existence. He answered on the third ring "speak" and the sound of his voice echoed of the walls of his one room prison,

" Yea this is Frank Bryson, I'm about 30 minutes away, headed toward the residence of one Bob Miller, is it okay to proceed?" the expert in Hydrology and underground aquifers asked.

"Proceed to residence but park your car on the gravel road running adjacent to his property, I will pick you up there" David answered and quickly disconnected the phone,

Just as the classic song that served as his ring tone predicted people will lie, lord people will cheat for the love of money, the pockets of large gas companies were so deep that David could buy the expert opinions of doctors, shrinks, and scientist like Frank Bryson; in fact, gas companies secretly employed more folks than the federal government. Oh God he loved his job having judges, politicians, and officers of the Law on payroll gave him great power to manipulate and control, and sometimes David had to pinch himself to remind himself that he was a mere mortal.

David pulled his powerful black charger next to Frank Bryson's small compact car, and yelled at the anxious, timorous, petite man to hop in his sleek, muscle car. As soon as the Lilliputian man had his seatbelt securely around, David floored the gas pedal and the charger fishtailed down the gravel road kicking up a trail of dust that swirled around them like some weird tornado. David glanced over at his honored guest, and noticed a scowl on his triangular face, so David handed him a wad of hundred dollar bills, the first of his installment payments from the Abbott gas company. The transformation of the man's face with instantaneous, and the large mouth broaden into a wide grin which threaten to escape the boundaries of the man's meager jawline.

Bob Miller's home was tucked back off County road 108, about 200 yards from the curvy narrow back wooded road. They turned onto Miller's rather lengthy driveway, David noticed the complex series of graphs, charts, and notes that Bryson had on his lap, and was reminded of one of one of the few bits of advice that his long departed daddy had told him "if you can't dazzle them with brilliance baffle them with bullshit." Bob Miller's home place was composed of a modest ranch home, with a bright reflective red tin roof, as the centerpiece, his company's equipment including two large trucks that were sitting idle in a spacious barn that had a matching red tin roof. The barn sat about 500 yards to the left of the home, and had an adjoining car garage with a matching red tin roof added on to the back quarters. David noted the orderly design of the buildings and knew right away that he was dealing with an extremely conservative personality, who didn't want or like any deviation to his redundant and boring lifestyle.

"Keep your water table explanation simple no complexes jabber about tectonic plates influencing aquifers. I don't want Miller so confused that he has to take an extra strength Tylenol, when we leave." David instructed

David stressed as he climbed the three steps leading to the front door. The small mole like Frank Bryson just nodded his head and grunted like some sub-servant slave. The stunning beauty that answered the door, after the doorbell chimed their presence did not surprise David. The dossier he reviewed thirty minutes ago had photographs and a vivid biography of each family member, but when Jennifer opened the door David realized that her picture did not do her justice. She was wearing a pink Nike jogging suit complete with a low top that reveal massive mammary glands with beads of sweat forming on her olive skin.

"Hello gentleman welcome to our humble abode. Bob is waiting on you out back on the patio". She invited them in the Foyer, which was decorated with the pictures of three teenagers ranging from ages 15 to 18 years old. David was ecstatic to know that Bob and Jennifer loved and adored their offspring; why else would they have a natural shrine built for them upon entrance to their home? Subliminally suggesting their children came first in their lives, David though that convincing Bob Miller to rescind the annoying ban on hydraulic Fracturing was going to be like shooting fish in a barrel!

David shuttered at the thought of his last analogy. He was slowly being countrified and wished he could expedite his mission, but then he peered into the brilliant blue eyes of Jennifer Miller and decided that he was in no hurry to leave.

CHAPTER 11

Bob Miller was waiting for them poolside underneath a umbrella that shaded his massive frame from the bright autumn sun, his shadow reaching toward the house like some macroscopic extension of his already gigantic body. He wore sunglasses covering the windows to his soul, which made it extremely difficult for David to gauge Miller's demeanor. Bob Miller was smoking a Cuban cigar and blowing smoke rings in the air, like a person that did not realize that he was flat broke or was he trying to project an image of a good ole country boy who is widely successful?

Bob Miller had on a white Polo golf shirt that barely skirted his 20-inch neck, and black Khaki shorts, that revealed hairy ape like legs that were propped up in a chair in front of him. As David and Sloan approached the table, a large booming voice greeted them.

"Well if it's not Abbott gas's henchman come to pay a visit to a small town city commissioner. I wonder what they could possible want from a small political pawn such as myself?" Bob Miller asked sensing that this was his time to exert power over a major oil corporation and by God He was going to make them beg at his feet! David sensed the man was a control and power freak, so He replied in his most submissive voice

" Yes thank you Sir for allowing us to meet with you on such short notice," He glanced at Bryson trying to discern if this PHD of hydrology had the common sense to be taking mental notes on how to handle a self-absorbed prick like Bob

Miller.

"Ah old Black Bart made it crystal clear to me that if I didn't meet with you, that it would be political suicide, so I didn't really have an option did I?" Miller asked as he blew smoke that drifted up into David and Bryson's face.

David coughed a bit, and he wanted to choke the life out of this fat retard, and then ravish his beautiful wife, but replied, "My name is David Barret and this is Dr, Bryson, professor at Duke University in Raleigh, North Carolina. Dr. Bryson is an expert in Hydrology and does consulting work for Abbot Natural Gas Company".

"Listen I know why your here, but your trip was in vain, I will continue to support the moratorium on hydraulic fracturing in Stokes County" Miller aggressively stated taking off his sunglasses and lying them on the glass tabletop.

David noticed the defiant stare coming from Miller's eyes, and noticed his wide shoulders tense up like a snake ready to pounce on its prey. David also noticed the yellowing around Miller's eyes, and knew the man in front of them would be dead in a year, David guessed that liver or colon cancer cells would overcome his Immunity system within a year laying waste to his vast army of white corpuscles, making his lovely wife Jennifer a wanton widow. David had to contain his unbridled joy at the thought of a lonely, sex deprived widow, but he calmly returned Miller's stare and asked

"Why are you so opposed to an industry that will make Stokes County richer than Saudi Arabia?"

"I have done massive research on the Barnabas and the Harnett Shale operations and the shale lies several hundred feet deeper than the aquifers, but they are still having problems with the back flow water contaminating wells in the area. The shale here in Stokes County lies at about the same level as our precious water tables, and I cannot in good faith vote to put Benzene, Radon, and a host of other Carcinogen chemicals in my Neighbors water supply!" Miller concludes his verbal wrath by blowing a huge smoke ring right in Bryson's face.

"If I may interject here Mr. Miller, but first let me say that I'm very impressed by your research," Frank Bryson praised as he quickly unrolled the geologic maps of Stokes County aquifers. David Barret smiled to himself he did indeed have the right horse in Bryson. He motioned for Miller to peer at the map, as he explained the complex science of Hydrology

" As you have so intelligently mentioned the great shale bed of Stokes county lies about 100 feet down, and your water table is around 80 feet in depth, and I agree with you is too close for any type of extraction." Bryson continued, "But the largest aquifer in Stokes County is protected by an Aquiclude or Aquifuge, which is a solid impermeable wall underlying between the shale extraction and the precious water source of Danbury and the surrounding area"!

David thought Bryson presentation was brilliant turning a complex science into something so simple that even this missing link idiot could understand. Miller stared at the Map, but shrugged his massive gorilla like shoulders and amplified his disbelief, in such a manner that his mentor Bill O'Toole would be proud of.

" Ah bullshit, You talk all this Hydrology crap to me, but I know your both on Abbott Gas bank roll, and I listen politely to your expert, but it's time for you all to get the hell off my property now"! Miller's yellow colored eyes expanded to impossible dimensions and for a minute Harvey Sloan fearing for his life was already vacating his seat.

Time to switch to plan B, so David calmly remained in his seat and asked Miller "How is your trucking business Bob?"

"None of your Damn business asshole, now get off my

land," Bob Miller shouted, and David though the man was going to slump over with a brain Hemorrhage, which would have saved him from the painful chemo treatments in the very near future.

"Now Bob simmer down, I am here to assist you in the moment of darkest need", David said as the retrieved Miller is trucking company's financial documents from his briefcase. Bob Miller was on his feet ready to remove David Barret from his poolside lounger, when Jennifer Miller screamed from the patio door, "Put your pride aside for a minute Bob, and listen to what Mr. Barret has to say!"

"Mr. Miller your trucking company is bankrupted, the bank is going to repossess your home, and you have a wife and children that are depending on you to make a rational assessment of your current financial, so check your emotions at the front door!" David calmed said as he laid the balance sheet and profit and loss statement from 2016 on the table in front of a shocked and embarrassed Bob Miller.

"How did you get my companies financial information?" Miller asked his face contorted into a mask of puzzlement.

" I just went online to Dun and Bradstreet website and downloaded it, took about five minutes, so Bob all your potential customers, suppliers and vendors know your broke that's why no one will accept your Bid on Jobs" David replied sympathetically.

Bob White terrible secret was out; his giant shoulders began to shake. He hung his head and his sobbing was unmanageable. Jennifer Miller rushed to her husband's side to comfort him, but being a southern macho man, he pushed her aside. David Barret, a fourth degree Black belt in Karate had to control his impulse to beat the caveman to death, but would severely damage his brilliant operation. Bob Miller was now at his lowest point, a desperate, broken, and beaten man, David knew it was the perfect time to spring the trap and make Bob Miller his pawn.

"Bob I can help provide a solution for saving your home, business, and provide you with the financial security to send your children to the best universities in the country," David said in a serene tranquil tone. Bob Miller studied David face for the slightest hint of a con job, or elaborate swindle, seeing that David Barret was very serious he just said one word, "How?"

That David lived for the conquering of the beast, "Bob, Hydraulic Fracturing is very complex, it requires massive quantities of sand, chemicals, and water, which equates into about up to 500 tanker and dump trucks for a single frack." Now, Bob can you imagine your bank account, if Miller trucking was the only trucking company that Abbott gas had on its payroll?" David asked hoping the man's primitive mind could make the connection.

David and Frank waited for the proverbial light switch to go on, and finally Bob Miller turned and stared at David like a returning savior,

"Ah so if a vote to rescind the moratorium on fracking, you can guarantee me all these jobs?"

"That's right Bob, all your problems will just go away" David glancing up at Jennifer Miller, who was standing behind her man. David could not understand how this beautiful woman could be so loyal to such an asshole, David wondered if it was love or fear that motivated this goddess. He would definitely have her before this mission was over.

David went on to explain that the Abbott Gas company had many friends at the Department of Transportation in Raleigh, and they were going to insure the Miller Trucking company was going to snare the majority of jobs in Stokes County, regardless of the competitions bid. David peered into the eyes of Bob Miller, and knew that Miller was still undecided. It was time to drive the final nail into the proverbial coffin.

"Bob and Jennifer you have some beautiful children, couldn't help but notice the pictures as we walked in the front door. They look about Collage age"? David asked baiting the final trap.

"Yes, Bob Jr and Katie are seniors in High School, and Melody is a sophomore. They are all very bright, Bob Jr wants to study Law, and Katie is looking for a career in Nursing". Jennifer Miller answered her brilliant blue eyes beaming with pride.

"Dr. Bryson what is the tuition at Duke for a year" David asked the silent man still petrified from cave boy's outburst.

"Well at least 100,000 grand a year" Bryson said with renewed conviction. David like a good salesman just shut his mouth and let the Miller think about how it would break their children's heart to deny them their dreams. Bob Miller looked into the eyes of his mate, as her eyes filled with tears, and he slowly turned around nodding his head in surrender, and calmly said, "Tell your unmoral employer that they have their proxy!"

David Barret wanted to cement the deal, so he pushed an envelope full of bills with Benjamin Franklin's image on them over to Bob Miller, and calmly explained

"This will pay off your mortgage and assist you in buying more trucks for your growing business" David then silently stood and He and Sloan excused themselves, as he glanced at Jennifer Miller he noticed a look of deep gratitude mixed with sheer attraction and lust. He smiled and nodded at her as if mentally consenting to an extra marital affair; he always played a little while on the road, after all it was always a great stress reliever. When they were finally out of the Miller's home, Frank Bryson was babbling something about more money.

David blocked him out completely as the Lyrics of the Ojays Money, Money played repeatedly in his mind. It was great background noise as he silently congratulated himself on the successful completion of the first phase of his operation. He knew the second phase of his plan would be dangerous because it included a meddling FBI agent, that he had seen being interviewed on the local news station. He had done research on her, and she had a very impressive resume, David also knew that Black Bart would not rest until they eliminated the royal pain in the ass Bill O'Toole.

CHAPTER 12

It was almost dusk when Kelli and Sam arrived at the estate of Bart Whitescarver. Sam peered through the large oak trees at the large Gothic looking structure at the end of Delta Church Road. In the dying light of a fall afternoon, the house bore an uncanny resemblance to Barnabas Collins mansion on his boyhood favorite show Dark Shadows. Sam shivered as he thought of the hellish vampire visiting him in the many nightmares of his youth, and tried to hide his deep sense of foreboding that suddenly pierced his soul from Kelli. Kelli peered at the mansion that seemed to move between the trees, like some large animal trying to escape capture. Kelli was concentrating so hard on the ghostly mansion, that she did not notice the front gate rapidly approaching. She slammed on the brakes coming within inches of smashing into the ancient Iron Gate. A man of darken skin tone ambled out of the guard shack, looking agitated at the interruption of his peaceful meditative napping.

"Agent Kelli Ryan and Agent Sam Jenkins here to see Bart Whitescarver, Kelli announced in her best authoritative tone." The man with dark curly hair, and a thick mustache just glared at them with some serious serial killer eyes vacantly replied

"Master Whitescarver is expecting you" as he went back to the guard shack to open the electronic gate he stared at Sam Jenkins as if he was a new life form. The gate opened and Kelli gunned the engines of the powerful Suburban lurched forward, once they had traveled 100 yards Sam Jenkins blurted out in his best Spanish accent " Master Whitescarver is expecting you!!!" and He and Kelli burst into laughter at Sam's spot on impersonation.

The home was a monstrosity, to Kelli it resembled the mansion in her favorite movie of all time Forrest Gump, but with a darker personality, She believe that some homes like the one featured in the Amityville horror took on an evil toxic vibes of the inhabitants. The hairs on her arms were standing straight up, she felt a chill travel down her spinal column, and she knew that soon she would be standing in front of a demon in human camouflage. The front of the home center attraction was a stacked Virginia stone fireplace that arched skyward from the ground to a Cathedral Ceiling. A wide Oak Balcony encircled the home, and as Kelly reached for the ancient brass lion door knocker, she spotted Black Bart youngest son playing contently on the deck totally oblivious to the guest below. Hugh Clerestory windows encased the door on both sides, so Kelly could see the dark skinned man approach the door, and to her shock he was the exact duplicate of the security guard at the front gate, Kelly thought that Black Bart found a way to clone servants or maybe there was a sale on twins at the border crossing.

The security guard clone opened the door and with about the same emotion of his twin brother, announced that Senor Whitescarver was waiting for them on the back balcony. Kelly noticed the reclaimed pine floors, and the crystal chandelier that hung 30 feet above them. As she began to climb to the black walnut staircase that connected the two floors, her mind was working overtime to process her surroundings. Kelli knew by the design and extravagant furnishings of Black Bart's home, that Black Bart valued money, power and prestige more than God himself did; in fact, Kelli knew that in Bart's narcissistic mind, He was his own God. As she reached the top of the stairs, Kelly glanced up, and was horrified to see the head of Shaun O'Toole mounted on a trophy wall directly in front of her. She was horrified as the blood shot eyes of the recently departed Shaun O'Toole glared at her. The decapitated head not knowing of its death seemed to be screaming, mouth wide open, drool dripping down its chin pooling on the beautiful pine floor. Kelli grasped Sam's arm and pointed to the ghoulish shrine, Sam calmly said "Best looking 12 point buck mounting that I have the pleasure of viewing, I simply must get the name of the Taxidermist that created this masterpiece". Kelli was horrified my her partner response, and as about to voice her extreme displeasure and confusion, when she turned back toward the wall and was shocked to see a normal man cave, with a mounting of a twelve point buck, a grizzly bear, and a mountain lion decorating Black Bart's study.

At that very moment, Kelli knew that her PTSD was going to be a serious distraction to this case, and as soon as she met with Director King, she would submit her resignation. As Kelli contemplated her fate, a booming voice echoed through the study,

"Ah I see that you're impressed with my hunting skills. Do you hunt anything besides humans Agent Ryan"?

Kelli whirled around and was shocked to see a beastly, bulging man with a large cranium and gleaming reptilian like eyes that held in a predatory star. As if she was, a tasty insect caught in a spider's web. Kelli turned and introduced herself and Sam Jenkins and informed Black Bart this was not a social visit, and they would be questioning him about his Son's eerie demise, but also the dismemberment of Shaun O'Toole.

"Let's go sit on my back porch, and listen to the ancient Dan River, which like time will run for eternity," Black Bart spouted like some country boy poet.

Kelli knew the reason why Black Bart wanted to sit on the porch, was because the darkness would conceal his reptilian eyes, making it more difficult of Kelli to discern the truth. As soon as their gluteus Maximus hit the cushions of the fine

Queen Ann chairs, Kelli asked,

"Who would want Chad dead? and why in such a horrible manner? Dehydrating his remains to the point that he resembled an Egyptian pharaoh in the tombs of Giza" Kelli asked watching the dark reptilian eyes for emotion.

"How the hell do I know what kind of psychopath would get pleasure out of murdering someone that way, but I would start with extreme environmental terrorist like Bill O'Toole or that damn Paul Williams!" Bart almost screamed in Kelli's ear.

Kelli hesitated, because she was taken by surprise by the sudden shift in Black Bart's personality from a back wooded poet into a raving bi polar lunatic,

"Oh so your implicating your formidable opponents on the hydraulic fracturing in Stokes County right away, how Convenient?" Kelli asked masterfully cutting through all the bullshit.

Black Bart studied Kelli face for a moment and thought to himself how he had underestimated the intelligence of the women in front of him, but then he realized that being a male chauvinist pig had made him blind. He would play his cards closer to his vest, and definitely tell David Barret that there was a new threat in town to their masterful plan.

Kelli realizing that she had Black Bart on his heels, then asked " Since you thought that Bill O'Toole might have murdered your son, would it not be easy to seek revenge for his murder by killing and dismembering Shaun's body in order to match the grisly condition of your Son's corpse?" Kelli asked looking defiantly into Black Bart's diabolic stare.

"Ah please, I have sense enough to know that, because my deep hatred for Bill O'Toole that I would be the number one suspect and I deeply resent the questioning here." "So get the hell of my property now!" Black Bart voice echoed throughout the second floor of the mansion.

Gloria Whitescarver, unaware of visitors scurried out to the back porch, "What can I get for you dear?" The wife-servant said as she suddenly appeared behind her husband.

Kelli looked up a poster child for the battered women syndrome; she had that shattered look of a completely beaten woman both emotionally and physically. Gloria Whitescarver eye was blackish purple from a recent beating, and upon seeing that Black Bart had guest she subconsciously tried to cover it up with her hand and mumbled something about falling down in the kitchen. Kelli's hatred for Black Bart intensified, and Sam Jenkins tensed in his chair willing his hands to his side, instead of wrapping them around Black Bart's neck,

Kelli remained in her chair, listening to the sound of the rushing water river below them, had a very calming effect on her soul, and she relished the sense peace and tranquility that invaded into her sub consciousness, silencing the beast of her PTSD. Black Bart was livid, and stood his massive 6'5" frame was quivering with rage, because the two federal agents were not responding to his demand, and all egomania Narcissist hate to be ignored. Sam Jenkins stood with the veins in his forehead and neck protruding out like flowing rivers underneath his skin, his eyes of steel resolve seemed to neutralize Black Bart's anger. Kelli knew that with most cowards, once confronted by another alpha male would back down. Kelli had one final card to play before leaving

"What about a sample of your DNA? so we can compare it to trace DNA the lab found on Shaun O"O'Toole" Kelli asked. Black Bart stared at Kelli with intense hatred, and Kelli could feel the searing heat of Bart's anger.

"To hell with your DNA sample, unless you go get a warrant, and since I own this county that's highly unlikely, besides I heard through the grapevine that the O'Toole boy was dissected like a frog in a High School Biology class"! Black Bart said with a fiendish grin.

Kelli wondered how Bart knew that detail, but she then remembered that Sheriff Brown was a friend and obedient servant to Black Bart. She then realized that Bart was too evil to have any friends, so she mentally corrected herself and labeled Sheriff Brown one of Black Bart's robotic henchmen!

" Do yourself a favor Mr. Whitescarver, and look of the term mitochondrial DNA analysis, and I promise we will be back with that warrant before your primitive mind can grasp the concept, so just practice opening your mouth so I can collect my sample" Kelli said in a stern and menacing manner.

Sam Jenkins did not like the wild look in Kelli's eyes, but as he turned and glanced at Gloria Whitescarver, he noticed a hint of a smile and a look of hero worship directed toward his Boss.

" Oh I forget Stokes County chief coroner has determined the time of death for Shaun O'Toole around October 11, about three days after your son's body was found, so the million dollar question on everyone's mind is where were you on the day in question?" hmmm Kelli added for amusement!

"Listen Bitch, I don't have to answer any of your damn questions, in fact this is your last interview with me, from now on you will confer with my lawyer, this is harassment," Black Bart said reaching for his cell phone.

"Such bad language, for the extremely well educated intelligent heathen that you are, and I wouldn't mind speaking to your lawyer because I am sure he is a hell of a lot easier on the eyes than you"! Kelli stood and walked toward the door leaving an utter path of destruction behind her, then she turned and said

" If I come back and there are any more bruises on your wife's face, I promise you a will drum up bogus federal charges on you so severe, by the time your boyfriend lawyer gets you out of prison you will not have to push any more when you take a shit".

Kelli was still fuming when she and Sam headed back down the driveway, and didn't say anything until they had cleared the ancient gate at the bottom of the hill, she turned and smiled at her friend Sam Jenkins and asked " Now didn't I make a wonderful first impression?" Sam nodded his head and silent affirmation, but he was secretly concerned that Kelli had pushed an extremely, unbalanced crazy man too far.

Sam had no idea how justified his thought process was, because the moment they left the mansion, Black Bart was on the phone with his new mentor David Barret.

"I want her dead yesterday, Black Bart screamed into the phone, in fact I am willing to put a 50,000 bounty on her head".

David had done some extension research on Kelli Ryan, and wanted to get rid of her too, but it was nothing personal she was just too damn brilliant for her own good, there were very few folks that scared David Barret, but Kelli Ryan was one of the rare human specimens that did.

"Ah don't worry your purty head Blackie Boy, I got a diabolical plan to get rid of the damn FBI pest, and you're Tree-hugging, save the frigging whales, global warming fruitcake Bill O'Toole at the same time".

Black Bart slammed the phone down mad because of the blackie boy comment, but again so glad to have the mind Magician on his team for the interim. He hated that David Barrett could always end their conversations with conflicting emotions, on one hand Black Bart despised him but on the flip side he admired his brilliance, yea it was a mental quagmire, a true love/hate relationship.

CHAPTER 13

The Pine River Motel was located about five miles off of curvy highway 8, nestled up against a cinnamon-red forest of Maples and ancient Oak trees. The motel was Inspector King's choice because it was remote and far removed from the turmoil that was gripping the small towns of Walnut cove and Danbury. When Kelli and Sam pulled into the ancient motor lodge, they knew that by its design, the hotel dated back to at least the 50's. They passed the office, and traveled under the arch, which connected two completely separate wings with twelve rooms each. A water fountain with small marble birds perched for eternity decorated the courtyard that separated the two wings. Black walnut benches circled the fountain so that young lovers could sit and admire the naturalistic setting.

Kelli thought as they pulled into the courtyard that Pine River Motel was a strange name for a motel. Since neither shaded the Motel pines nor had a cascading river to help coax her to sleep after a long and stressful day. Upon entering the courtyard, Kelli noticed that light escaping Agent Running Deer room, so she visualized the hard working agent burning the midnight oil, researching or processing evidence that had been collected during his trek to Vade Mecum springs. She had emailed Running Deer notifying him of the 6:00 am debriefing, and waved good night to Sam as he enter the last room on the wing on the other side of the commons. Inspector King, being an ex-army officer separated the team like a fire team on patrol with plenty of space between rooms. The main idea was if an intruder or killer wanted to take them all out in the middle of the night, they would have to set more than one booby-trap or explosive device. Kelli turned the key on the old fashion door, half expecting to be incinerated by an improvised explosive device, and breathed a sigh of relief as she stepped into the darken, musty, smelling room.

Kelli reached for the light switch, after flipping it on she almost wished there had been a bomb, because it would have saved her senses from the hideous onslaught of a room frozen in time. The two double beds were covered with rustic looking quilts that look like they came from a Saturday morning yard sale. The floor was covered with a blue rug that was faded and stained with God knows what, and two rickety chairs made of black oak pushed against an old cedar desk completed the ensemble. Kelli phone began to vibrated with urgency, She took the generation 7 out of her front pocket, and recoiled when she noticed that she had missed seven calls from Jake. She shuttered to think of Jake's emotional state, He would be livid with her not out of trying to control her but worried to death about her safety.

Kelli called Jake on face time, and like magic, the larger than life Jake Ryan appeared on her phone. The visual image of Jake scared her more than Brian Cox corpse sitting up in the Stokes County Morgue, Jake eyes were red, and his usually well groomed blond hair was disheveled, his face was caught in a frozen mask of intensity and tension,

"Damn you could have at least IM me, sent an email, or smoke signal or something," an exacerbated Jake yelled into the phone.

"I'm so sorry baby, this case consumed my entire thought process, since I landed in Greensboro, I can't believe it's almost Nine" Kelli replied in the most soothing voice she could trying to defuse his anxiety.

The soothing voice of his mate calmed Jake down significantly, he put his lips against the phone screen and comically asked his queen to give him as kiss and to Jake's utter and complete surprise Kelli complied by kissing the phone screen, even though Jake knew Kelli had a thing about germs. He closed his eyes and visualizes holding her and kissing on the nape of her neck, but this fantasy increased his longing for her. He slowly lifted his gaze of love into her eyes and explained why his heighten sense of anxiety,

" It's just that I worry about your Post Traumatic Stress Syndrome, and coupled with the unofficial report of several law officers losing their lives in Stokes County, North Carolina has caused me great stress baby" Jake said secretly worrying that his man card might be revoked at any time.

Kelli winked at her lover and said with a small hint of amusement, "Ah baby don't you worry your pretty little head about this tough G women."

Jake was secretly concerned about some kinda of weird role reversal, cleared his throat and asked Kelli to give him a rundown of her day, so he could give her some expert, insightful advice thus saving him from looking unmanly and bounteously weak. Kelli recapped her eventfully day, purposefully leaving out the video from Donnie Miller's body camera, which displayed the hideous beast straight out of a horror novel. Kelli felt bad about withholding information from Jake, but if other members of the investigation could not pass along facts of the case to love ones, then Kelli would feel like a hypocrite if she did not follow her own mandate. She did not want to put any additional stress and anxiety on an already disquieted Jake. Kelli explained her theory that the killings were carried out by two separate killers, because the Modus operandi or the killer's method of operation was distinctively different at each crime scene. The placement of the body parts of Sean O'Toole was methodical indicating some kind of planning, while the massacre at Moore's knob was a similar to an erupting of a volcano of fury and wrath.

"One crime was a planned execution with a lethal warning; the other was a crime of pent of rage that had been building for years. The victimology seems unrelated as well, killing of police officers and Brian Cox seems to indicate a hatred for authority, while the killing of Shaun O'Toole seems related to his family's opposition to Hydraulic Fracking. In the slaughter at Moore's knob, we are looking for a violent deranged killer, with a lengthy rap and an intense hatred for authority. The Shaun O'Toole killer will have ties to the Fracking industry, possibly even a professional killer hired by the Gas Company," Kelli summarized leaving out the part about the violent deranged killer having an uncanny resemblance to big foot.

Jake listened intently, typed copious notes onto his HP15 Hewlett Packard laptop, digesting both the details of the case and formulating theories in his quick deductive mind.

"Kelli I am going to do extensive research into this agent Briggs jerk, because he reminds of the certain pain in the ass agent that almost cost us our lives on Portsmouth Island North Carolina," Jake said sternly.

Kelli almost laughed at the intense scowl as he peered into her husband's face, but then felt a sharp wave of nausea when she thought of the deceased agent Walker. She didn't know if the nausea was from the hatred she had for Walker, or for the repulsive way he perished.

"Black Bart is definitely a person of interest in Shaun O'Toole murder, and I am definitely going to do solid research on him. I believe that there is another angle to this case besides the hydraulic fracking issue."

"Why do something as morbid as dismemberment and then distribute the body parts along the four highest peaks of the Sauratown Mountains?" "Why go that grandiose level of display? " Then it came to Jake and he inhaled sharply, he looked up at Kelli with a sudden look of enlightenment,

"Kelli have you ever heard of a Roman Slave named Spartacus?" Jake asked his eyes penetrating through the phone.

"Sure that was a Thracian gladiator that led a slave revolt against Roman" Kelli replied shocking Jake with her knowledge of History.

"Very good, didn't know you were a student of Ancient Roman history" Jake complimented as if speaking to one of his high school students.

"Ah teach don't get carried away, I'm a big fan of the AMC channel and just saw an old fifties movie starring my favorite actor Kirk Douglas playing the lead role as Spartacus, great movie by the way!" Kelli added sounding like a Hollywood movie critic.

"Kelli after Spartacus was crushed at Lucania in 71 BC, thus ending the Third Seville war. Many of his followers were crucified along the Appian way which spans from Rome to Capua, 117 miles of men nailed to crosses". Jake spread his arms for dramatic effect.

"Great history lesson Jake, but what in the hell does all this have to do with my case?" Kelli asked crossing her arms as if to mock Jake's drama flair.

"Well my beautiful sex kitten, many ancient Rome scholars believe that Spartacus body was decapitated and quartered, with his arms sent to the Northern Province of Dacha, and to the Siva, the southernmost boundary. The legs were sent to Britannia in the west, and Armenia the eastern most province, The placement of Spartacus at the dismembered body at the four corners of the Roman empire was a warning to any Roman slave entertaining the idea of leading another revolt" Jake lectured, crossed his arms indicating the the history lesson of ancient Rome was now complete.

Kelli blinked her eyes, and comically asked, "Should I be looking for a professor of Ancient Roman History?" eyeing

Jake with mocked suspicion

Jake laughed and sternly responded, "Your killers are sending a warning cease and desist or you will be next. It could be the oil companies sending a message to all the environmental groups in the area, but I don't think so, there is another angle to this murder." "It's a warning, but to whom?" " It just doesn't have the fingerprint of the corporate America, more like organized crime or a gang!" Jake said longing looking at his wife's beautiful face,

"Well done my Hero, now get down her Saturday, so I can rewarded you," Kelli said seductively, briefly flashing Jake her ample breast"

"Ah baby can't make it this weekend; we have out homecoming game against the Murray Falcons. Moreover, I have to chaperon the dance Saturday night. I tried like hell to get out of it, but all my peers in the teachers' lounge pointed out that I have never chaperoned a dance in my five year tenor here." Jake face clouded up with disappointment.

"That's OK baby, but if you're not here in the next weekend, I'm divorcing you." "Because I will be sooo lonely Black Bart will start looking good to me," Kelli laughed into the phone.

" Oh don't you worry my love, I am planning on taking a couple of sick days, because it's going to take more than two days to take care of your insatiable sexual desire" Jake said taking off his shirt and demonstrating his washboard abs.

Kelli turned and darkens the lights, and stripped down to her panties, and purred into the phone "Oh Jake give me a play by play description of what your devious intentions are!"

The two lovers spent the next hour describing and showing their partner how much they missed each other. Life is so cruel, because Jake and Kelli should have been wrapped in each other arms confessing their love for each other, since at that very moment a diabolical plan was being formulated to separate these two souls forever!

PART 4

Trails, Tribulations, and Terror

CHAPTER 1

At 9:00 am the morning of October 18, the noble Stokes County Commissioners rescinded the moratorium on hydraulic fracturing in Stokes County, North Carolina. A unanimous motion passed the decision, and within minutes, these 10 trusted public officials had endangered the drinking water of several thousand hard working, God-fearing citizens. The word was spread through social media like wildfire, and local news stations scrambled reporters and camera crews to the county seat of Danbury, hoping to capture the angry voices of the townsfolk. Within about two hours, livid citizens lined the street across from the courthouse protesting this unconscionable act of treason.

A couple of protest signs suggested violence response to any attempt to frack on sacred land surrounding the Dan river, already compromised by the coal ash spill of 2014. One clever sign declared in big red letters, "I heard rumors that Fracking causes Cancerous tumors", another sign read "Tar and feather our County Commissioners". Several local environmental groups like the Blue Ridge Defenders, and Stokes County citizens for clean water were circulating petitions for signatures hoping to get North Carolina Department of Environmental Quality or DEQ involved. The DEQ had assigned a commission called the oil and gas committee to research Hydraulic Fracturing and determine if the processes as environmental safe for North Carolina. As with many committees designed to protect our precious natural resources, the committee slowly morphed into a group vulnerable to special interest groups. The special interest in this case was large oil and gas corporations wanting to reap large profits of the great shale concentrations of the central Piedmont of North Carolina.

When a local Television reported asked a local citizen about getting the DEQ involved, and his impressions of the oil and gas Committee, the old boy spit some tobacco in his spittoon, and cleverly retorted,

"I trust them about as much as a hungry wolf guarded a chicken house" he then walking off carrying a sign saying "Hey Dumb asses you can't drunk money."

David Barret circulated among all the infuriated protesters, feeding off their anger, their sense of outrage stimulated his deep-seated psychological need for disorder and chaos. He was euphoric knowing that he had completed the first phase of his mission, but unfortunately, he could not rest. The next phase of the operation was much more complex, because he was now a modern day prospector searching for land to mine this liquid gold. He now must attended a meeting in the midst of his arch rivals, and then through telekinesis plan a method to assassinate Bill O'Toole, the head of the serpent that protected the land.

The old Tobacco barn sat about 50 yards off a dirt road, its tin roof reflecting the silvery moonlight back into space. The barn strategically divided Bill O'Toole's 2,000-acre ranch into almost two equal halves, once it was the center of bustling activity, now its ghostly image cast a surreal shadow over the landscape. The barn was a relic from the past, used to air cure burley tobacco, before taking it to the tobacco floor to be auctioned off to buyers representing large companies like Phillip Morris out of Winston Salem. The 3,000 square foot barn had nine tiers or wooden beams running the length of its frame, and could house many acres of tobacco. Men would off load the tobacco from a wagon pulled by a John Deere tractor.

A team of four farm hands would straddle the tiers; the

man on the lowest tier would bare the brunt of the labor handling every stick containing five or six tobacco stalks. He would reach down and grab the stick from the field hand on the wagon, then he would turn the stick vertical to the man on the next tier, until the stick was in the hands of the lucky field hand straddling the top tier about 50 feet off the ground. This human elevator could hang at least 1,000 sticks a day, but it was back breaking labor that a few native American sons wanted any part of today.

Bill O'Toole decided that tobacco was just too much of a labor intensified crop, so he converted the acreage that was used for tobacco production to grazing land for his cattle, or soybean production, He was irked by the fact that Black Bart stole most of his Mexican labors with the promise of higher wages about 10 years ago. His hatred for Black Bart began then and had been slowly building with volcanic intensity, and soon, very soon Bart Bart's day of reckoning will arrive with deadly repercussions.

The only occupants of the monstrous relic of yester-year were field mice and a family of great horned owls. The owls nest was high in the rafters, and there were two baby owlets that kept mom and dad busy feeding and protecting the brood. The large nocturnal beast would hunt at night, swooping out of the rafters, their yellow eyes gleaming and pinpointing small rodents with their animal binocular vision, their 54-inch wingspan enable them to claim their dish of choice with stealth like quickness. After the Moratorium on Fracking was rescinded, this serene barn was transformed into a meeting place of an elite, powerful group of men and women who would spearhead the environmental protest to the on-slaught of greed and corruption, which threatened their most precious natural resources. The area around the barn served as a crude parking lot, but the cars that were surrounding the old barn looked distinctly out of place, Mercedes E class, Lexus RX350, and BMW 5 series, served as a notice that this was indeed a meeting of the powerful and elite of Stokes and Rockingham Counties.

At about the same time that Jake and Kelli were having their red hot teleconference curiosity of Facebook, Bill 'O'Toole stood at the podium, trying to suppress the inner rage that comes from losing a son, and then be double crossed by Bob Miller and Tammi White. Bill suppressed his emotions because the delivery of his carefully prepared speech had to be made with a calm and steady voice. He stood in before those that were passion about preserving the land known as the Dan River basin, and despite their power and wealth detested the encroachment of gas companies that threatened their North Carolina version of the Garden of Eden. Bill O'Toole surveyed the group while they sat on the pews in front of him, which were divinely bequeathed to him by preacher Robby Hawkins, who had positioned himself directly in front of his hero, eagerly awaiting the message that would lay the foundations on how to save God's earthly kingdom from destruction.

Bill O'Toole stood before the group, looking like a cross between a Celtic King, and a robust lumberjack, his biceps bulging against his brightly checkered flannel shirt, and his bright red beard shone with an angelic illumination when the cracks in the barn emitted the brilliant full moon. Bill cleared his throat giving the non-verbal sign that he was calling the meeting to order. Through a voice that resembled the thunder from the heavens, he outlined a three-tier plan to arrest Horizontal Drilling in Stokes and Rockingham counties. Before starting, Bill warned them of a great Horned Owl that had taken residence in the old barn, and strongly suggested that those that wore hats to leave them on!

"First we will go into our delay game like Duke does when they have a 10 point lead over North Carolina with only two minutes on the clock. We will petition The North Carolina Department of Natural Resources to delay fracking permits submitted by gas companies, citing that we need to codify rules governing Horizontal Drilling. Secondly, during this delay, we will seek to convert land from the private sector to the public trust, creating common law doctrine that protects water rights, like the 1000-acre tract that Paul Williams manages along the Dan River. Paul Williams hand shot up in the back of the room, and that's when Bill noticed a tall figure standing in the shadows of the hay loft about 50 yards from the main body of the group. He was about admonish the shadowy figure, when Paul Williams question broke is train of thought,

"That is going to take several years Bill; we will have to file an environmental review through the NEPA." "How long do you reckon that will take? Considering it's a branch of the federal government, and we all know how long it takes Federal government to accomplish anything, we all might be dead!" Williams question was received with applauds and a collective amen. Bill O'Toole's looked Williams in the eyes with a stare that would scare the most deranged serial killer and calmly said

"As I stated before the meeting all questions and ideas will be discussed once the foundation of our protest is outlined, then we will brainstorm."

Bill O'Toole stern response silenced the crowd, and Williams seemed to want to put on a cloak of invisibility. Bill O'Toole glanced back to the shadowy figure he had noticed a couple of minutes ago, but the specter, ghost, or a figment of his imagination was gone! Bill thought maybe he imagined the image, God knows the stress and mourning that comes from losing your youngest son would send a lessor man to a deep, dark place.

"Finally we are going to submit some zoning ordinances to the Stokes County Planning Commission, prohibiting gas companies from setting up drilling rigs, hydration units, or missiles on certain parcels on land. Each frocking site consumes 3 acres of land, in which 40,000-gallon barrel pools, and massive sand storage tanks, which will turn our county into a wasteland. Since eminent domain has been found unconstitutional, it is our job to educate large landowners of the negative impacts of fracking, so we can deny gas companies the land that we hold sacred".

Just as Bill was going to finalize plan, the inner confines of his mind urged him to shouted out "Shaun O'Toole", Bill recoiled as if copperhead snake had bit him, but he managed to stay silent,

"In the interim we can get the EPA to intercede, but the most important thing we can do is educate the large landowners and gets petitions circulated and signed to present to the Environmental Protection Agency".

As Bill started to field questions the deep in the cortex of his brain wanted him to scream out SHAUN O'TOOLE, Bill went to one knee, and many of his peers left their seats fearing that Bill was having a stroke or a nervous breakdown or both. Bill quickly regained his composure, and asked everyone to take a seat. Bill's brilliant blue eyes were ablaze with a deep passion that emitted both strength and passion as he say

" Listen we are going to take about a five minute break, before answering questions and starting the brain storming session, so help yourself to coke or coffee in the back." Bill said as he raced to the back were the stranger had been standing, knowing that that shadowy demon had something to do with his mental meltdown.

David Barret stumbled out of the barn five minutes before Bill concluded his plan. He was in a complete panic mode, as he neared his car the full moon cast a shadow the ground, that seemed circled around him. David became alarmed, thinking it was the great horned owl preparing to collect his scalp. He ran and opens the car door, once inside the safe confides of his muscle car, he peered up into heavens and was completely amazed by the bright stars in the constellation of Pisces the fish, but saw no demon bird summoned by the considerable mental powers of Bill O'Toole mind. He dismissed the shadow as a product of his vivid imagination, still in shock after sensing the considerable psychic ability of his formidable opposition.

The double agent Sheriff Brown had tipped off David Barrett about the meeting on O'Toole's property. He took an awful change going, but he learned so much about his enemy. Many great generals like Patton, Westmoreland or Napoleon always preached the importance of knowing the strengths and weakness of your opponent. David learned that O'Toole was a great leader and had a superb plan, but the main reason that O'Toole had to die was that Bill O'Toole's mental toughness was completely resistance to David's mind control attempts.

In the barn, David set out a powerful telekinetic wave to the O'Toole cerebellum commanding him the shout out the name of his murdered son, hoping that the outburst would cause Bill's followers to question their leader's sanity. David was petrified, when not only did O'Toole not respond to him, but also sent a mental response that sent shock waves through David's Corpus collasum commanding him to "GET OUT, OR DIE." David shuttered as he gunned the powerful engine of the Mustang GT, realizing that before his mission was over Bill O'Toole, or he the great mind magician would not have a heartbeat. As he peered back in his rear-view mirror, he saw an enormous turkey vulture in the silvery moonlight circling the barn high overhead, and he thought maybe animals have psychic vision too, because somehow this thing knew that Bill O'Toole and anyone else that gets in his way would be dead very soon!

Bill O'Toole stood outside the barn peered into the

night, trying to use his new mental abilities to visualize the license plate of disappearing car, as it sped away into the vast darkness that was only inherit to a rural setting. Bill O'Toole thought of the great shift in his Brain as the mental interloper tried to control his thoughts. It was as if a great tractor beam was sent from an alien life form, first probing the frontal lobe of his brain for an opening, then once inside this telepathic virus began to control and insert power over his thoughts.

Bill thought about how terrified he had been when this alien being began to wrap its tentacles around his brain stem, but then deep in the recess of his mind a power came surging forth. A psychic rush came forth and like white corpuscles fighting infection in the body, completely vanquishing the enemy and sending it slithering away in fear. Bill sensed two emotions as the mental trespasser left his mind, surprise and fear, and that is when Bill projected his wrath mentally shouting at the interloper to leave or die. Bill was both terrified and excited; he discovered a power that had lain dormant within his soul, and now was erupting like a spring storm during a time of immense upheaval in his life, was this sign from God? His thoughts were interrupted by the sound of a passion debate between his devoted followers inside the barn.

As Bill O'Toole entered into the barn, he could hear the voice of the greatest conspiracy theorist in Stokes County. "They are all shape shifting aliens, determined to mine all our resources and then consume us like tasty vittles." Gus Williams shouted at anyone that would listen to his ranting and ravings. Everyone knew that Gus believed that the Apollo 11 never landed on the moon, instead was staged in a huge warehouse. Gus gleefully points to the US flag movement in the video sent back Apollo 11 as proof of the swindle, because the atmosphere of the moon is completely void of oxygen. Gus also believes that the US Government was somehow involved in the Kennedy Assassination and 9/11.

"Damn it listen to me, the Dotard administration is nothing but a bunch of greedy billionaires that don't give a damn about the environment. They are opening up the Arctic National wildlife animal refuge, which is going to increase the melting of the arctic glaciers. Once the Ice caps are gone, the human race will soon follow. We are all Dead men walking". Gus shouted the last sentence with such dramatic flair, Bill wondered if Gus was auditioning for some screenplay.

"We all appreciate your passion Gus, but We need to address issues a tad bit more local." Bill O'Toole interjected calmly knowing that Paul Williams little brother had only one canoe paddle in the water.

Before Bill could speak, again Judge Bacon raised his hand, Bill Nodded his head for the Honorable Stokes County Judge to rescue him from the onslaught of insanity the Gus had inserted into this vital meeting.

"Gentleman and ladies from a legal standpoint, I believe most of the county commissioners are afraid of being sued by the gas companies" Judge Bacon hesitated for one moment, because he knew that he would be interrupted.

Gus Williams did not disappointed him as he shouted from the back of the room

"How in the hell is that going to happen?" Gus Williams was now standing his hefty arms crossed in front, his huge face crimson red.

" Well if a landowner sells the mineral rights of the land to the gas companies, then the gas companies can sue by citing inverse condemnation, which is simply saying the by blocking hydraulic fracturing the County is undermining the value of the land, thus cutting valuable profits, which is a big no in a capitalistic society" Judge Bacon summarized .

" Well if someone tries to drill in my backyard, I'm going to light their drill rig up like a roman candle" Gus Williams once again shouted from the back of the room, and the thing that scared Bill O'Toole the most is that no one in the room doubted the crazy man's conviction.

Bill glanced at his watch, it was about 8:00 pm, and he decided it was a good time to adjourn the meeting, reasoning the spouses would be getting a little suspicious, and he did not want to risk any addition derailment by crazy Gus.

"Listen, I am going to adjourn this meeting. We will do more brainstorming Friday night, If you have any father ideas or questions you can email or holler at me on my cell. I appreciate your attendance, this is going be a long fight, but we must prevail for the sake of our future generations! Please pick up the minutes of this meeting when you exit. They will be passed out by my friend and Pastor Robbie!"

Bill ignored Paul Williams who was walking rapidly toward him, He suddenly felt very tired and drained, and so he dodged Williams by exited out the door directly behind him. Once outside, He sharply inhaled the cool October air and thought about his son Shaun, and wondered how his new gift was going to help him find and butcher the monsters that killed him.

CHAPTER 2

The couples were lying under the satin sheets, caressing each other with a hungry passion that was insatiable. The man's bedroom was upstairs in an old farmhouse that had been in the man's family for generations, and even though he owner had spent thousands of dollars in renovating the house, an ancient presence still permeates throughout the building. He held the women tightly, knowing what a special species resided within her, a monstrous entity that would be the centerpiece of his revenge. He thought of her as vehicle for his destruction, as a Trojan horse, which housed his most devious intentions. She stirred his manhood with her beauty jet-black hair, and her almond shaped eyes that contained not only the light of her soul, but also the viciousness of the beast within her.

"My exotic queen they will be coming for you soon, but don't be frightened, because the temporary sacrifice of your freedom will be the springboard that launches your people into salvation," he whispered in her ear. He moved his hand in a circular motion along the small of her back, and the touch of his gentle hand calmed her mood. Accalia trusted this man with her very soul, he had entered her life at the same time she had felt the quickening of the beast within her. As if they were ancient souls intertwined for eternity, she instinctively knew this small gentle man would protect her with the last ounce of his lifeblood.

She stirred and got out of bed, sliding out of the bed with the grace of a gazelle, her hips, ass, and breast were perfect. He considered himself and expert on the female anatomy, because he had seen thousands of naked female cadavers over the twenty years as he had worked as the Stokes County Coroner. Dr. Drake set this plan in motion about a year ago, when this dark haired beauty was sitting in his Anatomy and Physiology class at Stokes County community college. He instinctively knew by her intense, glowing, black eyes that she housed the creature that would avenge the great injustice cast on the Drake family by Black Bart's soulless grandfather Jack Whitescarver.

Jack Whitescarver had cheated his own grandfather Roy out of almost 50 thousand acres of land during a drunken poker game in one the many backrooms of the Whitescarver Mansion. After word spread of Jack's royal flush being created by pulling ace out of his sleeve, The Drake men were furious and the whole incident, which almost blew up to be a heated feud between families. The feud threaten to turn into a bloodbath like the infamous Hatfield and McCoy feud, which stained the beautiful rolling hills of West Virginia and Kentucky with blood from both clans, but the politically powerful Whitescarver family had Stokes County Sheriff office in their back pocket.

Several of the Drake men were arrested, and thrown in jail, but Jack Whitescarver graciously drop all charges after a plea deal was reached, and all the Drake clan had to do was cease and desist from any further violent reprisals. The great poker incident pretty much died down, but the anger lingered subconsciously in the hearts and minds of Drake offspring for a couple generations. Finally, he Stanley Drake had the instrument of his family's revenge lying in his arms; Dr. Drake smiled to himself, as he thinks of his brilliant plan to send this creature, like a heat-seeking missile into the heart of Black Bart. He can only imagine the shock and awe on his ugly face, when Black Bart learns this freak of nature shares his own DNA.

At exactly 6 Am, Sam Jenkins, and John Running deer

were meeting with Kelli in her room at the Pine river Hotel, since this antique motel did not have any kind of conference room, or computer room like many hotels that cater to the business guest. Although the remote motel did have limited Wi-Fi, or internet capabilities, reception was sporadic if best. Kelli's team needed to tap in vital information from CODIS or other sophisticated FBI databases at any given moment, so this motel would only serve as an emergency temporary command center. Kelli would speak to Director King about moving the FBI command center to the abandoned hotel at Vade Mecum springs, as the Goliath three story resort Inn would be ideal for FBI operations as the investigation heats up in intensity. The mammoth building would large enough to house the large FBI team that would be necessary to process a vast outdoor crime scene.

"Agent Running Deer update us on your trip down to Vade Mecum springs?" Kelli asked her gaze fixed on the burly, bronzed skin Cherokee Indian. Sam Jenkins thought that Running Deer resembled the Indian chief of the 1980's commercial, which condemned the trash littering along American Highways, and waterways. The famous Chief in those commercials has one tear rolling down his noble, proud face as He witness the deflowering of the beauty of his native land.

Agent John Running Deer proceeded to tell Kelly or the strange substance found along the path of the beast that marked the path of the wolf-creature like magic, gleaming in the moonlight like fairy dust. He bagged it and gave it to the FBI crime lab via a forensic technician that was shadowing him. I also ordered the technician to take impressions of both the animal prints and the human prints that we found along the way, again expediting the prints to our makeshift crime lab in Greensboro.

"I came along a ravine that appeared to be the resting place for the creature. The recent rain had softened the dirt, and the impression of where the creature had lain was immense in diameter. I measured the dimensions to be 10' long and 6 feet wide" John Running Deer gleamed at his peers with shining black eyes, which burned with an unnatural intensity. Sam Jenkins softly whistled at the Length and girth of a creature that just might come calling on them a pitch black night.

"We did find some dried blood stains within the impression, so the technician meticulously collected the samples. We sent all the forensic samples to the crime lab, and we should be getting a DNA profile on the killer with the next 72 hours. I tracked the partial footsteps to highway 8, where the scent of the beast and trail abruptly stopped." Agent Running Deer deep bass voice echoed off the walls of the tiny hotel room, as if he was speaking from a point high above them. Sam Jenkins seriously doubted that Running Deer could pick up a scent Forty-eight hours after the slayings, and then he realized that Running Deer was a full-blooded Cherokee Indian, whose warriors are known for their legendary tracking capabilities.

Kelli was excited to have John Running Deer on the team; his insight into Native American culture should prove to be invaluable in a case that increasing seemed to be intertwined with Indian culture.

"John when you saw the pictures of the mounds of bones piled on the observation deck on Moore's knob, you mention a Cherokee shape shifter named Hi'cictawi'a, could you tell us more about this creature?" Kelli asked, looking directly into the dark, brooding eyes of the huge Indian. Kelli did not believe in the supernatural, but after having viewed the monstrosity on the body camera on deceased Deputy Miller's vest, she did believe in human mutants capable of hideous acts of evil.

"The Hi'cictawi'a legend was born along the Trail of Tears, which was part of Andrew Jackson's Indian Removal Act. The march was over 1200 miles long, and 4,000 Cherokee died on it, including a powerful witch doctor named Dakota Blackclaw," John Running Deer said in a low mono-toned voice, as if he were in a trance.

Running Deer explained that Dakota Blackclaw had been an extremely powerful medicine woman who sometimes would use black magic to fight evil spirits like the Raven Mocker, an ordinary evil spirit that would consume the life of sick and dying people. The Raven Mocker would then increase its own life expectancy by adding the years from the aged or sick person. This shape shifter walked among the living, and many believed it to be very ancient looking with a face wrinkled like old dried up leather.

"It was a very busy shape shifter because along the Trail of Tears hundreds of my brethren were dying daily from starvation and dehydration. Many bodies were scattered along the trail, discarded like human trash, left for vultures, coyotes, and wolves to consume." John let out a low moan, as if an arrow had pierced his heart.

Kelli looked at him with compassion and pity. "John, if this is too painful, you do not have to continue."

John Running Deer, an Indian warrior, a man of strength and courage, locked eyes with her and replied,

"I am a professional FBI agent and will continue to tell you of this legend, because if we are indeed dealing with this shape shifter this information could be vital in saving your life: in fact record all of this for future reference." John then continued with the legend of Hi'cictawi'a.

"Dakota wore a necklace of owl feathers around her neck, and her moccasins were made of cougar hide, as these two creatures were worshiped by the Cherokee for their wise and noble appearance. Dakota Blackclaw was called into the Chief's tee-pee, where his infant son lay dying in his mother's arms. The chief asked his most respected medicine woman to protect his son from the Raven Mocker, who had been seen lurking around the tee-pee, and when approached, it sprouted wings and flew away mocking the chief with a loud, shrieking rant. Dakota began to care for the infant son, burning cedar and pinewood around the child night and day, chanting non-stop to keep evil spirits away. But as Dakota dozed off for a few minutes, the Raven Mocker slipped in like a thief in the night and snuffed out the life of the infant, claiming the many years of the child's life for its own." John Running Deer paused as if he was building the tension for the dramatic end of the tale.

"The chief, angered by the death of the son, asked his witch doctor to place a curse of Dakota, condemning her soul to the Underworld. The next day while marching along the steep Blue Ridge Mountains, Dakota slipped and disappeared over a mountain ledge. A few companions witnessed the incident, and they stopped and prayed for her soul in the afterlife for a few minutes. Soldiers screamed at them to move on, so in fear they shuffled away, saddened not only by the loss of a great medicine woman, but by the realization that their lives had been cheapened by this monster called the Trail of Tears." John Running Deer paused for a second, perhaps to catch his breath. Kelli and Sam were transfixed by the tale and sat there silently as if they were frozen in time.

"Dakota's soul was sent to the Underworld ruled by a demon called Tavgina, who wanted Dakota to bear his children. Tavgina had come to respect the savage Cherokee warrior for his bravery in battle and felt that the offspring of a powerful Cherokee medicine woman and a demon could defeat any of God's angels. Because of her status and position while alive, Dakota had been given free will, and she refused Tavgina's advances because she still possessed some goodness. The demons around her often told her of bloody massacres of defenseless women and children murdered by the white man, while most of the warriors were gone off hunting or fighting the palefaces. In 1863, after the slaughter of the two hundred-fifty Shoshone Indians during the Bear Creek Massacre in Idaho, Dakota finally agreed to have Tavgina's male children if he would give her a daughter who would avenge these mass murders in the most lethal, hideous manner possible. In order to impress Dakota, Tavgina agreed to bequeath his daughter with special demonic powers, like mind control that crippled her prey mentally while she consumed them like a tasty morsel. Hi'cictawi'a's power would always be greater during periods of great threat to the Cherokee." As he finished, John Running Deer was so visibly shaken from recanting this seemingly impossible tale that his bronze skin had taken on an ashen color.

Kelli, who didn't believe any of this Cherokee mythology, but at the same time she didn't want to disrespect John Running Deer's emotional testimony, asked the only rational question that, flowed out of her mind.

"John, there are no massacres occurring now. Most Indians have gambling casinos on their reservations, like the one in Cherokee. Why is Hi'cictawi'a appearing in this part of Stokes County?" Kelli asked perplexed.

John Running Deer stared at Kelli for a long time before answering. "Kelli, understand that the Cherokee has much reverence for Mother Earth. We believe that the humans of the middle earth belong to mother Earth, and that everything is interconnected. We believe that the trees and the long man's sustain life for millions of the middle earth's plants, animals, and humans. These resources are the lungs of every living creature of the middle earth and must be held sacred. There is now an attack on Mother Earth. Serpents carry gas and oil through ancient burial grounds. Hydraulic fracking is poisoning long mans from coast to coast and fish and wildlife are being poisoned by drinking from the long mans. Drilling for oil off North Carolina's coast will unleash terrible destruction on marine life, destroying oxygen-giving plankton and creating red tides of algae. Hi'cictawi'a is here because North Carolina is the epicenter of the attack on Mother Earth, and she will fight with unparalleled rage, because she is defending it not only to protect her people, but for the survival of Mother Earth, the one thing that Cherokee hold sacred over everything else!" John Running Deer's eyes were illuminated with a passion that Kelli had never witnessed.

"So, a Cherokee medicine woman made a deal with the devil, and this Hi'cictawi'a thingy killed those deputies on Moore's Knob because they were destroying the landscape by night hiking?" Sam Jenkins asked tactlessly.

"Ah, Agent Jenkins, that was a great attempt at sarcasm!" John Running Deer exclaimed "The deputies are collateral damage, killed partly because they remind Hi'cictawi'a of the paleface soldiers she mutilated centuries ago, but also to send a warning of terror to all those coming to desecrate this sacred land. Those men working on the well pads will be her prime target," John said in a low tone, as if he were trying to defuse tension between Jenkins and himself.

Kelli, sensing the tension between Jenkins and Running Deer herself, asked a very benign question. "John, what do you mean by 'long man?'"

"Very simple', Kelli 'Long mans are the rivers that provide fresh water to millions, and they are like time, because they are eternal and will run forever." Running Deer's response was coated in a tone of deep reverence.

Just as Kelli was formulating another question, her cell phone rang. She recognized the number immediately. Inspector King was calling to pick the brain of the FBI team. "Hello, Inspector, What can I do for you?" Kelli inquired.

"Well, it seems that Agent Briggs has solved the case in record time. He has just picked up Accalia Blackclaw as a person of interest in the massacre on Moore's Knob!" Inspector King's voice had a very boastful tone.

"Inspector King, what did you say the last name of the suspect was again?" Kelli asked, knowing the answer.

"It's Blackclaw, some common Saura Indian name. Why?" King asked, perplexed by Kelli's odd question and the tone in her voice.

A sudden chill went down Kelli's spine, but she managed to tell Inspector King not to start questioning the suspect until she arrived at the Sheriff's Office. She then turned to her team, and both men could tell by the look on her face that their investigation had just entered the second dimension of the twilight zone.

CHAPTER 4

About the same time Kelli received the message from Inspector King, David Barret was driving his Ford Mustang with extreme prejudice, disregarding speed limit signs as if they were suggestions instead of the law. David was on a mission. He was now a land prospector, acquiring land so his employers could stretch their tentacles of greed deep into the virgin land of Stokes County. Gas companies could no longer cite eminent domain as a reason for acquiring land for fracking, since many land owners were fighting back with appeals centered on inverse condemnation. Many landowners felt that their compensation for the land was woefully inadequate and that hydraulic fracturing greatly damaged the land for future generations.

David had an appointment with retired Marine Colonel Jeffery Anderson, who was a Medal of Honor recipient for flying his damaged US CH-46 Sea Knight into heavy small arms fire to help evacuate the US Embassy in Saigon, South Vietnam on April 29 and 30, 1975. Colonel Anderson had sustained shrapnel wounds to his buttocks and legs but had managed to safely land his disabled craft on the deck of the USS Forrestal, which waited for both American and South Vietnamese evacuees in the Gulf of Tonkin. The T58 turbo shaft engines of the US CH-46 were hemorrhaging hydraulic fluid so badly it pooled on the deck of the aircraft carrier. The damaged helicopter looked like some mechanical beast that had lost a knife fight.

The Forrestal's captain, who had been unfortunate enough to be on US Airways Flight 1549 in 2009, compared

Anderson's heroics to those of Captain Sully Sullenberger's miracle landing on the Hudson River. As a witness to both those miracle landings, Captain Russ Gates explained, "both these pilots' landings were miracles that were accomplished by God's most courageous angels with nerves of steel,"

Operation Frequent Wind had been an 18-hour operation, evacuating over 7,000 Americans and South Vietnamese people from the clutches of the Viet Cong and the Southern Liberation Front. Captain Anderson was credited with saving several hundred lives during those two days, despite extensive wounds. Unfortunately, Colonel Anderson was also a gold star parent, having lost his son Jeff Jr. in the mountains of Afghanistan in 2002.

Captain Jeff Anderson Jr. was an Army Ranger dedicated to capturing Osama Bin Laden, mastermind of 9/11. A Taliban sharp shooter killed Jeff Jr. during a CIA sanctioned mission near Tora Bora, Bin Laden's vast underground cave hideout deep in the Afghan mountains. A week earlier, a Navy P3 Orion, while conducting reconnaissance in the remote Afghanistan Mountains, he used sophisticated computer imaging software to pinpoint Bin Laden's location. The 75th Army Ranger regiment mission was to capture or kill the Al Qaeda leader, but had missed him by three days. Captain Anderson had been transmitting the calamitous information to his superiors when the sniper's 7.62 round obliterated the occipital lobe of Captain Anderson's brain. Even though the sniper's bullet was fired from a distance of 1,312 yards away, the Afghan sniper and his crew were hunted down and massacred with extreme prejudice. His team loved Captain Anderson, and there had not been a dry eye in the room when his body was shipped back to Dover Air Force Base in Delaware.

David was running late, and he knew that being tardy for a meeting with a career military man could be the kiss of death. Colonel Anderson was a legend, a 1973 graduate of the US Naval Academy in Annapolis, Maryland. He had been a Naval midshipman in his second year of the Academy when being a Marine began to dominate his thought process. His transition to Marine aviator was seamless, and two years later his young wife pinned on his wings emblazoned with the words Semper Fi, which means "always faithful", something that Jeff Anderson had proved to be to both his wife and his country over his many years of service.

David began to drive slowly through the exclusive, well-groomed neighborhood aligned with expensive homes. David geared his muscle car down to a slow crawl, because if the military-minded Jeff Anderson were outside, he would frown on any breech of discipline or control.

David slowly turned the corner and was greeted by a large white iron gate that acted like a sentry on post. It denied entry to those who were deemed unworthy. The gates suddenly swung open before David could enter the secret code he had been given. He could feel the Colonel's stare penetrate his car, as if eyes peered into his soul. David shook off his deep-seated feeling of foreboding as being highly melodramatic.

As his car maneuvered down the driveway, David was amazed by the immaculate grounds encased by a black iron rod fence around its perimeter, and the white pillars that were spaced about ten feet apart that supported the entire structure. He recognized the precision and orderliness of the domain, and he suddenly remembered from his astronomy class the professor not only stressing the vastness of universe, but the exactness of the universe in accordance with mathematical calculations. It seemed to David that both God and Jeffery Anderson loved precision and order, and David would use that perception of right and wrong, black or white, as the cornerstone of his deception on this decorated war hero.

The driveway turned into carefully laid brick that must have been very labor-intensive for some bricklayer, because there had to be at least 20,000 bricks stretching from the front porch to the two-car garage that extended out from the left corner of the massive home. The house itself was an impressive feat of architecture, and to David the white house made of stone that stood before him was a miniature replica of the President's residence at 1600 Pennsylvania Avenue.

He stopped the car about twenty feet from the door and admired the symmetry of the home. Four bay windows with black shutters divided evenly by two massive columns, which protruded out five feet from the expansive oak front door. The sloping black tiled roof was at least 40 feet in height and is connected by a triangular-shaped structure that had a dark circled vent in the middle. Giant pillars encased in Italian travertine supported this triangular-shaped portion of the roof. The pillars formed the front porch. The structure reminded David of The Eye of Providence, which is God watching over humanity, and wondered if Anderson had some kind of God complex.

Just as David began open his car door, two of the biggest Doberman pinschers he had ever seen charged out from around the backside of the house, eager to devour this mere mortal who had the audacity to invade their kingdom! The larger of the two dogs, jaws spewing vile, disgusting fluid, lunged at the car door a millisecond after David closed it. David, despite his training with bomb sniffing dogs in Fallujah, recoiled in terror.

"Zeus, Apollo, HEEL!" The strong authoritative male voice of the master echoed throughout David's car even though the windows were rolled up. David looked out the window, and the two canines from hell were sitting on their hindquarters as completely still as if they were carved in stone.

"It's safe to exit your car now, Captain Barret; you have my word as a man of honor!" The author of the words standing before him was the legend-in-the-flesh, Jeffery Anderson.

David glanced at the mountain of a man who stood there. He was at least 6'3" and 280 pounds of pure muscle, with bulging triceps and biceps, and with legs as big as tree trunks. As David exited his safe-space, he began to contemplate the sanity of trying to mind control a humanoid of such immense proportions, and silently wondered if he might end up as Doberman pinscher poop by the end of the evening.

Colonel Anderson extended his extremely large and well-tanned hand and bellowed, "Ah, the Mind Magician in the flesh! It's an honor to meet you!"

David grabbed the colonel's meaty paw, and the gigantic hand magically turned into a lethal weapon crushing David's hand like aluminum can. Colonel Anderson sent two messages with his greeting: First, which he had done an extensive background search on David; and second, that he, the great Colonel Anderson, would assume the dominant role in any social interaction between the two of them.

After shaking the colonel's hand, David quickly studied the Colonel's face for any sign that he could convince Anderson to allocate his prime acres of land, which geologists insisted were pregnant with enormous amounts of shale, to the gas companies without using any subliminal or hypnotic suggestion. After studying the Colonel's strong manly face, complete with a strong chiseled jawline and dark gray predatory eyes, he concluded that it was going to be a long day indeed!

He turned to the Colonel and praised him on a beautiful home in an exceptional, pristine location. "Ah, you haven't seen anything yet. The entire property backs up on Saint John's Lake. heck, I've got jet skiers coming by getting lunch or dinners to go, and the best thing today is that my wife Sandy has taken our grand-kids to the beach, so we have the place all to ourselves!"

As the Colonel announced that they were all alone, he playfully slapped David, winking at him as if he was letting him in on a private joke. David laughed heartily, but something in the Colonel's playful wink seemed cold and distant, and suddenly the great mind magician's blood began to chill. He wondered if it had been a terrible error in judgment to visit this man alone. As the colonel began to show David the interior of his mansion, David's mind thought back to the Doberman pinscher poop and his cock-sureness began to fade like the setting sun on a warm July evening.

"Care for a scotch or beer?" Anderson inquired as he showed David the interior of the mansion, which featured a mammoth Virginia stone fireplace and an interior balcony that ran the entire length of the second floor.

"Naw, been watching my alcohol consumption since getting out of the Army," David replied.

Those long days on the Iraqi battlefield had almost turned him into a raging alcoholic from the sorrow of losing so many of his brothers, plus the loneliness of being away from his wife for a year had seeped into his soul. He knew that many service men and women still battled the raging demon of alcohol even after returning to the civilian world. David began hoping Colonel Anderson would get inebriated; drunks were so much easier to hypnotize.

"Suit yourself," Colonel Anderson replied. "I'm going to satisfy my screaming demon of alcoholism with a good shot of my friend J&B." David breathed in sharply.

Anderson had seemed to read his thoughts! Then he realized that the comment was a mere coincidence. Why was he being so paranoid and full of anxiety? Then it came to him: it was October 24, just a week before Halloween. He then silently laughed at his last thought, because he, David Barret, a man of superior intellect, did not believe in anything that originated within the Druid or Celtic cultures.

Colonel Anderson returned from the bar with his scotch in hand, and they walked out the folding glass patio doors. The granite tile that encased the small swimming pool and elevated Jacuzzi impressed David. The outside enclosed bar was furnished with a large bedlam sofa, a large screen television, heavy duty mahogany chairs, and a majestic villa wood fireplace for football gazing on cool fall Saturdays or Sundays. But what caught his eye more than anything was the lake, which glimmered in the late afternoon fall sunlight.

There was a gentle breeze that blew in from the lake, stirring the leaves on the four live oak trees. These trees resembled gigantic beasts guarding against any encroachment from an unwanted guest that might emerge from the lake on a cold dark night. The trees were dressed in their finest fall attire; golden and sangria red hues cast a beautiful reflection on the lake. Suddenly David relaxed in his chair and realized that the conditions were perfect for a little hypnotic trance action, with the brilliant sunlight glittering off the water and the gentle breeze making the kaleidoscope of colors seem to come alive. He believed that Anderson's arrogance, deepened by Scotch, would combine to make his mission an absolute success.

CHAPTER 5

About the same time that David was being entertained by retired Colonel Jeffery Anderson, Kelli and her teams entered the Stokes County jail, and were confronted by Sheriff Bobby Green, Sheriff Brown's hastily chosen successor.

"Well, it's about time you federal slackers arrived!" Green snickered as he led them to the two-way mirror that allowed them to peer into the small interrogation room. A young Native American woman, who appeared to be in her mid-twenties, occupied the 10x10 foot room. Her face was turned toward them, and she seemed completely oblivious to fact, that federal agents were observing her. Kelli stared at the haunted eyes of the young woman and was struck by the vacant stare her eyes emitted. Kelli at first thought that she might be catatonic state, and then she had a premonition that these ancient eyes might have existed since the beginning of time and had witnessed many horrors. Kelli felt a shiver go down the length of her spine, but that shiver turned to intense heat when her nemesis, Agent Briggs, entered the viewing room.

"She has had that catatonic stare since we brought her in a couple of hours ago, and because of the overwhelming physical evidence against her, we were able to get a warrant for her DNA. We have expedited the sample to the SBI crime lab in Raleigh and should have the results within 24 to 48 hours. We almost had to water board her so she would open her mouth!" Briggs jokingly said. He winked at Sam Jenkins and added for dramatic flair.

"She can go twenty minutes without blinking her eyes,

very spooky stuff!"

"Agent Briggs, let me ask you a simple question." "Does that poor creature even remotely resemble what we witnessed on Deputy Miller's body camera?" Kelli stared at Briggs incredulously.

"Well, maybe she suffers from Schizophrenia or Dis-associative Identity Disorder! I have heard of cases of superhuman strength and facial deformities while folks are in their alter personalities," Briggs replied loudly, again pissed off by his perception that Kelli was questioning his judgment.

"Agent Briggs, have you lost your mind? For that young, lean, slight woman to resemble the beast we saw on Deputy Miller's body camera, she would have to be possessed by a demon of some sort! Surely you must have some concrete evidence on her, and if not, I will go release her myself!"

Kelli was enraged that Briggs had arrested what seemed to be a disturbed woman. Sam Jenkins was hopeful that his boss would simmer down, because he sensed that Briggs, if pressured, could explode like a roman candle on a hot July afternoon.

"Damn! You're so arrogant!" Agent Briggs said. "Of course I have firm reasons for bringing her here! First, she was picked up around 4 a.m. on Highway 8 just west of Vade Mecum Springs the morning after the deputies were slaughtered on Moore's Knob. She was completely naked and covered in blood and mud. A local truck driver, John Walker, picked her up and wrapped her in a blanket because she appeared to be on the verge of hypothermia. We expedited the DNA found on the blanket to our crime lab and got the results of the test this morning. Deputy Miller's and Mack Peters' DNA were all over the blanket!" Briggs explained in a heated rant as he stared directly into Kelli's eyes. Kelli was stunned by Briggs statement, unable to respond. Briggs added one final insult.

"Guess you're just pissed off that we won't need any more federal intervention here! We have the techniques and expertise and don't need any federal interlopers in this case."

"I thought I had told you to back off; this is still a federal investigation!" Kelli replied, trying to control her rage for this male chauvinist pig!

Just as Running Deer was starting to wonder if he would have to step in between the two, Kelli's phone rang. It was the crime lab at Quantico; they had the results from the Bio-geographical Ancestry Analysis of the fang that had been found embedded in Miller's femur. The technician calmly told Kelli the results, and Kelli asked Agent Briggs if he knew Accalia's heritage.

"Yeah, everybody knows that her mother was a fullblooded Cherokee Indian, and her daddy was rumored to be of the Caucasian persuasion," Briggs replied indignantly. Kelli was too stunned to speak. Briggs description of Accalia's rumored heritage matched the analysis from the crime lab perfectly. Kelli slowly turned and looked at the young, slender Native American woman, whose eyes suddenly appeared to glow with an inhuman stare. To Kelli's horror, one eye winked at her as if to select her for its next target.

CHAPTER 6

The two men sat near the shoreline of Saint John's Lake making small talk about wives, career choices, different commands they had been attached to while serving honorably, but they both were appraising each other, sniffing out weaknesses or strengths in each other's characters. They were like two prizefighters circling one another in the opening rounds of a championship fight. Anderson was the first to land a jab.

"I have done some extensive research on you, Captain Barret. You were able to undermine so many insurgent plots to kill our boys in Fallujah in November of 2003 that they called you the 'Mind Magician'. I am very aware of your mind-reading capabilities and your telekinetic powers." " Tell me, Captain Barrett, is that why you are here? Are you trying to acquire my land for the environmentally disastrous practice of hydraulic fracturing, which has caused several thousand spills of carcinogens into the aquifers of states that make up the Harnett Shale?"

David shifted in his chair and gazed at the late afternoon autumn sun, as its ultraviolet rays were now directly on the Equator. He turned to peer intensely at Anderson.

"Now, that's very astute of you, Colonel Anderson. I have come to take your land, rape your women, and pillage your community," David replied with a completely serious face.

After a moment of stunned silence, Colonel Anderson burst out laughing at David's audacious remark, and suddenly both men were laughing together like lifelong friends. Anderson slapped David on the knee and announced that he was going to get another round of scotch. As the colonel got up, David asked him for a cup of hot tea with a spoon.

"Hot tea, when you have the option of alcohol? Man, you must have lost your manhood in Fallujah!" Anderson said with a slight smirk.

"I Just promised the wife that I wouldn't drink on this trip. I just need something to combat the cool wind coming off your pristine lake," David added sheepishly.

Anderson gave him a weird look reserved for lost, pitiful souls that had surrendered their man-card to pacify their spouses out of fear of losing half their wealth.

"YOUR TEA IS COMING RIGHT UP, MRS. BARRET. Make sure you hold your pinkie up when you drink it!" Anderson replied, laughing hysterically. David also began to laugh with gusto, but for entirely different reasons. He realized that he had developed a bond with the gruff helicopter pilot and that Anderson did not realize he was becoming a willing participant in his own demise.

Upon his return, Colonel Anderson handed David the tea, complete with spoon and saucer, but could not resist saying, "Be careful, it's hot, and I wouldn't want you to burn your precious hands." Anderson laughed loudly again. David knew that he had lost face with this cocky, arrogant man, but also knew that his stellar military record would manage to uphold some degree of respect from Anderson. His host then proudly announced that his mind was impenetrable to hypnotic suggestion, and suddenly David felt like a weight had been lifted from his chest. He knew that Colonel Anderson was exhibiting a self-defensive strategy because deep in his subconscious, he knew that David Barret would have him barking like one of his Doberman pinschers before his visit was over.

"Yes, Colonel, I work for Abbott gas, which I'm proud

to say is committed to decreasing the dependency of the United States on foreign oil, particularly from countries that belong to OPEC. After 9/11 it was discovered that the vast majority of the hijackers came from Saudi Arabia, the de facto leader of this organization that is responsible for two-thirds of the world's oil production." David said in a deep tone, trying to capture the focus of Anderson's conscious mind, slowly stirring his hot tea and making sure the spoon hit the sides of the cup in a rhythmic pattern.

"So, what you're saying is that there's a connection between countries that sponsor terrorism and where major gas distributors in the United States purchase petroleum? How utterly brilliant of you!" slurred Anderson.

It was now or never. David had to activate an unconscious response right at that moment. "Yes, Colonel, and this is what also got your son Jeffery Jr. killed." David's voice sounded like thunder from the heavens, accusatory and stern!

Anderson recoiled as if he had been shot. His eyes looked as if they were going to explode out of their sockets; his large carotid arteries seemed to pulsate with a life of their own. David watched the man's reaction and was ready to be beaten and fed to his new best friends Zeus and Apollo!

Colonel Anderson, Medal of Honor winner and Bronze Star recipient, started to sob like a newborn baby and began to rock back and forth. His eyes glazed over, and his face contorted into a demented-looking mask. David had recognized those signs before, because they marked an individual on the cusp of a hypnotic trance. Anderson stared at the shimmering lake and began to mumble his confession to a specter that David could not see.

"He didn't want to go into the military. In fact, he just wanted to coach football and be a damn history teacher! But he could see the bitter disappointment in my face as I told him that if he did not enlist that I would disown him. The military is a tradition in the Anderson family, and no son of mind would dream of breaking that tradition. Ah, hell, he would be alive today if I hadn't been so bullheaded!" Jeffery Anderson was a broken man; guilt was eating up his soul, and David, being the ruthless that bastard he was, was going to capitalize on this war hero's grief.

It was time to lead Colonel Anderson's subconscious to the desired outcome. "Colonel, if you side with those damn environmentalists and prevent hydraulic fracturing from occurring on your land, you are helping to fund terrorist organization like Al-Qaida, and ISIS, and more decent men like Jeffery Jr. will perish. On the other hand, if you allow fracturing on your land, innocent American lives will be saved! You can take the funds that Abbott gas is prepared to allocate to you and build a memorial to Jeff Jr. right in the middle of downtown Walnut Cove if you want to."

David repeated this condensed statement about five times to the subconscious mind of Colonel Jeff Anderson.

"If you chose to deny fracturing on your land, you are siding with Al-Qaida and ISIS, but if you chose to allow fracturing, you're saving innocent American soldiers' lives...men like Jeff Jr."

David snapped his fingers and the drowsy, drunken Jeff Anderson was suddenly a super big believer in fracking in Stokes County. Anderson's conscious mind would not comprehend this fact until the representative from Abbott Gas showed up at his front door with a contract to lease 500 acres of prime land pregnant with abundant shale for several thousand dollars per acre, and royalties for every cubic meter of gas brought forth from the bowels of his land. Retired Colonel Jeffery Anderson, who had been so ardently against hydraulic fracking in Stokes County less than three days before, would sign the binding contract without any hesitation!

Three days after David left the Anderson estate,

he received a phone call from Abbott Gas that retired Colonel Jeffery Anderson had signed the contract, allowing Abbott to begin cultivating his land laden with abundant shale. Hydraulic fracturing was to begin on his property within a week. David hung up the phone and breathed a sigh of relief.

He had just left Jed Jackson's home, a hog farmer that had had the great fortune of inheriting 1,000 acres of land that was greatly coveted by Abbot Gas. Jed Jackson was furious with President Dotard, after the ruthless president had proposed a 25 percent tariff on Chinese goods entering the United States. The Chinese government had responded by imposing a 25 percent tariff on aluminum, machinery, and pork, which could cost Jackson several hundred thousand dollars in revenue. Jackson was furious, since he and all his cronies had helped Dotard carry Stokes County during the last election. He had even supported Dotard during his tumultuous first year in office. Jackson had explained to David that supporting Dotard was kind of like wanting a bowl of chili soooo bad, that when it comes back from the kitchen with a finger in it, you keep your mouth shut and eat it anyway!

David was Johnny-on-the-spot, explaining to the angered Jackson that he could more than compensate from any loses accrued from the tariffs by leasing out his land to Abbott Gas; the royalties alone would make up for the lost revenue from the unfair tariffs. Jackson had been so excited by his new-found savior, David Barret that he signed the contract offered by Abbott Gas on the spot! Ah! David's ole daddy had always said that timing was everything. Maybe in hind sight his daddy was not such a dumb ass after all.

David could not rest, however. He had just delivered to Abbott Gas two crown jewels that they had coveted. The last crown jewel would be David's greatest test, because the land belonged to Bill O'Toole, the head of the serpent that demonstrated great ability to resist his psychic invasion. Just then,

David's phone began to play Money, Money, and he answered the ring tone in his usual cocky, arrogant manner.

"Hello, Bart, guess you heard that I closed both Jackson and Anderson. I think congratulations are in order," boasted David.

"Naw, not really impressed. The biggest jewel is still out there, and if you can convince O'Toole to sign a contract, I will kiss your arse!" chuckled the slightly unhinged Whitescarver.

"Ah, you don't have to worry about puckering. And I'm glad, because I don't want your nasty mouth touching any part of my body because Bill O'Toole will be dead in less than a week," bragged David.

"So, you're going get a professional to do the job?" inquired a clueless Black Bart.

"Naw, his own son is going to do him in. Folks do desperate things when they believe that they're being disinherited," laughed David.

"That is the most cocked up plan I have ever heard!" exclaimed Bart.

"I don't care to hear your negativity, just get your ass over to the Weston Law Firm and get a package from the chief administrative assistant, Shelia Carter. She knows you're coming," ordered an annoyed David. David disconnected the phone call and started to recite his mantra "for the love of money a woman will sell her precious body. Money, money, Some folks got to have it." He then he said to himself, Thank you, Satan, for unadulterated greed!

One week earlier, Shelia Carter, administrative secretary to Paul Weston for over twenty years, had been in her office going over some newly completed irrevocable trusts, probate avoidance trusts, and a couple of qualified income trusts, and she smiled at the ironic humor that family members trusted each other so little during the settlement of an estate. Shelia had a special gift, a laser-focus attention to detail, which allowed her to pinpoint any commissions of errors or omission of essential information that the highly compensated paralegals might have made. In fact, no estate planning document ever left the highly successful law office until Shelia Carter had signed off on it. She looked down into the lowest cabinet on her outdated metallic desk and noticed a large manila envelope resting on top of the paperwork that she had neatly organized to perfection. Shelia Carter was a neat freak, otherwise known as being anal retentive to the max.

Shelia opened the envelope and to her amazement, several layers of $100 bills were staring her in the face. Shelia's eyes were transfixed by the stack of money, her face was flushed, and she looked around nervously like a pack rat that had just discovered a pound of aged cheddar cheese! Since it was Friday afternoon, she was alone in the office. But Shelia, being one who always erred on the side of caution, tucked the package under her shirt and scurried off to the privacy of the women's bathroom. Once she opened the stall doors and sat on the very expensive toilet seat (because the generous Paul Weston wanted his employees to crap in comfort), she opened the envelope and counted out twenty thousand dollars!

A small typed note simply directed her to make a copy of Bill O'Toole's will onto a jump drive and pass it off to Bart Whitescarver on Monday of next week. After completing her task, she would be rewarded with another twenty grand! Shelia was beside herself and was outraged that someone would sneak into her office and try to bribe her into breaking lawyer-client privilege! She went back to her desk and picked up the phone to call Paul Weston and tell him about the security breach at the office. The phone rang two times on the other end, and suddenly it occurred to her that her youngest son would be leaving for a private college next fall, and that her daughter's newborn baby girl, born with Down's Syndrome, would need around the clock care, so being the solid family woman she was, Shelia gently put the phone down.

Shelia had tossed and turned all weekend, thinking about how the Affordable Care Act was irresponsibly being replaced, and that her daughter might be drowning in insurmountable debt. She also knew that college tuition was increasing ten-fold, and how she was underpaid because she did not have a college degree like those paralegals whose work she had to double-check. She rationalized that the bribe money was back pay for her years of dedication to a firm that did not appreciate her. She decided that Monday morning, she was going to betray the man who had put enormous trust in her for twenty years, and in doing so would break the law for the very first time in her life.

She had heard of Bart Whitescarver. Most folks called him "Black Bart", but never to his face, because they were fearful of this evil man whom some suspected was the devil incarnate. Shelia was not intimidated or frightened, and if he messed with her too much, she would blackmail him for the much needed money for her family. Shelia had no idea of the soulless monster that she was dealing with, nor of the organization that could make her family disappear like dust in the wind.

The following Monday, October 26, Shelia started her life of crime by handing off the 128GB flash drive to Black Bart right in front of White's Drug Store at 7:30 a.m., exactly one hour before the Weston Law Firm opened. The interchange was very comical. Black Bart, dressed in a black trench coat, fake mustache, and sideburns, dropped the flash drive onto the pavement after Shelia had handed it to him with the skill of an all-pro quarterback in a Sunday afternoon football play. When he bent down to pick it up, he split his pants and knocked his fake mustache off! The scene was like an episode of Keystone Cops part 2! Finally, Black Bart scurried down the street, anxious to get the flash drive to the legal experts employed by Abbott Gas who were going to create the forgery that would cause a son to kill his father.

CHAPTER 7

The forensic evidence proving that Accalia was the killer was overwhelming. The DNA from the blanket that the trucker had used to shroud Accalia's body was covered with the DNA signature from the deputies who had been massacred on Moore's Knob. The Bio-geographical Ancestral Analysis matched Accalia's genetic footprints perfectly, and if Accalia's DNA matched that found on the fang embedded in Peters' femur, then it was a slam dunk case, the kind that state prosecutors dreamed of. Despite all this physical evidence, Kelli could not bring herself to believe that this 5'6" woman who might weigh 110 pounds soaking wet could have committed such a hideous crime.

Kelli had studied various interrogation techniques at the FBI academy in Quantico that had snared serial killers like the Zodiac Killer, Ted Bundy, and Charles Edmund Cullen, the Angel of Death; but this meager woman sitting before her did not remotely seem to be a threat. She had dark, piercing eyes that seemed to stare right through Kelli's soul, and a bronze skin tone that enhanced her exotic beauty. Kelli knew that Agent Briggs had not coaxed a single word from this petite and terrified suspect, so she was going to use an oldie but goodie interview technique commonly referred to as the GOOD COP/ BAD COP procedure. Kelli was going to try to befriend and comfort the young woman. Showing compassion and empathy, she was going to gain the young woman's trust. She knew that this technique was going to be a long shot, but Agent Briggs, being the general ass he was, had actually already set this technique into motion.

Kelli asked the woman if she heard voices, or had time missing in her schedule that she could not account for. The former question related to the condition of Schizophrenia, and the latter question was a classic sign for Dis-associative Identity Disorder. Kelli felt like an idiot asking such questions because no mental illness would explain the creature she had witnessed on Deputy Miller's' body cam. Suddenly the young woman held out her hands, seeming to want to hold Kelli's hands. Although it was against FBI protocol, Kelli grasped the offered hands as an act of compassion or perhaps an attempt to bond with the petrified young woman of a different race and color. That act of kindness almost cost Kelli her life. It was as if a psychic lighting rod had been placed in Kelli's cerebellum. Later Sam Jenkins and John Running Deer would tell her that her eyes had rolled back into her head, and she appeared to be channeling some kind of ghost from the Netherworld, like a medium at a séance!

Kelli recoiled in the chair. Suddenly she was back in the cave on Portsmouth Island, and Jeremy Locklear (alias Hercules) was snuffing her life out by smothering her with his gigantic hands that covered her nose and mouth in a vice-like grip! Just as she was succumbing to her fate, she was whisked out of her body, floating high above the Trail of Tears, with a front row seat to the deaths of many Cherokee Indians as they died of starvation and famine. Finally, she floated high above the massacre of several hundred women and children from several different tribes: Cherokee, Apache, Blackfoot, Shawnee, and others, being raped and killed by white soldiers in US Cavalry uniforms. Then nothing, until she heard Sam Jenkins' voice full of fear and worry, screaming that she had a pulse and was breathing normally. Kelli finally came to with the faces of Jenkins and Running Deer hovering over her like her angels of salvation. Kelli, very confused and traumatized, tried to get up, but the paramedic and EMS technicians pushed her back down.

Sam Jenkins was the first to speak. "Kelli, they are taking you to Stokes County Regional Hospital to run some tests and to observe you for the night. The paramedic seems to think that you suffered some kind of stroke. Jake has been contacted and is taking the first plane bound for Greensboro." Sam's calming tone tried to sooth a distraught Kelli.

The paramedic gave Kelli as sedative and she relaxed as they loaded her into the ambulance... that is until she looked into the night sky and saw the face of Accalia Blackclaw staring down at her with a look of two emotions: satisfaction, and deep, deep hatred.

CHAPTER 8

Early in the morning on Tuesday the 27th of October, Mercury Johnson stepped into the dimly lit waiting area of Gate 23B like a dignitary or a person bequeathed with a royal bloodline. She was tall and lean and moved with the grace of a panther stalking its prey. She had creamy olive complexion and light green eyes, coveted by many women of the African-American race. Her perpetual tan was a gift from her father who hailed from Nigeria, and her ivory skinned mother from the Netherlands. Mercury was a product of the N&N concoction, and she was damn proud of it.

Mercury Johnson walked pass the bars that aligned the B terminal, shaking her head in dismay at all the folks who needed to down liquid courage to get on an aircraft. She herself had plenty of courage, the kind that was forged under the label of being bi-racial. That, combined with determination and persistence, allowed her to be one of the best risk assessors within the Environmental Protection Agency. Many industrial and manufacturing companies guilty of dumping toxic chemicals into lakes, rivers and streams felt the stinging wrath of this righteous hellcat who would never take a bribe or settlement.

Bill O'Toole waited in the reception area reserved for people picking up friends and relatives, claiming them by holding up a hand like they were bidding on some precious commodity. Bill noticed Mercury immediately. His constant phone calls to Brad Decker, head knocker with the EPA, paid off, as his relationship with Decker had over the years. Decker had been O'Toole's bunk mate while they both served on the

USS Forrestal in '85. Brad had finally relented and had sent his best: a woman named Mercury Johnson. Besides, the Feds were very concerned about the coal ash spill on the Dan River in 2014. Brad Decker knew that the combination of the coal ash spill and the run offs from hydraulic fracturing could be a death sentence to a river that served as a source of drinking water and recreation to folks both in North Carolina and in Virginia.

Bill was smitten by the exotic beauty. When she suddenly smiled at him, her smile was like the sun coming out from behind dark rain clouds, dazzling bright! She grabbed his hand and Bill O'Toole, big ole Irish mountain man, was surprised by the immense strength emitted by such a gorgeous woman. Mercury exuded strength, honor, and grace without being pretentious, and Bill O'Toole suddenly knew that this woman did not care about corporate greed, power or money and would fight for injustices wrought on the average citizen.

Neither one of them noticed the heavy-set man at the baggage claim; he was lingering in the shadows taking pictures of them with his cell phone. If Bill had seen him, he would have recognized him immediately as the newly unemployed Sheriff Brown. As they turned to exit the baggage area, a man with a frazzled appearance and dark bags under his eyes bumped into her, but Mercury could tell, it was accidental, because the man looked like he was in a complete daze brought on by stress or complete dedication to get to his destination. Mercury had no idea that the man's name was Jake Ryan, and that in the very near future their paths would cross again at a place called Tory's Den and that one of them would not survive.

During the short 45-mile trip back to Danbury, Bill O'Toole learned much about his greatest weapon in the war against the decimation of the land.

"I am officially here to document King Power's process in

capping the coal ash ponds along the Dan River, especially in the Belew's Creek area. The coal ash dumping that polluted the Dan in 2014 is just the tip of the iceberg. Hexavalent chromium and arsenic, both cancer causing chemicals, are believed to come from coal ash ponds, but now some hottie-tottie professor in Raleigh says that hexavalent chromium is a naturally-occurring chemical. Naturally occurring my arse, That's like saying herpes in humans is naturally occurring!" Mercury shook her head in disbelief as Bill laughed heartily at her analogy.

Mercury continued by saying that unofficially she was coming to Stokes County to ensure that the gas companies followed federal guidelines when installing the drilling rigs. "I want to make sure that these fracking sites are at least 500 yards from any body of water, including lakes, ponds, and rivers. I also will be checking the casing or cement around the well bore, making sure that it will be strong enough to contain all the flow-back water returning to the surface from the frack site. The flow-back water contains all kinds of chemicals that may be causing cancer and leukemia in Texas, Pennsylvania, and other areas that allow hydraulic fracturing." Bill liked the stern, dedicated tone in Mercury's voice.

"Why doesn't the EPA regulate these dangerous carcinogenic chemicals?" the confused man inquired.

"Well, because these chemicals are protected by trade secrets, which like McDonald's protects their 'special sauce' from being replicated by competitors. This is a brilliant strategy to not only keep the public in the dark, but also to stymie regulation from the EPA. Ah, capitalism at its best" the agitation in Mercury's voice inundated the car.

"Sooooo let me get this straight. Say a well explodes. medical personnel arriving on the scene will have no idea what kind of chemical monsters they're dealing with?" an amazed Bill O'Toole asked.

"Give that man a cigar!" Mercury said, gently laughing. Her companion let out a low whistle and shook his head back and forth, like a man repulsed by eating a piece of rotten meat. They drove in silence for about thirty minutes, then out of nowhere Mercury asked,

"Bill, have you ever heard of the yellow lance mussel?"

"Naw, can't say I have. Why?" Bill asked with an inquisitive look on his face.

"Well, this three-inch mussel is protected under the federal Endangered Species Act and could be the reason for the legal showdown over the planned Gulf Coast Pipeline. This mussel has been disappearing at an alarming rate. speculation is that these natural filters are disappearing because of increasingly tainted water in rivers, streams, lakes. They filter particles of algae sediment and bacteria; they are nature's filtration system. They are like canaries in the coal mines that hinted at deadly methane and carbon monoxide." Mercury told Bill O'Toole everything he needed to know about the yellow lance mussel!

Bill suddenly remembered Paul Williams and his wildlife preserve and exclaimed excitedly, "Hey, Mercury, we have a nature preserve about 10 miles east of Danbury. My friend Paul Williams has complained about how selenium adversely affects the mollusk population in the Dan River, and how the arsenic and mercury released after the 2014 coal ash spill are killing the endangered red wolf, small raptors and coyotes that drink the waters of the river."

"Fantastic! That may be all we need to block hydraulic fracturing along the Dan, however until I do more in-depth analysis of the river condition, I want you to make sure that you get every citizen in Walnut Cove and Danbury to sign that petition banning fracking along the Dan. We must educate the public on the environmental dangers of fracking and the unleashing of dangerous chemicals into underground aquifers in the region."

As Mercury said this, she presented a photo of a tall, lanky, handsome man in army camouflage.

"Have you seen this man recently around in town observing protests, or perhaps at one of your meetings?" asked a suddenly serious Johnson.

Bill O'Toole studied the photo for what seemed an eternity to Mercury and finally responded.

"Yep I have seen that fellow hanging around with Black Bart Whitescarver. He comes from a powerful political family that has been entrenched in the area for years. Bart is also my main nemesis and arch enemy, because he is a strong proponent of hydraulic fracturing in the area. I also believe him to be the man who murdered my youngest son Shaun, and for that he is going to suffer tremendously before he perishes." A wild-eyed O'Toole had spoken in an almost inhuman voice.

Mercury Johnson looked at O'Toole for a long time with a compassionate gaze, trying to deduce if his commitment to killing Whitescarver was a sign of a truly unhinged man who could jeopardize her assessment, or that of a grief-stricken father releasing emotional pain. She decided on the latter and calmly said,

"The man in the picture is David Barret, otherwise known as the 'Mind Magician', and if he is here, we both could be in grave danger."

"Why is that?" an alarmed O'Toole inquired.

"Well, David Barret is ex-military and is considered to be a very dangerous man. The oil and gas companies hire him to do all their dirty work, which usually includes using his very impressive array of hypnotic and psychic abilities, which according to his dossier borders on mind control. He is ruthless and cunning, and will stop at nothing to achieve his goals of converting beautiful land into toxic cesspools of carcinogenic wastelands. He has shown up repeatedly in areas like Texas, Oklahoma and Pennsylvania, and has been successful in turning these areas into goldmines for the gas companies, raping the land for its high concentrate of shale. In his wake, he has left families broken by his deception. In fact, some folks just disappear for good!" Mercury glanced at O'Toole with a look of pure hatred and disdain as she described David Barret.

Bill O'Toole suddenly breathed in deeply as he realized that David Barret had been the man hidden in the shadows of the barn when Bill was laying out the plan to stop fracking in Stokes County. He then realized two things: One, that David Barret knew every detail of their plan to stop the gas companies' efforts to frack in Stokes County; and two, that Bill had a target on his back because a ruthless psycho had marked him for extermination.

CHAPTER 9

Jake drove like a maniac, obsessed by his desire to be by the side of the woman he cherished. Highway 8 snaked through the small hills surrounding Danbury, and Jake was doing about 65 in a 45 mile an hour speed zone. One of Sheriff Green's deputies flipped on his blue lights and a hot pursuit ensued. According to Jake's GPS, he only had two miles to go, so he floored the Dodge Challenger he had rented at the airport, and the muscle car responded with a thunderous roar as it fishtailed for about 100 feet, finally straightening out on its path to Stokes County Memorial Hospital. Jake smiled and thought this small town has never seen a police escort done in reverse! Jake's arrogance was short lived however, as the deputy, being a hometown boy raised in the area, knew of several shortcuts to the hospital. He nearly t-boned Jake's rental car in front of the hospital! As an ex-police officer, Jake knew exactly what was coming next, so he stopped the car, put his hands in the air, and waited for the deputy to order him to get out of the car.

Kelli, sitting up in her hospital bed, had witnessed the whole episode and calmly said, "There is my knight in shining armor now. Sam, would you and John please go down and make sure my husband is not thrown in jail? Kelli pleaded. "If he is thrown in the pokie, it would ruin the romantic weekend that I have planned!"

"Sure thing, Kelli," Sam replied as he headed out the door, immediately followed by John Running Deer.

When Sam and Running Deer arrived on the scene, Jake

was laying face down, spread-eagled on main Street. A crowd of curious onlookers had formed across the street, wondering if this was a wanted, dangerous criminal that was being captured. Both Sam and Running Deer flashed their badges and walked over to Jake. Sam knelt down beside the man on the ground and spoke to him as if they were in Jake's living room. "Hey, Jake, how ya been, old buddy? You are looking good! That football coaching must be agreeing with you."

"Hey, Sam, glad to see ya, man! It's been a long time!" Jake exclaimed excitedly. "Would you please tell these idiots who I am, so I can get off this nasty street? It's affecting my sinuses." Jake kind of sneezed and gagged out the last sentence for dramatic purposes.

Just then, Sheriff Bobby Green and SBI Director Jordan King walked out of the Sheriff's Office, which was right across the street from the hospital. Sheriff Green's authoritarian voice boomed off the archaic hospital walls. "Stand down, Deputy Allen. That's no way to treat our guest, especially one who is a decorated police veteran."

The deputy relaxed and placed his nine-millimeter glock back in his holster, still keeping a wary eye on the "fugitive".

Jake slowly got up, and with a nod of gratitude to the sheriff, bound up the steps of the hospital, running like a deer during mating season. Jake feared for the worst— tubes, needles, possibly a respirator. He rounded the corner and burst into the room, which contained the most precious element on earth---his Kelli. He was shocked to see his wife radiantly smiling at him as if he was a clown in a three ringed circus!

"Hello, my beautifully frazzled husband!" Kelli Said. "You always know how to make an entry, don't you? But these folks here don't like us very much, anyway, so can you tone it down please?" Kelli then laughed, and it was music to Jake's ears.

He rushed to her, kissed her lips ferociously, and hugged her so tight Kelli thought she was in the vice grip of an Anaconda.

"Jake! Jake! You are about ready to cut off my oxygen! Kelli screamed. "You keep on squeezing me and they'll be calling a code blue to this room for sure!"

Jake got hold of himself about the time Sam, Running Deer, Inspector King, and Sheriff Green reached the door. He finally let go of his queen and stared into her exquisite green eyes. He had a tear running down his cheek, but quickly wiped it away when he sensed other male species in the room!

He whispered to her ear, "Baby, you need to drop this investigation and come home."

Kelli looked him in the eyes and replied softly, "We have all weekend to discuss this, because I have rented a small cabin for us, complete with a fireplace, bear skin rug, and much bent up passion that needs to be released."

Jake looked at his queen who beamed with self-assurance, courage and determination, and knew that his reason for living would not be gracing the comfort of their love nest again anytime soon.

CHAPTER 10

About the same time that Kelli and Jake were having their tearful reunion, Bill Jr. walked into the Danbury Post Office feeling very cheerful and euphoric. It was the start of fall break at Wake Forest University and he was riding high. Classes were going great, he was on pace for achieving a perfect 4.0 grade point average this semester, and his super attractive Alpha Delta Pi girlfriend was accompanying him to his best friend's house for the annual Halloween party there, which always turned into a drunken orgy. His buddy Todd had already promised that he and his girlfriend Courtney could stay at his house, because the church-going ultra-conservative Bill O'Toole would highly disapprove of his son's indiscretions.

As he walked into the post office, several folks expressed their condolences to him on the death of his little brother Shaun. "That FBI woman agent and her team have any suspects in mind?" asked the super nosy Ellen Givens.

"Naw, Dad's supposed to meet with a couple of agents later on in the week," replied a preoccupied Junior, struggling to open his private PO box that guaranteed his independence from his snooping parents.

"Ah, the federal government agencies are so incompetent, even more so with the new commander in-chief. He doesn't know his asshole from a hole in the ground," Rudy Brown said in a high pitched voice. Rudy was the only mechanic to town. He was a whiz kid when it came to fixing cars, but he had not gone past the sixth grade. Bill Junior had the urge to correct Rudy's English, but decided that it would not be prudent to piss off the only good mechanic in town. Damn, he was glad he was a college-educated genius! Besides, everyone knew that Rudy always spoke tough to hide his insecurities for sounding like a pubescent girl.

Junior finally got the box open, retrieved the contents, and started for the door. He opened the door and started to step outside when he heard the gossipers whispering behind him.

"I'm sure that Bill Senior was livid when his favorite son was murdered. And I bet he wishes Junior was murdered instead. That boy looks nothing like Bill Sr. I heard a rumor that Junior was not even Bill's son! How ironic they named him Junior. Should have just called him what he is---a bastard!"

Junior whirled to angrily chastise those circulating such vicious rumors, but when he turned around no one was behind him. Those vicious words were either products of his imagination or the manifestation of a tortured mind.

Junior sat in his car and separated the junk mail from the legitimate looking mail, when a correspondence from Weston Law Firm addressed to his father grabbed his attention. The postmaster must have accidentally placed his father's mail in his box; after all, they did have the same name. Junior looked at the large manila envelope for the longest time, debating with himself whether he should invade his father's privacy, which ironically is why Junior had gotten a post office box in the first place.

Finally, the dark side won, and he tore into the envelope expecting to see changes in his father's will, giving him the portion of assets reserved for the recently departed Shaun. Oh, the transformation of Junior's face was epic when he discovered that he, the firstborn son, had been completed disinherited! The rage built up, and he almost ripped the will up when he realized the law offices would have electronic copies of the original documents and would simply mail out another copy. Junior did not notice Black Bart standing across the street witnessing the young man's emotional meltdown, waiting for the pinnacle of Junior's volcano to erupt. Finally, when Junior slammed his fist into the dashboard of his brand new Corvette, Bart made the call because if he had learned anything from the mind magician at all, it was that timing was everything.

Black Bart had forged an alliance with Junior about a week before, calling him up and offering an olive branch of peace by offering to buy Junior lunch. Now Junior did not care much for Black Bart, but Bart was politically powerful in Stokes County. Junior, also having future political ambitions, he decided to accept Bart's invitation because he was not one to burn bridges. Besides, they were on the same side of the hydraulic fracturing debate in Stokes County.

During lunch, both men had agreed that hydraulic fracturing was going to be an economic boom to the area, and in the process was going to make them as wealthy as oil sheikhs in Saudi Arabia! Therefore, when Bart called at the pinnacle of his hatred for his father, Junior did not even consider the perfect timing of the call that was going to use him as a scapegoat in a diabolical plan to assassinate the man whose seed had given him life.

When Junior answered the phone, Bart quietly said, "Hey, Junior, ole buddy, how's it going?"

"Ah, I'm fine," Junior said, barely able to contain his seething anger against his father.

"You don't sound so good, brother. What's up?" Bart asked almost puking in his mouth, having to address an O'Toole in such a civilized tone.

Junior, in the heat of rage, confided in Bart, telling him how his father had double crossed him and written him out of his will, most likely because Junior opposed him on the hydraulic fracturing issue.

"That bastard, I know that you have been a good and faithful son! Bart said in a smooth tone. "I tell you what. Meet me in Barker Park in 10 minutes, and I will save your inheritance and help you become financially solvent," Bart barked, capitalizing on Junior's anger and his perceived betrayal by his father. Junior, in an agitated rage, threw the Vet into reverse and gunned the car's powerful engines, squealing his tires and leaving the faint smell of burnt rubber as he charted a course toward pure destruction and betrayal.

Barker Park was in reality just a wide spot off Highway 8, with a couple of picnic tables about 100 yards off the road. The main attraction was a scenic view of the Dan River and a place where the kids can get their feet wet.   When Junior pulled up, he saw Bart's beat up old Ford Ranger pickup truck. It always amazed Junior that people with real money never flaunted their wealth. People like Bart were misers and penny pincers, thinking that all their money was going to buy them a ticket into heaven.

Junior pulled up beside Bart, and the grisly old coot motioned for him to get into the truck. Junior climbed out of his high school graduation gift from his father and opened the door of the truck. He was immediately repulsed by the scent of wet dog. He tried to hide his displeasure because the meanest SOB in Stokes County was sitting close enough to strangle the life out of him, which was rumored to be the fate of anyone who crossed Black Bart, the earthly carnation of Satan himself.

Junior was shocked when Bart slapped him on the back and bellowed, "Good to see you again, Junior! Never thought I say that to an O'Toole! I'm sorry for that smell; my old dog Jake was riding with me this morning, and Jake don't like baths," Black Bart said with a shit-eating grin.

Junior felt like he was going puke and wanted to jump out of that old truck. "What the hell is this about, Bart? I'm a busy man," Junior replied through clenched teeth, still thinking about having been disinherited.

Black Bart motioned for Junior to open the glove box. When he did, a giant wad of cash fell into his lap.

"There is about 40 thousand dollars in cash there, all in $100-dollar non-traceable bills," Bart informed him. Bart went on to tell him that the Abbott Gas wanted his father's land badly and knew that Bill Sr. would rather burn in hell before surrendering his land to them.

"So, what the hell do they want me to do?" Junior asked. After a moment of silence, his mind suddenly grasped what Black Bart was asking him to do, and the cold, vacant look in Black Bart's eyes confirmed his darkest suspicions!

Junior was outraged! He was going to get out and slam the door in Bart's face when he thought about the disinheritance, the cold betrayal of his father. He could not move, frozen with grief and pain, but most of all with unbridled, uncontrolled greed.

"Listen, Junior, there is another $60 grand after the job is done, and we will make sure that your father's will has you listed as the sole beneficiary."

This was a lie, because Junior would be having a terrible accident right after slaying his father. Just call it Karma, thought Black Bart.

"How in the hell are you going have my father's will changed?" asked Junior, showing all the signs of agreeing to the diabolical deal.

"Ah, Junior, my friend the 'Mind Magician', who works for Abbott Gas, has very valuable resources at Weston Law Firm, and has judges, politicians, and even the Federal Government in his back pocket. The truth is that in these dark times people without souls are soooo very easy to corrupt! Why back in the day I had no competition for the blackest, most empty soul; now it seems like everyone is in my immoral brotherhood!" Black Bart then laughed and the heinous odor that was exhaled deepened the stench inside the truck.

Without another word, Junior grasped the wad of cash and exited the truck, thus the agreement was non-verbal and binding. He had just been conned into murdering his father. Junior should have known in his heart that his father would never betray him, but the shock of the forged will and being locked in a close place with unspeakable evil had worked its dark magic.

Black Bart started his truck and caught up with Junior as he was getting into the car that had been given to him by the man he was going to kill. "Oh, one more thing" Bart said in a low tone. "We want it done within a week from now. Call us on this, when it's over," and he handed Junior a tracFone. Bart then smiled like a pedophile that had just tricked a little child into getting in the car with him. As Bart drove off, Junior suddenly felt sick, and he vomited alongside the road. It was as if his soul was trying to purge itself from the hellish monster it had just encountered.

CHAPTER 9

Kelli was the center of attention, Sam, John Running deer, and Jake were crowded around her bed, while inspector King and Sheriff were standing in the doorway, when a heavy set masculine looking nurse burst through the door nearly knocking Inspector King and Sheriff Green out of the way.

And the look on her face dared anyone to object with her demand. She reminded Sam Jenkins of nurse Ratchet in his favorite movie One Flew over the Cuckoo's Nest starring Jack Nickelson. As the others filed out of the room, Jake boldly explain to the overbearing nurse, that he was Kelli husband, and He was not going anywhere! John Running Deer half expected to see the buff nurse grab Jake by his trousers and toss him headlong out into the hall.

"I said everybody clear the room, including you Cowboy" the nurse scowled, snarling her massive nose

"I am staying beside my wife," Jake said with voice raising a decimal.

As John Running Deer looked back he saw a fearful sight, the nurse hands slightly curled was standing toe to toe with Jake. Jake was a good two foot taller than the short, stout looking Nurse. Nurse Ratchet clone looked up to Jake with a Clint Eastwood smile as to say, "Go ahead Punk Make my Day". Just as world war three was going to erupt, Dr. Bracket walked into Kelli room and gave the aggressive nurse a "stand down look", and the nurse quickly and quietly left the room.

"Sorry about that Nurse Owens is a great nurse, but she would never receive awards for Ms. Congeniality" Dr. Bracket said with a slight frown on his face.

"Hey Kelli how are you feeling today? You gave us all quite a scare yesterday, But I have some good news the MRI of your brain came back completely normal. There is no sign of a stroke or any Neurological damage to any region of the brain including the areas that are responsible for your keen investigative skills. Your vitals, Heartbeat, and blood pressure, are stable. All labs test that look for abnormality in your red or while bloods cells are negative. So young lady, I have no medical reason for your seizure yesterday, could have been brought on by stress, working a mass murder scene is not very relaxing I sure!" Dr. Bracket chuckled at his lame remark.

Jake's made of a face behind the doctor's back, which Kelli knew to be his "He is a dumb ass" look. The doctor then declared Kelli healthy, and the process for her discharge in the morning had already started. The Doc then stood up and announced that he had many other patients to see, so He told Kelli he wanted to see her in a couple of days, shook Jake's hand , and he quickly left the room.

Jake felt sorry for the Doctor with the limp handshake, who had to confer with many more patients before the day was out, because the hospitals administrators had to pay the bills. He then realized that no matter how affluent, wealthy or educated one is, if they work for someone else, like puppets on a string, once the boss barks "Dance Monkey Dance" you comply. Kelli sighed in relief. She has planning a grinding 15 hour work today tomorrow, which included interviewing Bill O'Toole, setting up a new command post old two story hotel at Vade Cum springs, the large building would be perfect place to set up forensic lab in close proximity to the crime scene at Moore's Knob. Kelli also had to collect black Barts DNA, because she would wager her career that there would at least a familial DNA link to the fang embedded in Deputy Peter's femur.

Kelli was telling Jake about the cabin on Shadow lake, which would be their weekend love nest, when Inspector King walked into the room, and spoiled Kelli's vision of her future with the FBI.

" Hey Kelli, your one resilient lady, we all thought you had a massive stroke yesterday, and twenty four hours later you are the picture of health, glad you are among the living" King said with a forced smile.

"Thank you Inspector King, I would like you to meet my husband Jake Ryan, who saved my career and life on my last mission eight years ago." Kelli grinned looking up at Jake with sparks of love, and admiration.

"Jake. I am very proud to meet you! I did some research on that case on the Outer Banks of North Carolina, your superior investigative techniques are very impressive, and your bravery and courage under extreme pressure were commendable," King said looking a Jake, with a hero worshiping stare.

Jake feeling very uncomfortable with all the praise calmly replied, "I appreciate all the praise Inspector King, but Kellie deserves all the credit, her attention to detail is what saved the case!" In fact, Kelli deductive reasoning skill was working in overdrive as she asked

"I'm sure your here for more than a social visit, Inspector King what news do you bring from my superiors at FBI headquarters?" Kelli asked already knowing the answer!

" I will get directly to the point, Paul Jacobs wants you to stand down for at least three days, because he wants to review all the hospital lab reports, also he is going to send down an FBI Psychologist to assess your mental health to make sure this incident is not linked to your PSTD. I have lobbied on your behalf, explaining to Jacobs that your expertise in dealing with the special circumstances around this case is essential in solving it." King said appearing to be visual shaken by the thought of Kelli leaving the area.

The phone rang beside Kelli's bed; it was Jacob's confirming what inspector King had just relayed. Jacobs told Kelli to stand down for four days, while he made a decision on her fate. He also explained that she was to meet with the FBI psychologist in a couple days; he would be emailing her on the exact location and time of her appointment. He also mentioned that she should seek a place of relaxation and spend some time with her husband. The phone line went dead, as Jacobs disconnected the call!

" Ah Kelli look at the bright side, we can spend the four days on shadow lake, going over this case with a fine-toothed comb, while I take care of your other needs" Jake said with a mischievous gleam in his eyes!

King also offered some comfort, "Kelli I agree with Jake, this time will allow you to step back and examine the case from an objective standpoint, allowing you to see it from different perspectives."

Kelli looked at both men, as if agreeing with their comforting suggestions, but her mind was racing as she thought of her team, and the objectives that they must accomplish in her absence. Agent Briggs already had the prime suspect in custody, but her rational logic mind knew that the small slender Indian women was just a patsy, like Lee Harvey Oswald, and was being offer up like a sacrificial lamb to cover up a vast, terrifying conspiracy. Kelli's mind was trying to convince her heart to give up this case, and to scurry back to the safe confines of her office at the profiler training academy in Quantico VA, but then the visions of Brian Cox lying broken at the bottom of Moore's knob flashed through her skull like some cheap horror film. Kelli realized that she would never voluntary leave Stokes Country until this case was solved. Finally she looked at inspector King and asked

"Inspector King you mentioned that there were special

circumstances in this case. Would you care to elaborate on what kind of special circumstances surround this case?"

Without Batting an eye, King confirmed that he was indeed on the same page as his lead FBI profiler,

"The supernatural" he uttered the words in a small voice usually reserved for a child's terrifying nightmare.

Kellie was in the process of being released into Jake's custody, when Running Deer and Sam Jenkins stepped into her room. Sam cleared his throat and announced, "SBI Agent Briggs had secured Accalia DNA and it matched the blood found on the ground in the ravine near Vade Mecum springs, but her DNA does not match the fang embedded in Deputy Power's Femur! In fact Accalia Blackclaw DNA is not found at the crime scene at Moore's knob!" exclaimed and excited Jenkins.

Kelli pondered the shocking news, and mentally prepared a list for her seasoned team to accomplish in her absence.

Kelli told the men to get out their cell phones and list the following tasks to be accomplished while she was on a temporary sabbatical. "First get with the FBI response recovery team and let's re walk the grid up at Moore's knob, there is still good forensic evidence there, but an outdoor crime scene especially one of that size is already about 70 percent corrupted. The park has been closed for two weeks now, and we are running out of time. Governor Buddy Gray has already called and wants the part reopened ASAP. Second, get Black Bart's DNA, I do not care if you have to tail him for 24 hours, anything he picks up or drinks from, I want it bag and tagged. I will bet my government pension that his DNA will at least be a familial hit to Accalia Blackclaws. Third, get the lab technicians to set up a mobile lab at the hotel at Vade Mecum springs, it will serve as our command center, so get the Tech geeks to get us online with FBI databases, like CODIS. Fourth, interview Bill O'toole find out as much as you can about Shaun O'toole , friends, hobbies, and most importantly folks that might want him to be void of a heartbeat. Five, scour the part of the river, in which Chad Whitescarver body was found, because I think we missed some crucial evidence there. Finally interview Dr. Drake the ghoulish county corner, and find out how a corpse of Chad Whitescarver could be void of any water molecules!". Kelli Continued, "I want a complete report of your progress every four hours, Is there any questions?"

Sam being accustomed to Kelli's strong work ethic just replied " No Ma'am", John Running Deer looked like he has in shock. Jake felt kind of sorry for him, but knew John Running Deer was a top notch agent and would break his back getting Kelli's orders accomplished.

" As for me gentleman, I will be working nonstop reviewing this case with a very seasoned detective-husband, who is gifted in so many skills in a remote romantic location" Kelli said winking at Jake.

Both Sam and Running Deer laughed in unison, while Jake could barely control a growing erection. Just as Jake was fantasizing about his reunion with his beauty wife, when her cell phone rang it, was Governor Grey calling to demand that Kelli lifted her federal quarantine of hanging rock state park. The quarantine of the park now in its ten day had cost the State of North Carolina several hundred thousand dollars in additional manpower that was required to insure no trespassing on several thousand acres of land that was now part of a federal crime scene investigation. Kelli calmly explained to the governor that the federal government would reimburse the state, when the investigation was over.

" Hell I will be retired and in the grave, when and if the Feds repay us for this infringement of our states sovereignty. Just look at poor Puerto Rico, many folks on the island do not have electricity a year after Hurricane Maria obliterated the Island." Governor Gray's voice boomed off the walls in the small hospital room. Kelli calmly told the governor " Good Night" and disconnected the phone call, not because she didn't want to put the fear of God and the Federal government into Gray's heart, but because it was a hospital environment and she didn't want to disturb patients recovering from their illnesses. It was nearly 9:00 pm , when Nurse Owens announced the visiting hours were over, and everyone but Jake was to clear the room, judging by her mild tone, and her accommodating attitude toward Jake the hospital administrator must have had a few choice words for nurse Ratchet.

As she entered the room, she calmly asked Kelli if she realized that she had a big fan club,   Kelli grinned at Nurse Owens, and thinking that it was her lame attempt of joking with her.

" Yes my fans adore me" but the words died in her throat , when Nurse Owens opened the drapes to her room. Kelli's room faced the parking lot, and the hospital powerful lights which protected the staff leaving the hospital in the middle of the nigh illuminated the parking lot. Kelli could make out a large contingency of folks actually protesting her presence at the hospital, holding up signs telling the Federal Government to keep their hands off their land, which was a clever reference to a female abortionist lobbyist plea. Kelli being the lead investigator for the FBI, was now a target for any unhinged resident looking for revenge!

Kelli smiled and calmly said " rather catchy slogan wouldn't you say Jake?"

" Ah Kelli my beautiful hellcat, you are always making friends and influencing people." Jake said smiling with a hint of sarcasm on this face. They both laughed in unison, but later on as Jake slept beside her in a comfy pullout chair, Kelli had a vivid dream that the townsfolk were chasing her with lit torches, like the monster in Mary Shelly's Frankenstein, and leading the pack was a tiny Native American Indian woman that strongly resembled Accalia Blackclaw.

CHAPTER 10 /
SHADOW LAKE

Friday morning October 30, was a typical mid fall morning in Central North Carolina, crisp, and clear with a heavy frost on the ground. The color of the sky was Royal blue, or as local folks say "Carolina blue", with a clarity and brightness that is not unique to autumn. Kelli woke to the sound of the heated debate between Jake and Nurse Owens on who would wheel Kelli out of the hospital, because Dr. Brackett had just released her from the hospital.

"MR. RYAN IT IS HOSPITAL PROTOCOL FOR HOSPITAL EMPLOYEES ONLY TO OPERATE THE WHEELCHAIR". Nurse Owens whaled.

Kelli alarmed by the tone of Nurse Owen's (alias Nurse Ratchet's voice), ordered Nurse Owens and Jake to cease and desist, and suggested a compromise between the two. Sam Jenkins fought hard to contain a laugh, when he wheeled Jake's car to the front of the hospital, and saw Jake with a death grip on the left side of the Wheelchair, while Nurse Owens had an equally tight grip on the right side. Jake opened the passenger door, and gently ushered Kelli inside, all the time staring at Nurse Owen with look that would petrify a harden criminal. He went to the other side, and thanked Sam for his valet service, and after checking his precious cargo's comfort level, slowly pulled out of the hospital parking lot. After leaving a frowning Nurse Owens and a smiling and waving Sam and John Running dear in the rear-view mirror, Kelli exhaled a sigh of relief glad to be released from her bondage. She nuzzled up to her man, and tried desperately resisted the urge to rip Jake's clothes off during the one hour trip to Shadow Lake.

They were silent for the first few moments of the trip; Kelli turned and peered into Jake's steel blue eyes, and could feel his love for her, and his intense desire to protect her. She also could feel a profound sadness within him, and chastised herself mentally for being so selfish, maybe she would relieved if the FBI shrink found her to unstable to complete her investigation. As if sensing her pain, Jake tightened his arm around her, and pulled her so close to him; it seemed as if they were one organism, joined forever by a shared soul.

Shadow Lake was formed about 14,000 years ago, when the last ice age receded and exposed carved out land, which quickly filled with melt water. The Saura Indians believed the lake to be a place of significant spiritual relevance, because the shadows cast down from the high ancient peaks surrounding the lake resembled their Gods of the netherworld.

Jake and Kelli cared not for the relevance of the lake; their focus was on the cabin nestled against a natural outcropping of quartzite, and partially hidden by the Canadian pines and Frazier furs that encircled their weekend love nest. As they pulled up to the rustic cabin, smoke was already bellowing out of the ancient stone chimney. Mr. Turner the resident caretaker had been hard at work preparing the cabin for their second honeymoon. They did not even carry their luggage in with them, because they did not want the passion in their loins to be imprisoned for another moment. Once inside the cabin, neither noticed the two bottles of red wine in the ice bucket resting near the roaring fire, or the romantically scented rose and lavender candles sitting on the table, because they were locked in an embrace that emitted a heat that could melt the deepest snow on Mount Everest.

They made love with wild abandon, trying to consume every morsel of their energy. Their bodies moved in complete harmony as if in tune to eternal music that only two souls interlocked for centuries could hear. Jake's manhood was thrusting deeply into the love spot that Kelli reserved only for him, and Kelli screamed with ecstasy with every mind bending orgasm. The two lovers would take temporarily take a break to sample the energy giving fruit on the table like Adam and Evil sampling the forbidden fruit in the garden of Eden. They arrived early afternoon, and made passion love until the sun was setting like a glowing sphere behind the ancient peaks of the Sauratown Mountains. They were hot and sweaty so they both took a cool, sensuous shower together, which led to another highly exotic bout of lovemaking. They both laughed at their lustful exercises, as they rested on the pillow top, deeply cushioned, king-sized bed and slowly their pillow talk turned to the topic of a case that bordered on the supernatural and had taken the life of their mutual friend Brian Cox.

As Jake caressed Kellie naked back, he told her of Brian Cox funeral, and how Brian's wife clung to his shoulder and sobbed with unspeakable grief. Brian's three grown sons spoke eloquently of their father's unconditional love for them, and his dedication to God, family, and to his strong commitment to protecting the citizens of North Carolina. The small Catholic Church in Maneto could not hold all the folks that came to honor a hometown hero, so the Church set up rows of chairs outside the church, and podcast the service to those outside.

Many Law officers from all around the state, including Jake gave stirring testimonials of Brian's bravery under fire, and after the playing of "Danny Boy" on the bagpipes to honor Brian's Irish heritage there was not a dry eye in or outside of the church. Kelli noticed that her husband had grown quiet, as if caught up in a moment of unbearable grief. Kelli then told

Jake of the heartbreaking funerals of Donny Miller and Mack Peters, the two sheriff's deputies that had been massacred on Moore's knob. The young lawman, who were well respected in Stokes Country left behind six children under the age of ten years old, their young wives were trying to cope with the loss of their husbands, while at the same time trying to comfort their young children. Kelli admired their bravery, and secretly wondered why Sheriff Brown chose an order a suicidal night mission!

As if their mind were linked, Jake as the obvious question, "Why send valuable resources out on a dangerous mission in the middle of the night?" Jake then made an intuitive jump in logic, "I think Brown was trying to link the Murder of Shaun O'Toole and the Massacre at Moore knob together". Kelli looked at her husband with a puzzled look, and asked

"Okay, Sherlock Holmes what is your reasoning for such a hypothesis?"

Jake kissed his beautiful wife on the forehead and replied, "Ah my tough FBI profiler, I'm just thinking out of the box, you know my specialization is divergent thinking." Jake said laughing. "He continued the murderer of Shaun O'Toole wanted to remain hidden, and what better way to accomplish that than to link the murder to a high profile crime like the slaughter of two native sons and a state bureau of investigation agent?" Jake asked his voice raising a decimal.

" Kelli I would find out who Sheriff Brown associates are, bug is phone, assign an agent to follow his every move, find a way to get a warrant for his computer software" Jake encouraged. "FBI forensic specialist can even search deleted files." Kelli then told Jake about issue that gave her great concern and stress.

"Doctor Drake the medical examiner of Stokes County is going to rule Brian's death a suicide," Kelli blurted out, suddenly aware of her bad timing,

"What!" Jake almost shouted,

"All the bones in Brian's legs were shattered, along with his all the Metatarsals in his feet, and according to Doctor Drake those injuries are consistent with Jumping" Kelli summarized like a third year med student. Jake was stunned unable to process what he had just heard.

"Kelli that ludicrous, during a 2,500 foot fall, Brian's body could have flipped over many times. I just wondered what motivation Drake has in ruling Brian's death a suicide?"

"That's another great question Jake". Kelli replied mentally making notes of Jake's powerful insights into the investigation.

Kelli then turned toward her husband, looks deeply into his baby blue eyes, and asked the question that would deepen the complexity of an already strange case.

"Jake do you believe in mind control, or the ability to control the actions of others with telekinesis" Kelli asked her eyes glowing in the shadows of the room.

"Oh sure like some character on the X-men, or the dude in that old movie the Manchurian Candidate that was brainwashed?" He asked looking at Kelli with a worried look in his eye.

"Come on Jake, how did cult leaders like David Koresh at Waco, or Jim Jones of the Guinea tragedy get there followers to drink the Cool Aid laced with poison?" Kelli replied briefly taken back by Jake's sarcasm.

"What are you trying to tell me that someone with great mind control abilities made Brian jump off a 2,500 foot peak?" Jake asked incredulously.

" No Jake not someone but something," Kelli replied in a hush tone and then preceded to tell Jake of the black magic of a Cherokee Indian shape shifter named Hi'cictawi'a. Jake sat in silence and listen to Kelli recite the legend of Hi'cictawi'a as told by Agent Running deer, he listened as Kelli stressed the words cannibalism, hypnotic mind control, and described a beast that was over nine feet tall and resembled a werewolf or Bigfoot with a very bad disposition. After Kelli breathlessly completed this tale of pure fantasy, Jake wondered if Kelli's post-traumatic stress syndrome had intensified under the stress of the investigation.

Kelli could tell by the look on Jake's face that he was thinking that she had become unhinged, so she quickly slip out of the nice warm bed slipped on a robe and walked out the room. Jake was sitting in the bed, silently chastising himself for being so transparent, when Kelli came back in the room with a laptop that she had downloaded the contents of Deputy Miller's body camera, which depicted the last terrifying moments of the young officer's life. Jake sat transfixed, and his eyes widen incomplete and utter horror as he witness the onslaught of pure evil.

Jake was speechless after viewing the video, but his eyes being the windows of the soul pleaded with his young wife to walk away from this investigation and never look back, Jake surprised Kelli, and shutdown the laptop, and quietly said that he was exhausted, and needed some sleep. Kelli then noticed the time, it was almost 4 Am, was it possible that they had spent almost twelve hours together? Jake turned down the bed and slipped in between the sheets, Kelli laid down beside her soul mate. Jake pulled her close and held her tight as if he was protecting her from the wrath of the beast that he observed on the death video. Kelli would have been surprised to know that Jake was not at all sleepy, but was using this downtime to think of a brilliant strategy to convince his stubborn, strong willed wife to walk away from a nightmare.

As Jake and Kelli slipped into a spasmodic sleep, the winds began to stir high upon the ancient peaks. It descended like a steam locomotive down the mountain, whistling through the Canadian Pines and Frazier Furs building to a climatic frenzy near the base of the lake, echoing the name Hi'cictawi'a, and creating It's horrifying image on the still, calm waters of Shadow Lake.

CHAPTER 11 - HALLOWEEN

Mac McKenzie, frack job supervisor for Abbott Gas stood on hallow ground, observing his crew as they positioned the drilling rig on the three-acre piece of land mysteriously bequeathed to Abbott Gas by retired Army Colonial Jeffery Anderson. McKenzie knew that Anderson was strongly opposed to hydraulic fracturing, and he had expected a long contentious battle with the strong willed Colonial.

McKenzie suspected that David Barrett, AKA the mind magician had used supernatural techniques to persuade Anderson to betray his neighbor Bill O'Toole. McKenzie had worked with Barrett before, and frankly, the man scared him to the point that McKenzie secretly wondered if David was a demigod with 666 engraved on the back of his skull.

Mac McKenzie had worked his way up from being a lowly roustabout, or unskilled laborer, to part of the drill crew or roughneck, and over the past 20 years had finally gotten the coveted status as frack job Supervisor, and he always demanded perfection from his subordinates.

" Dam it Jones get that trench dug so we can connect the hydration unit to the drilling rig, if you takes you any longer than 30 minutes to get it done, pack up your shit and considered yourself unemployed!" a red faced McKenzie yelled at new hire. McKenzie knew that he could push the new folks to near exhaustion, because they were eager to prove themselves, but more importantly, he wanted to weed out those that would slow down the completion of the set up. The blender, hydration unit, and missile all need to be attached to the drilling rig so that the chemicals, sand, and water can be sent at 100 PSI thousands of feet underground. This high pressure concoction breaks apart the shale releasing natural gas, which is then send to the surface by reverse osmosis.

After completion of the setup process, McKenzie thought the drill rig connected to a vast network of trucks and equipment resembled his terminally ill uncle in the critical care unit at Vanderbilt in Nashville Tennessee. Uncle Ben had tubes, monitors, IVs, connected to every region of his decaying, dying torso, and Mac McKenzie knew that his uncle would be deceased before this frack job was completed.

McKenzie was about to unload another burst of obscenity laced instructions to his new hire, when an ominous shadow appeared on the ground in front of him! He turned expected some kind of ravenous demon from his past moving in to devour him, but it was Mercury Johnson, an entity that was much more terrifying and disturbing than a flesh-eating demon could ever be!

"Better check the thickness of the cement casings that you're putting in the well-bore, because wells in the Barnabas and Harnett Shale's are leaking like sieves. The back flow water is bubbling up with carcinogens that I detailed in my report to congress, and they will determine if Abbot Gas is in violation of the any environmental mandates concerning fresh water."

"Ah agent Johnson, nice to see you too, about that violation thing, you know the old saying money talks and bullshit walks," McKenzie mumbled with a comical smirk!

"Ah so you think Abbot Gas is paying off members of Congress?" Johnson asked the question loud enough for the recorder on her cell phone to pick up. Suddenly big mouth Mac McKenzie was lost for words, and was as silent a corpse in the morgue!

Mercury suddenly changed her line of questioning, "What Kind of chemicals are you pumping down into the fine folks of Stokes County water supply? She asked?" "Are half their population going to have leukemia or cancerous tumors in a year?" Mercury asked keeping the meticulous badgering going.

"Listen Mercury you know that our ingredients of this and other frock is protected by trade secrets, Abbott Gas is not mandated by any laws to disclose any of those chemicals to the general public or to the mighty EPA!" McKenzie say raising his voice in defiance. Mercury knew that McKenzie was conscious of the stares of his crew and wanted to display his power over this pawn of the highly bureaucratic Federal Government. McKenzie unaware that he had been played was totally unprepared for what came next!

" Mac, you see all those protesters over there about a half mile away, holding up signs like BOB MILLER SOLD HIS SOUL TO THE DEVIL, AND WE WILL FIGHT FOR CLEAN WATER", Mercury said with a slight grin on her face.

" Oh yea, environmental protesters, they don't understand that fracking helps this country keep up with the energy needs of a modern high tech society, and at the same time defangs countries like Saudi Arabia that sponsor global terrorism. They are just a bunch of bleeding heart snowflakes, out of touch of reality searching for their safe room!" Thundered McKenzie and his crew applauded his verbal comeback.

Mercedes could barely contain her extreme joy, as she explained to this pompous ass that the land the protectors were standing on belong to Bill O'toole, the harshest critic of hydraulic fracking in Stokes County.

" Mac, Bill O'Toole has given the Federal Government permission to install monitoring wells on his property, in fact just envision these wells sampling the groundwater to detect seepage from your fracking site." Mercury continued and she noticed that big mouth Mac had paled and become deathly quiet.

"If our Geologist detect any Benzene, Cross Alpha, Ethyl Benzene or any other carcinogen in the soil, we will find Abbot Gas in violation of the Clean water act of 1972, and shut your entire operation down!"

Mercury sensing that her message was received loud and clear, turned to leave, but could not resist one parting shot.

" Ah Mac might as well shut the operation down, several pipelines like Atlantic Coast and the Colonial have been delayed because of the potential contamination of habitats of several endangered species along their protected path of their construction. In fact the three inch yellow lance mussel have just delayed the mighty Atlantic Coast pipeline, so even if you frack several cubic meters of gas it not going anywhere Baby" Mercury concluded with her own personal dig.

Mac McKenzie stood trembling with rage as he watched the flamboyant federal agent get in her government issued black Sudan and gunned the engines, as a final insult to his manhood. Mac McKenzie fumbled with his cell phone, punched in a few digits, and on the second ring a the strong masculine voice of David Barrett answered the phone, and strangely just of the sound of the voice of the Mind Magician calmed him, much like the voice of the master calms the spirit of the most vicious canine. Mac relayed the message delivered by Mercury to David; the phone went silent for a few minutes as David mentally formulated his plan to get rid of this pest.

"Hey Mac don't worry about that distraction, just get your installation done in 24 hrs. or I will give you something to be really terrified about" and suddenly the phone line went dead.

David was alone in his office, as he contemplated the fate of Mercury Johnson, she was indeed a formidable adversary, and he respected her tenacity, he had knocked heads with her plenty of times, and she had caused great disequilibrium in his other operations and campaigns. He knew she could not be bribed and like Bill O'Toole was completely resistance to mind control. She and that FBI special agent Kelli Ryan just had to disappear, after all he was not called the mind magician for nothing. Stokes County was so abundant that he could not let anything or anybody get in the way of completing his mission.

He could just round them all up; tie them up in some ole tobacco barn, and blow the building up with some C-4 activated by remote control, and then he thought that would be to messy bits of body parts everywhere. The crime labs of the FBI would soon match the DNA samples to the agents no matter how minuscule. Bill Jr. was going to take his own father out, and the two Federal Agents would just have to mysteriously disappear. He would bury them deep under the coal ash at Belews creek. David then remember the two Agents disappearing in the deep woods of Mississippi in the Mid-sixties trying to infiltrate the KKK. He then thought of the book "Mississippi Burning" in his High school history class, which detailed how the bodies of the two agents were eventually recovered, and several of the KKK members were brought to trial. David smiled to himself and thought about a new edition of the book called Stokes County Burning, except in this version agent Ryan and agent Johnson bodies will be lost forever in the residue and debris of a toxic environment hastened by man's unparalleled greed.

CHAPTER 11

Kelli woke the brilliant fall sunlight streaming through the large bay windows in the master bedroom. Jake, who could sleep through a nuclear blast, was still snoring with wild abandon. Kelli sipped out of bed, glancing at the alarm clock on the table is was 7:00 AM on Saturday October 31, and she needed a jog to reduce the stress of a demanding, mysterious, and deadly investigation. She searched her luggage and found her running gear, which included spandex pants, a bright yellow cascade thermal vest with a hoodie, and of course, her prized Nike running shoes, Kelli put an energy bar in her running pants, kissed Jake on the forehead, knowing it would not wake the slumbering Rip Van Winkle. She opened the front door and was met with brilliant sunshine, and crisp clear fall air. Once outside Kelli began to do exercises to stretch out her hamstring, quad, and calf muscles, all the time hearing the voice of her High School track coach Bill Jacobs screaming " Good stretching insures great performance."

Mr. Turner, the cabin's caretaker had told her of the running path that circled Shadow Lake and he estimated that the distance around the lake was about three miles. Kelli turned toward the path entrance and began to jog slowly, giving her body time to increase heart rate and her lungs to increase the oxygen in her blood, these physiological changes needed to be made gradually in order to complete the run in about 24 minutes. Her goal was about an 8-minute mile not bad for a woman approaching 40 years. The fallen leafs crunched under her confident stride, the air was brisk, and the sun was shining brightly creating sparkles on the lake that seemed to move. It was as if the sparkles were dancing in and on the lake.

The magical season of fall sent waves of euphoric joy from deep in her soul to hypothalamus region of the brain, which then decodes outside stimuli and then assigns emotional response such as fear, anger, grief, or joy. After about an hour, despite a light breeze Kelli began to feel a bit overheated, she stopped to take her light jacket off. Kelli was listening to her favorite country music song "Somewhere with you" by Kenny Chesney, but had to take the ear buds out to get the jacket off. That's when she heard a soft crackling sound about 200 feet off the path, her sharp keen eyes followed the sound to a husk of a large Hemlock tree that had been a victim of a strong wind as it descended from the ancient peaks high above her. The tree was completely barren, and its limbs were protruding out grotesque spider legs touching the ground at impossible angles. Kelli turned back to tie the jacket around her midsection, when out of the corner of her eye she saw that long dead Hemlock tree began to twitch, and then to her complete and utter horror began to move straight for her. The same region of the brain that produced the soothing emotion of Joy had morphed in complete unbridled fear, soon Kelli's cerebellum was in charge, and it commanded her to take flight.

Being a special agent Kelli would have normally processed her surroundings and left in a controlled but rapid pace, but her PTSD kicked in, and Kelli for the first time in her life, ran back to the cabin in complete and utter terror. She could hear the tree beast trashing through the woods in attempt to end her life with extreme prejudice, even though it was several yards away, Kelli could feel its utter hatred and contempt for her. It not only wanted to snuff her life out, but crush her bones, and spread her lifeblood on the ground like a farmer's spreading manure on barren, unproductive land. Kelli was in an extreme panic mode; she was breathing in quick shallow spurts, and knew that she was near the stage of hyperventilation, which in this situation would be a death sentence. She suddenly heard the voice of Dr. Sloan echoing through her mind, calming her through his assurances that this flight was irrational because trees are inanimate objects and do not stalk humans. Kelli began to slow almost to a slow jog, and calmed herself down by using many of desensitization techniques that Dr. Sloan had armed her with, and suddenly the trashing in the woods ceased.   She turned around half expecting the monster Hemlock tree branches to wrap around her. She was relieved to see nothing stalking her, and suddenly realized that her vision was manifestation of her PTSD. As she near the cabin, Kelli could smell the sweet aroma of her man cooking her a hearty breakfast. Kelli then smiled to herself and wondered if Jake would suspect anything if she consume a fifth of Jack Daniels with her scrambled eggs!

The same morning that Kelli was being stalked by a long dead tree, Rod O'Neil, one of the 45 prisoners at the Stokes County detention center was delivering breakfast to the other inmates. Rod was incarcerated for breaking and entering at a local convenience store. He was not looking for cash, just the golden nectar of the Gods, cold beer, because old Rod was a falling down old drunk, who was completely harmless. Sam Meadows the jailer felt sorry for the old coot, so he allowed Rod to work in the cafeteria hoping that it would give the old boy a sense of self-worth.

Old Rod was happily whistling as he delivered the trays filled something that barely resembled food that only imprisoned folk that were half-starving would consume. The grayish mush was supposed to be biscuits and gravy, but to Rodney it appeared to be balls on a platter that even flies on a hot July afternoon would ignore. Rodney liked taunting his fellow intimates with his temporary freedom, so he banged on the bars jail cells like a sadistic pet owner harassing a caged animal. He loved messing with the new prisoner a slightly build Indian women named Accalia, He despised all minorities, but he held a special hatred for native American Indians. His ex-wife had been a full-blooded Saura Indian, and had left him for his best friend, thus beginning Rodney's long slide into the wonderful world of alcoholism.

Rodney banged on her door the loudest, sliding the tray into the slot that allowed the prisoner to claim their prize three times a day. Rodney had heard that this Indian bitch had killed three folks on top of Moore's knob, and that intensified his hatred for her even more. He was not scared of the redskin, why he would skin her alive, if he could get his hands on her. So he shouted at her door with the manliest tone he could muster.

"Here you go Pocahontas, hope you choke on it" He yelled with a loud, evil tone.

No response just a low moan and a strange shuffling sound emerged from the cell. Ah, Rodney thought to himself, he caught the wench masturbating in her cell. To his surprise, little Rod began to harden, as he thought of the naked, bronze skinned beauty naked body grinding against her fingers or better yet some type of dildo. He could not contain his lust, so like some peeking tom; he moved the food out of the way, so he could get a front row seat to his own personnel X-rated movie.

What he saw next would haunt him for the rest of his life, and eventually drive him from the wonderful world of alcoholism to the terrifying world of insanity. Rodney would be transferred from the county jail to the sanatorium over in neighboring Eden within twenty-four hours after seeing that no human should ever witness. He opened the slot and peered in, the thing inside was on all fours crawling around the cell, like something from the third dimension of hell. He had seen the exorcist several times, but this thing made Linda Blair look like some kind of Girl Scout. Its body was contorted in a manner, which made the bile surge through his mouth. The body was arched at an impossible angle, the legs were pointed toward the back wall, but the upper torso, arms, head and shoulders were pointed directly at him. He tried to turn away and run; his false bravo had evaporated; now the coward in him was begging him to flee. He was transfixed, as if the thing in the cell had control his mind and it was forcing him to stare into its eyes.

OH, GOD ITS EYES, THERE WERE NO IRIS, JUST THE WHITES STARING AT HIM BECKONING HIM INTO INSANITY. The creature head had pivoted and was turned upside down in complete 360 degrees from the shoulders, forcing its neck to twist at an impossible angle. Saliva was dripping from the things mouth running down its chin and pooling on the floor. It kept chanting "Nudadequa" repeatedly and flickering it tongue in and out like a copperhead snake that Rodney spotted on the Dan River on one hot August afternoon. After the thing made sure that Rodney had slipped into the realm of insanity, it release him from his mental bondage. Old drunk Rodney, now turned into stark raving insane Rodney ran down the hall screaming and moaning at the top of his lungs, alerted the entire staff. They gasped in horror at the beast they encounter, but were finally able to sedate with enough tranquilizers that would kill a prehistoric T Rex, the most feared dinosaur of the Cretaceous period.

Several hours later, after the chief Psychologist viewed the video taken by the officers sedating the pitiful frail, small Indian women, Dr. Paul could not explain the body contortions with a diagnosis of acute Schizophrenic, because that diagnosis did not explain the superhuman strength of the women. He could not explain the stalking action, or how the body contorted into something that appeared to be inhuman. Dr. Paul, through his many clinical observations, could not shake the feeling that he was witnessing the women having some kind of out of body experience. Her body was there physically, but her mind was somewhere else stalking something for which it has deep consuming hatred. The doctor had also researched the word NUDADEQUA, and it appeared to be the Cherokee word for November moon. The doctor pushed back from his desk and suddenly had an uneasy, loathing feeling about super, blood moon that was forecasted to usher in the new month of November.

CHAPTER 12

Kelli paused for a moment before entering the cabin, in order to get her breathing and emotions in check. She opened the door, and caught a glimpse of the love of her life slaving over a hot stove cooking a breakfast that Chef Ramsey of Hell's kitchen would be proud.

"Well good morning rip van winkle", Kelli said softly, making sure her voice did not give away the extreme trauma that she had just endured.

"Ah my love muffin, did you enjoy your morning torture? Normal human beings like to sleep at least until eight am on their days off, besides had to make sure you weren't around to mess up my culinary masterpiece." Jake said in his own charming fashion. Jake turned, smiled, and held out his manly, muscled; arms and Kelli flew into his arms and braced him with a fierce hug, glad to be in the arms of the man that would protect her with his life. Jake held her for several minutes seeming to sense that his wife was troubled and frighten.

"Whoa, what's wrong little lady?" Jake said in a woefully, horrible impersonation of the Duke.

Kelli was silent for what seemed eternity, debating on whether to tell the truth about being stalked by a long dead tree, but in the end decided that her disclosure of a cannibalistic, mind controlling, satanic beast last night was all that Jake could deal with right now,

Kelli steeped back and looked at Jake with big, tear filled eyes and whispered

"Jake, I am terrified,"

Jake faced clouded over, his cheeks began to turn to a fiery red, and his big hands began to clinch with a sudden rage thinking of the bastard that had scared his wife.

"Baby who or what frighten you, if it was someone on that running path, I will hunt them down, and rip their windpipe out" Jake said already heading for the front door.

"Stop worrying Jake! You are the one scaring me so bad, with the God awful impersonation of my hero and idol John Wayne; in fact he would be rolling over in his grave with disgust!" Kelli said bursting out with laughter, Jake suddenly aware that we was being played lunged at her playfully and chased her down the hall. Kelli made it to the bathroom, and playfully shut the door in Jake's face.

Jake stood at the door wondering if she was going to invite him to shower with her, got his answer when she told her lover boy to get in kitchen and make a western omelet that John Wayne himself would be proud. Kelli wanted Jake to shower and then make love to her, but she needed her solitude to gather her composure. Jake would see right through the mask of calmness that was barely concealing her fear, and ask her a thousand questions finally forcing her to reveal that her PTSD was out of control. As the hot stream of water cascaded down from the showerhead began to chase the tension from her body, she thanked God for the acting classes that she had taken in college.

After a delectable breakfast, Kelli was calmly describing the itinerary for their Saturday, which included a brief stop in Mayodan NC for the small river town's annual Halloween festival, and a trip down the Virginia creeper, a sixteen-mile downhill cycling adventure. Jake rolled his eyes, and simply asked if they could just stay in bed and fine new ways to entertain each other. Kelli looked at Jake with her puppy dog eyes and mouthed the words please and that was all the convincing

Jake needed. He got up from the table to change clothes, and was greeted by two red flannel shirts neatly spread out on the bed.

" Really Kelli we will look like a couple of lumber jacks for the Yukon Peninsula," Jake bellowed but Kelli could tell by his bellow that Jake was secreted flatter they would match!

" Ah my love muscle, you know the old adage, when in Rome do as the Romans" Kelli squealed delighted to spend the entire day with the love of her life.

The Dodge Challenger that Jake rented from the airport roared to life, as Jake turned the key in the ignition. He knew that the 320 horses under hood would cover the 40 miles to Mayodan at the blink of an eye. Jake gunned the engines as his beautiful wife neared the passenger door, he wondered how he could ever live his life without her. Jake knew that something or someone had spooked her on that trail, and he knew that he was going to her home with him, even if he had to carry her over his shoulder!

Kelli was treating Jake a brief history of the town of Mayodan, as they drove the thirty minutes to the Halloween festival.

" The town is at the junction of the Mayo and Dan rivers, thus the name Mayodan. The township was mostly a mill community , and operated Mayo Mills, which slowly evolved into Tultex mills. In 1911, the Mill at Avalon burned to the ground, and the townspeople of Avalon simply used logs tied to mules to move the houses to Mayodan, since Avalon Mills and Mayo mills had the same owners" Kelli read from her smart phone.

"Ah the first MOBILE homes," Jake wisecracked crossing his eyes in a comical class clown fashion. Kelli ignored Jake and continued her history lesson. " The town of Mayodan been on the banks of these two rivers for over 200 years, and was a vibrant community until Chinese cheap imports , and NAFTA closed many of the mills in the mid-eighties, and have brought high unemployment rates that still persist even till today," Kelli read in a suddenly depressive tone.

As they crossed over the bridge, the small river town came into view, and Kelli noticed that some of the brick building had an architectural design of the 1800's, she could almost envision the bustling textile town of yester year. They parked their car near the city library, which had hay bales stacked in the form of a studious owl concentrating on a book perched on its lap. The book was labeled, The 200 year history of Mayodan NC, the artwork was so realistic that the eyes of the owl seemed to follow them down the street. As they neared the two streets closed off for the festival, Kelli's sense of smell was aroused by the scent of popcorn, cotton candy, funnel cakes, and hot dogs and hamburgers being cooked on an open grill. They strode hand in hand in their matching lumberjack shirts, trying to dodge all the children dashing around in their Halloween costumes, walking hand in hand with her man, Kelli suddenly realized this moment enhanced in the clarity of fall, would forever be a cherished memory.

Jake ran to the Ferris wheel like a 10-year-old child, pulling Kelli with him, saying something about conquering her fear of heights. Kelli, playfully dragged her heels, and forged a look of complete terror. The attendant opened the door to the steel cage that would transport them almost 30 feet off the ground, while staring at Kelli like a wolf would eyeing a piece of filet mignon. Jake noticed the wolf like stare of the attendant, but considered the stare a compliment to his super attractive wife. The cage rocked slightly due to the slight wind, as it lifted them higher toward the crest of the Ferris wheel. Jake and Kelli cage stopped at the top, and both Kelli and Jake drew in a sharp breath as the Sugar maples and Oak trees in their zenith of fall colors greeted them. They also had a bird's eyes view of the convergence of the Dan and Mayo rivers, for which the town of Mayodan was named.

The beauty of the scene and heighten sexual arousal which always peaks in the fall, caused the two to kiss with a red hot passion that could melt the ice cap at the Arctic circle. Both lovers would be horrified to know that two beady predatory eyes were locked on them, with the intensity of a multi-pixel camera. Black Bart made a mental note of the passionate kiss between Agent Kelli Ryan and her husband, because he knew that strong love could be powerful control mechanism. Bart smiled as he thought of his ole daddy say-in " Son the devil is in the details!" His thoughts were interrupted by his ball and chain.

" What you staring at honey, some kind of UFO or you dreaming about our intense love making session last night" Gloria Whitscarver asked

" How did you guess baby, ain't love a beautiful thing?" He said playfully smacking his wife of 40 years on her ample butt.

Jake and Kelli moaned as the Ferris wheel started to move again, which was probably a good thing because a few more minutes, and they would have both been arrested for indecent exposure. As they near the exit point, Kelli noticed Bart staring at them with evil intensity, and had a sudden impulse to question him some more in front of all the fine folk of Mayodan. But she chose to ignore him and walked right by him like he was invisible, for she was not going to let that piece of shit on the shoe of humanity ruin her perfect day with her man.

They browsed around the festival for another hour, checking our vendor booths that were selling items ranging from jewelry to knives. They stopped to watch the famous pumpkin roll, and listen to local ghost stories, but soon Kelli noticed that people were staring at her and whispering behind their back as they walked by, and suddenly Kelli had the urge get as far away from there as possible.

" Let's go Jake, ready to take you on your next adventure?" Kelli whispering trying to suppress her urge to run

" Ah my love, back to the cabin to finish what we started on the Ferris wheel?" Jake answered completely oblivious to the open stares of the townsfolk.

" Keep on dreaming my love, soon you will heading down a mountain on a bike at a break neck speed for sixteen miles", Kelli laughed as she grabbed her soul mates hand and headed for the exit. Jake just shook his head and began to wonder if his wife of eight years had progressed from having PTSD into full insanity.

CHAPTER 13

As they climbed Interstate 77, toward Wytheville, Virginia, Kelli was amazed by the vastness of the valley below her, it was so clear she could make out the city of Winston Salem, which was about 35 miles away. The Sauratown Mountains, Hanging Rock, and Pilot Mountain were in highlighted in a cloak of colors ranging from crimson red to medallion gold, Kelli involuntarily squeezed Jake's hand as the clarity of fall beauty made an impact on her mind and soul. Jake took his eyes off the road momentarily, alarmed by Kelli's sudden tight grip on his hand, and glanced at his radiate, stunning wife staring at him with such loving intensity that her emerald green eyes were brimming with tears of joy, and deep unbridled love.

Kelli, forever the tour guide, began to give Jake a brief synopsis of colorful history of The Virginia Creeper, which stretches 34 miles from Damascus to Abington Virginia, and use to carry Lumber, Iron ore, passengers, and supplies up the mountain all the way into North Carolina. The creeper construction was started in 1907, and by 1918 stretched all the way to North Carolina. Unfortunately, a late winter storm destroyed part of the creeper in 1977, but the state of Virginia, in their infinite wisdom converted the creeper to a Bike trail. The economy impact of his trail, which passes over 33 trestles and bridges and passes over the tops of beautiful Red Spruce Forrest has been a gold mine for the towns of Damascus and Abington Virginia.

" Dam I have to ride a bicycle for 16 miles, Kelly I know you think I'm superman, but I will not have enough energy to make sweet passionate love to you. And pedal a bike for 16 miles" Jake exclaimed excitedly. " So, which one would give you the most pleasure?" Jake said glancing at her with a mischievous grin.

" I think I will chose the bike ride, never have done that before, but I have DONE you many, many times" Kelli laughed.

The look on Jake's face was priceless, at look of abashed astonishment, and utter surprise flashed across Jake's face, so before Jake could slip into a deep , dark depression. Kelli explained that she could have both.

" Ah my love muscle, we are going to take a shuttle from Damascus to the top of White Top Mountain, and coast downhill for about 13 miles, unfortunately you will have to pedal the last three miles. Jake, if you can't pedal three miles, and then make wild, animal love to me you're fired," Kelli said with an evil gleam in her eye.

" OH Jake by the way, why do you think they called it the Virginia Creeper?," by the way your answer will determine my arousal level at the end of the ride," Kelli asked with a wicked smile. Jake was solo surprised that Kelli lobbed him such an easy question, with such important consequences hanging in the balance, blurted out without considering all the options,

" I guess loaded with all weight of passengers, lumber, and iron ore, the train crept up the mountain" ! Jake bellowed confident that the answer would secure him a deeply satisfying time with his love muffin.

" Jake it's just not your day, the Virginia creeper is also named for the wild flowers that grow near its tracks" Kelli answered almost felt sorry for her love Muscle.

" Fell right into the trap set by the mean ole FBI agent" Jake mumbled, faking a look of pure despair.

Upon arriving in Damascus, and 30 minutes after

taking the shuttle up the Mount Rogers, they were standing at white top station, with their rental bikes pointing downhill. Jake bellowed a yell, that would have made Tarzan jealous, took off like Lance Anderson in the Tour de France. The seven percent grade of the mountain, allow for almost a no pedaling downhill trip. The amazing trail traveled through an astonishing and dizzying array of fall colors, and the roaring river crashing over huge boulders heighten their sexual arousal that had been initiated on the Ferris wheel at the Mayodan fall festival. After passing over a high trestle, nearing 200 feet off the ground, and high above the deciduous forest peaking with fall colors, the two lovers could not contain their animal lust for each other. They hid their bikes behind a thick mountain laurel bushes, strategically placed there by divine intervention. Kelli grabbed the blanket that she had covertly hidden in her backpack, and Jake smiled knowing that his queen had planned this liaison from the very beginning of their romantic day. They made love by the roaring river, passion rose from their bodies, like the river water hitting the massive boulders. Kelli's orgasmic screams of pleasure where muted by the roaring current of the river. Afterward as they rested beside the river, Jake laughed and then whispered to his soul-mate,

" Thank God for the river, or we would have been arrested" and they both laughed in unison.

Kelli then looked into the crystal blue eyes of the soul that she would love for eternity, and whispered " Jake thank you for the most wonderful day of my life, I will love you for eternity."   Later around 7 pm as they were traveling down Interstate 77, Kelli noticed the massive size of the moon as it illuminated the entire valley below her.

"Jake look at that huge moon, it has a red glow around it"

'" My love that is a super, blue, blood moon, happens about every 150 years. It a massive super moon, and because it's orbit is taking it closer to the Earth than any other time;

It is fourteen percent bigger and thirty percent brighter than a regular moon. It is a blue moon because it is the second full moon in October. Finally it's a blood moon because the earth is sitting between the Sun and Moon, thus the red twinge surrounding it". Jake said finishing his seminar of the lunar positioning on Halloween night.

" You are a man of infinite knowledge and wisdom Mr. Jake Ryan, and your all mine," Kelli whispered nibbling on his earlobe.

" Whoa little lady, how am I supposed to concentrate on my driving"? Jake asked

Jake then turned his attention to the great Sauratown Mountains, it silhouette in the silvery moonlight looked like a body, and then he said, " Pilot Mountain looks like a decapitated head, detached from the rest of the body".

Kelli turned and looked with Jake in amazement, because that was the first thing that she thought the day Director King picked them up at the airport. She then realized that great minds think alike, or at least those that souls are linked for eternity.

Kelli than received a text from Sam , explaining that according to the lab report on the DNA found near on the ground near Vade Mecum springs did not match those found at the top of Moore's knob!!! Suddenly the moon that was so magical and awesome had taken an ominous turn in her mind to a moon of terrifying horror. Kelli had no idea that her premonition was on point , because before this super moon disappears from the heavens , two Federal agents will vanish and a son will try to assassinate his father.

PART 5

BAD MOON ARISING

November One, 2017

CHAPTER 1

As they laid intertwined in each other arms, Kelli decided to notify her boss Paul Jacobs that was no need to send a panel of FBI internal affairs, which included three shrinks to evaluate her ,because she was going to resign from the case. The last day spent with Jake had convinced her that this case was poison to her marriage, and she was not going to let anything interfere with her relationship with the snoring Rip van winkle sleeping next to her. Kelli had her mind made up. until the apparition of Brian Cox appeared before her, and through some kind of telepathic communication begged her to avenge his death and bring his killer to justice. The ghost of Brain Cox was weeping sending a shrill yell through Kellie brain, begging her not to let his death be labeled a suicide , that label would tarnish his career and have terrible financial consequences denying both pension and insurance benefits to his offspring. The ghost then sat on her midsection howling like a banshee, bringing her out of her deep sleep. Kelli sat up in the bed terrifying, shaking but unbelievably with a resumed, tenacious desire to avenge the death of her and Jake's beloved friend.

The next morning Kelli woke up early in the morning, dedicated herself to work from dawn to dust meticulously on an extremely mysterious case with increasing supernatural overtones. Jake still sleeping in the adjoining bedroom, and would be extremely valuable asset with his divergent thinking skills, otherwise known as thinking out of the box. Kelli reached for her ninth generation government issued smart phone, a phone issued by the FBI immune to any hacking by any spy technology. Sam Jenkins on the second ring,

" Hey Sam have you missed me?" Kelli asked with a slight twinge of guilt for deserting her crew during a very critical stage of the investigation.

" Always miss your sharp analytic thinking and deductive reasoning skills chief!" chuckled the good-natured Jenkins.

Kelli always getting to the point asked her trusted colleague to give her an update on the case, she needed that information to formulate her plan of action if she was allowed to be lead investigator in the case. Sam gave Kelli a complete run down of the objectives that she had listed before she was released from the hospital.

" OK chief it was a brilliant idea to re-walk the grid where Chad Whitescarver's mummified corpse was found, because Running deer found the same traces of the minerals that he found along the ridge line after the slayings on Moore's knob, connecting the two murders! We also have been following Black Bart daily trying to get him to leave some of his DNA behind on anything he touches, like a coffee cup or fast food wrappers, but he is as nervous as a whore in church. He makes sure that he takes anything he touches with him, but Running Deer is tenacious and believe we will get a sample soon. I have however been able to get warrant to secure his cell phone records, and he was in constant contact with a Pedro Gonzales about the same time that Shaun O'Toole disappeared. We all scoured the Moore's knob area, and didn't find any additional evidence that will assist us." Sam continued with his list of accomplishments since Kelli went off the grid.

"We interviewed Bill O'Toole, still in much grief over losing his son, but he indicated that his son was acting skidish, like he was terrified of something. He gave us a list of Shaun's friends and acquaintances, and we are in the process of interviewing them right now. We have set up the command center at the hotel at Vada Mecum Springs, also assembled a cell phone surveillance team, and have CODIS, VICAP up, and running. Finally, Dr. Drake interview was short and sweet, as he refused to answer any questions about his family's bad blood with the Whites carver clan. We did pull his employment records, and found that he was a professor at the same Collage that Accalia Blackclaw attended." Sam exhaled on the last sentence as if he was extremely fatigued by the lengthy review

" Great job Sam, get Pedro Gonzales and Dr. Drakes fingerprints posthaste and run them through CODIS, also get your hands on some stingrays, or IMSI devices that will stimulate cell towers in the area. We can then trick Gonzalez's cell phone to send calls, texts, and data streams right to our front doors! " Kelli continued, "Also put a tail on Sheriff Brown, I want you to get a warrant for his cell phone records, he is definitely a covert operative for Black Bart! Finally compile those interviews with all of Shaun acquaintances, and get a list of employees and colleagues at the Stokes Collage that knew of the inappropriate relationship between Drake and Accalia and email me that information by the end of the day!" Kelli suddenly heard her secret weapon begin to stir in the adjoining bedroom, so she thanked Sam and Running Deer for their hard work as she disconnected the call.

CHAPTER 2

Kelli turned to see the most beautiful man that she had ever seen enter the room, and she silently thanked God for giving him to her. " Ah my love muscle looking hot even at 8:00 o'clock on as Sunday morning!" Kellie purred.

" I don't feel like your sincere with your accolades, and I believe that action speaks louder than words" Jake smiled and held out his arms. Kelli rushed into the arms of the only man she would ever love, and kissed with a passion that a wife that a wife usually reserved for a husband returning from battle. They made love with wild abandon, almost breaking the king sized mahogany bed that had until today held up under a savage onslaught for the last couple of days.

"Guess they can take it out of my deposit" Kelli gasped between their loved sessions, and then exploded with Laughter.

After they both had taken a hot shower, Jake announced to Kelli that she should come home with him, and leave this case to someone not affected with PTSD.

" Kelli I have seen the cracks in your stoic personification, you are in no mental state to continue this case. I want you to come back home with me".! Jake said sternly looking deeply into her emerald green eyes.

Kelli was surprised by Jake's demands, because he had never tried to control her before, " Jake I agree with you, but I feel that I owe it to Brain Cox and his family to find his killer and clear his name. We owe it to him since he saved our lives nearly eight years ago on Portsmouth Island." Kelli said with tears welling in her eyes.

" Kelli I can appreciate your loyalty to Brian, but this commitment to Brian may be affecting your ability to be objective , and objectivity on this case. That thing I saw on the deceased sheriff's body camera is not human, and I have a very bad feeling about how this case is going to end." Jake pleaded his cheeks turning a bright red, his light blue eyes sending out lightning bolts of passion.

" Ah Jake we have conquered the supernatural before, that's why I am uniquely conditioned for this case, besides when I meet with the internal affairs department tomorrow they may agree with you, and I will be in loving arms by tomorrow evening." Kelli continued her plea to stay on the case.

"Jake, you know that I'm a fighter being the daughter of a special forces solider, and I simply just can't through in the towel." Kelli voice amplified with strong conviction convinced her Husband that she was not going to walk an away from a fight, even it cost her life.

Jake shrugged his shoulders and thought of the famous cliché "It is the very things that you love about someone, that can irritate you the most about them." He then looked down at his beautiful wife, radiating with a mixture of deep love for him and strong will of conviction, that he finally nodded his head and said " What the hell we standing here dong idle Chit chat, lets solve this dam case" Jake said demonstrating one of his lit up room smiles.

"Ah that's my love muscle," Kelli laughed kissing her man on the lips with a passion that would stop a speeding bullet. Jake listen intently as Kelli relayed the information that Sam had passed on during their 30-minute phone call. Jake wrote some notes on Kelli laptop as his wife debrief him.

" Kelli that's great news about the weird mineral particles appearing at both Moore's knob and location of Chad Whitscarver body on the Dan River, because it links to two crimes together. I believe that you are putting too much emphasis on Black Bart, put your resources on Sheriff Brown, he is the missing link. He sent Brian Cox and the others to their deaths to cover up crimes committed by Black Bart's henchman. We have a slender Indian woman in custody, and I believe she is just a scapegoat, set up to distract law enforcement from the real killers. That thing on the body armor camera of the murdered those deputies was and still is being controlled by Black Bart and David Barrett". Jake concluded

"So Jake do you actually believe any mortal man could control that thing we witnessed on the Deputy Miller's body camera? And how did that slender scapegoat's DNA get in that gully near Vade Mecum springs?" "Finally Kelli asked and the Deputies DNA that were murdered on the blanket the trucker gave her to keep her warm?"

"Kelli that a tough questions to answer until more lab work can be done." Jake said, the wrinkle on his forehead deepen.

"Ah Jake those were the easy questions, how is that the DNA from the fang embedded in Deputy Powers femur does not match the DNA found in the Vade Mecum Springs area?" Kelli asked her green eyes glimmering like emeralds.

Kelli then completely shocked Jake by telling him that the way the DNA could differ is that Accalia Blackclaw was not suffering from Disassociate personality disorder, but that she was the physical shell for a Cherokee Indian shape shifter called Hicictawi'a.

"So Jake you are partially right Acacia Black claw is indeed a scapegoat, but it's not for Bart Whitcarver or David Barret, but for the violent and cruel Hicictawi'a shape shifter"

"I believe that the psychic visions that I witness in the interrogation room and the visions that made Brian Cox jump off Moore's knob were generated by Hicictawi'a, and I fear that we have just witnessed the tip of the iceberg of its power.

CHAPTER 3

About the same time Kelli and Jake were having there intense debate, Bill Jr. was waking up with an intense hangover, after drinking too much tequila on Halloween night. He and his current girlfriend were wrapped up in the sheets in the upstairs bedroom of his best friend's house; his girl was still passed out in a semi-comatose state. Bill Jr. sat up in the bed, glanced at his cell phone and somehow managed to suppress his fear, his father the man with the immense heart and volcanic temper had expected him home two hours ago. Since Shaun was murdered, his dad had been over protective of him, as he examined his phone more intently he noticed that his father had left several voice mails. Filled with adrenaline, Bill sprang outta of the bed, hurried to get his clothes on, and flew down the stairs, open the front door and ran to his car. He gunned the engines, waking everyone in the house, except for his slumbering girlfriend, who was now stranded about 50 miles from her home.

As Bill Jr. sped down the road, he slowed down and grinned as he thought to himself "Why am I speeding down the road? That ole Bastard will be dead tomorrow!" Then Bill Jr. began to laugh hideously, yep that AK47 complete with bump-stock in the trunk, which had mysteriously appeared in his car one bright sunny day was going to help him to not only murder is father, but to slaughter him. Black Bart had texted him, and the unholy alliance wanted Bill Sr. assassinated on Monday, November 2. They wanted Bill Jr. to make it look like a professional hit, a double tap two to the chest and one to head, but Bill Jr. was so angry with his father for disinheriting him that he was going to unload the whole magazine on his father. Bill Jr. laughed insanely to himself, as he thought of the body of his father riddled with bullets. Ah, yes a professional hit done by a compulsive killer, who wanted to do a thorough job. When Bill Jr. got home and his father was racking him over the coals being late and not calling, Bill Jr. just stared at his father with a blank look on his face, thinking about how he was going to place a round right in his Dad's big ole trap.

"Dam it Junior there are some hogs that needed to be fed this morning" Bill Sr. raged. Bill Jr. just stared ahead listening as his father chastised him, but his Dad had just given him a great idea,

"Hey Dad how would you like to be Hog shit" he thought almost bursting out laughing.

" Now Junior I have to meet with several folks later on today in order to stop those dam permits Abbott Gas are filing to frack here in Stokes County.   Mercury Johnson, from the EPA has a brilliant idea to at least temporary halt Abbott Gas drilling on Colonel Anderson property. Drilling on that property is going to start tomorrow, unless we can get a judge to sign this injunction. She is going to use some endangered animals on Paul Williams land reserve to slow down or stop drilling in Stokes County. I will be gone most of the day, think you can handle the chores at the ranch while I'm gone?"

"Sure Dad". Bill Jr. answered flashing a brilliant smile, because his Dad has unwittingly given him great information to give his new employers.   Bill stared at his Son, and then gave his wife Beth a worried glance, his son was acting very strange, even for him! Maybe his brother's death how a greater impact on him than he thought. Maybe he was on Meth, which was a terrible problem here in Stokes County. God he wished he could get his hands on the bastard that was cooking that shit. Little did Bill senior realize that he was going to get his chance very soon.

CHAPTER 4.

Deputy sheriff Jackson almost burst out laughing, when he saw the small, weasel looking man with the huge bifocals sit down with Accalia Blackclaw. He was about thirty years her senior to the stunning looking petite, dark skinned beauty, but there they were holding hands in the visitation room of the jail like two love drunk honeymooners. The visitation room was very small and only had three tables that the jailbirds could get unconditional love from family members. The love was definitely unconditional because, coining a saying from his dear departed daddy, "Most of these drug addicted inmates were not worth the power to blow them into hell," thought Deputy Jackson.

Deputy Jackson had heard all about the Indian women being possessed by some kind of demon. She drove poor ole Rodney O'Neil insane by contorting her body in a way, which was not humanly possible. Although it was not polite to stare, Deputy Jackson could not take his eyes off the bronzed skin beauty.

Dr. Drake looked intensely into his secret weapon's eyes not out of love, but to telepathically instruct the beast within her.

"IT IS ALMOST TIME TO AVENGE YOUR PEOPLE, AND THE SUPER NUDADEQUA WILL PROTECT YOU. THE EVIL PALEFACES DAVID BARRETT AND BLACK BART WHITESCARVER ARE YOUR PRIMARY TARGETS; THEY MUST BE KILLED IN THE MOST VIOLENT MANNER. THEY ARE THE ONES RESPONSIBLE FOR DRILLING DEEP IN THE HEART OF MOTHER

EARTH; YOU KILL THEM AND THE VIOLATION INTO THE HEART OF MOTHER EARTH WILL CEASE. YOU ARE THEN TO GO TO THE FRACKING WELL PAD ON COLONEL ANDERSON'S PROPERTY AND Completely DESTROY IT, KILLING ANY ONE THAT TRIES TO STOP YOU." As he was giving instructions to Hicictawia, Drake could feel the soul of Accalia screaming in pain and agony to stop all the killing and he felt a pang of quilt and sorrow for her, but shrugged it off for she was just collateral damage.

The moon was just too strong, and Accalia after all was just a human shell, she was too weak like a jellyfish trying to fight off a tidal wave. Dr. Drake kissed the hands of his beautiful Accalia, then dropped her hands and started to get up, but he was violently grabbed by Accalia, who was trying to wrap her hands around the good Doc's windpipe! Deputy Jackson acted swiftly and tased the object of affection with extreme prejudice. As she fell to the floor, Jackson will never forget the pupils of eyes as they elongated to the point that they looked reptilian. He suddenly remembered the book he had read several years ago that claims that the Nation's capital is controlled by alien reptilian shape shifters bent on destroying the entire human race and a cold shiver ran down the length of his spine.

Dr. Drake witnessed the spectacle of Accalia being handcuffed and roughly manhandled with a cold detachment; after all, he was a raging sociopath and did not have any human emotions. In fact the only two thoughts he had as he got into his Jag was how he masterfully manipulated Accalia to bring forth the destruction of Abbott Gas, David Barret, and his nemesis Black Bart simultaneously, and how glad that he bribed his contact at Black Bart cell phone provider to place a small bug on his cell phone.

CHAPTER 5

Upon viewing the video from the visitation room, Dr. Paul ordered Accalia to be placed on a thorazine drip for four hours, so he could observe her symptoms and diagnose her condition with higher accuracy. During his twenty year career, Dr. Paul had thousands of patients and had been successful in his diagnose of all of his patients eventually, but Accalia condition wouldn't fit into any of the personality disorders, including the famous multi personality disorder. Although she did exhibit Schizophrenia and bipolar symptoms, these conditions were also ruled out. Dr. Paul soon began to believe that the only condition that fit all her symptoms was a possession by another entity, whether its origins were demonic or extraterrestrial he could not ascertain.

As he observed her, he could sense a quickening of something deep inside her. Her eyes were glowing like the super moon that was shining through the small windows of the observation room. He watched her now, as she stood on the only chair in the room, peering at the moon with great intensity. For a brief moment Dr. Paul had a foreboding premonition that this meek , slight Indian was going to start baying at the moon like some deranged werewolf from a B rated horror film. She seemed to be drawing power from the moon, as if the moon was like large batteries charging her for an impossible mission. He also notice a deep sadness within her soul, and under sedation, she would cry out in agonizing pain " No More Killing"!. She seemed to be in deep conflict with the entity that consumed her, her human side was very kind and compassionate, but that good side was slowly being consumed by a force that came directly from the bowels of hell. Dr. Paul slowly began to understand that Accalia's possessor was being empowered by the super moon in the heavens, and that once the thing reached its fully charged state, which unholy terror was going to consume the entire Dan River valley!

CHAPTER 6

As the chilling rain battered the windowpane, Kelli and Jake spent most of the day Sunday diagramming the complexities of the case, labeling each facet of the case from crime scenes to the possible unsubs.

"Kelli we need to find out all we can about Mr. David Barrett, my research indicates that he is a bad Hombre, with no conscious. So far he has been successful in getting the moratorium on fracking rescinded and obtains many of the acres of land, that Abbott Gas coveted, including the land of staunch opponent to Hydraulic Fracturing Colonel Anderson." As soon as Jake mentioned David's name he shuttered, because he was horrified by the thought of what the mind magician could do with Kelli's fragile mind as she battles the demons of PSTD. She would be like putty in his hands. Jake then mentioned the mummified corpse of Chad Whitescarver, and the complete draining of intercellular fluid from the corpse.

"Trust me, Doctor Drake is the missing link on this, draining a body of fluids is done every day by a mortician, so hello Mcfly, who is the only ghoul that has the medical knowledge accomplish this?" Jake asked dramatically arching his eyebrows like Sherlock Homes.

"Great ideas Jake, so on the list of unsubs we have David Barrett, Black Bart, Abbott gas, Dr. Drake, and Sheriff Brown. I'm going to subpoena all their computers, cell phone records, and put a tail on Drake and Brown"

"You forgot Accalia Blackclaw and that shape shifter thingy," Jake asked looking sharply at his spouse

"No I didn't, one is an innocent victim and the other is a horrifying terrorist that is fighting injustices brought upon its people. Well Jake it's going to be a big day tomorrow, what do you say we turn in early?" Kelli said turning toward the bedroom.

"Dam Kelli it's only 8:00 pm, it's too early to go to sleep" Jake said pouting like a small child. Kelli winked her love muscle and asked, "Who said anything about sleeping?"

Jake then turned that frown into a smile, and kicked of his shoes and ripping off his shirt beating his wife into bed, which has had its box springs severely tested in the last two days. After making passion love, they fell asleep cradled in each other arms, totally unaware that a covert evil operation was striking with malice into the heart of the resistance.

CHAPTER 7

Mercury Johnson was masterfully driving the lumbering, monstrous black suburban around the hairpin turns on Hwy 8; the government issued vehicle was fantastic for urban areas, its sleek design and V8 engines intimidating the mere mortals with 355-horsepower, causing them the scatter like cockroaches. The over-sized SUV was difficult to control on this narrow winding stretch of road , and Mercury wished that she was back home in her new Toyota Corolla.

The huge super moon was illuminating the road, so headlights were optional, Mercury laughed as she thought of the idiot drivers that drive without headlights even when there was a moon. Mercury was in high spirits, her meeting with Bill O'Toole and Paul Williams had deepen her resolve to file a petition against fracturing in Stokes County, she reasoned that if snails and bats could stop the mighty Atlantic coast and Colonial pipelines, the list of 10 endangered species on Paul Williams preserve would stop Abbott Gas dead in its tracks.

Mercury was in deep thought, as she reflected on how the current administration in the white house seems to have deep disrespect for laws that are in place to protect the fragile ecosystems throughout the Country. The new President has cut EPA spending across the board. He even threatens to dismantle environmental laws that lay the foundation for protection of our most precious renewable resource clean fresh water. The Clean Water Act of 1972 is under intense pressure to be modified to accommodate our countries mad desire to cultivate domestic fossil fuels like oil, gas, and coal. Mercury was so deep in thought, that as first she did not notice the red and blue flashing lights rapidly approaching her SUV from behind.

Mercury quickly checked her speed, and confirmed that she was indeed driving the speed limit, mostly because if one did not conform to the speed limit they would end up cutting down trees with their front bumper. Mercury then reasoned that the police officer was in hot response to a 911 call or a crime in progress and would pass her. Mercury slowed the suburban down, but to her amazement, the police car slowed and then turned on its siren. Mercury deeply aware that she was alone on a rural highway late at night, reached down underneath the seat for her .45 caliber Smith and Wesson, and stopped the vehicle on the shoulder of the road.

The lights from the cop car reflected on the crimson red, and canary yellow fall canopy of colors, highlighting them in a visual stunning fashion. The officer exited his car with his glock in one hand and a flashlight in the other. Mercury wondered why the officer even had a flashlight under such intense moonlight. Mercury froze in the car, and shouted into the night air identifying herself as a Federal Agent of the EPA. Mercury looked in the rear view mirror, and was surprised to a man with a receding patch of gray hair, and amused herself by thinking "I definitely could out draw this old geezer".

"Ma'am please step out of the car, with your identification and car's registration," the sheriff ordered.

"Why are you stopping me, I was not breaking the speed limit!" Mercury quickly responded.

"I'm sorry your vehicle matches the description of a stolen SUV reported stolen from Walnut Cove about an hour ago. I am sorry for the inconvenience, get out and show your me your ID and registration, and I will let you go" the officer explained in a gentle and calm voice.

"Why don't you just enter my license plate number into your dash board computer?" Mercury asked her uneasiness increasing by the minute

" Well ashamed to say, but my system is down right now, county budget does not allocate funding for high tech computers and such, in case you haven't noticed were kind of in the sticks. Just show me your government ID, so I can send you your way. I'm sure you better things to do" the sheriff chuckled. Mercury was getting rather impatient, it had been a long day and this unplanned stop was preventing her for some much needed pillow time.

"Okay lets compromise, holster your weapon and I will retrieve the documents you desire" Mercury said sternly, so the sheriff would not mistake the steel determination in her voice.

"Sounds fair to me" the elderly sheriff complied holstering his weapon and slowly but cautiously approached the SUV. Mercury watched the Sheriff Brown approach, his name-tag becoming more legible as he got closer. Mercury relaxed a bit, but still had the safety disengaged on her 45. When Sheriff Brown approached the driver's window, he tapped gently on the window glass with his flashlight, expressing his desire that Mercury roll down her window. Mercury hesitated not ready to erase the last barrier between her and the potential serial killer. Mercury rolled down the window just enough to pass the documents to the sheriff. With the help of the bright moonlight, the Sheriff was able to review the documents with the naked eye.

"Everything seems to be in order, but do you have the vehicle registration?" He then added his reasoning for the request "just to prove that this is a government vehicle". Mercury looked at the aged police officer with disbelief, but turned to retrieve the paperwork from the glove box, which in the spacious cab required Mercury to take her eyes off Brown. Brown knew that the window of opportunity would only last a second, so he brought his 9-millimeter handgun up to eye level. Mercury indistinctly knew she was in deep shit, so as she straighten up she pushed all her weight against the driver side door. She violently pushing the door open against a shocked Brown, who was standing within a foot of the door. The impact of the door knocked Brown back, and the panther like speed that Mercury pounced upon the older man with almost superhuman speed.

The first strike was a front kick to Brown's family jewels, and as the good sheriff was doubled over, the second strike was a roundhouse kick to the left temple of Brown's over-sized cranium rendering the senior cop unconscious on the cold, hard cement of Hwy 8. The man hiding in the tree line could barely contain his laughter, He had neglected to tell that narcissist, bull headed old fart, that Mercury Johnson was a fourth degree black belt, but playtime was over and he knew that he had little time to clean up this mess. He walked out of the woods, calm and collected; he was dressed in special ops black, from head to toe, with a ski masked pulled over his face. He saw Mercury retrieving her cell phone from her purse, and he just couldn't let her complete that 911 call, so he brought the rifle to a prone position and fired the tranquilizing dart which found its mark on Mercury's left hip.

Mercury had just reached her phone, and about a millisecond from dialing 911, when the dart struck her, she felt as if a bee had just stung her, and the last thought she would have before she was rendered unconscious was "why was there a bee out on a cold night in November?"

The man in black reached down and placed the ammonia cap under the napping Sheriff's nose. The old bastard began to stir, and the man in black just threw back his head and howled at the moon like a caged animal, the sound didn't sound human except for a tad bit of unbridled joy and amusement. The look on the bewildered Sheriffs face was priceless, as he shook his head violently to remove the cobwebs of a nasty ass kicking.

" I heard of sleeping on the job, but seriously Sheriff right out here on lonesome Highway, why you could have been run over!!" laughed the man in black.

"What the hell happen?" asked the obvious concussion suffering Brown

"Well I'll tell you Sheriff, you just got your ass whipped by a 120 pound Woman. Now get your old ass up and help me put your ass-whipper in the back seat of that black SUV, or can you see colors yet?"

Sheriff Brown wobbly got to his feet. He resembled a prizefighter that just TKO-ed in the eighth round, but through super human strength, or just wanting his man card back, helped load the unconscious agent into the SUV. He started to walk back to retrieve the police car.

"What the hell are you doing? Leave that dam car were it is, nothing more obvious than a stolen police car, taken by recently fired Sheriff. She must have kicked your last brain cell lose."

He was proud that the whole kidnapping, had only had taken about ten minutes. When the local police arrive, they will just find an abandon police car that had been whipped clean of fingerprints, as if the cop car was in eternal pursuit of a phantom that it will never catch. The old wives tale says there are mysterious happens under a full moon, but under a super full moon someone always disappears.

CHAPTER 8

Jake woke early Monday morning, squinting as the sun shone through the only window in the bedroom, he indistinctly felt for his for the love of his life, but only could fell the residual heat left from her beautiful body. He called her name but she did not answer. His heart leaped in his chest worried that she had decided to run around the lake again! Jake had a weird vibe about Shadow Lake, the place just exuded evil. Jake heard Kelli's voice from the adjoining room, her voice had an excited, high pitch tone, as if the news she was receiving was very shocking. Jake hurried to the door, and quickly locked eyes with his soul-mate,

"Thank you Inspector King. Thank you for your support, yes I will see you at 10.00 am" Kelli then disconnected the call. She got up and buried her head in Jake's shoulder, and told him to put his big strong arms around her, and never let her go. She explained to Jake that Agent Mercury Johnson, of the Environmental Protection Agency had disappeared on Hwy 8 late last night, a special BOLO was issued for her late model Suburban this morning by the State Police. She never returned to her hotel room last night after her meeting with Bill O'Toole and Paul Williams.

"Our friend Sheriff Brown's signature is all over this abduction. A police car was reported stolen from the lot near the police substation around seven this morning. No, sign of a breaking and entering, which leads one to ascertain that it an inside Job. Sheriff Green, sent deputies out to arrest Brown, but it seems are Ex- sheriff is in the wind, he has vanished into thin air." Kelli said. "Inspector King was just calling to inform me that he will be attending my consultation with the office of professional responsibility, or OPR. He also gave his unwavering support, and stressed that I need to stay on the case more than ever now." Jake held his wife for a few moments, looked down at his most prized possession, and lied!

"I now have got to take a shower, and catch my flight back to civilization, and you my brilliant profiler have a hearing to attend." Jake looked at his cell phone it was almost eight am and his flight left Piedmont International airport at 10 Am. After he showered and shaved, he meet his wife at the front door and gave her a warm embrace.

"I truly hope that the OPR finds you competent to continue the investigation," Jake whispered in his soul mate's ear, luckily, Kelli did not see that his fingers were crossed behind his back. Jake kissed his wife lips passionately and silently wondered if he would ever see her again. Kelli watched Jake as he walked to the car. She gave him a forced smile and wave, and shouted

"Hopefully I will see you tonight!" He shouted with a wide Jake grin on his beautiful face. Kelli faked a laugh, and silently wondered if she would ever see him again!

CHAPTER 9

As the Kelli walked up to the Old Stokes County Courthouse on Main Street, she was amazed by the 1800 architecture, the ominous building of power conveyed a message of abandon all hope, judgment is upon you to those poor souls that passed through its massive doors. The building was monolithic with four huge white thirty-foot pillars, supporting a triangle shaped structure with writing that advises one to Be Just and Fear Not. The old heavy oak door was in the middle behind the pillars, while there were six windows on each side of the door. The windows were symmetrically perfect; the lower windows were directly underneath the upper windows. The strangest design was the large concave looking structure at the very top, with two circular windows which were again perfect in their symmetrical design, to Kelli the concave structure has a like a giant human head with two beady eyes staring down on her!

"Whoa you nut job, you haven't even reached the front door yet" Kelli thought silently admonishing herself.

The courthouse was beautiful on the inside, with two-spiral staircase made of Black Cherry wood winding their way down to the ground floor. The administrative offices of Stokes County public schools were located on the second floor, while the lower sections dealt with minor civil disputes. The New Courthouse a mile down the road, constructed in 2003 dealt with the due process of law concerning misdemeanors and felonies. Kelli rounded corner, and bumped into Doctor Sloan, and a wave of relief washed throughout her body.

"Dr. Sloan thank God for coming, there trying to lynch me here," Kelli said laughing.

"No problem Kelli, in fact I was ordered here by senior agent Jacobs. He wanted to make sure that you had some type of defense." replied Dr. Sloan while eyeballing Kelli for any outward signs of stress that could be linked to...

"Did I make this trip in vain Agent Ryan?" Dr. Sloan asked his eyebrows arched.

"No flashbacks, or visions or twitches doc, I am fit as a fiddle," Kelli said lying through her teeth. She had several weird encounters like the one on the plane, in the morgue, at the lake, but her mind rationalized those episodes as stress from the case. They rounded the corner, and entered the magistrate's room, which now was converted to a small courtroom, perfect for the ambush by police internal affairs FBI counterpart the OPR.

Three top psychologists from the anti-terrorist unit were positioned in the front of the room, their microphones placed auspiciously in front of them. They were directly in front of Kelli, and seemed to be glaring at her with a burning intensity. They seem to be watching for any physical signs of PTSD manifesting in her body language. Kelli took her seat between Dr. Sloan, and Dr. Paul, and Inspector King of the SBI was sitting directly behind her. The court stenographer began to record as Dr. Garcia, PHD in Psychology began to ask a litany of probing questions, and the pace of the questions seemed to be designed to bring to the surface any symptoms of PTSD like angry outbursts, or nervous twitching.

Kelli answered each question rationally and professionally, with no outward signs of becoming unhinged, inspector King was very impressed by Kellie demeanor under pressure. The panel then turned its attention to Dr. Sloan, who listed all the desensitization and reprocessing therapy that had been successful in treating Kelli. Dr. Sloan had repeated rather sharply that he would never authorized Kelli for the mission if the cognitive and exposure therapy had failed. Dr. Sloan spoke for at least thirty minutes with passion and empathy, and when he indignantly took his seat, no one in the room questioned his loyalty and commitment to his patient.

Dr. Paul then was brought to the chopping block, as Chief Psychologist of the Stokes County Detention center, and who had been observing Accalia Blackclaw since her incarceration. Although his first diagnosis was simple schizophrenia, or possible dissociative identity disorder, he changed his opinion to demonic possession after witnessing the video taken after Accalia drove fellow prisoner Rodney O'Neil mad. Dr. Paul went on to argue that because of her possession Accalia was a psychic lighting rod, capable of transferring horrifying images into others subconscious. He then offered his professional opinion that it was Accalia psychic gifts, not PTSD that was responsible for Kelli's nervous breakdown in the interrogation room. Dr. Helen Holt, or the OCR, laughed at Dr. Paul and asked

"So doctor you are suggesting that we all are dealing with a simple case of demonic possession, should we call in a Catholic priest to treat your modern day Linda Blair?" After Holt's sarcastic remark, the entire panel laughed, but the laughter stopped when Dr. Paul turned off the lights and played the video of Accalia's body twisted and contorted at impossible angles. Oh Yes, Dr. Paul had just stumped the panel. The OCR felt the ramifications of a case that pressed the boundaries of sanity.

Finally, Inspector King testified that although the SBI had arrested Accalia's for the massacre the case was multifaceted and had several layers of investigation to peel back. He also mentioned that an EPA inspector had disappeared this morning and Kelli was needed more than ever in an increasing bizarre case.

" So Inspector King, You want an agent that barely escaped with her life eight years ago, and still is suffering from the trauma of that case to lead another investigation into the paranormal and supernatural?" asked incredulously Dr. Helen Holt..

"That is exactly why she is perfect for this case, Agent Ryan is a brilliant agent and her dealing with the supernatural just make her the most dangerous weapon that we have at our disposal. I recommend that she be allowed to continue this case, and if I am wrong I will surrender my pension!" Inspector King then nodded at Kelli and sat down.

"Inspector King, why is agent Ryan still needed?" You have a suspect in custody!" Dr. Holt asked. Inspector King then turned off the lights, and showed the body cam video of Mack Peter and Donnie Miller's slaughter, and suddenly the room was deathly quiet. Inspector King turned the lights back on, and calmly asked Dr. Holt in a calm Perry Mason's voice,

"Now Dr. Holt does the small, frail, women in custody even remotely resemble that beast from the third of dimension of hell?"

Dr. Helen Holt eyes were dilated from pure fright, as she whispered a quivering "NO", and all her peers were so glad that DR. Holt finally understood that they were not in their ivory towers of academia, but where in the of harsh reality of the real world. Kelli could have kissed Inspector King on the cheek at that moment, because she knew that if were not for Dr. Sloan, Dr. Paul, and Inspector King She would be boarding the next flight home.

In the end the OCR panel of Doctors, voted to allow Kelli to stay on the case, Kelli felt euphoric and exonerated as if a weight had been lifted off her chest. Kelli shook each man's hand, and she wanted to hug him but that would have breached FBI protocol. Inspector King winked at Kelli and said,

284

"Now that I put my neck out for you, get your Ass to work"

Sam Jenkins and John Running deer clapped their boss on the back, and congratulated Kelli, but as she turned to greet them, she sensed a malevolent spirit and a cold shill ran down her spine. Kelli thought "whoa get a hold of yourself, you just were reinstated, don't screw up by being weak."

" All right team you heard the man let's get back to the grindstone, John Running Deer, and I will go out and question Bill O'Toole , because He and Paul Williams were the last to see agent Mercury Johnson. Sam you get over to Vade Mecum Springs, and make sure our new headquarters is operational. Sam make sure those IMSI catchers have arrived, I have a feeling that they will be imperative in solving the case." Kelli said with a strong confident voice, hoping the OCR crew would hear her, and understand that they had made the right decision.

Kelli was thrilled for the opportunity to exonerate Brian Cox, but also to arrest Black Bark Whitescarver and David Barrett, because she knew that they were the evil puppet masters pulling the strings. If Kelli had known in 48 hours she would go missing, and one of her team would cease to have a heartbeat, she would have wished OCR had sent her back home to the security of her man's sinewy arms.

Dr. Paul, who was caught up in all the celebration, as he felt felicitous about helping the slender, pretty FBI Agent, that he did not noticed his pager going off. He finally felt the vibration of the annoying vice of modern technology. He scanned the number, and mumbled a few words of prayer, because the page came from the guard on duty that was assigned to Accaila Blackclaw. Since the episode with Rodney O'Neil, Dr. Paul had ordered a guard posted to Accalia's cell 24/7. Dr. Paul hurried from the courtroom and crossed the street to the New Stokes County Jail, He was standing in front of Accalia's cell, berating the Sheriff's deputy for alerting him to watch Accalia sleep on her worn out cot.

"What the hell is wrong with you, I come over half expecting to find half the staff dead, and a missing patient!" shouted an annoyed Paul.

"Sorry Doc, but you said to report to you any deviations in behavior. Its dam near three O'clock in the afternoon, and she had not budged a muscle. She is usually up when the rooster crows, chanting some Indian mumbo jumbo. It's like she saving up her energy for something big," replied portly Deputy Larry Harris.

"Deputy Harris I gave that young lady enough sedative to make a horse sleep until the second coming of Jesus, just answer one simple question is the patient breathing normally?"

"Yes Doc resting right peacefully, too peacefully if you ask me" replied the indignant corrections officer.

"WELL NO BODY ASKED YOU, NOW I HAVE GOT MORE IMPORTANT BUSINESS TO TAKE CARE OF, DON'T HAVE TIME TO STAND HERE JAWING WITH YOU!" Paul shouted as he stormed out of the room.

"Dam what an ass, old lady must have shut down the nooky outlet" thought Deputy Harris as he nervously glanced at the semi-comatose, slender Indian women in the cell.

Doctor Paul should have listen to the Deputy, because Accalia was not in a coma, she was dreaming of her evil father, the man who beat her poor mother, stomping on her like a piece of meat, calling her demeaning names like Indian Squaw, and red-skin piece of crap. Ah, Hicictawi'a was going to dance on the bones of her sperm donor, crushing his bones into powder. She was indeed recharging and storing her energy, because under the protection of the super blood moon, Hicictawi'a was going to turn Stokes County into a war zone, many of the palefaces would die, and her people would finally have their revenge!

CHAPTER 11

Bill O'Toole's massive estate was so beautiful; it should have been featured on a hallmark greeting card. A double black fence, with enough space in between for Bill's professional trainers to walk the thoroughbred horses, encompassed the main grounds of the home. The home was more like a compound with horse stables, and barns surrounding the main living quarters, the layout of O'Toole home reminded Kelli of the pictures of southern plantations that she had seen in the history books. As they passed through the main gate, Kelli was intrigued by the design of the massive horse stable, five cylinder domes about 12 feet high were arranged in the shape of a pentagram on the roof. These structures were visible from HWY 108, and seem to sublimely suggest to the passing motorist that this was the O'Toole kingdom, and He and his family were the royalty in Stokes County. As Kelli and John Running Deer approached the Mansion, Kelli could not escape the comparison to Bart Whitescarver estate, which exuded a presence of evil, while O'Toole ranch gave her a relaxing feeling of inner peace, harmony, and love. Kelli was not a metaphysical person, and she did not believe in psychic intuition, but she could not the feeling that she had just entered the spiritual plane of righteousness.

The mansion had four massive columns spanning the front of the home, and an enormous fountain in the front. The fountain having an equine design, as a large bronze horse in the middle spewed crystal clear water high in the air. Kelli was about to ring the door, when a beautiful women with an hourglass figure. Identified her as Beth O'Toole opened the door and smiled broadly, showing off picture perfect teeth, and sparking green eyes.

" Hello Kelli, and agent Running Deer, we have been expecting you, welcome to our humble abode" Beth seemed to pause for a moment perhaps waiting for someone to grin or laugh, The home was anything but ordinary, with a crystal chandelier and spiral staircases greeting a visitor as the entered the home. The home had a decorative ceiling with touches of granite and marble throughout the home. Pictures of Amelia and Ann the twins, in there riding attire as they competed in riding competitions, saturated the wall. There were action shots of Amelia guiding her horse of a series of jumps.

"I'm sure you're very proud of your girls" Kelli felt almost obligated to exclaim.

"Yes our children are our precious commodity, even the boys when they were young have several trophies from several riding competitions around the world" Beth hung on the word "Boys" too long, as if her mind could not process that she now only had one son. She quickly changed the subject of conversation.

"Bill is in his study waiting for you, when you conclude your conversation; He will give you a brief tour of our property. We are quite proud of the 1,500 feet of the Mayo River, which forms the southern boundary to our property."

"I have to attend to my daughters, at their age, they are very High maintenance," Beth laughed, but her laughter sounded hollow as Kelli sensed that pain and sorrow locked her heart in a vice grip. Bill O'Toole stood as they entered the room, and vigorously shook Agent Running Deer's hand,

"Agent Running Deer good to see you again, thought that I gave you and Agent Jenkins enough leads to keep you busy for at least a month!" laughed a good-natured O'Toole.

"Well you were such an interesting character, that I simply had to introduce you to my supervisor Senior Agent Kelli Ryan", gesturing to Kelli.

Kelli held out her hand to shake and Bill O'Toole gently took her hand, and kissed it, as if He was meeting Royalty for the first time. Kelli was embarrassed by the old-fashioned gesture, but when she looked into the deep blue eyes of Bill O'Toole, she instinctively knew that she was meeting a man of immense strength, both physically and emotionally. She was magnetically drawn to a man that possessed great Charisma, a natural born leader, a man that others would sacrifice his life for others. Kelli was shocked that she felt those vibes so strong, upon meeting him for the first time, it was not a romantic crush but a deep bond a daughter would feel for her father. She felt that if it had been century early, she would be looking into the eyes of William Wallace himself, the avenging angel of Scotland.

"Thank you for seeing on such short notice Bill, Running Deer and I are here to question you about the disappearance of Mercury Johnson, an agent of the environment protection agency. I understand that she was meeting with you and Paul Williams the night she vanished." Kelli asked quietly but sternly. Kelli could sense deep sorrow exuding from Bill O'Toole's gaze, because of the loss of his youngest son. His stare seemed to penetrate her soul, as if he was probing her subconscious for additional information.

"Yes Mercury had met with Paul Williams and me in order to generate a proposal to stop the commonwealth pipeline, which would carry fracked gas from North Carolina to the processing plants located in the Gulf of Mexico. We have been unsuccessful stopping Abbot Gas from drilling in Stokes Country by convention methods such as rezoning laws, and denial of permits. The gas companies have such deep pockets, that they able to influence State officials with bribes. Environmental groups have stopped both the Atlantic Coast Pipeline and the Colonial pipeline due to the pipelines damaging the habitats of protective species of Bats, Grey Wolves, Yellow lance Mussels, and snails. The logical thought process is if we can terminate the means of transporting the fracked gas to processing plants, then Abbott Gas will have no other options than to stop all hydraulic fracturing operations in Stokes County" Bill summarized passionately.

" Mercury Johnson was sent here to insure that King power was adhering to EPA cleanup standards at Belews Creek, why was she assisting you on abolishing Hydraulic fracturing in Stokes County?" "What was your relationship to her?" Kelli linked the two questions together in order to get an answer based on emotion instead of logic.

"I asked Mercury to help us because; I know that like me, she is an environmental warrior that is dedicated to saving this planet from destruction. I know that she is completely impervious to pressures and bribes from special lobbying groups, her integrity is impeccable, and I believe that those qualities are linked to her disappearance" answer O'Toole in a slightly elevated tone".

"So you and Mercury were two souls linked in your struggle to save the planet? Sounds a little melodramatic to me," Kelli said in a tone that was cool and calm.

Bill stood behind his desk, his eyes blazing with a passion, his color in his cheeks turned a crimson red, and monstrous hand opened and closed, for a minute Kelli was frighten that she had just let a caged beast of his cage. He glanced at John Running Deer, whose body seemed to tense for a confrontation. Both were very surprised with the large hands began to tremble and shake, and then delivered the most articulate, powerful rationalization for the theory of global warming that both had ever heard.

"Agent Ryan and John Running Deer, please listen to me, and please don't interrupt until I am done speaking. The ten warmest years globally have happen since 1998, with 2014 being the hottest year ever since thousands of meteorological stations, buoys, and ships have been keeping record since 1850. The most destructive and powerful hurricanes to punish the United States have happen in the last 10 years started with Katrina and Harvey in 2005, and cost this country 250 Billion dollars in damages. Wow! guys if FEMA didn't have to pay billions to rebuild American cities destroyed by intense hurricanes that are the byproduct of global warming, then we could build a wall on the border of Mexico that would stop the flow of illegal drugs into this country." Bill reasoned.

"Fossil fuel like coal and gas have contributed to carbon dioxide into atmosphere, but not to the extent of the methane gas, which is released during the hydraulic fracturing! In fact there is a direct correlation of mean average temperature spiking and the onset of fracturing in the Mid 90's." He stood up and placed the charts and graphs in front of the two agents, a decade of data that definitely tracked the correlation between global temperature increases and the increased reliance on fracked gas! While Agent Ryan and Running Deer were looking over years of data tediously collected by Bill O'Toole, he continued his lecture.

"Agent John Running Deer, the Cherokee people have for centuries understood the theory of interconnection, or that the environment, society and economic systems are inextricably linked, and if there is disturbance or disruption in one these systems the other two will be affected. It is the classic domino effect. Please let me illustrate, I will give a simple breakdown of the three systems in action, First, the environment: Nifty-Five percent of the thickest Arctic ice is now gone, so what use to reflect the sun's ultraviolet rays is now allowing absorption of the heat from the sun. This phenomenon allows for rising of ocean levels that flood many

Island nations. (Second): social impacts thousands of people are suddenly homeless, leaving their homeland in search of a habitable place to live. These immigrants, refugees arrive at other countries borders demanding entrance thus causing violence, wars, and social unrest. (Economic) Thriving coastal Megalopolis like New York or Los Angeles are flooded, shutting down large financial centers, like Wall Street. Just remember how Hurricane Katrina or 911 disrupted financial transactions around the globe.

Bill paused for a moment -, before preceding his rant. "Ash and Walnut trees in the Great Smoky Mountains are being killed by beetles that migrated from Asia, the colder climate in the Smokies ten years ago would have killed these varmints, Now because of global warming, these Asian interlopers are killing my trees" Bill concluded with his eyes bulging in their sockets.

Kelli began to think that Bill O'Toole was having some kind of mental breakdown, which was understandable after losing his Son, and he was having an apocalyptic vision like Apostle John, who had written the book of Revelation while on the Island of Patmos. While she appreciated his passion, Kelli needed to get the questioning back on track,

"Bill we understand your passion, but we need to question you about Mercury Johnson disappearance, can you tell me about any conflicts that Mercury may have had before vanishing?"

" Agent Ryan, Mercury had an altercation with a foreman named Mac McKenzie at the Anderson Drilling site about two days ago, She informed that the EPA was going to put monitoring wells on my property to control the chemicals that they were using during their Fracs, I would start by questioning him. Oh, Mercury was kidnapped by those that wish to destroy this land bequeathed by the creator to my children and grandchildren, and I swear on my daddy's grave that I will defend this land with the last drop of blood in my veins " Bill O'Toole answered with a voice that sounded like the growl of a wounded bear.

Realizing that they had consumed two hours of valuable time Kelli got up, shook Bill's hand, and thanked him for his time, but Bill was insistent of giving his new allies a brief tour of his property. Kelli initially declined, but sensing that Bill was going to be a tremendous asset to the case hesitantly agreed. On reflection, Kelli was glad she agreed to the tour, because in about five hours the daytime observation would assist her in visualizing the crime scene in which a son attempted to assassinate his father.

CHAPTER 12

It was 5:00 PM, Deputy Harris was doing last walk through inspection of the prisoners on his floor, before the second shift came on duty. The lights came on in the facility, because even at 5:00 pm, the late fall day was turning Grey, but the brilliance of the super moon lit the sky like a giant flashlight in the heavens. Deputy Harris walked past Accalia cell at a brisk pace, not wanting to see any distraction that would delay his departure from this stinking hellhole, because Deputy Harris was still angry at Dr. Paul, and frankly "Scarlet", he didn't give a dam about Paul's star patient, in fact if she was hanging from the ceiling, he would not intervene. He would just let the second shift boys handled it.

As the portly deputy Harris walked pass Accalia cell, he noticed that she was sitting upright, facing him. Her eyes were illuminated with a strange glow, and her hair seemed to be on fire, but that was not the reason that Deputy Harris stopped dead in his tracks. The girl sitting on the bed was his baby girl Jenny, who when she was just three years old was kidnapped and brutally murdered. Deputy Harris conscious, rational mind knew that the thing sitting on the bed was an optical illusion, brought on by stress, and the misery of losing a child, his subconscious mind wanted the impossible to be reality, so he could hold his baby girl on more time! She held out her arms, and in a small child's voice whispered,

"Hug me Daddy, I am soooo alone"

Deputy Harris, crying with unquenchable Joy, unlocked the jail cell, and in his hurry left the door wide open, rushed into the arms of his child , crying out " daddies here, daddies here it's going to be alright"

As the beginning of the hug, Deputy Harries felt Joy, relief, and love swell up in his soul, but something was wrong as he felt a sharp pain in his carotid artery. Accalia sunk her sharp fangs into his neck, and suddenly the joy turned into horror, and the last conscious, rational thought Deputy Harris had was that his brain, heart, and soul was being absorbed by a creature straight from the bowels of hell.

Accalia absorbed all the layers of Harris skin from the epidermis, to the dermis, and finally the subcutaneous layers, cells were absorbed down to the mitochondria , all organs, tissues, and even hair follicles were absorbed, and so like in the Movie " The Body Snatchers" from the 1950's, Accalia WAS deputy Harris. All that was left of deputy Harries was a quivering mass of cytoplasm, which Accalia rapidly covered up with her blanket. Accalia calmly got up and walked out of the jail cell, and using Harris keys unlocked the door to his ward, so Deputy Allen could relieve him.

"Hey what's going on big guy? How were our guests today? Anything to report?" asked a spry the new deputy sheriff.

Harris walked past Deputy Allen, as if he was invisible, neither acknowledging him or his questions, later Allen would testify the Harris resembled a zombie from his favorite show "The Walking Dead." Asked why he did not report the incident, Deputy Allen responded the Harris must have had a terrible day, and he did not want to put any additional pressure on his mentor. Cameras in the parking lot would show Harris walking right past his car, and into the woods across from the jail. The guard watching the cameras just thought that portly deputy wanted some exercise, and had chosen to walk home... The walking home seemed to be a rational explanation, until his supervisor later that day explained that

Harris lived a good twenty miles away.

Once deep in the woods, Hicictawi'a steeped out of its man's suit. It changed from Harris's 5'10" frame into its mammoth 9-foot frame. The super Moon had transformed Hicictawi'a to a beast on steroids; it muscles quivering with kinetic energy. Its blood red eyes seemed to glow in the moonlight, unable to contain it's savage hatred, It reared its head back, and released a howl into the night, that seemed to announced to the humans in Stokes County that their night of unholy terror was about to begin. Dr. Drake rocking on his front porch of his home four miles away, heard the blood curling howl, ah music to his ears, finally after all these years Black Bart was going to feel the wrath of his indigence.

PART 6

The Quickening of the Beast

CHAPTER 1

Hicictawia bound off into the deep woods, and an ancient presence guided it like a modern GPS to the outskirts of Bill O'Toole ranch. The thoroughbred horses, chestnut in color bucked against their stables creating an awful noise. These horses were the descendants of the great Secretariat, which won the triple crown of horse racing in 1973. The stud of the ranch was the great-grandson of the huge, chestnut colt that beat the rest of the field by 21lengths in the Belmont Stakes, which help it to achieve horse racing immortality. It was around 6:30, and Bill was sitting down with his family at the supper table.

"Hey Junior will you please go out and check out those horses?" "Someone or something spooked them" Bill glanced at his son with a look that meant it was not a request but a commandment. Everyone in the home including Bill's twin girls new how much their father cherished his horses. Some men covet expensive cars like corvettes, or Lamborghini, but Bill third love behind God and family was his horses of the exotic bloodline of a champion.

"Sure Dad, be back in a minute" Junior replied as he rose from the table. Bill and Beth exchanged glances, as if to agree in unison that Bill Junior was indeed acting strange, usually he would have argued passionately that he would comply with his father's wishes after dinner. Bill just assumed the Boy was maturing into a man, and did not want to cause any more drama so soon after Shaun's passing. The minute Bill Jar was out the door, he was cussing his father was a barrage of profanity, spewing words of hatred for his father who had betrayed him. Bill Jar resentment for his father had grown immensely since discovering that he had been written out of the will, the angry now was like the molten lava building under Mount St. Helen's before it erupted. Bill Junior hurried to the place the AK47 had been hidden, and evil thought then entered his mind "Why stop with his father? he might slaughter his entire family, including those whining little sisters of his."

Bill Jr. did not even check the stables, for he was like a heat-seeking missile heading straight for the old tobacco barn, and his hidden stockpile of instruments of death. Black Bart instructed him on not leaving any forensic evidence behind, like fingerprints or DNA, so Bill Junior slipped on the Latex gloves before he entered the barn. Bart also instructed him to pick of any spent ammunition, because the SBI or FBI with sophisticated equipment could match the rifle to the bullet casings.

Black Bart explained that the rifle had no serial number, and was a product of the black web, so no research on gun purchases could be linked to them, so bullet casings was the only way that the rifle could be linked to the crime. Bart then explained to Junior to do the hit very quick, leave the rifle buried outside the Barn, one of "his" crew will be back to retrieve it. Finally get away from the ranch, meet with close friends to establish an alibi, since the body would not be discovered until later, coroner will have to estimate time of death. All these principles of Murder 101 paraded in his head as he waited in the cold, smelly, old barn, at least the barn had some light as the rays of the super moon penetrated the cracks in the wood planks that made up the ancient walls. Suddenly Bill Jr. heard a noise directly above him, and wielded the rifle toward the spot and shouted absurdly

"I have a rifle, and I will blow your brains out" but lowered the gun when he realized it was just the wind. Bill Jr., was agitated and a tad bit spooked, but he stoically waited like a good solider anxious to end the life of the man that had given life to him,

"Honey shouldn't you go out and check on JR?" "He has been gone for over an hour," Beth asked with a worried look on her face.

" Okay everything is quiet over in the stables, no wonder Junior was so anxious to help, he probably used the check on the horses as an excuse to run off to his girlfriend's house" Bill said with a slight grin on his face.

"Oh Bill trust your son", after all he is your blood" retorted Beth with a wink.

"If you say so, you know what they say momma's baby, daddies maybe" Bill laughed as he went out the door, barely evading the shoe that Beth threw at him.

Bill searched the stables, his prize possessions were quietly eating their dinner, but looked up at him as if to ask "so you bringing us some dessert?" There was no sign of Bill Jr., so Bill was getting ready to walk back to the home, when he heard a noise from the Old Tobacco barn. Junior raised the AK 47, when he heard his father walk to the old barn door; he put his finger on the trigger, and took a deep breath. Bill Sr. opened the door, and his 6'3" frame was bathed in the silvery moonlight, Junior thinking that the sudden illumination was a sign from heaven, that he was doing the right thing. He was about to squeeze of the shots that would blow the back of his father's head off, when Hicictawi'a leaped from the bottom tier, like a deranged Tarzan, knocking Jr. to the ground, causing him to fire blindly toward the roof of the barn. Junior was so shocked that he did not realize that he was bleeding profusely from his arm, the beast then raised its razor sharp claws arched in the high in air ready to strike the fatal blow that would separate Jr. into two pieces.

" NO" Hicictawi head turned to the man that had

telepathically communicated with it, for the centuries that Hicictawi had walked the earth, no mortal human had ever mind chatted with it. Hicictawi'a lowered its claw and walked toward the man. As it walked toward the man, it sensed an ally, a man that had purity of heart, and man that loved the land as much as any of its people, a man that would cherish the water, and hold sacred the ways of the Cherokee.

Bill O'Toole was in awe of the beast that stood over 9 feet tall, and resembled was a cross between a werewolf and Bigfoot , but he also was getting psychic vibes from a beast that it was enraged by generations of white men that had slaughtered and enslaved it's people. Bill felt empathy for the beast, which was a manifestation of evil deeds and debauchery that had been committed against a people that only sought peace and serenity.

"Spare my son, oh great one, I know your pain and anguish, but I also know that you are a noble warrior that does not kill women and innocent. My son is not a solider, please spare his life" Bill used the last bit of his telepathic strength to convey the last message to Hicictawia.

Hicictawia hesitated for a moment, and spoke telepathically "Your respect, empathy, and compassion has spared you your son's life. Continue to fight for Mother Earth, now I must go to punish those that bring destruction to this land". It when took a giant leap through the barn doors, and it disappeared into the night. Bill Sr. ran to his Son, and even though his son had tried to murder him moments ago, cradled his son head in his lap, and told him that he loved him and forgave him, as he applied a tourniquet to his son's wounds.

"Dad forgive me, I'm sorry," Junior said to this father repeatedly.

" Junior save your strength, I am going to run to the house and call 911, you just hang on Son" Bill then got up and ran like a man possessed to his house, praying to God that he would be able to save his son's life.

CHAPTER 2

Kelli working late at Vade Mecum springs, the three-story hotel had been converted into a makeshift FBI command center. She was doing research on David Barrett, trying to find information about his military exploits, and his unique psychic gifts. She was impressed by his stellar military evaluations, seems that Captain David Barrett had saved countless lives in Iraq; Kelly discovered that David Barret was a Silver Star recipient, for heroism with distinction in battle. As she her research intensified her fear of David Barret began to increase, his clairvoyant skills would be magnified tenfold because of her PTSD, she would have to be very cautious around him in order for him not to slither into her mind.

An urgent call on her cell phone interrupted her thought process, it was Inspector King,   "Hello Agent Ryan there has been a situation at O'Toole ranch, I suggest you get your team assembled and get there ASAP. Sheriff Green and Agent Briggs are already on site. Good to have you back on the case Kelli, I have all the confidence in your abilities," Inspector King added before he hung up the phone.

"Thank You" Kelli offered before realizing that King had hung up the phone.   Kelli then paged John Running Deer and Sam Jenkins had ordered them to meet at the O'Toole ranch in thirty minutes.   As Kelli arrived on the crime scene, several local and state vehicles were parked at the O'Toole mansion, their flashing red and blue lights illuminating O'Toole's home in an eerie nightmarish manner.   Kelli headlights picked the two familiar member of her team.

"Hello gentleman glad you could make so quickly on short notice, let's head over to the barn, and walk the grid of the crime scene," Kelli ordered.

Agent Briggs was lingering in the shadows processing the crime area, when Kelli and her team walked through the barn doors. John Running Deer knew that a confrontation was intimate, because of the bad blood between the two.

"This is a Federal investigation, remove your CSI team from my Site" Kelli thundered as she walked into the room.

"Not anymore seems as your director Jacobs and my boss have reached an agreement. Seems the SBI and the FBI are going to join forces on this one, we are now teammates. "Agent Briggs could not conceal his amusement, and was a proud owner of a large grin.

Just as Kelli was going to lay the riot act, her cell phone rang it was Director Jacobs.

"Hey Kelli congrats for your victory of the OPR team, I am glad you're still on the case. Kelli, because of the scope of case and the large geographic area that needs to be searched, the SBI and FBI evidence response teams are joining forces. I am appointing you lead agent over the Federal team, while Director King is appointed Special Agent Briggs the lead over the state resources. I understand that there is some bad blood between you and Agent Briggs, and I want that to cease immediately."

"You are operating as a team now, sharing investigative materials, including any DNA sampling. Do I make myself clear Special agent Ryan?" Jacobs asked with a hint of aggravation in his voice.

"Crystal clear Sir." Kelli replied biting her tongue determined to wage this war at another time.

"Great, carry on Agent Ryan, oh by the way this case has gotten the attention of President Dotard, as he has requested that Governor Kristy to order the National Guard to be deploy to the area. In addition, the Governor is also ordering Marshall Law for the Stokes county area with a mandatory curfew to be in effect from dust to dawn. Inform the local Sheriff to enforce the curfew with his deputies; if any problems arise, the National Guard will intervene. I cannot stress how important this investigation is to National Security". "Are there any questions Agent Ryan?" Jacobs asked the tone of his voice indicating that Kelli needed to ask no questions.

"No sir" Kelli responded glancing over at Agent Briggs, who had a look of pure unadulterated joy on his face. Jacobs replied "good" and the phone line went dead.

CHAPTER 3

"Agent Briggs what have you got for me Sir" Kelli asked almost gagging on the last word, but she wanted to show professional respect for her new partner.

Briggs proceeded to explain the AK-14 had been used in the shooting, and many spent bullet casing were scattered on the barn's wooden floor. He also went on to explain that there was no serial number on the weapon, so it was untraceable.

"Seems like Bill O'Toole has a new summertime ventilation design for his barn", as he pointed to the roof above them, that had been pierced by several rounds of the assault rifle, when Junior was knocked to the floor by Hicictaw'a.

"Was there any Motive for the shooting?" Kelli asked trying to understand why a son would try to kill a father, who seemed to spoil his children with unconditional love.

"Well Bill Jr., is fighting for his life over at Stokes Regional Hospital, so he not going to be much assistance in discovering a motive". Agent Briggs replied with a hint of sarcasm.

They both walked over to Bill Sr. who still seemed to be in shock. and questioned him about the incident. Agent Running Deer asked Bill Sr. some questions concerning the physical description of the beast, and was convinced that Bill O'Toole and Son had encountered the powerful Cherokee shape sifter Hicictaw'a. He was amazed that both Bill and his son were not sent screaming into the Underworld.

"Any reason Bill that junior would try to murder you?" Kelli asked point blank

"No Junior and I had our differences like any father and son, but never in my wildest dreams would I ever believe that my oldest son would want me dead" Bill replied in a distraught voice.

Kelli could sense that he wanted to get to the hospital to be with his son, so she compassionately dismissed him, much to Agent Briggs's chagrin.

"What the hell did you let him go for?" asked a pissed off agent Briggs

"Well agent Briggs. it easy to determine that Bill O'Toole's is traumatized by tonight's events, and as a trained profiler, I know that any information gained while someone is stressed is irrational and senseless, I am simply giving Bill time to clear his head" Kelli answered as if she was speaking to a special needs student. Besides, Kelli knew indistinctly that David Barret and Bart Whitescarver were behind this assassination attempt of Bill O'Toole, because Bill O'Toole was the charismatic leader of the organization that could prevent them from power and wealth, and that is always an excellent motive for murder.

About a half mile away, rough neck John "Big Boy" Parker was supervising two lowly roustabouts as they prepared for the first frack on the Anderson property, the well bore had been encased with cement to insure a " Safe Frack", and a preliminary pressure test of the high pressure pumps was successful. These tests were EPA mandatory that ensured that dangerous chemical from product water would not leak into underground aquifers, polluting the good folks of Stokes County drinking water. Big John, was always amazed how environment propaganda made it appear that gas companies was bringing forth the hounds of hell bent on contaminating landowners water supplies. The truth of the matter was the wells bore when almost a mile down in the earth's crust much deeper than any aquifer, But this Stokes County site was a different animal because the enormous amount of shale was much closer to the main aquifer, so Abbott Gas had to be very Cautious.

Once the Wellbore got to its intended depth, it makes a right turn and continues for about half mile, thus creating the name horizontal drilling. Six fracks opened up by perforating guns would occur on this half mile circuit, so John was taking an inventory of isolation plugs, perforating guns, and sand that would keep the fracks open long enough to get all the precious natural gas out.

Big John completed his inventory, and was famished, and was licking his chops thinking about the diner down the street from his hotel, where he proudly explained to the head waitress, who seemed to stare at his massive stomach,

"That one who has a giant tool, must have an equally impressive tool shed", then John bellowed on of this famous laughs that could be heard down the street. He called for the two morons that he had sent to the hydration unit that would eject enough water to service a town of 65,000 folks during the inaugural frack on the Anderson property in the morning. He yelled at them and got no response, he thought that they were hanging out in the woods smoking pot or crack, or anything else that helped them escape their meager existence!

"Ah Shit, they don't pay me enough to babysit morons" he murmured to himself. He turned to walk to the hydration unit, when he felt the first drop of liquid hit his shoulder, and his initial thought was the weatherman had not called for any precipitation changes tonight. He glanced at his shoulder, and saw the stream of saliva running down his chest. John mind rationalized that he was over 6'5inches tall, so whatever was standing behind him had to be over 8 feet in height. John's Survival instinct kicked in and he whirled to do battle with this titan, and much to his dismay he had guessed wrong and miss the height of this snarling beast by almost one foot.

CHAPTER 4

Kelli noticed Sheriff Green over in the corner of the room, speaking in agitated tones at someone on his staff at the jail.

"Pull the dam surveillance camera recording from the time frame, and call me back ASAP," He yelled into the phone. Kelli walked up behind that agitated Sheriff, and pecked him on the shoulder, Green whirled and his hand went instinctively for his glock.

"Whoa there Sheriff, what the hell is going on?" Kelli asked alarmed by the Sheriff's nervous behavior, clearly something had spooked him.

"It seems like one of my deputies was found in Accalia Blackclaw's cell. It was found quivering under a blanket on Accalia cot." Kelli was very confused by the terminology of the Sheriff, referring to another human as an it.

"What do mean it was quivering" Kelli asked in astonishment.

" Well Agent Ryan, seems as if the body of Deputy Jailer Harris was reduced to a massive amount of unrecognizable protoplasm, and subcutaneous fat quivering on the bed like a bowl of Jelly!".

Just as the Sheriff spoke these words, the surveillance video was sent to his phone, showing Accalia Blackclaw sucking on the throat of Harris, and slowly assuming his identity, the good Sheriff then slowly turned a ashen Grey, and turned and spewed his dinner of chili all over the barn floor. The video reminded Kelli of a B rated horror flick of the fifties called Invasion of the Body Snatchers.

Kelli knew that it was very bad timing, but as the sheriff recovered from his vomiting, she informed him that he and his deputies were to enforce a curfew on the fine folks of Stokes County.

"The hell I will, we are sending search parties out for a one Accalia Blackclaw, we will apprehend her by dawn," He arrogantly vowed.

Kelli did not want to confuse this Barney Fife clone by telling him that he missed Accalia Blackclaw by about an hour, so she explained that these orders were passed down by the Governor of North Carolina, and will be enforced by the National Guard.

"Remember Sheriff this entire County is under Marshall Law, and anyone out after sunset will be arrested." "Do you understand Sheriff?" Kelli asked her forehead creasing and a steely look of resolve in her eyes.

"What the hell am I going to tell all these folks keep them indoors all night? These are country folks, and they are used to their freedom!" Green explained.

Just then, on cue the answer came from God himself! The building shook with a violent repercussion of a ferocious explosion. Everyone one in the barn hit the ground, but Kelli ran to the door and witnessed a huge fireball on the Anderson property. Kelli ripped out her phone and called 911, and told the operator about the explosion. She identified herself as an FBI agent, and told the 911 operator to activate any fire department within the radius of 50 miles.

"Make sure they have self-contained breathing apparatus or (SCBA), and hazmat suites, because they will be dealing with many unknown toxic and possible carcinogenic chemicals." Kelli then walked into the barn, and asked the dazed Agent Briggs to call Director King and ask him to get helicopters from nearby Raleigh in the air immediately.

Kelli then turned to a shell shocked Green, alas Barney Fife, and said, "Now you have your ammunition on what to tell the fine folks of Stokes County".

Sheriff Green looked at her with that perpetual stupid look on his face and asked

"And what in the hell is that?"

Kelli stared at the dimwitted Sheriff for a moment shocked by his stupidity,

"Unless they want to breathe in poisonous, toxic fumes, that may cause cancerous tumors and leukemia, they might want to keep their ass inside." After shocking Sheriff Green with her brash comment, Agent Ryan and her team walked out of the barn on their way to a burning hell on earth! Agent Briggs assembled a team of SBI agents and Sheriff Deputies and began to follow the fresh tracks of the beast! He called Inspector King, and asked for some search helicopters to be scrambled out of Fort Bragg. He then turned to Sheriff Green and asked him for the best bloodhounds he could find, because deep in his stomach Agent Briggs knew that all resources would be needed to track this massive creature.

CHAPTER 5

Kelli, Running deer, and Sam were on route to the well fire, when Kelli received a call from Leo Burns, Fire Captain of Station 15 in Danbury.

"Agent Ryan, we are in the process of evacuated all civilians in the hot zone, which in this case is mile from the Frack Site. This is not a well fire, I repeat, this is not a well fire, it's point of origin seems to be the chemical tanks, that are located about 200 feet from the well pad. We are using high-pressure foam to smother the flames, but need to get a list of chemicals that my people and first res-ponders are dealing with. Abbott Gas Company do not list the chemicals they use, and there are no Material Data Safety Sheets, so if any injured folks ambulance personnel do not know how to treat them. I have been trying to reach Mac McKenzie, frack supervisor, but my calls go unanswered." An obvious frustrated Burns yelled into the phone.

Kelli was angered by the fact the many gas companies don't list the ingredients of the chemicals they use on Frack Jobs, citing Trade Secrets that protect their "special sauce" from their competitors. As Kelli was talking their vehicle was stopped at the fire watch point, Kelli noticed a portly, obese man sweating profusely as he tried to get into his Hazmat suit, and she guessed that it was Mac McKenzie.

"Chief you need to monitor for benzene, and Methanol, and Uranium, I will be getting you a complete list of chemicals within 10 minutes". Kelli said calmly trying to pacify the anxious Chief. Kelli knew she failed miserably, when she heard the fire chief exclaim

"Need that information ASAP, it's a matter of life and death" and the phone went dead.

The rookie fire watch, flagged down their vehicle, Kelli showed the rookie their badges, and calmly got out of the car.

"Agent Ryan glad you're here, both SBI Inspector King and FBI director Jacobs, have notified us that you were on the way, we have your Hazmat suites and self-contained breathing devices here." Kelli ignored the rookie, and walked up to the struggling McKenzie. She held out her hand and introduced herself, while showing him her Badge; his face turned an ashen color.

"Mac McKenzie, Franck supervisor, now if you will excuse me, I have to get to my site." he replied arrogantly

"OH you're not going anywhere until you give the complete list of chemical that first responders and firemen are trying to contain at your well pad site." At this point of the riot act, McKenzie tried to interject. Kelli face turned a red-hot shade of red, as she physically pushed the bumbling Mackenzie to the ground.

" Now you listen, there are people putting their lives on the line less than a mile from here, so you are going to give me the list of the chemicals that are on site. or I am going to incite you with resisting a Federal investigation. You will be doing some serious time in a Federal prison you sniveling little twat".

Mackenzie realizing the magnitude of the situation produced a list of chemicals that were in his front pocket, spouting that he was going to give them to Chief Burns when he arrived on site.

"Judging by your wresting match with your hazmat suit, which would have been a year from now" Kelli said smirking at the wallowing idiot on the ground. When Mackenzie handed the list to Kelli, she noticed that 4 out of 5 chemicals on the list were highly carcinogenic, so she immediately phoned Chief Burns and told him the ingredients of the lethal chemical cocktail that his men were exposed to.

" Hey Running Deer, you and Sam get down to the well pad pronto, walk the grid and get back to me ASAP. I have enjoyed speaking with my new buddy here, think we will chat some more". Kelli said with an evil smile.

"YOU CAN'T KEEP ME HERE; THEY NEED MY EXPERTISE AND INSTRUCTION ON THE WELL PAD"! A furious McKenzie shouted.

" Ah calm down Mac, think you need to calm down and take a couple of breath mints before you stagger down there" Kelli replied hinted too the alcohol that she smelled on his breath. Mac realizing that Kelli held the key to his retirement in her hands became more compliant to Kelli's questioning.

"Listen Mac, Mercury Johnson disappeared a couple of days ago, after having a heated discussion with you, you wouldn't know anything about her disappearance would you?" Kelli asked looking for non-verbal reactions from Mackenzie.

"Hell no! She was harassing me at the Job site, just had to defend Abbot Gas and myself. She takes great pride in pissing me off" Mackenzie blurted out.

Being a trainer pro filer, Kelli looked for signs of lying, like rapid breath, nervous twitch, or rapid eye movement and saw no sign of deceit in Mackenzie body language.

"Do you know a David Barrett or Bart Whitescarver" Kelli asked looking for the same nonverbal signs of fabrication.

"Yea David Barrett works for Abbot Gas, I have worked

with him on several assignments. I'm afraid that I never heard of that Whitesharper dude"! Again no body language indicating deception

"That's Whites carver, and why do they call David Barrett the Mind Magician?" a tenacious Kelli inquired.

"I don't know, maybe he could answer these asinine questions better than me. Now can we please get down to the site? so I can do my Dam Job." Mac McKenzie pleaded

Kelli knew that Mackenzie was not going to truthfully answer her questions, but she did know that the big weasel would run back to David and black Bart and tell them the Feds are on to them. That information may send them into a panic, which may cause them to make mistakes.

"Sure Mac let's get down there, they do need you down there" Kelli said with reassuring Mackenzie of his self-perceived importance.

"Hey Agent Ryan, could we forget about the breath thing? I was just having a few drinks with dinner," a suddenly timid Mackenzie asked.

"Sure Mac just as long as you meet me at the sheriff's office for a little polygraph tomorrow morning" Kelli responded spryly, knowing she had Mac McKenzie by the proverbial balls.

McKenzie was about to object, when Kelli cell phone rang " Go " she replied knowing that it was Running Deer on the other end.

"Boss you need to get down here post haste, we just found something you're not going to believe," Running Deer shouted to be heard of the noise the firefighters working feverishly to contain a firestorm.

"Tell me now what the hell is going on" Kelli asked not sure if she wanted to hear the answer. "Ask Mackenzie how many men he had working on the Pad at the time of the explosion," Running Deer asked.

McKenzie heard the question and held up three fingers, and then he said "one roughneck and two roustabouts."

"I think we just found your two roustabouts" Running Deer replied.

"Let me talk to those two morons, so they can explain to me what the hell went wrong," Mac McKenzie yelled into the phone.

There was a long silence on the phone, and then a response from Running Deer that either Kelli or Mac McKenzie will ever forget.

"I'm afraid there both deceased, we found them hanging from a large tree. Their small Intestines were Cut Out and used as the hanging rope." Running Deer voice sounded strained with horror...

CHAPTER 6

Kelli and Mackenzie drove his Audi down to the Well Pad, and was greeted by fire trucks from five different counties working feverishly to starve this chemical fire of oxygen. Running Deer and Sam Jenkins were waiting for their boss with ghoulish looks on their faces, Kelli pounced out of the car and followed her team to the clump of trees about 300 yards away. Mac McKenzie leaped out of the car, and immediately headed in the direction of the chemical tanks, along the way he noticed that one of the perforating guns was missing from the inventory room, and all of a sudden, he had a very sick feeling in the pit of his stomach.

When Kelli arrived, an FBI forensic team were collecting DNA, trace Fibers, and hair from the ground around the two dead men. Kelli stared at the grisly sight, and almost heaved up her lunch. The men were propped up on a huge fallen Oak tree, which seemed to been dragged over for them to stand on, thus creating a supporting aid for the small intestines tied around their necks in a noose like fashion. The bloating of the faces and the awful stench of the digestive juices from the open abdominal wounds were too much for Kelli, and since they were far enough from the chemical fire, she removed her mask and vomited in the grass. Special Agent David Grant, trained as pathologist walked over to her, and gave her the gory details,

"The intestines were tied around these men's neck postmortem; they were killed by deep lacerations to their abdominal cavities. The length of the small intestine in an adult human body is 20 feet; the killer doubled the intestines round their neck thus hanging them 10 feet below the tree. The killer then dragged this huge tree over to prop the corpses up, as if it was trying to display its work to the public either to horrify or to boast its creativity. In my 20 years of crime investigation, I have never seen claw marks like the ones on these men bodies, Agent Ryan you are dealing with a creature with amazing strength and cunning, and judging from this crime scene, it enjoyed killing these men, and will continue killing till it's apprehended". Agent Grant spoke the last words in an elevated tone, as if he was in trance.

Just as Grant spoke these words Ralph Barton and Rod Lewis pulled up, lights still blazing and siren piercing the night air.

"Agent Grant are you and your techs done here", Kelli asked anxious to cut these two monstrosities down, before she heaved again. Agent Grant nodded his head yes!

"Make sure you get all crime scene evidence over to our new forensic lab over at Vade Mecum springs," instructed Kelli, making it clear this was \federal evidence, in case Agent Briggs showed up ordering otherwise.

Ralph Barton and Rod Lewis loaded the two deceased men into the ambulance, grateful for their breathing apparatus, which shielded them from the stench of men that had been dissected like rats in a high school Biology class.

" Hey guys get these bodies over to the Stokes County Morgue, want a report from chief Pathologist Dr. Drake, tell him want a complete Autopsy report ASAP, Thank you" Kelli added trying not to sound too bossy.

Mac McKenzie noticed that one perforating gun was missing, so he checked his inventory and sure enough on of the explosive charges to open on of the "Fracks" was missing. Mac McKenzie then knew how the terrorist sabotaged his job, by putting a loaded perforating gun under the largest chemical tank and detonating it! Alone in his office, Mac McKenzie noticed that the PSI around the flow back mani-fold was extremely high, which was weird because no " Frack" had taken place, and the flow back manifold controls product water loaded with chemicals and sand flowing back to the sur-face after the frack had been completed.

He ran out of the office, and walked about a quarter of a mile to the flow back manifold , and was amazed to see that there was a giant lump in the tube leading to the mani-fold, to Mackenzie it looked like a reticulated python had just devoured some very large prey, like a deer or a unfortunate human being. Mac McKenzie unscrewed the coupling of the large hose to the manifold and peered inside and to his utter horror stared into the eyes of John "Big Boy" Parker whose 6"5-inch frame had been stuffed into the hose. After the Fire team cut John out of the tubing, the thing that Mac Macken-zie will never forget was the grin on John's face, as if he was ecstatic about the fact he was right about the two lowly roust-abouts hanging out in the woods.

Hicictawi'a was about two miles away from the sa-cred cave behind the waterfalls, at a place the palefaces call Tories den, when it heard the baying of the bloodhounds that were tracking it. It would have stopped and ambushed its pursuers and ate the bloodhounds and drank their blood, but its vision had been impaired by the chemicals that were re-leased during the explosion at the franking pad. The dark night was beginning to lighten in the eastern sky, like the dying embers of a large campfire before it goes completely out. Hicicawi'a could hear the chant of the ancient medicine men in its mind. As it climbed the steep bluffs, and a deep feeling a reverence permeating in its warrior's heart, for it had struck a piercing blow into the heart of the greedy palefaces. It could the feel its human side starting to stir, like a fetus in a womb, trying to emerge into the light.

Hicicawi'a reached the massive cave behind the roaring, raging plume of water, and enter into the mouth of the dark cave, and then with the strength of a thousand mortals rolled a huge stone in front of the entrance, sealing itself and Accalia in a tomb of enormous proportions. It lay down on a giant slab of quartile, closed its eyes, and began dreaming of its final mission. It will kill the evil father of its human shell, and feed on the heart of the treacherous one that does the bidding of those that wish to desecrate the land of its ancestors. As Hicicawi'a slipped into a light sleep, it could hear the dogs sniffing a pawing at the huge boulder that protected its liar.

CHAPTER 7

The hunting cabin built on the high bluffs of the Sauratown Mountains was completely camouflaged, but not of colors, a deer hunter would wear to blend in with the forest, but of a type that would blend in with the mountain rock that surrounded it. The cabin itself was in a natural cave, so the ceiling was quartzite rock, but the sides and floor was constructed with red cedar wood, which was carried up an old logging trail by horse and wagon. The cabin was in essence the first man-cave, that helped Bart's father get away from the meddling of an over bearing wife. It was completely hidden from any helicopter or plane that passed over, and Bart had improved the covert location by placing several booby traps in the brush that encircled it. The cabin was the perfect place to evacuate to in times of an emergency, and to the desperate men inside their current situation was very serious indeed.

The men that sitting at the worn pine table were engaged in a heated discussion and Black Bart was livid of the failure to kill Bill O'Toole!

"Dammed if I don't have the FBI or SBI following every move I make, they have a surveillance team on me 24/7. I wouldn't be surprised if they have a picture of me sitting on the crapper, and it all because that FBI lady got a hard-on for me," bellowed an obviously enraged Black Bart.

David Barrett rocked back in his chair, uncharacteristically quiet. When the well pad exploded last night, that there would be no hydraulic fracturing in Stokes County now or ever, because of all the negative publicity around the explosion. News channels would feast over the disaster, and Abbot Gas would be in found in violation of several laws enforced by the EPA. And as Kenny Rogers so gracefully put in one of his country music songs " YOU GOT TO KNOW WHEN TO HOLD EM AND WHEN TO FOLD EM", so David decided to fold em,, leaving Black Bart and these other two idiots to be his scapegoats. He reasoned that Black Bart would be arrested for the attempted assassination of Bill O'Toole because JR would recover from his wounds and finger Black Bart for the conspiracy to commit murder. Agent Briggs and the hapless Ex-sheriff Brown would be linked to the kidnapping and murder of EPA agent Mercury Johnson. No physical evidence to either crime, and no money trail would led to him, because David had made sure that Black Bart paid off both Briggs and Brown for their treason to their professions.

David could be arrested for bribing public officials, like commissioners Tammy Allen and Bob Miller, but Abbott Gas, not wanting their secret weapon to go to prison, would send a team of gifted lawyers that would fight to have him acquitted of all chargers, the very worst scenario is that David would be put on probation. David had already purchased his plane tickets, and would be back home in his beautiful mansion in Colorado in a week, but first he had to tie up some lose ends namely the kidnapping of the pain in the ass FBI lady and the disposal of two bodies. In both cases the three idiots surrounding him would do the dirty work, he simply had to plant the seed in their little bitty brains.

"Hey Briggs what about that dam creature that interfered with the murder of Bill O'Toole, and destroyed the fracking well pad at the Anderson drill site?" Asked the frantic Black Bart.

"The blood hounds tracked the dam thing to a place the local's call Tories den, a small cave behind a massive waterfall. Tough hike in the middle of the night, but dogs stopped about

40 feet into the cave, blocked by a huge boulder". Exclaimed an obvious frustrated Briggs

"What the hell are you talking about? Tories Den is a mammoth cave, big enough to hide 50 or 60 Tories after they burned the homes of their arch enemies the Whigs during the period of the American Revolution back in the seventeen hundreds." Bart continued to give a brief history lesson, explaining the Tories were British citizens, living in North Carolina during the American Revolution. They were loyal to King George the third, and they would conduct night raids, burning the homes of their hated rival the Whigs, because the Whig party supported a complete break from the England. The Whigs sided with the American patriots, that infuriated the Tories, and they would show their displeasure by burning the homes of their hated rival and then hide out in a large cave concealed by a large waterfall, thus the name Tories Den.

"Must have been a cave- in then, because the cave I was in only went back about 40 feet," exclaimed a pissed off Briggs. David Barret knew that the timing was right to lay the final cornerstone of his plan, changed the topic.

" Thanks for the history lesson Bart, but you screwed up the murder of Bill O'Toole, and now we have a FBI agent breathing down our neck, so tell me big man what the hell are we going to do now?" asked an angry David Barrette, knowing that Black Bart fly into a rage. David knew that Bart would have already formulated a plan to compensate for his perceived incompetence. Black Bart stared at David Barrette for a long time, trying to decide whether to kill this prick on the spot, but then he decided to wait until the current crisis has blown over.

"Okay arrogant ass, we are going to kidnap that pain in the ass FBI women, and hold her for ransom!"

"What kind of lame bullshit plan is that?" a confused ex-sheriff Brown asked

"Well we need to get rid of her nosy ass and pain in the ass Bill O'Toole. Therefore, we kill two birds with one stone. Listen I saw Agent Ryan and her husband at the street festival in Mayodan, they couldn't keep their dam hands off of each other, obviously stone cold in love with each other. Love is a powerful motivating tool, We kidnap her and send an email to her husband explaining that if he wants to ever see is wife again, He must murder Bill O'Toole!!!!. I have done research on Jake Ryan, and he is an ex-police officer, and very proficient with various weapons, including sniper rifles" proclaimed a very proud Black Bart, obviously proud of his background research.

The room went deathly quiet. And agent Briggs calmly asked, "How do you know about the sniper rifle, is he a dam hit man?" Agent Briggs chuckled

" Well to answer your question smart ass, Jake Ryan did a two year stint in the US Army, and was the best marksman of his graduating class in boot camp, and he used a sniper rifle to qualify" Black Bart smugly replied, pissed off my Agent Briggs's remark.

"Brilliant plan" David Barret shouted forging a fake look of admiration. If Black Bart could read David's mind he would be shocked by his thoughts, which were:

" What a fucking moron, the killing of Bill O'Toole made no dam sense, the attempt to hydraulic fracking in Stokes county had failed the night those chemical tanks explodes, so killing Bill O'Toole the environmentalist and leader of the movement to ban Fracking in stokes County was a moot point. Black Bart's real motivation for killing Bill O'Toole was revenge was for the killing of his son Chad, which quite possibly Bill had nothing to do with. He would help plan the kidnapping and subsequent murders of two Federal agents, because these actions would tie up all the loose ends of the disastrous attempt by Abbot Gas to frack in Stokes County, and also ensure that Black Bart, Brown, and Briggs would further incriminate themselves".

"Okay men we will kill these two, and then bury these bodies under the tons of coal ash the Belews creek plant." David said endorsing Black Bart's plan.

David patted black Bart on the back, while quietly planning his departure in less than 24 hours after the murders, knowing that by the time these morons turned on each other during an intense FBI probe, which he and his wife will be on the beach drinking rum and coke. David then knowing how important self-preservation is to sociopaths joyously concluded the plan by saying

"Agent Briggs keep working close to the FBI bitch until you can nab her at a vulnerable moment, we will lay low in these fine accommodations. Boys you need to do three things in the next three days, brush up on your Spanish, get your passports, and work on your tans, because you are going to be living international in some exotic location for the next few years. I have recently purchased some plane tickets to get you all as far away from this God-forsaken place as possible". David said smiling. Ah, karma is such a bitch, because in less than two days, he and his cronies will be slaughtered in the most grotesque way.

CHAPTER 8

Kelli was working alone at Vade Mecum springs; the makeshift FBI command post had been set on in the Gothic looking turn of the 19th century resort hotel. The three floors had been divided into three sections, with a crime lab on the first floor, command center with computers systems operating CODIS and other sophisticated software on the second, and the third floor working on tracking GPS, Cellphones, and other mass communications technology. Triangulation of cell phones communication with cell phone towers have been very helpful in tracking criminals that have just committed crimes like murder, home break-ins, or robbery. After working the fires at the well pad and being traumatize by the unholy hanging of the two roustabouts, Kelli told Jenkins and Running Deer to go back to their rooms and get some rest. It was 1:00 am, and Kelli had just gotten off the phone with Stokes County Regional Hospital, Bill Jr. was still in a medically induced coma. His condition was upgraded from serious to critical, Kelli needed to interview him as soon as possible, because she knew that Black Bart and David Barrette was behind the attempted to murder of Bill O'Toole.

Kelli was extremely agitated with her staff; both Black Bart and David Barrett had eluded FBI surveillance teams and were in the wind. Kelli was definitely going to piss some folks off at tomorrow morning skull session. Just as she was about to turn in for the night on the comfortable looking couch in an emergency workaholic sleep room, her cellphone rang, and the only human being that she would EVER answer the phone at 1:30 in the morning was on the other end.

"Hey Baby, I miss you terribly the last few days, sorry been working 24/7 on this case, it's really heating up literally". Kelli said before Jake had a chance to say hello.

Kelli then proceeded to tell Jake about the supernatural escape of Accali Blackclaw, the attempted murder of Bill O'Toole, the chemical fire at the Anderson well pad, and the disappearance of Sheriff Brown, David Barrett, and Black Bart. Jake was quite for what seemed to be an eternity, then he calmly said

"Kelli I want you to be extremely careful, because I have a premonition that an attempt will be made on YOUR life, I demand that you come home!" Jake said in very stern voice.

Kelli was taken aback by Jake' stern request, but knew he was anxious and very worried for her, so she calmly replied

" Jake I also have a feeling that this case is about the break in a very big way, quite soon, and for the sake of Brian Cox, and all the deputies that have lost their lives, I must stay here until all the suspects are apprehended. In fact there is an arrest warrant on Sheriff Brown for the kidnapping of Mercury Johnston; we have search parties, helicopters, and drones searching the rugged Sauratown Mountains for all three fugitives and this Indian shape shifter creature alas Accalia Blackclaw!" Kelli surprised herself by revealing that she suspected that Accalia Blackclaw and Hicicawi'a were the same entity.

"Kelli do you remember Eric Rudolph?" Jake asked

"Yes" Kelli responded knowing the direction of Jake's point

"Well then you know that he eluded the FBI, SBI, National Guard in the deep woods of North Carolina for years, why do you think you can append a vicious shape shifter Indian that is in its ancestral homeland?" Jake asked

" Jake I love you, and I could use your assistance on this

case, so If you can get up here, please come my love as soon as possible, but I am not leaving as long as these fugitives are still at large" Kelli said her voice shaking with emotion.

" I love you baby, and I will ask for some vacation time, and will try like hell to be there with in forty eight hours, and stay away from that Briggs guy. "I got a bad feeling about him, so I will see you in 48 hours, going to let you get back to work now, love you my Queen." The phone line went dead with a strange clicking sound as if someone was listening to their entire conversation.

As if he knew they were discussing him, Kelli phoned hummed to life, Kelli not waiting for any kind of salutation, immediately asked in an extremely agitated voice

"Where in the hell have you been Agent Briggs? After the leaving the O'Toole property, I have repeatedly tried to call, text and email you, with no response. We are supposed to be a team which means communication and teamwork."

" Well sorry, stalking a big foot monster in the deep woods of North Carolina is quite time consuming, and the cell reception is nonexistent" Briggs replied, thinking not to mention was extremely busy planning your kidnapping and execution is quite draining too, he smiled a wicked grin.

"Don't want to hear any of your BS, just have your ass in here at 5:00 Am", Kelly shouted into the phone, before hanging up.

Agent Briggs than began to pray, even though he didn't believe in God, that tomorrow would be the day, that he show that bossy bitch who the alpha dog was in the pack, and oh God he also prayed that she resisted with a very bit of courage and strength that she could muster.

CHAPTER 9

Kelli arrived at Vade Mecum Springs at 4:45, surprised to see that Agent Briggs had already arrived. He was already calling Stokes Country Hospital, and was in the process of checking on Bill Junior's condition; Kelli thought that perhaps He was trying to make amends for his actions the previous day. The Nurse at the ICU unit relayed that Bill Junior was still in a medically induced coma, but doctors were going to bring him to consciousness in the next couple of days.

"Wow you're in bright and early this morning, sorry I jumped on you yesterday," Kelli said in a cheery tone, trying to put the past behind them. She was aware that it was going to take complete cooperation between State and Federal agencies to solve this multifaceted case.

"Hey it okay, should have tried harder to keep you in the loop, I think we are all feeling intense pressure from this case" Briggs calmly replied.

Kelli thought to herself that this was the closest thing to an apology, which she was going to get from an alpha dog like Joel Briggs. Agent Running Deer and Sam Jenkins strolled into the command center sharply at 5 am, not wanting to stir the wrath of senior agent Kelli Ryan. Just as Kelli was going to brief the team on their duties for the day, the phone rang it was Dick Dockens, senior special agent in charge of cell phone triangulation and IMSI catchers division, and his phone call was going to initiate a firestorm that would put many lives in peril.

"Kelli it was Brilliant idea to place that IMSI catcher near

Pedro Gonzalez residence, I have got a recording a phone call between He and Black Bart, which you have to listen to immediately!"

Dick Dockens, not being able to contain his excitement, shouted into the Phone. Running Deer and Sam heard the usually laid back Dick Dockens way across the room, looked at each other in shock.

"Calm down Dick, I will be there in 2 minutes", Kelli replied as she motioned Sam, Running deer, and Agent Briggs to follow her upstairs. Kelli almost ran up the staircase, like a track star on crack! Running Deer looked at the ancient staircase and prayed to the Gods of the upper world that the creaking staircase would hold their weight.

Dick Dockens was waiting for them at the top of the stairs, and led them into a spacious conference room, with two agents monitoring IMSI catchers, that stimulate cell towers within a twenty-mile radius of where they are placed. These stingrays intercept calls, texts, and data streams, and have been instrumental in napping criminals ranging from murders to terrorist.

" Pull up a chair Agent Ryan, because after you listen to this tape, I promise you will not have a moment's rest for at least 36 hours" Weaver laughed.

Agent Briggs glanced at Kelli, and noticed the veins in his nemesis forehead were bulging like large rivers underneath her skin, and her skin was flush with excitement. He was actually kind of turn on by the surge of adrenaline, and wondered if they could get to know each better while she was a guest at the hunting cabin. Dick Dockens pushed play and the first voice they heard was Pedro Gonzales,

"Hey Boss you wanted me to give you a call"? Pedro asked with timidly. Black Barters evil, hissing voice answered the meager question with pure adulterated disrespect'

"YEA YOU DAM HEATHEN, I GOING TO BE GONE FOR A WHILE, YOU ARE IN FULL CHARGE OF THE COOKING OPERATION, BUT DO NOT ANYTHING DIFFERENT UNLESS YOU HAVE MY AUTHORIZATION! YOU DON'T WANT TO END UP MISSING LIKE DAVID GARCIA DO YOU?" Bart then laughed, and it sounded like wicked, insidious music played from the bowels of hell.

Pedro had heard of Black Bart's molten rage, meagerly replied

"YOU CAN COUNT ON ME, SIR"

"I HOPE I CAN, I WOULD HATE TO HAVE TO CUT YOU UP AND FEED YOU TO THE HOGS. NO ONE WOULD EVER COME LOOKING FOR YOU, BECAUSE YOU ARE HERE ILLEGALLY! Then the recording abruptly stopped.

Kelli then turned to her team, her eyes ablaze with an internal passion that burned like a nuclear fire.

"Dick want you to get a GPS triangulation on Black Bart's cell phone, need to get the physical location of that phone, Sam, you and Running Deer go and round up Pedro Gonzales for questioning, I want him here yesterday!"

Agent Briggs and I will start the process to get a warrant's to search Black Bart's home, which I know will lead to an arrest warrant for manufacturing illegal substances, and capital murder." Kelli said very loudly! As Agent Jenkins and Running Deer left the room, Sam joked that he was happily to leave, because that shouting virus seemed to be contagious.

CHAPTER 10

Accalia Blackclaw woke up in the isolated cave, shivering with severe hunger pangs, and was very confused about how she ended up there. She remembers lying down in her jail cell, under the intense moonlight of a gigantic full moon, and then waking up shivering with hypothermia in an empty cave. Her thoughts were fragmented, but she remembered a blaze that partially blinded her. She sat up doing a physical inventory of any other injuries, and noticed burn markings on her legs and arms, but they were just first-degree burns, not much worse than sunburn.

She walked over to the huge boulder that seemed to be blocking her path to freedom, she put her ear close to the mammoth boulder, and could hear the thunderous crash of cascading water, and then she knew instinctively that she was behind a large waterfall. Suddenly a wave of despair and depression swept over her, she began to sway back and forth, chanting an ancient prayer for protection, and then an ancient voice rose up from her tormented soul, calming and frightening her at the same time. The voice command her to lie down and get her rest, for tonight under the brilliant moon she would feast on the blood and bones of her people's tormentors.

CHAPTER 11

Kelli and Agent Briggs returned to the command center, with the warrant to search black Bart's home and land for the Meth manufacturing site, and a disgruntled and angry Pedro Gonzales was there to greet them with a snarl and flirtatious stare. He was a tall, slender man, with tattoos revealing his anti-social personality all over his body, including his face and neck. His skin was tan, and he had massive veins protruding from his long arms, indicating that he was no stranger to manual labor.

Kelli looked into the man's hostile eyes, and knew that extracting information from this harden criminal was not going to be easy, unless she used sound interrogation techniques.

"Pedro what can you tell me about David Garcia disappearance?" Kelli asked sternly. Pedro stared at Kelli with indifference, and calmly responded with " Me no speaka English" as a wicked grin appeared on his face.

Kelli anticipating such a response calmly brought in the John Alverez, a trained FBI interpreter who calmly explained to Pedro that the feds had interrupted a call between him and Black Bart. He also told Pedro that ICE agents were on their way to detain, incarcerate, and deport his ass back to Mexico, if he did not cooperate with the nice FBI agent. Pedro demeanor changed dramatically, and the information that Kelli needed flowed from his lips like avalanche flowing down Mount Everest. For the next thirty minutes Pedro, speaking in Spanish spilled his guts to Alvarez, and Kelli did not interfere with the flow of vital information from Gonzales to Alvarez, because there would be plenty of time to cross-exam Gonzales later since he was not going anywhere. Kelli wanted to get the entire confession on tape, before Gonzales changed his mind and clammed up.

After he finished speaking, Alvarez debriefed Kelli for the next twenty minutes,

"Pedro said that Black Bart not only used the Mexicans for hard labor in the fields during the day, but had them cook Meth for him at night. David Garcia was the supervisor of the meth operation, and had killed Shaun O'Toole after he found him snooping around the manufacturing site".

"David thought that Shaun O'Toole was a rival, canvassing the area planning to rob and kill his team, and then assume the operations under his direction. David had worked for the Mexican drug cartel, and decided to cut up Shaun's body and place them on the highest peaks of hanging rock state park, thus displaying his corpse in the most grisly fashion. David knew that this diabolic action would send a warning to any other potential drug dealers in the area, and that the Whitescarver operation was going to be the only source of Meth in Stokes County. "

"David Garcia made two mistakes however, He killed an innocent man, and perhaps the worst mistake of his young life was the action was not authorized by Black Bart! Black Bart was furious at Garcia for the unsanctioned killing, so Black Bart pulled out a 9millmeter pistol and shot Garcia right between the eyes." Alvarez relayed the information of Gonzales story verbatim and when silent as he sensed Kelli final questions. Kelli was silent for a moment, and then began her questioning of Gonzales.

"Pedro, how did find out that Shaun was an innocent man? And that he was in the wrong place at the wrong time."

335

Alvarez relayed the question to Pedro, who calmly responded that when they found Shaun's truck and it several ginseng plants that had been illegally poached, and had just stumbled on the "Meth operation".

Kelli shuffled her feet, and then asked, "How many witnesses was there to Black Bart shooting David Garcia?"

Pedro responded by saying "three including himself."

"What did Black Bart do with David Garcia's body?" Kelli asked sensing that she really did not want to know the answer to that question.

Pedro looked up at Kelli, and said in perfect English. "He feed him to the Pigs", he then winked at her and threw back his head and laughed like a demon on methamphetamine. Pedro cleared his throat, and explained to Kelli that Black Bart convinced Sheriff Brown to send his deputies on a suicide mission in the middle of the night, because He needed to cover up Shaun murder!

"Black Bart wanted that big foot creature in the woods to be blamed for both the slaughter of the deputies and the murder and dismemberment of Shaun's body". Pedro summarized like a trained criminologist.

"Interesting theory Pedro, but how did Sheriff Brown know that Hicictawia would attack the deputies?" Kelli asked her eyes not betraying her surprise of Pedro's excellent command of the English language.

Pedro reacted with surprise when Kelli mentioned the name Hicictawia, because he suddenly had a name for the monster that had been haunting his dreams for months.

"Simple, Sheriff Brown called DR. DRAKE, who telepathically relayed to Hicictawia that Black Bart was part of the search team, knowing that Black Bart would be miles away from any danger."

Kelli was too stunned to speak, but finally asked "Dr. Drake, the Stokes County medical examiner?" she asked in disbelief. Kelli knew that Brown and Dr. Drake path had crossed many times during investigations that including autopsies, so the two may have developed some kind of relationship, that bond gave credence to Pedro's story.

"That's the one, apparently Dr. Drake hates Black Bart, and he has the ability to control that beast from hell like a Marionette!" Pedro replied excitedly accidently slipping into his native tongue!

CHAPTER 12.

Kelli left the interrogation room in order to do some research and put her plan of apprehending Black Bart and David Barrett into action. She first met with John Running Deer and Sam Jenkins, who had been observing the interview through a two-way mirror.

"Men I need you to go and round up the rest of Pedro's amigos, they can collaborate Pedro's story of Black Bart killing David Garcia. They can all so give us details of the Meth operation that Black Bart was operating".

" Hey Running Deer bring your Nike running shoes, I think a lot of Pedro friends are going to have a sudden urge to go on their daily run, when they see us!" Sam Jenkins laughed.

"Kelli after these men witnessed what Black Bart did to David Garcia, do you really think they will testify against him?" John Running Deer asked.

" Good question John, but when I started mentioning deportation, and immigration customs enforcement agents checking to see if they are legally in the United States, the unrighteous shall begin to confess their sins" Kelli replied in her most evangelistic tone.

Kelli then left the room and ran Pedro's fingerprints and palm prints through an international database called Morph, which since 911 has been used to track fugitives and terrorist wanted by authorities around the world. Within five minutes of inserting Pedro's prints through Morph, Kelli suspicions were confirmed seems bad boy Pedro had several aliases, and was a drug runner for the Mexican cartel. He was suspected of killing a couple of Mexican DEA agents working undercover in Guadalajara. Kelli suddenly had all the leverage she needed for Pedro or whoever he was to cooperate with the investigation.

Kelli reentered the interrogation room, confident that she had all the ammunition she needed for Pedro to show them where the Meth manufacturing site was. Kelli and agent Briggs sat down and stared at Pedro with a menacing stare, making the harden criminal very aware that he was in danger of returning to Mexico and facing the wrath of not only the corrupt police but the vicious Mexican cartel.

"So Pedro, or should I say Francisca Castellanos, are you ready to leave this country, where the prisons have very nice accommodations like free medical care, cable television, and three squares a day, or return to deplorable conditions in Mexican prison? You might even run into some old buddies from the Cartel, I am sure they will be very happy to see you. Oh by the way the United States has a friendly relationship with our Neighbors to the south, which means I can get you extradited to your homeland within hours." Kelli said in a stern manner.

Pedro's face paled when Kelli called him by his birth name, dam he hated technology with a great passion. Pedro knew that he bitch had him by the balls, so he calmly said

"How can I be of assistance Senorita?" Pedro said politely.

"Well I want you to testify against Black Bart, which will guarantee you another two to three years in our comfy prisons, and to escort agent Briggs and I to Black Bart's Meth operational site," Kelli said cementing the deal.

"When are we leaving? cuz I have an appointment with the jail's barber at 2:30" he replied winking at Kelli as if they were lifelong friends.

Kelli and Briggs left the room, started coordinating the plan find, and apprehend Black Bart, and to raid the Meth lab, hopefully both Black Bart and David Barret will be there. Kelli laid out the plan, which included several State DEA agents, and an FBI swat team. Kelli then used her cell phone to call Jake, and told him that he was right about the slaughter covering up the violent murder of Shaun O'Toole. Kelli also relayed to Jake that she was leading a raid on black Bart's meth production site.

"You are a genius my love. I will call later tonight after the raid. Hopefully I will be in your manly arms soon," Kelli said in a low voice, not wanting others to hear her unprofessional breach of protocol. While Kelli was preoccupied with her brief call, Agent Briggs went outside to an isolated spot of the grounds of the massive hotel. He had to get the information to Black Bart that the FEDS and the SBI was coming to arrest him. Being aware of the many string rays in the area, Agent Briggs simply texted #2 to untraceable track phone. The recipients of the text would be then getting the room ready for their very special guest, but more importantly have the roadside IEDS in place, and the three-passenger Gater Utility vehicle at Jacobs ridge gassed up and ready to move at 2:00 pm.

Agent Briggs then proceeded to get strapped with various weapons for the raid, and he also put on his Black ops suit, which he wore for his last successful abducted of a government agent. Agent Briggs was a very superstitious, and like a professional athlete always wore the same clothes if the preceding game or mission had been productive. As he entered the rally point, Kelli and several of FBI swat team were already assembled, and Kelli suppressed at laugh and asked

"What's the deal with the man in black costume?"

Agent Briggs agitated by Kelli's question, calmly replied, "Oh I always wear black during funerals or kidnappings."

Kelli looked at Briggs and thought what a strange, weird thing to say, but she then thought maybe that she heard him incorrectly. She did not have time to ponder the answer, or ask him to repeat himself, so she just slightly laughed and nodded her head. She had no idea that with that slight nod of her head, that she was giving Briggs permission to take her and eventually her life.

CHAPTER 13

David Barrett was sitting at the primitive kitchen table, drinking a cup of coffee when he received the text from Briggs concerning the arrival of their new guest at approximately 2;00 pm. David already planned the extraction and kidnapping of agent Kelli Ryan down to the last smallest detail. His sharp reasoning ability had already predicted the interrogation of Pedro Gonzalez and the raid on the Meth production site. He laughed to himself thinking that these mere mortals were so very predictable.

Sheriff Brown and Back Bart had planted the IEDs at Duncan's bridge, which spans the Mayo river, and although the FBI SRT van was armored, plated, it was not match for three IED's planted directly underneath it. Black Bart would also be there killing any agents that managed to survive the blast and the frigid Mayo river with an AR-15 assault rifle, there would be no survivors. Black Bart loved this part of the plan; he exclaimed that it would be like "shooting fish in a barrel".

David had also found an email address for Jake Ryan, by searching the internet, David found the high school where Ryan coached football, and was set to send him an encrypted message, which would also, blocked the computer's IP address from any FBI hackers. The email will include a video of his beauty wife in her new surroundings, hopefully frighten and panicked. The email would demand the assassination of Bill O'Toole, in return his wife will be safely returned to him. David knew that with fracking off the table in Stokes County, it may little to no sense to kill Bill O'Toole, but Black Bart had a personal vendetta against O'Toole. David reasoned that the poor SOB should get something for being the sacrificial lamb. The dumb ass did not even realize that the ransom note sent from his laptop would further incriminate him in the murder of Bill O'Toole, thus taking the heat off the mind magician. David then planned to kill the two agents later tonight, the murdering of Bill O'Toole will be in vain, because by time Ryan pulls the trigger his wife will be stone cold dead.

David walking into the living room of the cave-cabin and noticed Sheriff Brown snoring on the couch, and black Bart wrapped in bearskin asleep in the chair, but men looked very serene and peaceful. David stood in silence and noticed that every square inch of the walls of the cave-cabin was covered with some kind of animal hide, bear, bobcat, rabbit, deer and mountain lion. The heads of these beast, were stuffed and mounted over the fireplace, but Black Bart would not be satisfied until the head of Hicitawi'a, the Tasmania devil of Stokes County, was at the centerpiece of his macabre collection.

"Hey great white hunter prepare for another guest, just got a text from Briggs, we will be bringing our guest of honor to our happy hiding place around 2:00 pm. Are you sure that the internet or WIFI in this God forsaken cave will allow be to send this email? Our entire plan is contingent on Jake Ryan receiving that email!" David said kicking Black Bart's feet.

"Hell Yes, and if you kick me feet again, you won't ever have to worry about a dam thing ever again" Black Bart growled not appreciating being awaken from his beauty rest. David turned toward the slumbering Sheriff Brown and shouted

"Get your old fat ass up and gas the gater up, and while you're at it check on our VIP guest in the next room, she hadn't made a sound all morning. I just hoped she hasn't escaped, but watch out don't spook her she may get up and beat your old ass". David threw that last insult in for free because he uttered despised the "conceited ex lawman.

"Hope she kills herself, save us from killing her later, in fact you want me to off her now?" asked Brown his eyes shining in anticipation.

"Naw may need her in the video I'm making" David Barret replied like some Hollywood producer of a low budget movie.

Brown opened the door, and silently walked in the room, shutting the door behind him. David and Bart looked at each other wondering if the shutting of the door indicating that a rape was intimate. But then David just shook his head from side to side and said with a grin

"Naw old fat ass couldn't even get it up" and they both laughed in union. Which was something that rarely happen? David then had a terrible thought perhaps they were bonding, and he promptly stifled his laugh.

As Brown walked into the room, He could not help but to ask "how was the environment in the room? and if it had met Mercury's EPA high flu-ten standards?".

Mercury Johnson was lying on her side on the hard red pine floor, a piece of tape was placed over her eyes, and her hands and feet were bound, she appeared to be asleep. Brown walked over and removed the tape over eyes, tearing if off violently. Sheriff Brown, being the sociopath that he was, wanted to see fear and terror in Mercury light brown eyes. He instead was greeted with a steely gaze of defiance and molten hot rage. Sheriff Brown almost peed himself, and out of unbridled fear struck Mercury in the face with his closed fist. Mercury recoiled in pain and shock, but through a bloody grin told Brown that he punched like a "lil bitch"!

"I'll show you a lil bitch," Brown screamed as he drew his hand back to punch Mercury again, when David grabbed his fist and bent it behind him. David's face was full of rage, slapped Sheriff Brown across the face and told him to leave the room. David looked down at Mercury and showed compassion for the young federal worker, who was unfortunate collateral damage, and apologized for a coward that would strike a women, particularly a defend less one.

Mercury gave a David a stare that penetrated his soul, and actually frightened him slightly. Mercury then calmly said, "That's okay David, appreciate your kindness and for that I'm going to kill your last" and Mercury laughed with a high-pitched tone that unhinged David so bad that he re taped her mouth got up and shut the door quietly behind him.

CHAPTER 14

Agent Briggs led the handcuffed Gonzales to the waiting FBI black SUV, which was also armor plated, and placed him in the back seat, and gave him a thumbs up sign. Pedro knew then that He would be free very soon, and nodded back at Briggs. Agent Briggs slipped into the driver's seat, Kelli finally arrived after briefing the leader of the SWAT team. Kelli ordered the driver of the SWAT SRT Van to stay closely behind them, At 1300 hours on November 6; the super moon would make its final appearance tonight, but would be hidden because of a pending ice storm that was ushering in a strong cold front. The FBI caravan left Mecum Springs Hotel on their way to a bloody nightmare.

"The cooking site is only about 10 miles away, take a left on Boiling Springs road, and follow it for eight miles, then take a left on Duncan's bridge road." Gonzales commanded like a backseat driver.

Agent Briggs was only traveling about 60 miles an hour, but speed up considerably, when he reached Duncan Bridge road. Briggs checked the rear-view mirror, and as ordered, the van was right on his tail. He could see the intersection of Cedar Fork road and Duncan Bridge road about a quarter of a mile ahead. Cedar Fork Road intersected Duncan's bridge road right before the road crossed the Mayo river; Cedar Fork road branched off Boiling Springs road at about a 45-degree angle. Briggs glanced at Pedro in the backseat, and knew that his accomplice was ready to pounce. At the very last moment with blinding speed, Briggs cut the wheel to the left causing the car to swerve violently on to Cedar Fork road, while the SWAT van continued on Duncan Bridge road.

The explosion on the bridge rocked the SUV, and Kelli was caught by complete surprise. She turned in time to see the van explode into a huge fireball, and the bridge collapse. The two events happen so simultaneously, that they seemed to be connected. Kelli was stunned by Briggs' betrayal. She knew that she was in deep shit, so she turned toward Briggs and was about to deliver a blow to his solar plexus, when two strong arms wrapped around her throat, cutting off he oxygen supply, and before losing consciousness, the last image she saw was Briggs staring at her like a shark before it consumes it prey.

"Hey ease up on the strangle hold, she is unconscious. Don't want her dead yet!" Briggs yelled

"Oh that's my bad. I Just got carried away" Gonzales apologized before releasing Kelli.

Kelli's body slumped down in the passenger seat, and Briggs just had to check her pulse and make sure the idiot did not kill her prematurely. Briggs breathed in a sigh of relief, Kelli's pulse was slow and steady, just then Black Bart emerged from the wood line on the other side of the river, anxious to shoot some fish in a barrel. He watched the river for any survivors bobbing up like turtles sunning on a hot, sultry summer day.

Bart knew that there would be no survivors because of some deep trenches under the bridge. The combined weight of tactic gear, and weapons like assault rifle and shotguns would weight any survivors down better than cement shoes. As Briggs was scanning the water, he noticed Black Bart give him the thumbs down sign. Briggs pulled his 9mm out of his waistband, and turned toward Gonzales and said,

"Your employer just sent a message that he wished to terminate your employment, but he wanted to let you know it's not personnel, just business", and then Briggs dealt Pedro the same fate as David Garcia.

Briggs saw Black Bart get in a canoe and start paddling down river, He would paddle about 3 miles, then hike two miles up to the Cabin-cave. Agent Briggs hated Black Bart, but he did appreciated raw toughness and black Bart did epitomize the tough mountain man personification. He backed the car up, and proceeded on Cedar Fork road to his meeting with Brown. As Briggs approached, the terminus of Cedar Fork road Kelli began to stir, so he stopped the car and injected her with more sedative. He did not want her awake and thus harder to control as they ascended to the cabin-cave in the all-terrain vehicle.

Sheriff Brown emerged from the woods on the 3-passenger Gator utility vehicle that would transport them via the logging trail up the mountain.

"Dam thing even has power steering" Brown bragged as he pulled up next to the SUV. Briggs scanned the terrain; there was a sheer drop-off of at least 3,000 feet at the junction of Cedar Fork Road and the logging trail.

" Were not on some dam camping trip here, time is of the essence, so get off that dam thing and come over here and help me push this example of government waste off this cliff, but first come over and get our guest secured in the Gater." Briggs ordered.

After Kelli was strapped into the Gator, the two men pushed the SUV off the cliff; it careened down the mountain and exploded on impact as it hit the bottom three thousand feet below.

" Maybe the Dumb ass FBI will think we missed a turn, and spend all their time looking for us down there." as he watch the SUV burn leaving a smoke signal for the search party that would be looking for them.

" Ah don't worry about that smoke signal, we got some weather moving in starting as a rain and ending as Ice pellets later tonight" Sheriff Brown said sounding like a meteorologist on the evening news.

As they started on the bumpy trek up the old logging trail, both men believed that the inclement weather to be a sign from the Gods, that they will be protected from the wrath of the law enforcement agencies closing in on them, but they would soon learn that the weather would be an conspirator to their slaughter.

CHAPTER 15

Accalia was curled up in a fetal position, shivering with the onset of hypothermia, her starvation had driven her to eat small cave dwelling spiders and bugs. He had been dreaming of mother, who had died from the abuse that her father black Bart had inflicted on her. Her mother came to her in her dreams, comforting by singing to her as if she was a small child. Accalia opened her eyes, she could feel a deep stirring in her soul, the dark beast within her was beginning to stir. It chanted ancient Cherokee war chants inside her brain, and she suddenly realize that it was going to erupt like a sudden spring storm killing everything in its path. She knew that it had starved her, so she would consume every morsel of the meal that it would provide for her. That human flesh, blood and bones would be the only food that would satisfy her unquenchable hunger.

Briggs reached the summit of the mountain around 3:00 pm, and he and Brown wasted no time in getting Kelli into the Cabin-cave. Kelli was semi-conscious but she recognized Black Bart and David Barrett alas mind magician and she suddenly realized that David was going to destroy her mind before he and the others murdered her. She was quickly taken to the back room. She was laid next another unfortunate soul, and her feet and hands were bound with tape. Briggs removed Mercury tape from her mouth, so the two could communicate with each other. Kelli thought maybe Briggs thought that by having the two exchange words that it would heighten their fear thus creating the right environment for the mind Magician to first hypnotize Kelli. then her fear would bring forth her posttraumatic stress syndrome condition to reappear. David hoped to traumatize this brilliant agent enough to turn her into a psychotic basket case, thus sending a truly horrifying video of her to her loving husband. They both could hear the men discussing rather loudly about their impending burial under the tons of coal ash at the King power's disposal site.

David Barret suddenly walked into the room, and knelt beside Kelli, and he began to whisper in Kelli's ear in a rheumatic cadence, at first, Kelli resisted, but to battle this mental giant was futile and after only ten minutes, Kelli succumbed to his hypnotic chant. Mercury began to realize what David was doing to Kelli, and screamed

"Stop terrorizing her you sadistic bastard! If you're going to kill us, then why are your torturing her?" David paused for a moment and slipped the tape back on Mercury's mouth, and continue his onslaught on Kelli's soul by whispering into her ear,

"Hercules is coming for you, He is not dead! He is right outside your door, ready to snuff the life out of you".

Kelli felt a chill run down her spine; she began to feel as if she was suffocating. Her face began to contort into a mask of unbridled horror and repulsion. Saliva was running down her chin, and she screamed an unholy wail of fear, anger, and pure, pure terror! It is at that moment that David Barret pointed his cell phone at her and began filming the video that he would send to Jake. David began to laugh as he thought about the old cliché "that a picture was worth a thousand words", and he knew that Jake Ryan would move heaven and earth to kill Bill O'Toole.

David then left the room with his coveted prized video, and after the proper inscription, which hid the ISP from the recipient, sent the grotesque video to Jake Ryan. In the next room, Kelli was trashing back and forth, fighting an invisible entity, when Mercury grabbed her hand and began to deescalate the mental damage David had done. Mercury knew several techniques of combating PTSD from helping her brother, overcome his demons that possessed his soul, while being deployed to Iraq in the early 2003. Mercury used several desensitization methods to help Kelli to normalize her breathing and mental stability. Kelli reached out and grabbed Mercury hand, and Mercury then realized that a bond had been created between the two women, and their friendship was going to be a formidable opponent to David and his demonic clan.

CHAPTER 16

Jake was working on his laptop, during his three pm planning period, and was grading his seniors essay's on the causes of the cold war of the 1960's between the Soviet Union and the United States. He was about to award another strong F, when his new email notification pinged on his cell phone. Jake needing a distraction from the horror of the past hour, so he eyed the email address. He was going to delete it, because he did not recognize the sender's address, but a voice in his mind that sounded very much like Brian Cox has demanded that he opened it.

As Jake started watching the video, and he recoiled as if he was hit by an invisible bullet, and he inhaled sharply, trying desperately to shield his heart from the emotional pain of seeing his queen's face contorted into a mask of pain. Jake then saw the picture of the man that he had to kill, or his wife would be lost to him for eternity. Just when Jake was about to call Director Jacobs to send of a computer forensic team to trace the email back to the sender, the phone rang it was Dr. Brackett from Stokes County Hospital apologizing about the technician not recognizing the enzyme in Kelli's blood work that indicated that Jake was going to be a father. Jake felt like he had just been stabbed in the heart, because his wife and unborn child was in unspeakable danger. Jake left the school, without notifying any of the administrators in the main office, because he had no time to waste! As a veteran police officer, Jake knew that if a kidnapped victim is not found after twenty-four hours, the odds are that the victim would not survive! Jake immediately called Jacob's office, and as if he was expected, his call Jacobs answered.

"What the hell is going on Jacobs?" Jake screamed into the phone, taking the full brunt of his fury out on Director Jacobs.

"Calm down Jake, not in the mood for your drama, just lost twelve members of our elite Swat team. Divers just recovered their bodies at approximate 14:00 at Duncan's bridge in Stokes County. I have been consoling wives and girlfriends all afternoon and don't want to hear any of your BS!" Jacobs's voice was trembling with rage.

Jake relayed the information about the plot to kill Bill O'Toole, and that he was en route to Dulles to catch a 5:00 pm flight to Greensboro. He suggested that Director Jacobs place O'Toole in protective custody.

"Jake this is a Federal investigation, and if you interfere, I will have your ass arrested" Jacobs yelled into a dead phone.

Jake floored the accelerator, He had no plans to kill Bill O'Toole, first his conscious would not allow him to kill an innocent man, but the bastards that had taken his wife were fair game. He would not rest until his wife was back safely in his arms, and some preacher was reciting a eulogy over her kidnapper's corpses.

PART 7

Terror at Tories Den

CHAPTER 1 / 6:00 PM, NOVEMBER 6TH

In the cold dark cave, Accalia began to shiver as waves of hunger pains were cascading throughout her stomach. She succumbed to the pain in her stomach, and she laid down on the giant bolder that been her bed for the last three days. Her mother's sweet spirit swept over her calming her, but then the mysterious heat began to build in her exhausted body, consuming every cell, tissue, and organ system. The metamorphosis had begun, arms elongated, fingers turned to claws, and hair began to sprout over every portion of her body. Accalia began to sob, shaking her head in defiance willing the transformation to end, but then a strange chant of her grandmother Dakota Blackclaw calmed her by claiming that vengeance of her people would be fulfilled tonight and the beast would be gone forever. Once the transformation ended, Hicictawi'a leaped from the table, and with supernatural strength rolled back the boulder that sealed the tomb. The beast was covered with ice pellets, as it stood on the edge of the cliff, and howled down into the abyss. The howl was filled with so much rage and hatred that the windy, stormy night could not drown it out.

CHAPTER 2/ 7:00 PM, NOVEMBER SIXTH

Inspector King was there to meet Jake as he emerged from umbilical cord, which connected the United 727 to the main terminal. Inspector King noticed the Jake looked like a man on the verge of unraveling, and knew that the next five minutes were going to be very unpleasant! King saw the Jake's eyes were very bloodshot, and his hair was uncombed, his face was frozen into a perpetual look of worry and fear. As if his vision was impaired, Jake nearly knocked several people over as he hurried over to King; he was a man on a mission, a quest to save his young wife and their unborn child!

"What the hell is going on King?" Jake almost screamed as he neared the spot were King was standing.

"Calm down Jake! I will explain the situation in detail on our ride to Stokes County; this is not the place to discuss intimate details of this case." King said shocked by Jake's appearance and attitude. King then reflected over his 40-year career, and knew that the very best law officers were very intense and emotional.

"Jake I would like to introduce you to Larry Cole, He is from the FBI office in Raleigh, and is going to directing the search for Kelli. We have the finest joint team of FBI and SBI agents at Duncan's bridge, tracking your Wife and a suspected rogue SBI agent named Joel Briggs". King explained looking at Jake with a very worried expression on his face.

For the first time Jake noticed the man standing next to

King, He was massive over 6'3" inches tall with dark brooding features, dark almost black eyes, that commanded respect. His forehead protruded over his eyes, and formed the classic 5 head, of the classic cave dweller or Neanderthal.

"Jake, I have heard great things about your detective skills, I would be honored for you to assist us in the search for your wife," his thunderous voice echoed in Jake's ears as Jake shook the humongous paw of the gigantic federal agent.

On the car ride back to Stokes County, Inspector King broke the terrible news about the burned out carcass of the FBI black Sudan that was found at the bottom of 3,000 cliff named dead man's leap, about 20 miles southeast of Danbury NC.

Jake inhaled sharply, and exhaled only when King told him that the FBI response team found no bodies inside.

"We suspect the Briggs, and ex sheriff Brown, Black Bart, and David Barrett are the ones for kidnapping of special Agent Ryan and EPA Agent Mercury Johnson. We believe that they are holed up in a hunting cabin on Jonas ridge, but so far our surveillance aircraft has not been able to locate this cabin."

"Then what the hell are you waiting for get some boots on the ground searching for that cabin tonight?" Jake implored.

Inspector King turned around in his seat, so he could look Jake in the eyes,

"Jake there is some is a strong ice storm moving in, hiking the 4 miles straight up the mountain would be impossible, because of the ice and strong winds. The visibility would be poor, and we have information from a reliable source that Bart Whitescarver has booby trapped the entire area around the cabin. Jake, the FBI has already suffered eleven causalities today and we do not want to add to the body count by sending teams up there in the middle of the night. We have decided to wait until 6:00 am to conduct the raid on the cabin." King then turned around sensing the firestorm that was about to erupt. Jake could feel the rage as it coursed through his body, and he let out his unholy rant

"Dam you and your cowardliness, the strongest police force in the world is afraid of four men hiding in a hunting cabin, while my pregnant wife is in extreme danger. Well screw you all, I will assemble a team and assault the cabin tonight." fumed an angry and hostile Jake Ryan. Larry Cole then turned around and laid the riot act down.

"YOU WILL STAND DOWN, AND IF YOU GO ANYWHERE NEAR THAT CABIN TONIGHT, I WILL PERSONALLY ARREST YOU FOR ON FEDERAL CHARGES FOR INTERFERING WITH A FEDERAL INVESTIGATION!" Cole shouted then looked at Jake with a deadpan stare, as if to dare him to fisticuffs! Jake balled his fist ready and was about to deliver a blow to Cole's solar plexus, but then He realized that he would his pregnant wife no good by sitting in Stokes County jail. Jake calmed then asked, "Why did you mention that I could assist in the investigation?"

Cole's face then soften, because he had compassion for Jake, and simply replied

"Jake, I meant that I wanted you to use those great detective skills you have behind the scenes, by giving us your powerful insight into what is motivating these man, and strategies on how to capture them."

Jake then relaxed in the backseat, and began to formulate his plan to rescue his queen TONIGHT, because Jake Ryan would walk through the fires of hell to save his beloved. When Jake got to his hotel room, He called Sam Jenkins and John Running Deer, and asked them to help in rescuing Kelli tonight.

"Ah Jake both running Deer and I have been given the riot act by that new asshole Larry Cole, we will be terminated immediately if we help you in anyway. You know that I love Kelli, and would do anything to help her. In fact, Running Deer and I will be leading the rescue in the morning. Jake I deplore you to wait until morning; I have a family and can't risk my retirement pension," muttered an ashamed Jenkins. Jake could barely contain his disappointed as he asked Jenkins if he knew that Kelli was pregnant, and then he disconnected the call.

Jake then called Bill O'Toole, because he knew that Bill O'Toole knew that backwoods of Stokes County better than anyone. Bill answered the phone on the first ring and Jake relayed how Black Bart had kidnapped his wife, and was blackmailing Jake to kill him for the safe return of his wife. He then ask Bill O'Toole, if he would help him rescue his wife tonight... There was a brief pause on the other end of the line, and Jake was sure that Bill O'Toole was going to tell him he was nuts, and not to call him again.

"What hotel did you say you were in?" asked Bill O'Toole in a stoic but calm voice

"I'm in the River gate hotel" Jake replied with renewed hope.

" I will be there in one hour, and Jake I'm bringing all the cold weather I can assemble because trust me brother we are going to need it!" growled Bill O'Toole.

Jake disconnected the call, and slowly realized that the man that he was supposed to kill was going to risk his life to save his beloved queen. Bill O'Toole never said anything about traps, or the stormy, cold weather, because he was man's man. Bill O'Toole was the kind of man that would storm the beaches of Normandy on D-day, under withering machine gun fire with a gleam in his eye and a devilish smirk on his face.

Jake was busy getting his gear together, when there was a tentative knock on the door. Jake opened the door, and to his surprise Sam Jenkins and John Running Deer was standing at his door. Jake ushered the men into his cheap and ancient motel room. The room had no amenities at all but an uncomfortable bed with a cigarette burn on the bedspread. Jake noticed that both men were decked out in FBI issued cold weather gear, complete with Parka's and Bib coveralls. They both had huge backpacks packed with cold weather survival gear.

"Going somewhere gentleman?" Jake asked his face beaming with gratitude.

" Hell ya, couldn't let you have all the fun, besides those government jobs are a royal pain in the Arse, all that bureaucratic red tape, when you fill our request for leave or vacation," laughed Sam.

" What he said" comically retorted John Running Deer

Jake grabbed both men, and gave them a giant bear hug, and with tears in his eyes thanked them and promised them both that he would find them gainful employment if the feds let them go.

" No thanks Jake, don't want to be a custodian at some high school, because I would have to kill some of those smart ass kids," Sam laughed again

" Now enough of this mushy shit Jake, let's go save my boss" Running Deer interjected. Just then, there was another knock at the door, and Jake opened the door and there stood Bill O'Toole covered head to toe in insulated camouflage from head to toe. He then shoved a pack in Jake's face and told him to quit lollygagging on put it on.

At around 9:00 pm, after Jake changed into his survival gear, the men climbed in an FBI metal plated SUV, stocked with weapons ranging from 9 millimeters, to Assault rifles, and under the cover a fierce ice storm, they rode off like the four horseman of the Apocalypse.

CHAPTER 3/ 7:30 PM, NOVEMBER SIXTH

The fire was crackling, as Sheriff Brown walked into the living room of the cabin-cave. The temperature had dropped to near freezing outside, and inside the cabin, the temperature was not much warmer. Ice pellets carried in the cave by 30 mile an hour winds pelted the tin roof of the cabin.

" Well men been monitoring the search parties all afternoon on my scanner, seems as if both the SBI and FBI have called off the search until the morning because of a little ice and darkness, What a bunch of pussies". Brown said laughing like a three-day-old idiot.

" I guess it's our civic duty to help keep those two beauties in the back room as warm as possible," Briggs said with a gleam in his eye.

" You touch either of those women, and you're a dead man," David commanded looking at Briggs with a sudden look of intense hatred. Briggs had no way of knowing that David had witnessed his mother being raped by his father at the tender age of ten.

" Dam Chill out, I was trying to lighten the atmosphere of the room." a solemn faced Briggs exclaimed

David ignored the apologetic Briggs, as he laid out the plan to bury the bodies in the coal ash remnants at Bellows creek, and then gave each man their fake passports, identification papers, and plane tickets to separate tropical paradises. He also gave each man detailed instruction on how to vary their appearances with disguises. What he did not explain to them is that the airline tickets were a complete and utter fakes, and while the authorities were busy arrested these three stooges, He would be on a plane bound for an island off the coast of Belize.

CHAPTER 4/ 9:30 PM

About the same time that Jake Ryan had rounded up his posse, Hicictawia was standing outside the cabin-cave using its psychic ability to gather information about the four humans inside. It scanned the house , mentally searching for the gifted one, the one they call the mind magician. Hicictawia was planning a surprise attack, and was going to take out the greatest threat first. It wanted to catch David Barrett in a semiconscious state or in a deep sleep and control his mind, before David could ramp up his great powers.

David Barrett was mentally and physically exhausted, because last month had drained him of all his telepathic, and mind controlling capabilities. He was like a drained battery with very little strength left, and the only way to recharge his gifts was to sleep. The roaring fire, and the bearskin draped over his body, were great tools for the sand man. David Barrett closed his eyes and drifted off sleep, a fatal error that initiated an unholy slaughter. When Black Bart knew that David was in a deep sleep, He told Briggs to go have his way with Kelli Ryan. Black Bart hated agent Ryan with a deep passion, and the mental image of Briggs defiling her, gave the old man a raging hard-on. In fact, after he got through bashing David Barrett's arrogant head in, he would sample the fine government ass in the back bedroom. He figured it is the least the government could do, since he kept, illegal aliens gainfully employed and not on the street selling drugs or committing violent crimes like armed robbery.

Briggs opened the door the back bedroom and began to unzip his pants, his penis was standing rigid in anticipation of showing Kelli Ryan who the alpha dog was. He untied Kelli's legs, pulled her clothes off, and slid her panties down to her feet, the heat was building in his loins. He did not want to be premature, so he awkwardly mounted her, as Kelli screamed and cried out in pain. Just as Briggs was on the verge of thrusting into her, Mercury Johnson emerged out of the darkness, and sent a roundhouse kick to Briggs solar plexus. Briggs was on the verge of unconsciousness, when Mercury delivered the uppercut that caused Briggs to collapse at an angle, thus he was sound asleep before he hit floor right next to Kelly.

" Police rule number one dumb ass, always clear the room of any threats," Mercury shouted into the sleeping man's ear.

" How in the hell did you get out of those cuffs Mercury?" Kelli asked in bewilderment.

" Growing up with three older brothers, you learn many tricks! We have got get outta here," Mercury said as she began to untie Kelli's hands and feet. Mercury sensed they were in grave danger, as she helped Kelli too her feet.

" Something is wrong with my legs. "I can't move them." Kelli cried out. Mercury knew that Kelli had suffered mental anguish at the hands of David Barret and John Briggs, and even though nothing was physically wrong with Kelli's legs, her mind was crippled with fear had shut down her ability to walk! Mercury then heard an inhuman scream from the front of the cabin, and instinct knew that in order to save Kelli's life she had to escape without her.

" Listen Kelli, I am going out the window. I will be close by." as she lifted Kelli up and placed her in the only closet in the room.

" Just be as quiet as you can!". Mercury said locking eyes with Kelli.

Looking into her eyes, Kelli could see the tears of guilt

and shame well up in Mercury eyes. Kelli knew that in order for Mercury to save her life, she had to escape.

" Listen don't feel guilty for leaving me, trust me I have been in tougher situations," Kelli laughed thinking back to Portsmouth Island.

" Dam your one brave white girl" Mercury said with a bright smile, as she climbed out the window, draped in only a heavy blanket.

As the drama unfolded in the back bedroom, Black Bart hovered over a sleeping David Barrett, raised the fire poker over his head, and with one sweeping downward swing was going to end the life of the man that he despised more than any other creature on God's green earth. He was interrupted by the sound of feet shuffling around the front portion of the cave, He quickly turned to a wide-eyed Sheriff brown, who was excited about witnessing his first ever head bashing..

" Hey make yourself useful, and go out and check what's making that dam noise," Black Bart ordered.

" Ah shit it's nothing but the Dam wind, I would much rather watch you bash his brains in! by the way have you got any popcorn?" laughed a soulless Brown.

Black Bart lowered the fire poker, and walked over to Sheriff Brown and looked at him with a stare that turned Brown's blood ice cold, because Brown could see the murderous rage in Black Bart's eyes. He grabbed his coat, and went out the front door without saying another word, as if he was petrified that there would be a double head bashing.

Black Bart raised the fire poker again, and then the door burst open, because the beast that stood in the door way was so incredibly hideous that Black Bart held the poker in mid-air and began to urinate in his pants.. David awoke from a vivid dream of his beautiful wife, to a seductress holding firewood for the roaring fire. David smiled when he recognized the seductress as Jennifer Miller, the commissioner's wife, who was married to that coward Bob Miller, a poor excuse for a man. David thought the Gods brought her to him, so she could demonstrate to her the sexual prowess of a REAL MAN. Black Bart was shocked to observe the reaction of David Barrett, as he smiled and then blow a kiss to this nine foot, snarling, saliva drooling, werewolf holding the bloody limbs of the recently departed Sheriff Brown.

Black Bart then had a rare moment of clear mental processing, and realized that this thing before had the great mind magician in a hypnotic trance, and was given the arrogant bastard a taste of his own medicine. He was thinking that his idea was totally impossible nothing was more powerful than the great mind magician was. The beast looked at Black Bart with his hideous, black eyes and commanded Black Bart to sleep, and suddenly Black Bart dropped to floor, as if he had been shot between the eyes, hitting his head on the hard floor of the cabin/cave. During the split second that the creature turned its attention to Black Bart, David's quick mind began to stage a mental comeback. His psychic and telekinesis abilities began to surge back , and he suddenly came to the realize that he was in a mental battle with a creature that possessed the same abilities he had, and that he was engaged in a "BATTLE OF THE TITANS" and the loser of the battle would pay with their lives.

David thought that the thing in front of him was a DEEP FAKE, created by facial mapping technology to manipulate people's voices, bodies, and faces, somehow the FBI had entered into hippocampus and stole his memory of the provocative Jennifer Miller, who had aroused his sexual urges. David mind screamed him to counteract the power of the beast, but it was too little too late, David Barrett the great mind magician was going to be brain fucked by entity much more powerful than he was. David was about to submit to the beast as a submissive would to its master. Jennifer crossed the doorway and was in David arms, kissing him and stroking his manhood. The rational mind of David Barrett sunk back into the confides of his soul, and David was at the mercy of the powers of Hell.

Jennifer smiled at him and producer a razor, instructed David to start cutting himself as foreplay, and as David began to cut his way through his layers of skin, starting with the epidermis, then the Dermis, and finally the Hypodermis, thus skinning himself alive. He laughed as the razor peeled away layers of his skin, because of being in such a deep hypnotic trance, he felt no pain. David Barret had blood pouring from every pore of his body, and before his cardiac muscle mercifully stopped beating, He smiled and with blood, pouring out of his mouth confessed his undying love to Hicictawia.

CHAPTER 5- 9:45 PM/ NOVEMBER 6

Black Bart woke to ice pellets bouncing off the top of his massive head, there was a freezing cold wind caressing his face. He tried to scratch his face, but his arms and legs would not move. He then realized that he must be dreaming, and that he would awake from this nightmare at any moment, until He heard a women voice chant the words " e do da", the Cherokee words for father. His heart skipped a beat, and fear coursed through his body, like a raging river. He turned his eyes toward the sound, and looked up into the hatred filled eyes of his illegitimate daughter Accalia Blackclaw! The daughter that he ignored all her life, claiming that she was not his, but in his heart he knew the blood that flowed through her veins was of his genetic type. The recent intuitive feeling that all the evil that he had done would coming back to haunt him was appearing right before him in the form of his only daughter.

She spoke to him , through telepathic communication

" To the earth you shall return my father, for the laws of the universe command that you should pay for your sins. You are a demonic minion that will be sent to the underworld screaming, and grinding your teeth in pain. My mother died at your hands, now through the Karma of my ancestors, you will perish at her offspring's hands."

She then poured some sweet substance on his head, and

it filled into his eyes. Again, he tried to move his hands, but they were paralyzed. His daughter squatted in front of him, and placed a hand held vanity mirror in front of his face, then she shined a flashlight so he could see his reflection. TO BLACK BART'S HORROR, HIS HEAD WAS PROTRUDING OUT OF THE FROZEN GROUND, LIKE SOME KIND OF PLANTED EAR OF CORN!. To his Chagrin, the rest of his body had been buried underground, and when he opened his mouth to scream, assassin bugs into his mouth. Accalia knew that these small bugs would suck all the juices out of her father's body, devouring his eyes like tasty morsels. If he lived long enough, he would develop a sickness called Chagas, which would cause her demonic father's heart to stop.

The assassin bugs were feasting on the honey, hundreds of bites per minute causing the face and scalp of her beloved father to disappear. She knew the bugs would die soon from the subfreezing temperatures, but not before the demons from the underworld transported his father's soul to his eternal resting place. He could not scream, because the assassin bugs were crawling down his throat looking for a warm place to continue their feast. Accalia did not have to hear his pitiful scream of pain and anguish, because when she looked into his demon black eyes she saw that the extraordinary pain and fear purging his soul.

Kelli was Paralyzed with fear, she could hear something of massive size walk into the room, it's breathing sounded like the Chinook winds as they cascaded down the leeward side of the Rocky mountains. She curled up in ball, suffering from the symptoms of PTSD, alternating between burst of anger and deep fear. She clutched the butcher knife, ready to do battle with whatever opened the door to her hiding place. She heard a weird chant, as if the thing outside was casting some kind of spell, then she heard a snapping sound as if someone stepped on twig or stick while hiking in the woods.

She was not prepared for the monstrosity that opened the door, the thing was the most horrifying image that Kelli had ever seen. Its hellish red eyes locked on her with evil intensity, as it reached in with its claws to cut her body to pieces, but Kelli being a fighter to the bitter end lashed out with unbridled fury . The knife buried into the claw of the beast, but the beast reacted as if it was stung by an insect. It grabbed Kelli, who was screaming and kicking with all her strength, but Hicictawi'a picked her up as gently as a mother would a newborn baby. Hicictawi'a had decided to use Kelli as bait, using her set up a trap for the evil palefaces that wish to destroy it. It would lure them to its lair, and consume their flesh, using their souls to energize it.

Kelli looked around the room for a weapon, but only spotted Briggs lying on the floor. Kelli could not believe her eyes as she gazed at the deceased Briggs on the floor, something was terribly wrong. Kelli stared at the body of Briggs for what seemed like eternity, and then it came to her, He was lying on his stomach, but his eyes were staring back at her. His head had been twisted completely around like some nightmarish Owl peering at something behind it. She then knew that the snapping sound she had heard in the closet was Briggs vertebra snapping to accommodate the hideous body posture that he would be found in.

Kelli looked at Briggs again, and realized with great horror, that Briggs back was rising and falling, she then knew that Hicictawi'a had left a zombie behind to guard the hunting cabin. The presence was too ghastly for Kelli and she opened her mouth to scream, and that is when Hicictawi'a brushed its claw against Kelli's cheek mercifully sending Kelli into a deep sleep. Hicictawi'a then wrapped Kelli into a thick bearskin blanket, and then disappeared through the front of the cave into the black, frozen night.

CHAPTER 6

2:00 AM, November 7

John Running Deer was in the point position, clearing the path of any booby traps that Black Bart set on the trek up to Jonah's ridge. He had already uncovered one IED, and a bear snare on the route that Bill O'Toole knew led to the Whitescarver hunting cabin. Bill O'Toole had been to the cabin many years ago, when Black Bart and he were best friends instead of the mortal enemies they are today. The cabin was invisible from the air, because it was under the natural Quartzite rock that encased it, even homegrown hikers and hunters were oblivious to its consistency.

The group equipped with night vision goggles , were moving slowly up the spine of Jonah's ridge. They were spaced about 15 yards apart, moving in a condensed wedge formation, because of the rocky terrain. The group of men were moving like a tactical Army squad on a recon mission. Each man had an AR 15 assault rifle, several rounds of ammunition, and several explosive devices with them. After about 3 miles straight up, John Running Deer suddenly stopped, and motioned for the others. It was very clear by his animated gesturing that he had discovered something horrible. When his comrades were assembled, Running Deer shined his flashlight over to a line of Canadian pines, and underneath the pines, was a frozen human head protruding out of the ground like some gigantic deformed mushroom.

The men approached the head with caution, and as they got closer, Bill O'Toole knew that it was the head of his hated rival Bart Whitescarver. Running Deer knelt down and examined the head, the mouth was wide open frozen in an eternal scream of pain, and anguish. Running Deer and the others found dead assassin bugs in Black Bart's, throat, nose, and ears, as if the bugs tried to warm themselves in the bitter cold. Jake looked down at the remains of Bart's eyes, which had been consumed revealing the optic nerve leading to Bart's Brain, so it wasn't a stretch of Jake imagination to believe that the bugs had dined on Bart's brain before they succumbed to the cold.

" It's a method the Apache used to torture their enemies, except they used fire ants," Running Deer said, as he stood up sensing that their destination was very near.

" Dam even that evil bastard didn't deserve that" Bill O'Toole mumbled as he turned to face Running Deer. But after quiet reflection about how is own son had been quartered and laid out for display, Bill then added, with a devious grin on his face, " Never have been one to argue against the laws of karma though!"

CHAPTER 7   2:30 AM/ NOVEMBER 7

About twenty minutes after finding Black Bart buried in the frozen ground, with just his head piercing the surface, Running Deer followed a blood path to a dark spacious area directly beneath a saddle depression in the Quartzite rock. Bill O'Toole barked for Running Deer to STOP, because he had found the entrance to the cabin. Jake looked at the front door, it was the only obstacle separating him from his pregnant wife. He motioned the others to cover him with their AK47, as he got in position to kick the door in.

"Okay guys on the count of three!" Jake said loudly, unaware that the blood pulsing through his body, had caused his voice to peak at a high volume pitch. Jake executed a perfect frontal kick to the wooden door, the door broke away from the hinges completely, and to their horror, they peered at the mutilated, skinned carcass of one David Barret. His face was turned toward them, and they all were completed shocked by the position of David's mouth, because he was smiling as if he was in a state of euphoric joy. The men were completely stunned by the amount of blood caked in the small living quarters of the cabin, Jake proceeded slowly down the hall toward the back room, sweating profusely, his body on high alert ready to do battle with any demon he encountered. He dreaded opening the door, his heart was pounding, knowing that if he found his queen dead, He would simply put the rifle under his chin and blow his brains out.

He gently pushed the door open, and walked in the room sweeping his flashlight from left to right, and to his surprised relief the room was empty, as he turned to go, something moved with lightning speed and grabbed Jake by his arm. Jake spun around and was surprised to see agent Briggs face, but was amazed that his body was anatomically incorrect, because Briggs face and ass checks faced the same direction! Jake's mind was racing to make sense of what his eyes were seeing, when he heard Agent Running Deer screaming at him to get down. Somehow, Jake was able to get one knee, and was amazed to see Running Deer use his body as a launching board to propel himself toward Briggs. Agent Running Deer leaped at Briggs with a tomahawk in one hand and a knife in the other, and with a sweeping scissor motion crossed the two weapons on Briggs throat cutting his head off with the same precision as a guillotine.

Jake could not believe what he had just witnessed, and was shocked by the animal like quickness of John Running Deer.

" Thank you John, you just saved my life," Jake looked at Running Deer with a look of deep appreciation and hero worship. Running Deer, face smeared with blood was in the process of cleaning off his weapons, when Sam Jenkins came running down the hall, ready to defend his friends with his life. He stopped when he saw Briggs decapitate body sprawled out on the floor, and his head lying about five feet from his torso. Jenkins surveyed the room, quickly comprehending that Jake and Running Deer were safe, and simply said

" Never like that Briggs dude, seemed kind of Backwards, and overtly angry." Despite their surroundings of unspeakable horror, Jake and Running Deer starting to laugh like a couple of deranged lunatics! Sam the giant of a man just stood there with a look of extreme confusion on his face and said, " Now what's so dam funny?"

The men joined Bill O'Toole in the main room, watching the roaring fire with great concentration. When Jake asked Bill what he was staring at, Bill turned and calmly answered him.

" Well gentlemen since David Barret, Agent Briggs, and Black Bart Whitescarver have all been accounted for, I guess the burning limbs in the fire place belong to the late and great Sheriff Brown. That is very surprising to me, because I considered that bastard to be one of my best friends".

" Well looks like we just saved the Federal Government a ton of money, by not having to prosecute these losers," quipped Jake.

" Where in the hell is your wife and that missing EPA agent?" Bill O'Toole asked. And before anyone could answer, a soft voice behind them said,

" Well Agent Mercury Johnson is standing right behind you, and Jake's wife Kelli has been taken by an Indian Shape shifter."

The men whirled around a was surprised to see a women draped in a large blanket, clearly near hypothermia, and frostbite had turned her face and hands a deep crimson color. Mercury quickly added,

" I tried to follow but my hands and feet were numb by frost nip, so I turned around almost getting lost, until I found my way back to the cabin, and this group of merry men."

Mercury let out a slight giggle in-spite of her pain. Jake assisted Mercury to the raging fire, careful not to let her warm to fast. He also had Mercury dip her hands in some warm water, as she slowly warmed her feet by the fire. Bill O'Toole poured a hot cup of coffee from the pot brewing on the stove, apparently, one of the men was making coffee, and was slaughtered before he got his coveted coffee break.

Jake was pacing the floor, racking his brain to come up with a plan to save his queen, when John Running Deer, discovered the same sandstone in the cabin that he had found on the banks of the Dan river around the body of Chad Whites carver, and at the site of the massacre on Moore's knob.

" Show me those traces of that sandstone John!" Jake almost demanded. Running Deer showed the Jake the particles that have been found on the floor. Jake looked at the sandstone for several minutes, as he tried to retrieve from his brain the relevance of the substance , that he held in his hand. Finally Jake spoke,

" Gentlemen this is limber-grit, or bending rock, there are very few deposits of it in the world, and Stokes County is the only place in the United States that Itacolumite deposits are found. The largest deposit of Limber-grit in Stokes County is in a place called Tories Den, a hidden cave behind a great waterfall. Gentleman get your gear we are going to get my wife, and slay a murderous beast from the deepest confines of Hades.

" Whoa Jake slow down, we need to rest a couple hours, before hiking over five miles of very treacherous territory, and Mercury needs a at least two hours to warm her skin. We will be too exhausted to do battle with a nine foot beast!" Bill O'Toole said in a calm tone. Jake wanted to admonish Bill for even suggesting that they should delay the rescue of his queen, then logic superseded emotion, and besides these men had risk their lives voluntarily to save his wife. He knew after hiking up three miles from Cedar Fork road in an ice storm, which these courageous men needed time to replenish their strength through food and rest.

" If it is agreeable with everyone, we will leave at 4:30 AM." Jake said looking at the men for nonverbal signs of agreement, They all nodded in agreement, except for Sam Jenkins, who was snoozing loudly in front of the soothing fire. Fifteen minutes before leaving the cabin, Bill O'Toole laid out the plan to rescue Kelli.

" Tories Den has two entrances, but the second entrance is very small. Mercury you will have to crawl on your hands and knees, find Kelli and evacuate her as expeditiously as possible. While you are accomplishing that, Jake, John and I will be creating a diversion that will bring Hicictawi'a to us. This will allow you some time to complete your task." Bill O'Toole paused for a brief second, and Jake blurted out the obvious question.

" Just how in the hell are we going to the attention of that insidious beast, remember my wife's life is at risk here" Jake asked, his big Irish face reddening.

" Very simply Jake, I am going to be the bait to lure the beast from the cave," Bill O'Toole stated calmly, as if he was describing a Sunday walk in the park.

CHAPTER 8 8:00 AM NOVEMBER 7

As they neared Tories Den, the winds and precipitation stopped. Jake noticed that the sky was clearing, and a brilliant sunrise was illuminating the rift valley below them. Jake inhaled sharply not from lack of oxygen, but because of the exquisite sight that the creator of the universe had painted. The ice particles from last night storm had coated the Canadian pines with a thin coat of ice, and made pines sparkle like diamonds in the morning sun. He thought that maybe God was sending a visual gift of awesome beauty to help him cope with the terror and horror that he was about to encounter. He could hear the massive waterfall as cascaded down the cliffs to the Dan River beneath them. He began to realize that it was almost show time, and just maybe by the grace of God, that he would be holding his queen soon.

They were about 100 yards above the waterfall, when Bill O'Toole stopped. He opened his pack and brought out camouflaged binoculars, and brought them to his eyes. He swore a bit, as he turned the focus knob to bring his target into a clear, sharp image. He passed the binoculars to Mercury, so she could see the tiny opening that appeared to resemble a portal on a ship. In fact, Mercury had just returned from a much-needed vacation on a cruise ship, and the small opening reminded her of the small window in her stateroom.

"What the hell O'Toole, you expect me to slither through that tiny opening, I'm not a dam lizard or snake!" Mercury said with angry tone, due to the throbbing pain in her feet. The four-mile hike had enhanced the pain in her feet, brought on by her bout with frost nip.

" Remember we are still 100 yards from that opening, but it is bigger once you get closer, and It widens dramatically very quickly , within the first couple of feet." O'Toole said confidently.

" Oh so it's kind of like being born again, but not in a religious sense." Mercury added for comical relief.

" How you know so much about the dimensions of that opening Bill" Jake asked worried about the first phase of the operation.

" I shimmed through that opening , when I was about fifteen, and was about the same size as agent Johnson. I would not send her on this dangerous mission without being absolutely sure she could accomplish it." Bill said with urgency, disappointed the team did not trust his judgment. Bill quickly told the team about his initial encounter with Hicictawi'a the night his son was attacked in the barn. He told them about his telepathic bond with the beast, and how he, without speaking a word, had begged it to not to kill his son. Hicictawi'a had spared his son's life, and so he would offer two palefaces and a traitor Indian as sacrifices to pay homage to its greatness.

" SOOO, let me get this right, you are going to feed us to a cannibalistic monster?" Jake asked his eyes widening in a comic impression of someone in a state of sheer terror.

" Of Course not Jake, kind of bonded with you all" Bill O'Toole retorts as he reaches into pack, and calmly assembles a sharpshooter's rifle capable of hitting a target from 2,000 feet away.

" I understand you have some marksman ship abilities, which you acquired while serving in our US Army?" Bill asked

Jake, as he handed him the sleek weapon.

Jake whistled as he Remington 700 AC, complete with long-range scope, as he began to get familiar himself with the weapon he joked, " Gee Dad thanks for the great Christmas present!" He laughed. Bill O'Toole reached into the gift bag and retrieved another rifle identical to the one he had given to Jake. He proudly presented to Agent Jenkins " Here you go Agent Jenkins didn't want to leave you out!"

" So gentleman Agent Running Deer and I are going to summon the beast to an opening, that I is about 50 yard from Tories den, when it moves into the clearing, YOU gentleman will kill it in a withering crossfire. I have special ammo in those rifles that will pierce armor plates. Mercury once out get Kelli, you will meet us back here, this will be our rallying point once the mission is complete." O'Toole said with his voice rising with excitement.

" Brilliant plan Bill, but why are we trying to kill this thing from such a long distance?" both Jake and Sam said in unison.

" Gentleman Hicictawia has already demonstrated formidable psychic abilities, we need to be outside of its psychic reach," Bill O'Toole answered, stoking his massive beard as if he was lost in deep thought.

" How do you know that half a mile is going to be outta of its psychic realm of influence?" Jake asked

" Honestly, I don't" Bill responded, with a sly smile. Agent Running Deer said tactfully changing the subject.

" Soooo you said that you were the bait, you didn't say anything about me! How was I selected to be the snack of the day?" Agent Running Deer asked, winking his eye.

" Well Agent Running Deer, you have special meaning to Hicictawi'a. You represent a traitor, a Cherokee warrior working for the palefaces to desecrate it's people. It has a very special hatred for you, It will not be able to resist it's desire to dance on your bloodstained bones," Bill said with a wink.

" Well I just hope it likes red meat," Agent Running said with a look of forged terror. The entire team burst out laughing with wild abandon, knowing that they may not survive the day.

CHAPTER 9

9:00 Am, November 7

After a few words of coordination of their brazen plan from Bill O'Toole, Jake yelled   "READY BREAK", as if he was still quarterback for the University of Florida. Mercury Johnson headed toward the tiny opening in the cave, and Jake and Sam headed off in different directions with the sniper rifles slung on their backs. Bill O'Toole waited thirty minutes, and began to summed Hicictawi'a, He stepped forward and prepared himself mentally his telepathic communication path to the beast. He whispered to Hicictawi'a from the right posterior cortical part of his brain.

" OH GREAT ONE, I HAVE BROUGHT TO YOU SACRIFICES TO GLORIFY YOU, TO HONOR YOU FOR NOT SENDING MY SON TO THE AFTERWORLD. I HAVE LIED TO THESE PALE-FACES, AND TOLD THEM THAT I WILL LEAD THEM TO YOU! YOU MUST COME AND CLAIM THERE SOULS."

Hicictawi'a was in the process of positioning Kelli against the cave wall, like some kind of Barbie doll that a young girl would have on her bed. Kelli was unconscious, and had not stirred during the long run back to the cave. Hicicta-wia was exhausted from the trip, but immediately responded to Bill O'Toole request. It used its remote viewing capability to "SEE" Bill O'Toole and the traitor Cherokee that worked for the palefaces standing beside him. Hicictawia howled with an intense angry and hatred and lurched toward the entrance of the cave. It left its piece of human bait alone lying on the floor deep within the cave. It believed that no intruder would ever find her. Bill O'Toole looking down the clearing with his binoculars, witnesses Hicicitawia leave the cave heading directly toward him. Bill's mouth locked into a crooked smile as he thought "phase one of the operation was a great success."

Hicicitawia smelled out the betrayal after advancing only one hundred meters from the cave, but it continued toward Bill O'Toole, intent in playing with these mere mortals for its entertainment. As it approached the clearing, it cast the net of a hypnotic trance on Bill and Running Deer, Hicicitawia sent a web of telepathic orders to Jake and Sam. Both men had their sniper rifles trained on Hicicitawia, and had the creature in their sights. Slowly the men lowered their weapons, and placed the butt of rifles on the ground. and put the barrel of the gun in their mouth. Hicicitawia then commanded the men to pull the trigger. Sam Jenkins complied, blowing brain matter about twenty feet into the air. Jake hesitated, his strong will refusing Hicicitawia's command, because he had a burning desire to save his wife and their unborn child. At the last moment, Jake pulled the rifle from his chin, because no power on earth was going to stop him from saving his family. Jake Ryan a man of great heart, stood and roared at the beast with great intensity and defiance.

CHAPTER 10

9;15 AM, November 7th

Hicicitawia was stunned by the pale faces defiance, no mortal had ever refused its command in centuries. It would deal with that problematic human later, because right now it was going to be entertained by two gladiators fighting to the death. Bill O'Toole and Running Deer turned and glared at each other with great hatred, spit oozed out of their mouths like two rabid dogs as they circled each other. Neither man had a weapon, this was going to be a fight to the death Mano against Mano. Bill O'Toole was shorter than running deer, but was powerfully built, his massive arms were capable of delivering a blow that would not only render his opponent unconscious, but also be fatal.

Running Deer charged Bill O'Toole with blinding speed, but Bill O'Toole step to the side and delivered an uppercut to Running Deer jaw, which stunned the Indian. Running Deer fell to the ground, bleeding profusely from the mouth. Bill O'Toole was on top of the semi-conscious Indian within a split second. He straddled the hapless Indian, raining down blow after blow on defenseless John Running Deer. Running dear was almost unconscious, bordering on the throes of death, when his hand searching for a weapon. He found a huge rock embedded in the soil. He thanked his ancestors for the miracle, and closed his hand around it. He then brought it up against O'Toole's massive cranium, rending him unconscious. Hicictawia telepathically instructed John Running Deer to finish the Irishman, but then its psychic radar sensed a human presence in the cave. It slowly realized it had been tricked, and these humans had staged a distraction to get it out of the cave. Hicictawia howled with anger, turned and began running toward the cave, thus breaking the telepathic bond with John Running Deer.

John Running Deer, coming to his senses, look down at Bill O'Toole with great remorse, as he saw a large laceration on his forehead. Running Deer filled with rage, after seeing the serious wound on O'Toole head, picked up his knife and tomahawk, charged the beast, John Deer running at an inhuman pace, leaped into the air, and buried the knife deep into Hicictawia leg. John Running Deer was shocked to see the wound on the beast leg began heal immediately, and then disappear. The last thought that ran through Running Deer's mind was what kind of hellish beast was this, before Hicictawia claw ripped through his right arm, severing it at the shoulder. Hicictawia knew that the wound would prove to be fatal, and the traitor Cherokee would bleed out within five minutes, turned toward the cave and with an incredible leap was gone.

CHAPTER 11

9:30 Am, November 7

Kelli was sleeping soundly in the pitch-black cave, when the sound of footsteps echoing on the cave walls awaken her. She indistinctly looked for a rock to split the head of the hideous beast, which had tied her up in this freezing cold snake pit. Her hands were free, but her legs were bound with evergreen vines that had attached themselves to the quartzite rock near the cave entrance. Kelli was shocked to see the flashlight beams as they recoiled off cave wall. Could there be a human presence behind those illuminating beams of light?

Kelli tensed up, her fight or flight instinct took over, she was ready to fight to the death! Her senses were on high alert, her heart was hammering in her chest, her breathing was shallow and fast, she was ready to explode with a vengeance on the monster that had tormented humanity for eons. She exhaled with relief, when she recognized that heroic women that had saved her life in the cabin/cave.

"What you doing girl? I didn't know you were into spelunking?" Mercury laughed as she shined her flashlight on Kelli. Kelli allowed herself to laugh, as the flashlight seemed to warm her flesh.

" How did you find me?" Kelli asked in complete shock to see her friend alive.

" Girl don't you know us Black women, have an innate ability to find anything ,when we put our minds to it." Mercury said smiling at her new best friend.

" How you think we find our men, when they out there creep-in around on us?" "No more time for pleasantries, got to get you the hell outta here!" Mercury replied producing a large butcher knife that she had taken from the Cabin-cave, knowing it would come in handy later. Mercury quickly cut Kelli free, and then helped her to feet. Kelli first steps were wobbly, but her ability to walk had returned. Mercury laughed to herself, as she thought of the con man posing as an evangelist shout " It's a miracle!". Kelli glanced at her friend with a puzzled look, thinking that her newfound friend has cracked under the extreme pressure of their dire circumstances. Mercury looked at her with a large grin, and calmly said,

" Private Joke baby, myself defensive- mechanism when the shit hits the fan".

Just then, they both heard the ground shake near the entrance to the cave, and they both realized that a major shit was headed directly for them.

CHAPTER 12

" Quick, the Bitch is here." Mercury shouted as she led Kelli to the back of the cave, and the tiny opening that would serve as their portal to safety. As they neared the back of the cave, Mercury shined the light directly on the small opening, shouting at Kelli with an extreme urgency to shimmy through the opening. Kelli knelt at the opening and began to worm through the opening, which was spacious at the beginning but began to narrow as she approached light and freedom. Mercury watched as Kelli squirmed through the opening , and then sudden horror realized that Kelli was wider in the hips than she was , and that Kelli would need a major push in order to clear the opening.

Mercury knowing that Hicictawi'a was almost upon them, began to crawl toward the light, and just as she feared, Kelli was hopelessly stuck at the very end of the opening, in fact, her upper torso had cleared the opening. Mercury knew that they would both die in the cave, so with a superhuman strength pushed Kelli's feet, and prayed to Jesus that he would miraculous save them. To her surprise, she heard a popping sound, like a cork being pulled from a wine bottle, and knew that Kelli had cleared the diminutive opening. She saw the light cascading through the opening, it was like light shining down from heaven, bathing her righteous soul in its warm embrace!

Just as Mercury pushed her head, neck and shoulders through the opening, she felt the claws of the beast dig into her feet, she yelled at Kelli to grab her hands and pull. Kelli grabbed Mercury's hand and began to tug with all her might, but her strength was no match for the hideous beast from hell. Kelli watch with horror as Mercury began to disappear into the blackness, transfixed by the look in Mercury's eyes. It was not a gaze of fear and horror, but one of steel resolve and courage, Kelli then understood that Mercury was a person that she will remember and idolize forever.

As Hicicawai pulled Mercury toward it, it felt a superhuman kick, and to its complete and utter surprise the kick temporary caused it to lose a grip on its prey, but this human did not scurry toward the opening like a scared rabbit. Mercury stood on her wounded legs in complete and utter defiance and screamed at the beast,

" Come on you corn braided ugly Bitch let's dance," as she assumed her fighting stance waving the butcher knife with a death grip.

Hicictawi'a was incensed by the sheer arrogance of the human before it, closed in rapidly already tasting the blood of this brazen warrior. Hicictawi'a was upon this pitiful human with claws open ready to decapitate her. It lunged at arrogant intruder, but was surprised when with blazing speed, Mercury fell to the ground. The claw passed harmlessly over Mercury head, and before Hicicawi'a could counter, Mercury plunged the knife deep into Hicicawi'a underbelly. Hicicawi'a screeched with pain, shock and surprised, no human had ever inflicted so much pain on it in centuries. Mercury smiled as she watched the beast bleed out on the cave floor, but her smile turned to horror, as she realized that the wound had catheterized itself, and the tremendous flow of blood had stopped. Mercury knew that she must cut the head off this beast , or plunge her knife deep into its heart to kill it, but her complete and utter horror she could not move, she was paralyzed.

Hicicawi'a knew that it's "bait" was escaping, and so it no longer wish to play with this human, so it used its psychic power to freeze the warrior that had inflicted so much pain on it.. It stood before the human, silently worshiping her bravery, and strength. She was a tremendous warrior, so her death will be quick and painless, and Hicicawi'a will drink her blood hoping that her strength and soul would then flow through its body. Hicicawi'a raised it' claw and with one vicious swipe motion decapitated Mercury, and drank her lifeblood as it squirted from her carotid artery.

CHAPTER 13

10:00 Am, November 7th

Kelli waited for a few minutes, hoping that her Mercury would emerge from the cave, victorious over the soulless beast, but when she heard the inhuman scream of pain and anguish emerge from the cave like a thunderous wave, she began to run with wild abandon, her soul filled with grief and guilt. Hicicawi'a knew that it would not be able clear the small opening in the cave, shifted into a 20-foot copperhead snake and slithered through the hole on its belly. Once outside the cave, Hicicawi'a shifted back to a Wolf/ Bigfoot creature, smelled the air and knew that its prey was semi naked and afraid.

Jake ran toward the howl like a man possessed, He emerged on the ridgeline, and to his horror saw a large beast chasing his beloved wife. The beast was closing in, its claws were out and ready to slice and dice his queen. Jake was about 100 feet above the beast, so with an action of desperation Jake leaped off the cliff. He arched his body completely erect, like a speeding rocket, and placed himself on a collision course with the beast. Kelli could feel the hot breath of Hicicawi'a on her neck, and knew that the end would come mercifully quick. Just as Hicicawi'a raised its claw, deal Kelli the same fate it had dealt Mercury, a tremendous force screaming like a wild banshee hit it and knocked it off the ridgeline. Hicicawi'a felt itself falling through the air, and because of the swiftness of the attack could not react with any of its supernatural abilities.

Kelli watched in complete and utter horror, as

Jake, the essence of her life, rode on the back of Hicicawi'a down to the Dan river almost 500 feet below them. The hideous monster landed on a long dead tree branch protruding out of the water like a large stake. The branch pierced the heart of Hicicawi'a , and the beast let out a howl that would chill all the demons of the underworld. Hicicawi'a tried to shape shift, but its power had seeped from it like its lifeblood being swept down the river. As Kelli watched the human form of Accalia Blackclaw appeared, a tear flowed down Accalia's cheek, and a beautiful, peaceful smile appeared on her bloody face. Kelli, then understood that her tears were not born of pain and anguish, but of sheer joy, her sweet soul had finally been freed from a hellish nightmare. Kelli watched as the lifeless body of Jake was swept down the river. The pain was unbearable. her soul was screaming to be with her soulmate, so she steeped of the cliff wanting to be reunited with her love of her life forever, but strong hands grabbed her arms at the last possible moment and with superhuman strength pulled Kelli to safety.

Jake still alive and conscious floating on his back in the Dan river, watched as the strong arms of Bill O'Toole pulled his love to safety. Jake would take the vision of a man, with a grievous head wound, save his queen's life to the grave with him. The very man that he was ordered to kill, had saved his wife's life. Thorough the powers of the universe, or Karma his actions to preserve this man's life had in the end, saved the thing most precious to him. Jake's pain was numbed by the icy waters of the Dan river, he watched as the late fall leaves, swirled down from the heavens. The ice had covered the trees that lined the banks of the river, the brilliance of the sun lit the trees up, and they seemed to be on fire. Jake then thought about how he had read that the rivers were like time and would run for all eternity. The beauty of the scene prepared Jake to die, and he wondered if the river would consume him, allowing him to live forever! Jake then smiled and peace spread through his soul and he closed his eyes.

CHAPTER 14

November 9, 8:00 Am-3:00 pm

He had his arms around her, holding her so close that she could almost feel their souls intertwine. He kissed her lips with a tenderness and passion that she had never know, and she was ready to give herself to him in that miraculous way that God intended for a Husband and Wife to connect. Jake pressed himself against her, thrusting wildly inside her, and Kelli could feel herself nearing orgasm. The motion was at a wild frenzy, but something was wrong, Jake breath began to smell of rotten flesh, rancid, putrid in scent. Kelli opened her eyes and began to scream, a long piercing scream that seemed to last for eternity, but Hicictawi'a placed its claw over her mouth and muffled the sound. Kelli could not breathe, and just as her lungs began to explode into a million fragments, Kelli woke up. It was a nightmare, and then the memory of her beautiful Jake floating away from her for all eternity flooded her mind, and she grabbed the tear stained pillow, and began to sob, tears flowed down her face like the cascading water of Tory's Den waterfall.

She began to pray for another terror-filled nightmare to visit soon, because if that was the only way for her to feel Jake's arms, then she would bare that burden for all eternity. Doctor Rivers had given her sedatives to help her sleep, but her pain was unbearable, and the only thing that kept her from another suicide attempt, was the life that was growing inside her. Kelli knew that she would never hold her love again, but part of him was growing inside of her and she would honor her warrior by giving birth to his offspring. She had given into despair and grief for two days, lying in bed not wanting to live. The phone began to ring, but Kelli ignored it, not wanting her mourning to be interrupted. Suddenly an intense desire urged her to pick the phone up. She picked up the phone on third ring it was Paul Jacobs.

" Kelli, I have great news, they found Jake"! Paul Jacobs shouted into the phone. Kelli like Lazarus of the New Testament, suddenly came back the dead! She was too stunned for words, but then she smiled and silently thanked God for bringing her man back to her. Kelli cleared her throat and replied trying to hold back her tears,

" At least we can have a proper burial for him now!" there was a brief pause on the phone.

" There won't be any need for a funeral Kelli, because Jake is alive!" Jacobs shouted his voice filled with euphoric joy. Jacobs hear nothing for several minutes, then a scream of pure ecstasy and delight as the information was processed by Kelli's mind, so many questions flooded her brain, but all she could ask was "HOW DID HE SURVIVE?"

Jacobs told her that the ice-cold water had slowed down Jake's vital organs, to a point that his body was in hibernation. Jake survived because of something called Mammalian Diving Reflex, which slowed his heart rate, and breathing to a point that his brain needed less blood. Jake was in the water all most an hour, and was found by a fly angler near the town of Trenton, NC.

" Jake is one lucky hombre Kelli, The man that found him was a retired paramedic that gave Jake prolonged CPR, and knew not to warm Jake's body to quickly" Jacobs explained.

" Where is he Paul?" Kelli asked breathlessly.

" He is at Carlton County Regional Hospital, which is in Adairsville NC, 40 miles from Danbury NC. Kelli Jake has amnesia, so you might want to wait a day before you fly there," Jacobs said in his most paternal voice. Unfortunately, Paul Jacobs's advice was ignored, because Kelli was already on the way to Ronald Reagan Airport to catch the first plane to North Carolina.

Once Kelli arrived at Ronald Reagan International airport, she was stopped by a TSA agent, and asked to follow her to a small conference room near her gate. At first Kelli objected, and showed the women her credentials, but the agent seemed unimpressed and demanded that Kelli follow her. She was shocked to see Paul Jacobs standing in front of the room, appearing to be quite frustrated.

" Kelli I know you're in a hurry to see Jake, but you have to be debriefed on your last mission. a lot has transpired, since you went in your depressive Hiatus! You still have an hour to catch your flight, and depending on your attitude and, you may make your flight. It is all up to you!" Jacobs said glaring at her.

" Well it's my last debriefing, because I am retiring from the FBI effective today, should have left several years ago. but I was pig headed. My stubbornness almost cost my Husband life AGAIN!" Kelli could almost feel her PTSD raging like an angry bull. Paul Jacobs stared at Kelli, and wondered if she was truly serious about retiring, because she would be sorely missed.

Paul Jacobs looked at Kelli with great compassion, and explained to her that John Running Deer and Bill 'O'Toole were both still alive. Larry Cole, who was leading a FBI recovery team to Tories Den, heard gunshots, and directed the team in the direction of the shots. The team was only about 300 yards from a large clearing, and found Bill O'Toole and John Running Deer, both were in extremely critical condition. They were able to stabilize both men and get them evacuated by helicopter.

" John Running Deer had a severed right arm, but Bill O'Toole saved his life by placing a tourniquet around it, Running Deer lost the limb, but both men will survive and are listed in fair condition at Stokes County Memorial in Danbury." Kelli was very relieved to hear that both these brave men were still alive, and then it dawned on her that Bill O'Toole had saved two lives on that terrible day.

" What about Mercury Johnson and Sam Jenkins?" Kelli asked, her voice cracking with emotion. Jacobs stared at her for what seemed for eternity, before he spoke

" Kelli I'm afraid there both deceased. Sam Jenkins body was found about 300 yards from O'Toole and Running deer, dead of an apparent gunshot wound. Mercury body was found in Tories den, both bodies are still in Stokes County morgue pending Autopsy." Jacobs left out the details of the self-inflicted gunshot wound to Jenkins head, and the condition of Mercury's body, found in the cave with her head missing. The recovery team had found the head in a dark corner of the cave, fifty feet from her body. rodents and other cave dwelling varmints had already consumed her eyes.

" I guess that dam ghoul Drake is performing the Autopsy?" Kelli asked.

" I'm afraid that the CO medical examiner is doing the autopsy, ME Drake went missing, but was arrested in Costa Rico this morning for the murder of Chad Whitewater. Forensic evidence found on Whitewater body, and the condition of Whitewater mummified remains link him to the murder. He is being extradited as we speak." Jacobs paused for dramatic purposed,

" David Barrett, Bart Whitecarver, Sheriff Brown and Joel Briggs were killed in a terrible car accident this morning trying to elude authorities in the mountains of North Carolina," Jacobs informed her with a stone face, and a burning intensity in his eyes.

" Paul you know that's bullshit, I saw them being slaughtered by a Cherokee shape shiftier named Hicic-tawi'a the night that Briggs tried to rape me." Kelli said her voice rising.

" Kelli, If the public knew of a cannibalistic, wolf-big foot creature roaming the hills of North Carolina there would be mass panic, people would be terrified and the economic impact of loss tourism would be significant! The Governor and state officials in Raleigh have asked us to put the proverbial lid on the Shape-shiftier theory."

" So what about Jake, Bill O'Toole and John Running Deer. Did you erase their memory?" "They witnessed the slaughter at Whites-carver's cabin too!" Kelli asked not really sure, she wanted to know the answer.

" That's already been taken care of, memory can be manipulated" Paul Jacobs replied eerily. Suddenly Kelli was aware that she was in the midst of a terrible conspiracy, and her and Jake's life would be at risk if she did not do exactly what Jacobs wanted. Kelli looked at the clock, she had about 15 minutes to get to her gate, so she nodded her head in compliance to Jacob's request.

" Well then have a great flight, Director King will be meeting you in Greensboro, and Kelli you did a great Job, and the bureau will always be grateful." Jacobs said giving her a wink and smile.

Kelli promptly returned his gesture with a gesture of her own, her middle finger hyper extended as she headed off toward her gate. Just as Kelli began to walk away, She turned abruptly around and walked up to Jacobs, violating his personal space, and whispered in his ear.

" If you try and withhold Jenkins pension to his family, because of the coroners finding, I will contact a tabloid magazine and tell them a little story about an ancient Cherokee

Shape-Shifter" " Now go get my resignation papers in order."
Kelli then stepped back and walked away from a very angry
and shocked control freak.

Unfortunate Kelli's plane had a two-hour lay-
over in Conover NC, so Kelli exited the plane and went straight
to the nearest bar, for shot of Jack Daniels to calm her nerves.
Jacobs's actions made Kelli think of the popular show the X-
files, in which she was Scully being sworn to secrecy or she
would experience the wrath of the most powerful law enforcement agency in the world. Kelli ordered a double shot,
and settled in on the cozy bar stool. She looked around the
bar for possible FBI goons stalking her, but no one appeared
to be the least bit interested in her. They were just exhausted
business travelers, with enormous bags under their eyes from
sleeping in too many hotel rooms. Kelli turned her attention
to the television an attractive CNN news anchor droned on
about ICE raiding a Meth lab in Stokes County North Carolina.

" Several illegal aliens were arrested and
deported today after SBI raided a Meth lab on the property
of Bart Whitescarver, one of the men killed this morning in
a high speed car chase with federal and local authorizes. The
Men pictured here, Bart Whitescarver, David Barrett, John
Briggs, and ex Stokes county Sheriff John Brown were wanted
for the abduction and murder of EPA agent Mercury Johnson,
and for the Kidnapping of FBI special agent Kelli Ryan."

Kelli cringed as her and Mercury's picture flashed across
the television screen, she gulped down her drink, paid for her
drink and headed toward her gate, but not before toasting the
four and praying that they burn in hell forever.

Epilogue

Inspector King picked Kelli up from Piedmont International Airport, and during the two-hour trip, the two barely spoke. Kelli was still an emotional wreck, almost three days after FBI Swat and Evidence response teams rescued her from Tories Den. The silence was broken by King, as he personally apologized for the actions of SBI Agent Briggs, explaining the Briggs was financially bankrupted because of gambling debt that he had accrued over the years. David Barrett was using funds from Abbott Gas to pay Briggs and Brown obscene amounts of money.

" It's a shame that humanity will sale their soul for that mean green." Inspector King reflected.

" Agent Briggs owed some very bad folks that operated the casinos in Cherokee NC serious coin, and they had threatened to skin him and his children alive if he didn't pay off, but that fact does not excuse his treason." King said in a hushed tone almost ashamed to look Kelli in the eyes. Kelli grabbed King's tiny hand, and told him that he had nothing to apologize for.

" I am sure you put Agent Briggs through a tough screening process, sometimes things happen that are outta your control. free will is a bitch to control, just ask our creator in Heaven." Kelli replied like an ordained minister.

As they near Adairsville, the radio personality on the local radio station informed them that a hiker and slipped and fallen at Tories Den waterfall, and somehow had been impaled on a dead tree branch protruding from the river. Stokes County Medical examiner is ruling the death an accident, and identity is being withheld pending the notification of next of kin.

" Wow sounds like a freak accident" the co-anchor, exclaimed in the background. To which Kelli replied to no one in particular " They have no idea!" as she glanced over at King.

When they arrived at the hospital, Doctor Drainer called

Kelli into a small conference room, and explained to her that Jake was suffering from hypothermia and severe dehydration. He also incurred a lacerated liver and spine fracture from the fall that almost claimed his life. Finally, Jake has partial memory lapse, and has no memory of the 24 hours before his fall, so therefore, he may have problems recognizing you.

" In short your husband is very lucky to be alive, and we are not sure that he will ever walk again. He is in very critical condition, and is going in and out of a light coma. He is in ICU, and you will be only able to visit him in very short intervals." Doctor Drainer voice was stern, but his eyes were full of sympathy and compassion. An ICU nurse came into the room, and asked Kelli to follow her to Jake's room.

When Kelli first saw Jake she had to fight back the tears, he was hooked up to monitors, and IV tubes attached to both hands were pumping painkillers, saline solution, and medication into his bruised body. He had a cast around his upper torso, and oxygen tubes were taped to his mouth. Kelli noticed that his face appeared shrunken, as the skin around the eye was discolored, and for a terrible minute Kelli thought that Jake already resembled a corpse. Kelli stood in the doorway, unable to move, and then through a miracle, Jake's eyes opened and he motioned for her.

Kelli bent over him, confessing her love for him over, and over! The ICU nurse was almost brought to tears as she watched a true American love story unfold right in front of her. Suddenly Jake motioned for Kelli to come close to him, Kelli bent down so close she could see Jake's chest rise and fall, and hear his strong heartbeat. Jake then spoke to her in a raspy hoarse voice.

" My Queen, I love you with all my heart, but if you take another case in North Carolina, I will divorce you! I will also write you out of my will, and you will never see a dime of my vast fortune." Jake then smiled that beautiful, warm, cocky grin and hugged so tight that the air was almost forced from Kelli's lungs. Jake then shut is eyes and drifted off to sleep. Kelli laid there for a minute in his arms, relishing in the moment that she knew her superman, the center of her universe was going to make a full recovery.

One year later, Kelli and a partially recovered Jake, who was still walking with the help of a cane, were in an Arlington VA, listening to Bill O'Toole deliver a powerful speech on the evils of Hydraulic Fracturing, and Horizontal drilling. Several environmental groups like the Sierra club and Greenpeace hired Bill to be a public speaker, representing them across the country. These groups wanted Bill to explain what strategies that his small group of protesters used in defeating one of the most aggressive gas companies in the nation. The Sierra Club compared Bill's group to a modern David and Goliath story. They wanted other communities to use techniques that Bill O'Toole group used to fight off the greedy onslaught of those, that with to lay destruction to the most valuable resource on the planet- WATER.

" In conclusion I would like to submit a hypothesis, that the current administration is creating diversions of building a Border Wall, or Tariffs with China, or the personnel indiscretions of the commander-in-Chief in order to get the attention of the American public. While the American people are so preoccupied with these issues, I believe this administration is quietly dismantling environmental laws, like the clean water act of 1972. This erasing of laws to protect our precious water, allows big oil and gas reap huge profit by drilling in areas that a few years ago were off limits. It is the classic look one way, while we slowly get what we really want strategy. The oil and gas companies are only concerned about great profits, and their greed blinds them to the fact that if we don't have water, there will be no life on this planet." "Thank you for allowing me to speak to you tonight, and please get active because after all your grandchildren and great grandchildren are depending on you to save our planet." Bill then turned and walked off the stage to a thunderous standing ovation.

Kelli and Jake were unable to speak to Bill that night, because the media was hovering around him like vultures around a dead animal. Kelli called Bill several times, but always got voice mail. She decided to write a letter to Bill thanking him for saving her life and the life of her unborn son. She also wrote that She and Jake had named their son Jake " William" Ryan to honor a true American hero, She invited him Dinner, so they could thank him properly, but he never responded. She also called John Running Deer, and always received his voice mail. Kelli began to believe that Jacobs totally erased both Running Deer and Bill's memory, and they may not even remember her. Her belief was confirmed, when Running Deer called and politely called back and told her, she had the wrong number, that he does not know a Kelli or Jake Ryan. For a moment, Kelli was saddened, but then she shuddered as she thought of the agency that she served with honor and distinction now viewed her as enemy of the state. A shiver went down her spine as she thought of the great lengths that our government goes to cover up events that it deems to be a threat to national security.

Six months later Jake had completely recovered from the injuries he sustained nearly two years ago in North Carolina. He was driving to his new position as athletic director of a large high school in Alexandria, Virginia. He was receiving a fantastic salary, and even had time to work on his Master's in school administration. Kelli was now a stay at home mom taking great care of Junior, and seemed to relish taking care of their infant son. She was a natural mom, and had even joined a new mother's meet up group! Jake was obsessed by his inability to remember the circumstances that led up to his near death in the Dan river, and Kelli appeared to be very paranoid when they went out, which was very seldom. That behavior was extremely strange for Kelli, but he contributed it to being a new mother. Jake was in deep thought, when he looked up at the Arlington bank that displayed the time and temperature. The bold letters on the electronic sign indicated that it was 95 degrees, and the time was 10:00 am. Jake had to take a double take, because it was only the last day of March, and then Bill O'Toole's warning popped in his mind. Jake then gripped the steering column and thought of his infant son, and how this FRACKED UP WEATHER was leading to conditions that may make mother earth inhabitable.

The End

Made in the USA
Coppell, TX
24 November 2019

11862094R00236